Acclaim for *Kings of the Earth*

"In his masterful and compassionate new novel, *Kings of the Earth,* Clinch borrows from a true-life case of possible fratricide. Three elderly, semiliterate brothers live in squalor on a ramshackle dairy farm in central New York state. The prismatic narrative shifts time and point of view, and Clinch easily slips into the voices of his diverse cast of characters—a nosy, good-hearted neighbor, a police investigator struggling to do the right thing, and the brothers' drug-dealing nephew. Through evocative descriptions of the landscape—'a countryside full of that same old homegrown desolation'—and by imbuing these odd men with a gentle nobility and an 'antique strangeness,' Clinch has created a haunting, suspenseful story."

— *O, The Oprah Magazine* (Lead Title, Summer Reading List)

"True feeling seems to be out of fashion in contemporary fiction, and fiction is the poorer for it. Disaffection and irony may be the tenor of the times, but too much of it can leave you estranged and lonely. Then along comes Clinch, and we are once again safe at home, in the hands of a master. *Kings of the Earth* recalls the finest work of John Gardner, and Bruce Chatwin's *On the Black Hill.* It becomes a story that is not told but lived, a cry from the heart of the heart of the country, in William Gass's phrase, unsentimental but deeply felt, unschooled but never less than lucid. Never mawkish, Clinch's voice never fails to elucidate and, finally, to forgive, even as it mourns."

— *Washington Post*

"It's the sort of book you race through then read again more slowly, savoring each voice. Preston, the kindly neighbor who cheerfully admits he doesn't entirely understand the Proctors, says, 'Where a man comes from isn't enough. You've got to go all the way back to the seed of a man and the planting of it, and a person can't go back that far ever I don't think.' Clinch goes back to that seed and that planting, and readers will eagerly go with him."

— *Seattle Times*

"The power of *Kings of the Earth* lies in the intricacies of the relationships among the Proctors; neighbor and childhood friend Preston, who serves as something of a guardian angel; the drug-dealing nephew, and the police. Clinch is canny enough to move his characters through their own understated lives, hinting where he needs to as he skirts the obvious, and refusing to overlay a sense of morality on their actions. The landscape informs the story as much as the internal terrain of the characters does, giving *Kings of the Earth* a grounding that is missing from many modern novels. We know the events that lie behind Clinch's novel were real, and that the novel is not. But the realism here is no less, with writing so vibrant that you feel the bite of a northern wind, smell the rankness of dissipated lives and experience the heart-tug of watching tenuous lives play out their last inches of thread."

— *Los Angeles Times*

"Clinch's literary alchemy results in a stunning book. Because each chapter releases essential information, the book moves easily toward closure, but an intricate knot of story lines plays out through them. Recalling William Faulkner's *As I Lay Dying,* each short chapter is broken into a section that is told in the first person. Not only do we get the brothers' voices, we hear an entire rural chorus: the dead father and mother, neighbors, the sister, brother-in-law, lawyers and the police."

— *Dallas Morning News*

"This is a gritty but warm-hearted and beautifully realized novel about three old unmarried brothers who live together on a rundown dairy farm in upstate New York. Clinch addresses one of Faulkner's favorite themes in this novel—our ability to endure—and explores it in ways that are inspiring and poignant. Enthusiastically recommended for readers of literary fiction."

— *Library Journal (Starred)*

"In Clinch's multilayered, pastoral second novel (after *Finn),* a death among three elderly, illiterate brothers living together on an upstate New York farm raises suspicions and accusations in the surrounding community. Family histories and troubles are divulged in short chapters by a cacophony of characters speaking in first person. Alongside the police troopers' investigation, each player contributes his own personal perspectives and motivations. Clinch explores family dynamics in this quiet storm of a novel that will stun readers with its power."

— Publishers Weekly (Starred)

Advance Praise for Jon Clinch's *The Thief of Auschwitz*

"Jon Clinch's The Thief of Auschwitz is the intensely dramatic and moving story of how a remarkable painting enables two doomed parents to save their beloved teenage son from the gas chambers of Nazi Germany. Abounding with richly developed, surprising characters, The Thief of Auschwitz is itself a stunning portrait of how love of family, of freedom, and of art can triumph over pure, relentless evil. The Thief of Auschwitz, for my money, is the best and most powerful work of fiction ever written about the Holocaust"

— Howard Frank Mosher, author of *Walking to Gatlinburg* and *Where The Rivers Flow North*

"There is a painting of a child that figures throughout Jon Clinch's moving and fierce new book, one of many indelible and haunting images he paints in this story of one family's fight to keep love alive in a landscape filled with death. That painting will remain, like the story itself, in your heart forever."

— Robert Goolrick, author of *A Reliable Wife* and *Heading Out to Wonderful*

Acclaim for Jon Clinch's *Finn*

Named a best book of the year by the *Washington Post*, the *Chicago Tribune*, and the *Christian Science Monitor*.

Named a Notable Book by the *American Library Association*.
Winner of the *Philadelphia Athenaeum Literary Award*.
Shortlisted for the *Sargent First Novel Prize*.

"A brave and ambitious debut novel... It stands on its own while giving new life and meaning to Twain's novel, which has been stirring passions and debates since 1885... triumph of imagination and graceful writing.... Bookstores and libraries shelve novels alphabetically by authors' names. That leaves Clinch a long way from Twain. But on my bookshelves, they'll lean against each other. I'd like to think that the cantankerous Twain would welcome the company."

— *USA Today*

"Ravishing…In the saga of this tormented human being, Clinch brings us a radical (and endlessly debatable) new take on Twain's classic, and a stand-alone marvel of a novel. Grade: A."

— *Entertainment Weekly*

"Haunting…Clinch reimagines Finn in a strikingly original way, replacing Huck's voice with his own magisterial vision—one that's nothing short of revelatory…Spellbinding."

— *Washington Post*

"His models may include Cormac McCarthy, and Charles Frazier, whose Cold Mountain also has a voice that sounds like 19th-century American (both formal and colloquial) but has a contemporary spikiness. This voice couldn't be better suited to a historical novel with a modernist sensibility: Clinch's riverbank Missouri feels post-apocalyptic, and his Pap Finn is a crazed yet wily survivor in a polluted landscape…Clinch's Pap is a convincingly nightmarish extrapolation of Twain's. He's the mad, lost and dangerous center of a world we'd hate to live in— or do we still live there?—and crave to revisit as soon as we close the book."

— *Newsweek*

"I haven't been swallowed whole by a work of fiction in some time. Jon Clinch's first novel has done it: sucked me under like I was a rag doll thrown into the wake of a Mississippi steamboat…Jon Clinch has turned in a nearly perfect first book, a creative response that matches *The Adventures of Huckleberry Finn* in intensity and tenacious soul-searching about racism."

— *Bookslut*

"An important work that would be regarded as a major novel, even if *Adventures of Huckleberry Finn* didn't exist."

— Kent Rasmussen, author of *Mark Twain A To Z*

KINGS OF THE EARTH

A Novel

Jon Clinch

unmediated ink™

Grateful acknowledgment is made to Jalma Music for permission
to reprint an excerpt from "Murder in the Red Barn," written by
Tom Waits and Kathleen Brennan, copyright © 1983 by
Jalma Music (ASCAP). All rights reserved. Used by permission.

Grateful acknowledgment is made to Michael Ticcino for permission
to use a portion the image "Tendrils of Time" as cover art.
MJTiccinoImages.com

Originally published in hardcover by Random House, 2010.

Visit jonclinch.com to download a Reading Group Guide.

ISBN: 1481175408
ISBN-13: 978-1481175401

Version 1.0

FOR MY PARENTS, JOYCE AND WARREN CLINCH—

FOR ALL OF THESE OLD VOICES.

There's always some killin' you got to do around the farm.

— TOM WAITS AND KATHLEEN BRENNAN,
"Murder in the Red Barn"

KINGS OF THE EARTH

1990

Audie

MY BROTHER VERNON went on ahead. I woke up and felt for him but the bed was dry and my brother Creed was already up. He had his overalls on and he was telling me that I had to get up too because it was after four-thirty and the cows wouldn't wait. The bed was cold but it was dry. My brother Vernon was still in it and he was cold like the bed was since he had gone on. That left me here with Creed. It made me the oldest.

Preston

I WOULDN'T HAVE BEEN SURPRISED if we'd lost the both of them at the same time. Vernon and Audie I mean. That's how close they've been ever since they were boys. Vernon would lead the way and Audie would follow right along behind. Not that they were two peas in a pod, not by any means. Vernon was the brains of the operation and Audie had problems. Has problems.

I was sitting in the kitchen with my coffee and down the hill Creed opened the barn door the way he always does first thing, but instead of opening it and looking at the day and then going right back in he kept coming. I've known those boys since they were boys, I've lived right here alongside their place since the thirties, and they've always run in the same track. Everything goes the same today as it went yesterday. That's how it is around a farm. A farm is the master of you and not the other way around. So when Creed opened the barn door and came out and kept on coming instead of going back in, I knew something wasn't right. I believe I stood up at the kitchen table and said so to Margaret. I said something wasn't right.

He was coming across the field toward our place and I guessed by how he was coming that it'd be a good idea to meet him halfway if I could. I put my coffee cup down and I went out onto the porch and then I came back in to put my coat on because it was cooler outdoors than I'd expected it to be and I guessed I might be out there for a while. Creed had on that old wool coat of his that's torn up the back and covered all over with cow manure. It's either his coat or Vernon's. I can never remember. They all swap things around. It's the way they were brought up. Anyway he was wearing the wool coat. That house of theirs doesn't have anything much in the way of insulation, so they probably have a better idea of the weather outdoors than we do. That's why I had to go back in for a coat of my own. Outdoors is no different from indoors to them, except outdoors there's more breeze and it smells better. Even in the barnyard. I don't know if he slept in that coat or not but he might have.

That poor old boy looked like he was about to have a heart attack and I was glad I'd gone out so he didn't have to keep coming up the hill. "Vernon died in the night," he said. He was shaking a little, like he was about to have a fit. I'm no doctor but that's how it seemed. A doctor might tell you something else, or put it another way. "My brother's awful cold," he said.

So we went down. I got him turned back around and we went down the hill and in through the barn instead of up on the porch and in by the front door. Not that I think they ever lock that front door. I don't guess those boys ever owned a lock other than the one on that room they closed off thirty years ago. Why would they? But we didn't go in the front door anyhow. We cut straight through the barn. The cows were coming in all by themselves and they were complaining the way they will, but they were going to have to wait.

The house has just the one room that they use. Audie was on the floor and Vernon was in the bed. I wouldn't say he was cold but he wasn't much better than room temperature. It seemed to me he was stiffening up some. Creed didn't seem to mind my touching him, but I minded it enough for both of us.

I've been around death enough that it ought not to bother me, but now that I'm getting nearer to it myself it's different. It's different for an old man.

Audie was the one who needed a hand. He was curled up in a ball in his long johns and he was shaking all over like he was freezing to death. Moving all over, every part of him, the way his brother Creed had done outdoors but worse. Audie will do that some anyhow, just as a regular thing, but this was worse than usual. I said his name and he didn't say anything back. I got down on my hands and knees in front of him and I looked at him hard and I said his name louder. I made an effort to kind of bark it, the way Vernon used to when he wanted to get his attention. I slapped the floor with the flat of my hand and a cloud of dust rose up and I got a splinter but never mind that. He heard me and his eyes popped opened wide and he looked at me like he'd seen a ghost. Or like I was the ghost and he was looking straight through me at something else. Maybe Vernon, up there on the bed. Audie's pretty near blind and one of his eyes is clouded over some, but I've never seen anything so blue.

Audie

WHEN I CAME OUT onto the front porch they were turning.

A little wind had come up and they were all faced in the same direction and they were turning. I couldn't see them all that clear but I could hear every one separate. They all make a different sound. Every one. I didn't make them that way on purpose, but that's how they turned out. They can't help it and I couldn't help it either. They come out how they come out. Vernon says they're like children that way. They were turning in the little wind and I listened to them turn and I felt some better.

Donna

IT WAS MARGARET who thought to call the sister.

Margaret Hatch, who'd watched from her kitchen window as her husband walked down the hill between the houses and who'd kept watching when he didn't come back. Margaret, who'd watched as the sun came up and the shadow of her house gathered itself and pushed down the hill to poke at the Proctor boys' barn, and who'd moved with her coffee out onto the screen porch to keep on watching as the shadow withdrew a little and the heat of the day began to rise and the state trooper's patrol car came roaring up the dirt lane.

She figured the boys' telephone must work or else they couldn't have called the troopers, but she didn't figure they would think to call Donna. She was right. She looked up the number and stood in the kitchen and dialed. She wished she had a cigarette, and the idea of it surprised her completely. She hadn't smoked since Harry Truman, but she thought that right now a cigarette might be just the thing to calm her nerves.

*

The house smelled like cow manure and dry rot and spoiled food. Like tobacco and burnt rope and rat droppings. Like old men and sickness and death. Del Graham was the captain and he arrived first. He walked past the old man who sat rocking on the porch with his long white beard pooling in his lap and his hands knotted over his hairless skull, and he went through the open front door as into a mouth full of rotted teeth. The disarray and the stink. The order and the purposefulness gone to no use in the end.

Creed was sitting at the table alongside the neighbor, Hatch. Preston Hatch who'd made the call. The telephone was on the table between them, and they sat composed on either side of it like a formal double portrait. Titans of industry, awaiting a message from some distant outpost of commerce. The telephone was solid black, square and heavy. All business. The cord that connected it to the wall was wrapped in a kind of woven material that Graham didn't remember having seen for a long time. It looped easily and snakelike in spite of its age, and although it was frayed in places it looked made to last. The telephone was the old fashioned kind with a dial, rotary phones they called them, and the numbers under the dial were either worn away from use or obscured by dirt. He figured the second. Either way, in the absence of the numbers a person would need to count in order to make a phone call. Graham guessed that such a telephone probably didn't get much use, considering. It was a conduit to a world that had no business here.

The bed was in the corner beyond the table and the man on it had no pulse. There was one empty chair at the table and Graham came back and took it for himself. These two looked like individuals who could be trusted to know death when they laid their hands on it. He knew Creed by sight. He was the double of the old man on the porch except for a full head of hair pushed up crazily in some places and flattened down in other places. He looked about used up. His cheeks were hollow beneath his beard and his mouth was caved in. His nose was spotted and bulbous, something grown underground and dug up and left to wither. His pale eyes, heavy-lidded and sunken, were vague and weary of witness.

"So what happened."

"Vernon's dead. My brother."

"I know. I'm sorry."

"My brother Vernon."

"I know who he is."

Creed held a Red Man cap in his knobby hands and he wrung it. "He weren't dead last night when he went to sleep but he's dead now."

"We'll have some fellows up here soon'll take care of him. I live just down the West Road a little, so I came straight from the house. Those other fellows'll be right along."

Creed reached behind him, into a teetering pile of what looked like trash. He drew out a pouch of tobacco. "You mind if I chew?"

"It's your house."

Hatch touched Creed on the arm but only briefly. "You do what you like."

"This ain't no crime scene I guess." He fiddled with the pouch. "I ain't disturbing anything."

"Not so's I can tell," said Graham. He took off his flat-brimmed hat and hung it on his knee. He looked at Creed. Then with the palms of both hands he smoothed back the hair on each side of his head, as if he needed to.

*

DeAlton answered the telephone in his businesslike way and Margaret asked for his wife without identifying herself. It was no business of his who she was, and he didn't ask, and that suited her fine. Donna got on the line and Margaret told her that there was a state trooper at her brothers' place. Told her everything she knew: That she had seen Creed come out as usual and that she had seen Audie sitting on the porch. That she could see him there still or at least his legs, kicking. But that no, she had not seen Vernon. Not this morning. Not yet.

Now there were a couple more troopers and an ambulance too. That last had come slow up the dirt lane with its lights off. Donna had better drop everything and come.

*

The room was too small to fit everyone, although it had once been two rooms. The part near the door and the part by the bed were different colors and there was a ragged four-inch line dividing them where a long time ago somebody had torn down a partition wall. The headboard was pushed up hard against another door that was sealed with a padlock. The hasp on it was oversized and rusted and weathered down, and it had probably seen use on a barn door at some time. The padlock was rusted too from prior seasons in the outdoors. If a person could find the key for it in this mess he'd be eligible for some prize. It was surely rusted tight anyhow. A single solid piece of stubborn ruin.

Two troopers and two emergency technicians had crowded around the bed for no reason anybody could tell anymore. One of the troopers went out to his car and came back in and handed the other one a jar of Vicks so he could rub a little under his nose against the stink. They usually reserved the Vicks for around bodies a good deal more decomposed than this one, but Vernon had the same effect in that department whether he was alive or dead.

A little wind came up and the sheer lace curtain that hung over the front window pushed into the room upon it and fluttered some and died back. A creaking arose from outdoors.

*

Donna pulled up and parked in the dirt lane since there were no places left in the yard. The technicians had Vernon strapped onto a stretcher already and covered over with a sheet, and everyone had had to clear out of the house to let them angle him through the door clean. Not that it mattered how rough they were. Graham held the door and the two other troopers were up against their cars smoking and Preston Hatch was leaning on the porch rail next to Creed, who chewed and spat into the dirt yard and gave the impression of thought. Preston as short and round as Creed was tall and thin. Preston as pink as Creed was white. The pair of them an apple set against a parsnip, one clean and ruddy and the other dirt-rimmed and root-threaded, arranged for a kind of still life.

Creed spat and wiped his lip on his sleeve and spoke to his sister. "Vernon died."

"Vernon." Coming toward the porch.

"He ain't been so good lately."

"I know. I know that."

"I think he had the same cancer killed her."

Donna looked at Graham and saw him for the authority here and explained that Creed was talking about his mother. Her mother. A long time in the ground. "Where's Audie?" she asked.

Hatch looked around and noticed him gone for the first time and said, "Audie? I don't know. Maybe he's in the barn. If he is, he's the only one of us that's got any sense."

Audie

THEY ALL CAME OUT TOGETHER. They came out together alive and dead both. The humming of their talk and the grinding of their feet on the boards. The knocking of that plank against the doorframe like Vernon wanted something. I thought I would go feed the turkeys but the cows were calling from the barn all mournful. I heard them through the barn wall so instead of going out to the schoolbus where we keep the turkeys I pried open the track door and slid on in among them. I got a pail and the milking stool and I squatted down and took hold of the first teat that come to hand and I worked it. I was shaking some and a little of the milk caught me in the knee when it spurted out and it ran down my leg and reminded me how the bed was dry when I woke up. The bed was dry and Vernon was dead in it and I was the oldest, the oldest and left to follow him. But not all the way. Not yet.

Donna

GRAHAM STEPPED OFF the porch last. "Put out those smokes and give these fellows a hand why don't you?" He was talking to the other troopers. It was his way of giving orders. "Make yourselves useful."

Donna stood in the dirt watching the technicians set the brakes on the stretcher and check it and open the rear door of the ambulance. She looked woeful and aghast, collapsed in on herself.

"I'm sorry about your brother."

"I know. Thank you."

He reached in his pocket and took out a white card and gave it to her along with his name.

"They all sleep in that same bed, you know. Slept."

Graham fitted his hat on his head and looked out over the yard. At the bare dirt and the sprays of tobacco juice soaking into it. At the whirligigs turning in the breeze. At the collapsed fence and the fields beyond it and the dirt lane running through. He tilted the hat back on his head by a few degrees and he scratched at his forehead with two fingers and he tilted it back down. "This's a hard way to live," he said.

"I told myself I'd never come back."

"When was that."

"Whenever. Always. I'd imagine going off somewhere and wherever I'd got to I'd never come back. Wherever turned out to be two-year college. Then nursing school."

Graham looked at her and thought she wouldn't mind if he said it. "That makes you the black sheep."

"I guess it does." She didn't mind. It wasn't the first time.

The technicians had the door open and the front legs of the stretcher unlatched and sprung and they were getting set to slide it in, working slowly, as if it were the only job they would have to do all day. There was a time for urgency and there was a time for this.

"You never got a look at your brother."

"No."

"I was wondering maybe you would want to." He watched the men. "What with the nursing school and all."

Her right arm hung down straight along her side and she reached behind her back with her left to hold it by the elbow.

"I just thought."

"There's a thousand things that could have killed Vernon."

"I don't doubt it."

"God knows how he lived this long." She sighed and let go of her elbow and started down toward the ambulance, just to take a look.

Preston

I TOOK HIM to the hospital myself that one time. I had an old blue Nash 600 I'd picked up second-hand and I had him laid out flat in the back of it. Creed was in Korea then and the old man was long dead and Audie was every bit as useless as he is now. This was the spring of fifty-two. Early spring. The snow just gone in most places and in some other places not even.

Vernon and Audie'd taken the spike tooth harrow down to get it ready. It was an antique even back then. They were dragging it across the floor of the barn and a tooth caught and broke off, and it flew and it took Vernon straight through the calf. It came all the way through and half out the other side. The calf of his right leg. He never did walk right after that.

This was early in the day and I hadn't gone to work yet. I heard a howl from my upstairs window and I went down and opened the kitchen door and the howling hadn't quit so I went out. It was a man, I knew that. It wasn't any animal I ever heard of. I got my coat and I went out and I went straight down the hill through the mud and what snow there was. I followed that howl. I didn't even go by the driveway. It didn't occur to me. I just went right straight down.

Of course it wasn't Vernon. Vernon had himself propped up on that harrow with his leg on the crossbar and he had a piece of angle iron in his one hand. He began to beat on that spike in his leg and Audie was howling and he wouldn't let up. He beat on it and I hollered at him not to but he kept on, with Audie on his knees and shaking and howling all the while. Six or seven good blows and he drove that spike clear out the other side and it just fell down in the dirt and bounced once and laid there.

Audie kept shaking and howling and he wouldn't stop even though the spike was out and Vernon was limping toward the stall. The leg of his pants was red and there was blood on his boot and blood on the floor soaking into the dirt and into the straw wherever he stepped. I told him he had to let a doctor see it but he said no. Vernon'd never do anything you told him he had to do. That'd been his way since he was a boy. He shook out a feedbag and tore a strip off it and got him some baling twine and he rolled up that pantleg and wrapped the rag around where the spike had gone through and tied it off. A black hole on both sides, pumping. That's going to bleed I told him, that's going to keep bleeding and you won't stop it like that. You ought to at least put it up in the air I said, but there were chores to be done and he shut his ears to me. He said the sooner I get back to work the sooner that idiot stops his blubbering. He was right about that.

That rusted-through spike was broken off clean and there was no repairing it. Vernon kicked it out into the yard with his good leg and then he hoisted his brother to his feet and the two of them went to work side by side at the bench as if they had just one mind between them. Audie holding that piece of angle iron steady and Vernon hammering at it until they'd made themselves a pretty fair replacement for that rotten spike. Vernon's leg wasn't bleeding so much now or at least not so much that he was leaking everywhere. When they were satisfied with the hammering, Vernon fetched down a brace and bit and put a couple of holes in the top of it by eye and they mounted that old piece of angle iron on the harrow like it was made for the job. I'd say I'd never seen the like of it but I had. You see a lot, you live alongside those boys their whole lives.

Anyway, that wasn't the time I took Vernon to the hospital. That came later on, when the blood poisoning set in and he about died from it. He'd bandaged a piece of salt pork over the hole to draw the infection but it hadn't worked. Vernon rode in the back seat and Audie in the front. I drove fast and we had the windows open and Audie lost his hat. He didn't mind. I don't know that he even missed it. He leaned forward and watched the world go by a whole lot faster than he'd ever seen it go by from the seat of a tractor and he looked so happy. He looked happy enough to sing a song if he'd known the words to one.

1931

Ruth

EVERY SINGLE ONE of their children will arrive in the fall of the year. From December to April the house is an icebox—just the two little square rooms in front and the long narrow one behind, but it won't stay warm for anything. Not for all the wood in the world. Not with the stove in the first of the front rooms and the boys Vernon and Audie sharing a bed in other and the passage to their parents' little narrow hallway of a sleeping room going through there. Just a cut in the wall really. Not even a door to it and in the wintertime not even so much as a curtain, but the heat from the stove in the front room will give out rather than travel that far. Lester is forever promising to saw a hole in the kitchen wall to let the heat though but he never gets around to it. Instead he and Ruth work on the next child. Creed. That third boy still nothing but a temporary refuge against hard weather.

A house is going up on the next lot and it will be much finer than this one. When the workmen dug its foundation the summer before they measured it out probably half again as wide and twice as deep as the stone pilings under the Proctor place and they took it down six or maybe seven feet into the earth, which Lester said would help keep out the cold as long as they were smart enough to seal it off right. They might even put a root cellar down there if they had any sense, or a place for canned goods or any such other excess as the people who live in so grand a two-story house might accumulate. Ruth knows how deep they dug because she's had to pull one boy or the other out of the hole. But that was back in the summer, and now it is closed off and the walls are framed out and the whole place is boarded up weathertight and roofed over. They haven't cut the windows yet so it sits there on its little hill blind and poker-faced. It catches the light in the morning, and Ruth leans against the barn door looking at it and listening to the stretching sounds it makes as it grows warm and comfortable in the sun. Thinking what a shame it is to let such a thing stand empty even for a minute.

*

Once a week at most—usually Saturday night according to custom, although when Ruth married Lester she gave up any hope of going to church on Sunday morning—once a week she heats water in a pair of old cooking pots and a dutch oven and a teakettle on the black iron stove, and when it draws near to a boil she pours it out into a galvanized washtub and heats more and pours that out in turn until the bath is ready. The boys get clean enough, but considering the work of splitting the wood and stoking the fire and drawing the water from the pump and boiling it on that black iron stove with the rooster on the side, and considering how rapidly they get themselves filthy again, she has her doubts. She gets nothing but complaint from Lester for his role in it, and she has to wonder how long both of those boys will continue to fit into the galvanized tub anyhow. Two separate baths will be too much to manage. She can almost see Vernon handling his own in a year or two, but then there is Audie to consider. There is always Audie to consider and there always will be. He is like the poor, forever with us.

Five and six years old now, they're still a pair of tadpoles. Slippery in the soapy water. Where it slops over onto the board floor it freezes, and when she shifts her position for better purchase on one boy or the other her knees skid over thin sheets of it. Stuttering beneath her.

She stands them up one after the other and rubs their narrow bodies of bone with a towel thin as gauze, working from the top down with their feet still planted in the warm gray water. Then she lifts them out one after the other too and they stand in turn on the thin-iced floor and she finishes drying their lower parts if they have the patience for it. Then off they go. Chasing one another around the frozen house like the pair of innocent animals they are. Otters.

Their little wrinkled toes and fingers and other parts alien. Comfortable in the water or out of it, sunwarm or otherwise.

Bucket by bucket she empties the tub, making trip after trip through the front door and onto the snowblown porch and over to the edge of it the greatest distance from the barn, stepping to the rail and casting the soapy leavings into black air that freezes it into long curved glimmering sheets, lit by stars and falling.

Audie

MY BROTHER VERNON was bare and I was bare too and the old man hollered at us to quit horsing around. The old man was in his bedroom. He was drinking, but not from the still. We didn't have the still then. Creed built that later and he had plenty of help and the old man was gone on ahead or else he'd helped too and then he'd helped drink whatever came out of it. That was his way. He was handy but he was handy with a drink too. The old man hollered at us to quit horsing around but we didn't and he didn't stop hollering and I guess he didn't stop drinking either. My mother coming and going. My brother Vernon leaned over the washtub and put his hands on the rim of it and dared me to come around and give him a dunking if I thought I could manage it. I thought I could and I done it too but not quite. I come on around and my foot caught a smooth spot that was maybe ice and maybe not but either way it set me aspin and where did I go but into the stove. That old red rooster.

Lester

I GELDED A HORSE or two in my time and I cauterized the cut. I helped do it and I learnt how. This was over on the Middle Road with Lawson. He kept horses. I was just a boy. Lawson was a fast hand at that work, fast with the blade and fast with the iron both. You had to be fast. There weren't no other way. He showed me how to work the blade and the hot iron. The one to cut and the one to cauterize. You'd think it'd have a meat smell but it don't. I don't know why. All that burning that's what you'd think. There's noise when you first done it but after you was done if you'd done it right the horse'd rise up and shake all over and walk away. Just like that. You'd think there'd be more to it but there ain't. A horse don't know how to complain.

Them two boys of mine was making a racket in the front room and I told them to quiet down but they didn't. Maybe they did a little but it didn't last. I hollered at them one more time and it didn't change nothing but I didn't come out from where I was neither. I weren't about to. She was opening the door and closing it and opening it again, going in and out. That front room was about froze over and I had the curtain drawn against it and I weren't coming out from where I was no matter what.

At least I didn't meant to. But they set up a hollering, first one and then the other, and then their mother come back in and something clanged and she begun hollering too. I can't say if I judged it was important or if I'd just stood enough of their carrying on and hers too but either way I went. I put down the bottle and went.

What clanged was that tin pail. I seen it right off. Rolling across the floor bent, like that woman didn't care nothing for it and flung it hard as she could just to be shut of it. Like it was the pail caused everything. She had the young one by his shoulders and he was still hollering. All mouth. A hole big enough to drive a tractor through. And he was hopping too, just hopping up and down and hollering. I seen that rooster on his back like the one on the stove and red like it too and I smelt that smell I remembered from Lawson's place with that redhot iron. It weren't a meat smell but I remembered it the same. I took that boy up and I hugged him to my chest and I hauled him outdoors into the snow and I threw him down. That was the best thing for him. He kept on hollering and he tried to get up but I held him down. Oh how he hollered. If I'd had a knife I ought to've finished the job the way Lawson taught me. An idiot child like that. Done us all a favor. Got it over with.

Ruth

HER HUSBAND SAYS he ought to lay into her with that pail if she's going to be so careless of it. Look at the trouble she's brought on, with her filling the wash-tub and her emptying it, with her going out and her coming in. With her inexplicable commitment to hygiene. Look at what she has brought down on his family. He behaves as if that tin pail and her use of it are the cause of every woe he has ever endured in this world, as if by getting free of them he might enter paradise early. If he weren't so drunk, someone might get hurt.

Now they have Vernon alone in his bed and Audie in the front room alongside the stove. Ruth has made him a soft place on the table and has him laid out on it with his legs under a blanket and a couple of old burlap sacks over his bare arms and the rest of him uncovered. He lies on his stomach, with that rooster tattooed on his back throbbing in the soft light of the stove and in the hard light of the one electric bulb. He cannot keep quiet. He cries out from pain and he cries out for his brother Vernon. His mother strokes his leg through the blanket and he cries out over that too. His back gleams with an ointment that his father uses on the udders of cows. The old man was loathe to part with any but he acquiesced in the end. It smells like pine. Like Christmas in the house. At some point in the past Lester used the lid of the big round tin for some other purpose and left the rest to sit uncovered in the barn, so the ointment has flecks of chaff and clods of dirt and something that is probably bat droppings sifted down from the rafters in it, but she has done her best to pick them out.

She pulls up a chair alongside her son and she wants to touch him but she does not. She draws breath and lets it out. Even the passage of that little air over his raw back pains him. He calls out for his brother. For Vernon.

Audie

I FELT THAT OLD RED ROOSTER on my back and I saw its twin brother on the stove. I was lying on my belly with my head turned that way. I couldn't much move and I didn't want to. My mother was there. The stove was black and the rooster on the side of it was painted red and it was red from the heat too. I knew those two old birds were the same size and that they come from the same form and so when the one on my back got bigger in my mind the one on the stove got bigger right along with it. Bigger and drawing close. I didn't say anything about that.

1932

Preston

WE MOVED FROM TOWN when I was twelve years old. People out there called where we came from the city but it wasn't a city any more than I'm the King of England. It wasn't then and it isn't now. I've seen cities. I go to the VA hospital in Syracuse every six months. I've seen New York City on two occasions, and I've seen Washington from a tour bus, and one time I saw Montreal. That was with Margaret. We were on a tour bus then too just like in Washington, and we came through that town twice now that I think of it, but I'll just count it the once because it was the same trip. I've seen cities all right, but I didn't grow up in one. Cassius couldn't have been home to more than four or five thousand souls then and it doesn't have more than half again that many now.

On the other hand I suppose it depends on your point of view. When the Proctor boys talked about town they meant a wide spot in the road with a sign in front of it that said Carversville. I'd call it a village or maybe a settlement if that. A hamlet if that's still a word. Carversville is the same now as it was in those days: A crossroads with six or eight houses and a Methodist church and a tavern. A filling station and a store that never has anything you might want because they've always just sold the last one of anything and they ought to be getting more in two weeks. Anyhow the Proctor boys and the other folks around those parts called Carversville the town and they called Cassius where I came from when I was twelve years old the city, and there wasn't any changing their minds so you didn't try.

The Proctor brothers said I was a city boy and I took it for a compliment. They didn't mean any harm by it that I could tell. Besides, they were younger. Six and seven, to my twelve. I don't believe they meant it by way of a judgment. It was just a means to sort things out so you could look at them and understand them and see them clearer one by one. It was like keeping the cows and the sheep and the chickens all separate in your mind or in pens or wherever, each with its own place in the world and its own use.

That's what I think, although you can't ever really tell another person's mind. People say you have to know where he came from and that's true as far as it goes, but it doesn't go far enough. I know where those boys came from—I knew Audie and Vernon since they were six and seven years old, and I've known the last brother Creed from the hour he was born in that back bedroom until this very day—but that still doesn't mean I understand any one of them. Where a man comes from isn't enough. You've got to go all the way back to the seed of a man and the planting of it, and a person can't go back that far ever I don't think. Because there's always another seed behind that one and another planting of it too. All the way back to Adam. By which I don't mean to suggest that I'm a religious man. Margaret goes to church every Sunday but I just go along to keep her from getting lonesome.

So I was twice as old as those two when we moved here in 1932, even though today people take me for a good bit younger. I suppose that's because I'm the one who enjoyed all the advantages in life. The blessings and the benefits. My father owned a lumber yard and he built this house during the Depression when nobody wanted anything he had to sell. It was either make use of it or let it rot in the weather he used to say, so he kept his people on as best he could and he set them to work building this place. He had a little money saved up from doing a cash business all his life. He'd never put it in the bank so he never lost it. I don't know whether he was smart or just lucky and it doesn't matter much either way. Not then and not anymore. He drew up the elevations himself and the floor plans and all the rest, and he oversaw every bit of the work, and when it was all done the Depression was starting to lift and he sent his men back to the lumber yard. He and my mother hung onto the empty house in town until the war broke out and then they sold it for a nice profit. I was in France then and I didn't get to see it go.

We came in the summertime and Creed came in the fall.

Lester didn't put any stock in hospitals and I don't guess he could have afforded to if he did, so that was all right. I don't know how they could have gotten to the hospital if they'd wanted to. The only vehicle they had was a wagon without so much as a single round wheel on it. Put a woman in labor on a wagon like that and she'll be giving birth before you get her a half-mile down the road. Not that that would have troubled Lester any. The boys got hold of an old Farmall tractor once he was gone—this was while I was in France with General Patton—they got hold of an old Farmall tractor after the old man passed on and how they've kept it running all this time I can't say but they have. They had it when I came back. I walked home from the train with my bag over my shoulder and Lester was two years dead and they were all three riding that tractor around the yard like it was some kind of a carousel ride. God knows where they got the money for it. I used to kid them that they bought it with Lester's estate money.

Anyhow when Creed was born they didn't have much of a way to get to the hospital and Lester couldn't have paid for it if they did, so they let nature take its course. The same thing when Donna was born a couple of years later. I don't believe they so much as knew the name of a doctor. Like I said, I was the one who had all the advantages.

1970

Audie

THE BOY NEVER HAD WINGS that I knew of but he was flying.

Donna

SHE'D INTENDED TO BUY tickets for all of them, but they were too proud to let their little sister pay their way. She stood at the folding table in the high school lobby realizing that if she had thought to get the tickets ahead of time it would have been an end to it, but she hadn't thought. Vernon had money in the breast pocket of his overalls. He unsnapped the pocket and fished out the money and counted it. He put it back in and waited a minute and fished for it again and counted it all over. They had been the last in line for a while but it only seemed that way, because other people arriving to see the show would come near to them and scent the brothers and withdraw.

Vernon was chewing a wad of tobacco and Audie wanted some, but his brother wouldn't give him any because they would be in the auditorium in just a minute and what would he do with it then. Audie made his complaint and any number of people lingering along the walls of the big room turned their heads and looked. "Hush up and wait," Vernon said. "You'll forget all about that Red Man soon enough."

"Four adults," Donna said. Her husband, DeAlton, was out of town selling and wouldn't be back until the next afternoon. They would go together tomorrow night, just the two of them.

She put down two dollars and Vernon watched her and he put down six, placing each bill on the table as carefully as if he were putting it to bed, licking his thumb between one and the next. It gave him visible satisfaction. She thought that maybe letting her brothers pay their own way wasn't so terrible if doing it pleased him this much. She forgave him, and she forgave herself for having put her own satisfaction above his.

She spoke again to the woman with the cashbox. "Four. Please."

The woman looked from her to the pile of stiff bills that Vernon had laid out and back again. The bills were brown all over and flaking. Crusted with cow manure like bark. As if they'd been planted and fertilized and grown up all brown and green in some field.

Donna opened her pocketbook and took another bill from her wallet. "How about I give you a ten and you can just give me back two singles," she said. Scooping up the money she'd just put down and her brother's money too. Putting it all in her wallet where it wouldn't bother anybody. "Would that be easier?"

*

They took mimeographed programs from the smiling boy at the door and went in to find seats. The auditorium was brightly lit by mercury vapor lamps hung high overhead like captive flying saucers, pulsing all but invisibly and emitting a high thin sizzle. Most of the crowd didn't notice, but here and there some unfortunate blinked and poked a curious finger into his ear and felt suddenly overwhelmed by a sense of agitation and dread that dissipated only when the big lamps snapped off and the room was plunged not into darkness but into another kind of illumination altogether, the light of a hundred evenly spaced recessed bulbs on a bank of dimmers, promising relief.

"Thank God," said Donna to another young mother on her right. "I thought they were going to make us take the SAT."

"You and me both."

She and her brothers sat examining their programs, Vernon paging methodically and running his finger down one column after another like a speed
reader; Audie following his brother's example but going back to front, front to
back, whichever way the wind blew; Creed narrowing his eyes and puckering
his lips and flipping angrily past page after page in search of his nephew's
printed name. Donna found it first and showed to the rest of them. Also to the
woman at her side. "My son's Michael," she said. "I mean he plays Michael. The
youngest boy." Pointing. "His name's Tom. He's only eleven."

"I'll keep an eye out," said the other woman. "You must be very proud." She
might have flicked a glance past Donna and let herself size up the menagerie
she'd brought in with her for comparison against the prospective child, but it
was hard to say for certain. Donna didn't care anyhow. The orchestra such as it
was had trooped in and begun to play, and the lights overhead were fading and
the curtain was rising like fog, and on the stage thus revealed a thousand stars
twinkled beyond an open bedroom window. Three children lay asleep in their
beds. A tiny spotlight from somewhere over the shoulders of the crowd began
to dance along the dark wall of the nursery.

Donna slid forward in her seat and held her breath and sought out the
smallest of the three forms on the three high beds, the one that belonged to
Michael Darling. Her boy Tom. She had no interest in Peter Pan, the child who
could never grow up.

*

When Tom finally jerked into the air, the crowd roared and his uncle Audie
jumped clean out of his skin. All the pixie dust in Neverland could not have
raised him higher. All the lovely thoughts in London could not have lifted him
any more suddenly. And by the look on his face he was prepared never to come
down again.

*

Since this was a special occasion, the brothers had refused Donna's offer of a
ride and taken their old tractor the six miles into town. Vernon on the curved
seat of perforated steel, Audie and Creed perched on the running gear to his
right and his left. Audie's beard was long even then, and it streamed out behind
him like a pennant. Vernon's was shorter than his brother's by a foot and

roughly shaven above the lip in the manner of a haphazard Abraham Lincoln. Creed didn't have a beard at all in those days unless you counted what grew back weekly. Not one of them had yet gone white.

Now Donna wanted to drive them home. The springtime was well along but it was still chilly at night, even cold, and they weren't dressed for it. She said they could go on and leave the tractor in the high school lot, and she'd fetch one of them back for it tomorrow. They could pull it right around back by the cafeteria entrance. Nobody would care. Tomorrow was Saturday anyhow.

But there was a field to be plowed in the morning, and they couldn't afford her kindness.

She stood alongside them in the lobby as the crowd passed around them like water around stones and she tried to be reasonable. "Does that thing even have a headlight?"

"You bet," said Vernon. He reached into his pocket and pulled out a lump of Red Man and started on it, considering. "It's got a headlight all right."

"If I know you, it doesn't work."

"If it don't work, we'll go slow," he said. Which was true enough. They would go slow regardless.

"You wait here while I get Tom," she said. "Maybe he can talk some sense into you."

The three of them brightened at the idea, as if they were about to make the acquaintance of some favorite Hollywood star they knew from television. Andy Griffith maybe, or Little Joe from Bonanza. Groups of high school students passed them by, noisy and full of life, some with instrument cases in their arms and some still half in and half out of costumes. A few eyed the brothers like naturalists happening upon a rare species and a few sized them up like old jurists grown intolerant with the passing of too many years and the rest seemed not to notice them at all. The girl who had played Tom's mother flickered in and out of Vernon's vision and he recognized her right off, although she looked younger than he had expected. He thought she was pretty and he said so to Creed under his breath. Creed looked at him as if he'd just made a lascivious remark about their own sister, and he took a half-step away.

Audie

I HEARD VERNON SAY it wasn't pixie dust but wires, but I never seen any wires myself.

Donna

TOM CAME OUT carrying a canvas gym bag that belonged to his father. It was green and it said CASSIUS COUNTRY CLUB on the side and it bore the club's crest, crossed irons on a shield of gold with a white-tailed dear rampant. The bag was heavy and the boy hauled it that way. Inside it were his schoolbooks and his gym uniform and the harness of thick leather straps and cotton webbing and brass clips and sliders that he wore so as to be lifted up and swung out over the stage. The other cast members, older than Tom and at home in the high school building, kept theirs in their lockers and donned them in the boys' and girls' rooms before putting on their costumes. The director made an exception for Tom and let him change at home, which made for an uncomfortable car ride. He'd taken it off in the boys' room because it chafed, and with his free hand he was rubbing alternately at his shoulder and his crotch as he came.

The brothers cheered when he and Donna emerged from around the corner. Creed put two fingers in his mouth and blew a salute. Vernon fell to one knee and held his arms out. Audie stretched out his arms too but without kneeling down, as if Tom might possess the power to fly straight into them from where he stood.

"Hey," said Tom.

"Boy, you done great," said Vernon.

"You was a regular Buddy Ebsen out there," said Creed.

Tom smiled down at the floor.

"OK, Mister Movie Star," said his mother. "How about persuading your uncles to let me give them a ride back to the farm."

He tried but they wouldn't budge. Vernon said he didn't deserve to ride alongside a big shot like Tom so he'd just stick to the tractor. Creed asked Donna if she'd hired a limousine or some other such transport as befitted a luminary like Little Buddy Ebsen and when she said no he feigned disappointment and said he'd find his own way home. Donna screwed up her face and balled up her fists and told them that they could freeze stiff on that tractor for all she cared, but that didn't budge them either so she quit.

The lot was nearly empty when they went out. The sky was crowded with stars, millions upon millions of them hung in black space so deep as to transcend vision and confound it. Audie looked up and stumbled over a curb and windmilled his arms, falling and falling into the populous sky until Vernon caught him by the straps of his overalls and set him right. Donna and Tom got into the car and drove off. The brothers climbed aboard the Farmall and Vernon pulled out the choke and started it up and let it run for a minute. It shook like a dog fresh out of a lake. They shook along with it and the stars shook too on the backs of their eyes. After a while the engine smoothed out some and Vernon pushed the choke in and it settled down. Sparks flew out of the muffler and scrambled upward into the cold night.

Vernon hollered at his brothers to hang on as he jammed in the clutch and threw it into gear. The transmission had a kick like a mule and with that tricycle setup in front the whole thing turned on a dime no matter how old and illused it was. Vernon straightened out the wheel and they leaned to one side and came straight again and went lumbering down the access road to the highway, and once they were away from the lights Creed leaned over and shouted into his ear. "Turn off and go cross-lots why don't you," he hollered. "Save time." He pointed, his arm stiff in the starlight. So Vernon cranked the wheel, cutting north over the outer limits of the big lawn, past the tennis courts, leaving a three-part trail of dark ruts in the wet spring grass. If you can't take advantage of it now and then, why drive a tractor in the first place.

Preston

I SAW THEM coming up the road in the dark. The tractor had two headlights on it and only one of them seemed to be working and even that one was kind of dim and crusted over. It cast a yellow light that wobbled. I'd never seen it lit up before but all the same it's how I recognized them coming up the road. Who else would it have been? That one headlight was the only bright thing for miles around except the lamppost at the end of my little gravel driveway, the one I'd put on a timer a year or two before. Their farm was dark as always and the roads were dark too. The only light over there most times is the TV, and it was an old set when they got it and it gives off a blue light and they sit there in that light still. I don't know what all they get out of watching it. They just look at cop shows and lawyer shows like everybody else. I don't have much use for television, so I was sitting in the front room with a book in my lap when I saw them coming up the road.

I set down my reading and I went. I put on my jacket and I stood on the porch and I watched that little yellow light come passing back and forth up the dirt lane among the fields. If it'd been high summer and the corn was up I'd never have seen it, but this was in the springtime and there wasn't anything in the ground yet.

They rounded the one last curve onto that level stretch past my lamppost and in the light of it I saw Vernon at the wheel as usual, with Creed beside him holding on. They were both looking steady and hard into the night as if they'd been expecting trouble all the way from town and hadn't seen any of it yet but wouldn't quit looking out for it just in case. Behind them with his feet hooked on a piece of plowchain was Audie, balanced on the back end of that tractor like some kind of trick rider. He had his eyes shut tight and his arms out to both sides like wings, and he was flying. Flying on that tractor in the dark. All the way up the road from town.

1985

Audie

I ALWAYS KEPT at it just like I learned from Vernon. It's close work and I favor that. There's turning in the doing of it and there's turning when it's done. When we cut a tree we save a little out for the straight pieces. Vernon helps me put them up in the hayloft to dry out. Vernon or Creed these days if Vernon can't. It takes straight pieces for the turning and flat pieces for the other. None of them with knots if I can help it. I find a piece with a knot I burn it. I've got no use for knots. An old-timer named Driscoll keeps a sawmill over on the other side of town, down there in a little hollow where the creek runs by, and sometimes we take a nice piece down there and Driscoll saws it up and planes it smooth and then I've got my flat pieces. Sometimes I use paint and sometimes I don't. It depends. Sometimes I don't have any paint and sometimes I can't see to use it.

DeAlton

NOW THIS HAS GOT to be the shortest goddamned par three in the state. I'm sorry. I'm embarrassed to bring you out here and have you see it, but there it is.

I know you don't play much and that's fine. I understand. It's still good to get out, though. I never played much myself until a few years back and if I had nothing but this course to play on I don't believe I'd play at all. You start getting a little good it bores you right to death. Someday we'll go play Green Lakes. Now there's a course. It's a state park but it's a nice course all the same. Your tax dollars at work. Might as well make use of it.

Shit. That's all right. Take another ball and we'll act like it never happened. I got plenty.

You know who owns this land? Same old fellow owned it all along. He just leases it to the club. It takes a certain kind of individual to turn good farmland into something as useless as a golf course. I'd say it takes imagination. It takes a different turn of mind from other folks. He does all right with it though. He does all right. Don't you worry about him. Me, I'm the same way. I guess that makes me the black sheep of my family but that's all right.

No, you're fine. That's fine. You don't have to call fore if the ball's headed straight into the cornfield. Just kidding. Really. Here.

Anyhow, I'm the one struck out on my own. Went to work selling for Roy Dobson, as you well know.

Yeah, old Roy's still around. Absolutely. His name's on the building and he's still around all right. But he hasn't had a fresh idea in thirty or forty years, so he uses me to have his ideas for him. You didn't hear it from me but that's mostly what he pays me for. You know how it is. Sometimes a man'll have one good idea and he'll keep on riding on it as long as he can and you can't blame him for that, especially if it makes him a fortune. Roy's a fine gentleman and he's made his fortune all right. The only problem is he thinks since a cow's udder hasn't changed in a million years he doesn't need to change the machine that milks it. Like I said, I'm the black sheep.

Here, let me help you line this one up.

So I grew up in the muck on my old man's onion farm out past Wampsville, and as soon as I could cut loose I cut loose and I went. I never once looked back. Not once. My boy, he's the same way. He was born independent. It comes naturally to him and he can't help it. A while back I arranged things so he could come work for Roy, learn the ropes, come up through the ranks like I did, but he wasn't having any of it. Can you imagine that? It hurt my feelings a little bit, I don't mind telling you. Then Tommy took that two-year college education of his and what did he do with it but start working construction over in Utica. Can you imagine that? Talk about a black sheep.

Just go on tap that one in and we won't even count it.

He did get some of my instincts for the business world, though. That boy won't stay in construction forever, and you can bet money on that. Old Tommy's always got a couple of irons in the fire. Just like his old man.

Tom

IT WAS BETWEEN eight and nine and the shadows were getting long when Tom Poole came tearing up the dirt lane to his uncles' place. He parked the pale blue VW fastback in front of the barn and he jumped out and slammed the door behind him as if he hated that damned car, which he did.

"You working late?" Creed's high and reedy voice, from the shadows of the barn.

"I been working late and now I'm starting the second shift." As if it was his uncle's fault.

The construction project in Utica had gone into overtime, which was just perfect for making Tom's life miserable since he still had his plants to look after. His grandfather Poole had always said that there was no rest for a man who chose to make his way in an agriculturally-oriented endeavor, and the old man should have known what he was talking about since he was usually standing knee-deep in muck when the notion to pontificate came into his head. Tom hadn't ever paid him much attention and he'd certainly never thought that the old coot's useless wisdom would apply to him—first with his college plans and then with his construction job—yet here he was. Watching the sky and hauling fertilizer in a wheelbarrow. Calculating his yield and watching the market. Something told him that this was better than onions, but not by much. He hated onions. That was for sure. And he didn't hate dope, except for the work and the uncertainty that went into growing it.

"I been working late myself," said Creed, his voice whistling in the dark. He hadn't stepped out of the barn and he wouldn't. Let the boy come in if he had something to say.

But Tom didn't go in. Last year's crop was about used up and this year's was coming on and he humped up the hill behind the cow pasture to see what was what. Hoping that he could get it harvested and dried and cured before the old supply ran out and he developed a cash flow problem. He had his tools in his backpack. Not the tools from Utica, but his own. He knew he ought to take some other path up into the high field but there wasn't ever time. He ought to park his car over on the Middle Road and cut through the woods on the back side of Preston Hatch's property—either that or find some other way—but who cared. He hadn't ever been caught and Creed hadn't ever been caught running that old whiskey still out there either. History was on his side. History and habit and probably custom, too.

Up the hill he went and down a little tractor path that was more like a game trail than anything ever made by a man, and then on through a break in the barbed wire that passed for a gate. It sagged and it dripped rust. You could close it up if you had work gloves or if you didn't mind bleeding to death or if your hands were made out of elephant hide like his uncles', but he never bothered. He passed through it and walked another thirty yards in the low sun over fallow land. After a while he came to a little patch of woods. His uncle Creed's old still was hidden in the middle of it and his own marijuana plants were set all about the perimeter where they could get sun. The marijuana competed with fiddleheads and poison ivy and Queen Anne's Lace and a million other kinds of underbrush that he didn't know by name. It was a mixed blessing. Competition and concealment both. There was a time when he'd cunningly set the individual plants among the cornrows, hiding them in plain sight and thinking to put his uncles to work without their even knowing it, but the old men had surprised him and gotten up there with the harvester when he wasn't looking. A season's worth of grass, straight into the silo. He'd hoped the cows had enjoyed it. Since then he'd come to put his trust in nature. He made do without irrigation, contrary to the conventional wisdom, relying instead on a creek from up in the hills that fed this whole area and kept it all more or less green and yielded up this little copse of trees and brush. The creek ran over a couple of little waterfalls where he'd spent plenty of happy hours as a boy, and it still managed to bring him delight—if only indirectly—now that he'd put away childish things.

It turned out the plants weren't near ready yet, and he didn't know whether to take that as an affront or a reprieve. He was prepared to begin trimming them and carrying them down to dry in the hayloft, and he was sure as hell eager to start turning his crop into cash, but on the other hand it was pushing nine o'clock and the air was still godawful hot and he was just plain beat from the overtime. How come the dope business was turning out to be so much like farming, anyhow?

*

Vernon was on the porch, collapsed into a great big overstuffed chair. Damp clouds of cotton wadding leaked out of it along every seam as if something inside it had blown up. Vernon sat plucking little bits of the wadding with one hand, rolling them into little pellets between his thumb and forefinger and flicking them into the yard and then starting again. He'd been squinting into the failing sun and waiting for Tom to come down from the high field, down through the pasture and along the fence and into the barnyard where he might either turn toward the house or just get into his car and go. Finally he showed up. He came around the corner of the barn and turned into the yard and the old man spoke to him, his voice coming out with a deep and penetrating kind of squawk, like the voice of a crow slowed down. "Watch your step among them whirligigs," he said.

"I see them."

"You're always in a hurry."

"I'm a busy man."

"I guess."

A light breeze had come up. It pulled the lace curtain out through the window and Vernon brushed it away from his face with one hand. The whirligigs in the yard veered as if they shared one mind among them, rotating to face away from the wind and begin their slow turning. Winged pigs and cows and horses. Chickens and geese and ducks. They creaked in the failing light and the sound of them drew Audie's sharp face to the window from behind the curtain that his brother had pushed away. His eyes were vague and his long beard mingled with the lace curtain and he smiled through it as if he had just been reminded of something remarkable.

Tom came up on the steps and sat.

His uncle said, "I seen that crop of yours on television."

"I don't know what you're talking about."

"I seen it all right."

From the window Audie muttered something either oracular or idiotic. Maybe words and maybe not.

"I seen it on that Sixty Minutes last week. They was saying it might do me some good."

"I don't know what you're talking about, Vernon."

They sat for a minute and the wind kept up and the things in the yard kept turning. Audie said something to them, either to the things or to his relations, but he got no answer. Vernon worked at the chair. After a while a door opened somewhere and the lace curtain billowed out from the window and the door slammed and the curtain collapsed back in on itself.

Vernon did not so much as turn in the overstuffed chair. "That you, Creed?"

"Suppertime," said Creed, in from the barn, standing by the dead refrigerator in the dark house. He took a plate of butter from on top of it and swatted away flies and set it on the table. Then he opened the refrigerator and took out half a loaf of bread and put that on the table too. The refrigerator was jammed with stuff but not much of it was food and not much of that was still worth eating. Audie moved from the window to the table and scraped back one of the three chairs and sat.

Vernon flicked away a pellet of cotton batting and held out his hand. "Help an old man up," he said.

"If you sat on a straight chair," Tom said, "this wouldn't happen."

"You don't know."

"I work alongside men older than you forty hours a week. Plus overtime."

"Work," said Vernon. He smiled and wheezed. "I know about work. You couldn't kept up with me in my day."

"You've still got your day, old man." Tom stood and hauled Vernon to his feet. "It's still your day, as far as I can tell."

"I'm sixty years old."

In the kitchen, without turning his head, Audie offered something by way of disputation.

"So I'm fifty-eight then. He's right enough. I was born in the fall of twenty-five. I'm fifty-eight."

"That's not old."

"I got a birthday coming."

"I know."

"My own mother died at fifty-six." He shuffled toward the door. He was still half bent from sitting and he tilted forward, grimacing behind his beard. "She had the same cancer as me."

Tom just shook his head. "When'd you last see a doctor?"

"I ain't never seen a doctor. Not but that one time I got the blood poisoning."

"So how do you know what you've got. If you've even got anything."

"I know what I got. I seen it kill her. We all did."

Tom held the door for him. "Go on in and have your supper," he said. "Maybe it'll make you feel better."

"I'll feel better if you give me some of what you're growing up by the still." Vernon stepped into the inner dark. "That's how I'll feel better."

"I don't know what you're talking about," Tom said.

1960

Preston

I THINK IF they'd been left to their own devices those boys'd put her in the burn barrel with everything else and meant no disrespect by it. It'd been like something out of Homer. God knows they revered that woman.

Ruth

A PERSON CANNOT forever beat back the predations of time and the world. The house where she lives is the house where she raised up the children and the house from which she buried her husband, but it is not the same place. Her room in the back is a dank and airless cell. Her daughter, Donna, is gone and with her such standards of cleanliness and order as a woman will maintain. She ascribes it to that. Now and then Audie will slip into her room and reposition the lace doily on the bedside table or blow away a rime of dust that has gathered there along its edges but that is the extent of it. The extent of anyone's intervention or upholding on her behalf. He means well and she thanks him. When he is done he vanishes through the door that he and his brother Vernon hung in the cut hole so many years ago, when their father went on before them and a barrier between their bedroom and that of their mother was required. It was as if they had been waiting all that time.

In those days Donna slept in the first of the front rooms. The kitchen and the living room and whatever else was required of it. Her bedroom too, then, for seventeen years. In the winter she slept alongside the black and red stove and in the summer she slept beneath the blowing lace curtain. She grew up and she graduated from high school and she moved out to start college. She married DeAlton Poole and he paid for her to study nursing in Syracuse for all the good it has done her forbears.

These days she comes back to the house with her belly protruding, the child growing in her and the sickness growing in her mother. One to enter the world and one to leave it.

She comes in her minivan and she takes her mother to the hospital in Cassius. The old woman doesn't see any point in going but since it's Donna she goes. They sit together on a hard bench in the laboratory. Everyone in the hospital knows Donna and by now everyone knows her fading mother too. Ruth parts with three tinkling vials of blood, watching it drain from her arm and imagining that living within it are certain invisible creatures that she is better off getting shut of. If only she could rid herself of it entirely. One more part of her gone, although minus the sickness there might be nothing left. She asks her daughter the nursing school graduate why she cannot draw the blood at home and just bring the vials of it to the hospital herself without troubling an invalid to make the trip. That way she wouldn't even have to get out of bed. But Donna reminds her that after they have visited the drugstore they will stop for lunch at McDonald's or the Madison Street Dineraunt, her choice, and this takes a little of the sting out.

The nurse pulls the needle and covers the red spot with a cotton ball and asks Ruth to keep it there please, which the old woman does with a look of vast seriousness and intensity, holding her thin forearm as if it is the most precious thing on earth. Cradling herself to herself there on a hard plastic bench the color of poison. The puckered vein when the nurse returns to cover it over is a pale roadmap drawn on parchment, the road itself lost and gone, the map of no use to anyone. Not even as a memento.

DeAlton

WHEN YOUR FATHER DIED without a will it was ignorance, but if your mother goes the same way it's nothing but stupidity and pigheadedness. I know they're simple people, she's a simple person, and I don't mean any offense by that. But the law isn't particularly kind to simple people. It doesn't make any exceptions for them.

Hand me that ketchup.

Intestate is the word for it. It means without a testament.

Latin? Is that right? Latin? Well I'll be. You did get all the brains in the family. I don't mean any offense by that either.

Anyhow I talked with Vince over lunch at the Rotary. He'll do it for nothing. Professional courtesy. The truth is he does a little corporate work for Dobson and he'll probably just bury it, but he'll never say so. That's the kind of thing that if you keep it to yourself it's a favor and if you say it out loud it becomes an ethics violation. Nobody wants that.

It's not going to come as any surprise to her. She's been getting ready to die as long as I can remember. You're not going to hurt her feelings.

Vernon

SHE OUTSMARTED THEM city lawyers. DeAlton come out here with that Italian feller and this pretty little gal the Italian feller had with him carrying the papers. She was a little bitty thing. Looked like that Connie Chung on television. They come out here the three of them and they went on in her room like they owned the place which I guess they were trying to. But she wouldn't sign. She wouldn't sign. She laid there in the bed and she asked that Italian feller how about if she just turned the place over to the four of us before she went. There weren't no chance we'd throw her out. That Italian feller scratched his head and said he had to allow she had a point, and the little gal with the papers looked like she wanted to laugh but couldn't. DeAlton pushed them all back out to the car and they left.

Audie

MY MOTHER WENT on ahead. After they took her out I went in and arranged her things. I made up the bed. She always kept her clothes in the chest of drawers and I left them right where they lay. Creed came in and said it was about time we had the use of that furniture but I wouldn't let him. I wouldn't let him have the use of it. I was in her room and he came in with some things he wanted to put in that chest of drawers. He had some old hats and his winter coat and mine too and Vernon's, but I told him they could just keep on hanging in the barn the way they always did. There wasn't any reason to use up her chest of drawers that way. I asked him where we would put her things if we took them out and he said we ought to give them to the poor.

Preston

YOU HAD TO GO through Ruth's bedroom to get to the jakes. It'd been that way from a long time back, when Lester and Ruth lived there just the two of them. It was all right in those days I guess. Before the boys came and Donna. Anyhow the jakes was in between the house and the barn and you had to go through Ruth's bedroom to get to it. I would imagine there was a parade all night long with those four children.

When Ruth passed on and they closed up her bedroom, I think they were surprised at not having the use of it anymore. The jakes I mean. I don't think they saw that coming. They were pretty well occupied about her and I don't blame them. This was in the summertime. I believe they used the woods for a while, somewhere up by the still. They used the woods as long as the weather held but the seasons change whether you like it or not and they couldn't keep on that way forever. I'd see the three of them coming and going up that hill and down again one by one and I'd feel sorry for them, but I wasn't about to offer up the use of our facilities either. I could blame that on Margaret but I won't, since I felt the same way she did. It was a failing and I know it but there are limits to everything, even kindness.

What brought it on was that pretty soon Audie wouldn't come out of her bedroom for anything. That's why they had to close it up. She had an old caned chair by the bed and he sat in it and he wouldn't even come out to work on his whirligigs. A person who knew him would have figured that that work and those whirligigs were the things he loved most in all this world—those and his brother Vernon—but in the end that distinction went to his mother.

Donna

SHE WAS GLAD that her mother had passed away in the summertime, if you could say such a thing. The ground would be soft. Nobody ever got buried in the winter. She had been three years old the winter her father died, and although she believed that she remembered his funeral she knew that such memories may have been hearsay. Her mother's words made flesh. On the other hand she was certain that she did recall his burial, which took place one bright spring afternoon on a little plot of ground that bordered Hatch's woods. Her brothers dug the hole. The world was green, and stepping into the woods was stepping into a bottle. To put her father into that fertile ground was to be assured that he would rise up again. At some point in her youth she realized that she did not know where his body had been kept during the months following the funeral, and rather than have to find out she was glad that her mother had chosen to pass away when the weather was warm.

Her brothers dug this hole too, right alongside the other and sharing the headstone. Careful not to interfere with what was already there, hidden in the earth and not risen up after this score of years but still worthy of veneration. Preston came up and helped them map the hole with a snapline and a carpenter's square. He drove pegs into the ground and he strung the line and they worked within the perimeter of it, heading straight down. Audie didn't dig but sat vigil at some remove on an upturned bucket, keeping an eye on the hole. He had the look about him of a man considering not just what had to go down into it but what might come up.

The preacher who served the church in Carversville had another charge in Lenox and one more in Peterboro, and he was a hard man to pin down. During the week he was nowhere and on Sunday he was everywhere. For a while Donna wasn't sure that she could even get him. The undertaker from Cassius swore that he could find somebody else in a pinch but she didn't want a stranger. The preacher from Carversville was stranger enough. She thought his name was Tuttle.

Her mother's body went to the funeral home and stayed there overnight and came back again like something on loan, twelve miles altogether in the most luxurious conveyance she had ever ridden. Inside a box the whole distance. DeAlton paid for it. Someone from the state came out to assess the burial ground, a barrel of a man who paced off the yardage between Preston Hatch's wellhead and the hole and declared the operation unacceptable on account of something having to do with groundwater. Preston scoffed. He said he'd been drinking the remains of the deceased's husband Lester for twenty-one years and he wasn't the worse for it yet. Worse things died all the time up there in the woods and nobody cared. The state man had a face like a boiled egg and it ran with sweat in the sun and he didn't feel like arguing either chemistry or philosophy with someone he took for a bumpkin. Regulations were regulations, and the new hole was fifty feet short of squaring with them. Preston asked what the fine would be. The man from the state told him and Preston said he'd pay it himself. He volunteered to pay it himself right then and there if that was what it took and the man from the state looked tempted and he fidgeted some and put the forms back into his pocket but when all was said and done he didn't take him up on it. He just got back in the car and drove off. Preston went inside and drew himself a glass of water.

*

Tuttle drove up while Audie was prying the old hasp away from the track door on the side of the barn. Vernon had given him a hammer and a crowbar, and although the hammer had but one claw and the crowbar was too big the outcome was certain nonetheless. Audie would not have quit without Vernon's authority. He would not have quit even if he had understood the full import of his work: that his brothers meant to use the hasp to seal their mother's room against him. The nails that held it to the barn were old cut iron and they were driven into a solid oak upright and they screamed as they yielded inch by inch. They screamed and gave up their straightness, and Audie cursed them in his own way. If Tuttle minded or even understood he made no mention of it. He had certainly heard worse, for there is something about the nearness of death that shows men plain and unadorned. An individual may conceal himself before God but not before that. The preacher wore a straw fedora against the sun and he tipped it to Audie and he went on past. He knocked at the door but no answer came. He put his nose against the screen. It smelled of rust and he called through it into the dark but his voice in that small space was no larger than his knocking and it produced the same result. He wiped the reddened and checkered tip of his nose on the back of his hand and hitched up his pants and went down from the porch, on past Audie again and around the empty barn and up into the fields.

Creed was on the tractor, his silhouette atop the ridge making a slice against the sky. He saw Tuttle coming and he cut the engine and it took a while to quit. The ridge where he was working was a little bit of a walk, and although it took Tuttle some time to reach him he made no effort to climb down and meet him halfway. He sat in the sun and waited, and Tuttle came on slowly.

"I'm sorry about your mother." Tuttle said it without introducing himself, trusting that Creed would know him by his collar.

"She was dying for a long time."

"I guess we all are." Tuttle shaded his eyes and looked up toward Creed where he sat on the Farmall. "We're all dying from the moment we're born."

"I mean the cancer," Creed said.

"Right. Right you are. The cancer." There in the dry field with dust on his shoes, he turned and surveyed the landscape from beneath the shade of his hand. He turned his back on Creed and sighted down toward the barn. "I know she was a fine woman," he said. Such were the words that came under these circumstances. He said them with his back turned, as if to allow for some doubt that he'd even spoken. "I'm sorry for your loss."

"So how much for the job?"

Tuttle turned back. "What was that?"

"The funeral ain't until tomorrow so I guess you come about the charge."

"Oh, no. There's no charge. I appreciate the thought, but there's no charge."

"All right. She paid her debts and I won't have her go out owing."

"Oh, no. Never fear."

"All right, I won't."

Tuttle brightened a little. "You could make a donation, though. If you like." And then, by instinct, "The church is always in need."

"Vernon keeps hold of the money," said Creed. He put his foot on the starter.

"Actually, what I came for was to see if there's something you'd like me to say about your mother."

Creed pulled at his lip, brown teeth behind a brown hand. "She paid her debts," he said. "She done her best with the four of us. That's all."

"She did her best."

"It weren't easy." His eyes glassed over thinking it, and his foot bounced on the starter.

"She did a fine job."

"Just say that."

"I will."

Creed pressed the starter once and nothing happened and he pressed it again and nothing happened and then on the third try it kicked in.

Preston

IF THEY'D HAD any common sense they'd have waited a while to close off that room, but common sense was never their strong suit. I was up at the graveside for the service and I stayed to help put her in the ground. It was just the three boys and Donna and DeAlton and Margaret and me, along with a cousin of DeAlton's from over in Valley Mills. The seven of us and the reverend. He was a nice enough young fellow although I don't guess he had a lot of funeral work under his belt yet, and a good deal of what he had to say sounded like he'd gotten it out of a textbook. Like he was just filling in the blanks. Then again he didn't have much to work with.

Audie was quiet the whole time. He stood alongside his sister and she held his hand. I kept my eye on him and I made up my mind that he wasn't certain as to who was inside the box. I think he had a picture of his mother in his mind and it didn't include her lying underneath a coffin lid. After the reverend said his piece he held his Bible to his chest and started in on "Blest Be The Tie That Binds" and we joined in, Donna and Margaret and me. The boys tried to help but kept coming in late. There isn't a strong voice among them anyway. DeAlton just looked at the ground. I don't know about his cousin. I didn't look his way.

I'd helped Vernon and Creed lay out ropes under the box and we used them to lift it up a little bit and edge it over and let it on down. One of the ropes got snagged under the box and gave us a little trouble and I'd have just left it down there if it'd been up to me, but those boys were always great believers in waste not want not. Audie went down for it and came up grinning like a boy who'd caught a snake. He looked young.

*

We had a little reception on the screen porch out back. You could about see the grave from there for one thing. And anyhow you didn't necessarily want to spend much time in a closed room with those boys no matter what the occasion was. Margaret set out baloney sandwiches cut up small and macaroni salad and baked beans and a white cake. She put that last under a little screen tent she had that folded up like a parasol when you didn't need it, even though the porch already had screens. She set out some lemonade too. I'd told her earlier in the day that I was afraid the cake might make things a little too festive but the boys didn't seem to get that impression. They went at it like a pack of wolves. DeAlton's cousin ate a little piece of a sandwich and headed on home but the reverend stayed. He didn't have a wedding ring on his hand so he was probably figuring this would do him for supper. That's what Margaret said later. She guessed he lived from one potluck dinner to another, and this one was as good as the next. He didn't push the church on us any.

After a while we wrapped up the leavings in tinfoil and the boys took them home. If it'd been anybody else I guess we'd just let them take the plates and bring them back when they were done. Margaret said they ought to get at the baloney and the macaroni salad and the baked beans right off because they wouldn't keep in this heat. The cake would last but there wasn't much of it. They thanked her kindly and went off satisfied. Say what you want, those boys were brought up to be gracious. You can't take that away from them.

DeAlton went back to work and Donna went home and the reverend left too. It seemed to me there was a good deal more awkwardness over all those goodbyes than there had been up at the grave, I guess because the parties involved were all still among the living. Plus up there the reverend was in charge of things and he knew exactly how it was supposed to be done, step by step, even if he did get it out of a book. Afterward it's every man for himself.

They went down to the house and I sat with Margaret on the porch. The trash needed emptying but I didn't get at it right away. We hadn't done all that much, but we were about worn out. A funeral will do that to you no matter how old you are and we weren't old then. Not yet. We sat side by side and watched them go down the hill and across the little bit of pasture toward the house. Vernon gave his tinfoil to Creed and went around back where the old schoolbus was that they kept full of turkeys, and Creed and Audie went into the barn. I didn't know if they would keep going into the house but I figured they wouldn't because they'd have work to do in the barn the same as always.

It wasn't until I heard Audie carrying on that I knew they'd kept going into the house. Why Creed couldn't have waited to get the hasp mounted on her bedroom door I can't say. There's such a thing as a decent interval. Why he had to have Audie work on it I don't know either.

Creed

HE'S A GOOD WORKER but he wouldn't do that job. Preston come and give him some white cake and that calmed him down and then I done it myself.

1990

Del

I HATED LIKE ANYTHING to see them go put up that yellow tape. I knew it had to be done, but I hated to see it happen and I hated that I couldn't do anything to prevent it. You reach a point, though, beyond which it's all procedure. Some men take comfort in that but I don't. Maybe I will one day, but I don't now.

What were they going to find? Those three men lived there cheek by jowl all their lives and the place hadn't been cleaned in forever. There were fingerprints on that headboard older than I am. If you looked hard enough you'd find fingerprints of dead people. And I don't mean Vernon either. I mean the old couple, what were their names, Lester and Ruth. The parents.

The only evidence if you could call it that was on the body. I never noticed it myself, but I'm no doctor. The sister didn't notice it either even though I had her look. At least she didn't say. The medical examiner did his job, though, and what I took for sunburn turned out in his opinion to be sunburn and something else on top of that or rather underneath it. Burst blood vessels. Petechiae is the word he used. The blood vessels break from pressure, which can indicate asphyxiation. Strangling. You'd see them on the cheeks and on the neck and in the eyeballs, and Vernon had them in all three places. I don't know. They can burst from coughing too, as I understand it. And maybe a million other things.

It's plain that Vernon wasn't a well man to begin with. So I don't know. I think you'd have to have more than that to go on. But the medical examiner saw what he saw and they had to go out there and put up that yellow tape, regardless of what I thought. It was procedure. Plain and simple.

Donna

VERNON ONCE DREAMED his own death. He dreamed it one night in the bed with his brothers, and all the next day it would give him no peace. It hung in his mind like the lace curtain in the front window in the summertime, always in motion, never revealing itself entirely, flickering around the edges of his mind. It showed itself over and over, different parts of it in different orders, troubling stark snippets of black menace that would not let go. He saw himself dead in the bed and he saw one of his own brothers arrested and charged. He could not be sure which. It varied. He saw himself alive at bedtime in the comfort of his usual valley and he saw himself not waking up. He never saw himself dying but he saw himself dead. Dead with a brother on either side of him, the younger to one side and the youngest to the other, one of them to blame in the eyes of the law.

Because he could not shake the dream, he shared it. He sat on the over-stuffed chair which was his by right of seniority and he gathered his brothers onto the porch and he told them. One said, "It weren't me." So did the other. The first said it was the cancer. Had Vernon known the Judas if a Judas there was, it would have been easier but no more satisfactory.

"One way or the other I'm going soon," he said with an air of resignation and boding, and they offered no argument. He sat plucking bits of cotton batting from the chair and rolling it into pellets between his fingers. "Maybe I'll take a gun and shoot myself. Get it over with. Save you boys the trouble."

His youngest brother Creed said he would help by hiding the gun if he wanted. He would do whatever was required.

"Don't worry about that," said Vernon, "There won't be no need to hide it. As long as I go during the daytime, you'll be all right."

It is in the nature of visions to be communicated. Vernon told Preston Hatch, who told Donna because she had a right to know. She told DeAlton and a few people on her shift at the hospital, and before long it was everywhere.

Those brothers of hers. Who knew where they got their ideas. Certain individuals decided maybe they got them from one another, and that Vernon was doomed.

*

If the yellow tape was meant to prohibit contamination, it was put up years too late. Its only functions now were those of superstition and formality. The two troopers from Cassius who strung it up and the forensics technician from Syracuse who gave them a hand with it began their day with a cold professional air, but when the work was done they would go home to their families glassy-eyed and incredulous. Not one would describe what he had seen.

The bedsheets were yellow and brown, perhaps more so in the middle where Vernon slept but not by much. They smelled like ammonia and sulfur and cats, and when the men tried removing them they stuck to the mattress and pulled loose fiber by fiber, making a thin high tearing sound of disintegration. They separated and billowed into clouds that lifted slowly and hung in the air. The men coughed and were glad for their masks, sifting tatters of linen through their fingers and thinking about mummies. In the end they took the whole mattress.

The floorboards by the broken refrigerator, along the wall beyond which stood the jakes, were damp and rotted down to a soft mulch. A yellow haze of mold grew on it. The side of the refrigerator was mossy. The man from Syracuse said his Boy Scout training must be failing him because he'd been given to understand that moss grew on the north sides of trees and this was the east. One of the troopers suggested that maybe the conventional wisdom didn't apply to iceboxes. A coffee tin stood alongside the bed for a spittoon. Good to the last drop, said one of the troopers as he lifted it up. Another tin, the very mate to it but older, lay upset beneath the bed with its contents spilled like black varnish. Insects had died in the spreading tongue of it and they lay there still. On the far bedpost sat a cracked glass containing a quarter-inch of something that looked like turpentine and smelled the same. They dusted it and they took a sample of its contents in a vial. A plastic ashtray from the Olcott Tavern in Cassius sat on the table alongside a stack of ancient seed catalogs and girly magazines. There were ashes in it and spent kitchen matches and a cigarette butt that had no filter and was twisted up tight around itself and skewered on a piece of copper wire. They took that too.

Preston

THE TROOPERS WENT through that place like thieves. There wasn't any justice in it. Those Proctor boys don't own much and half of what they own those fellows took. They took the mattress, for crying out loud. I don't know where they're supposed to sleep but I suppose it doesn't matter since they're not supposed to go in the house. I guess the barn.

Who knows when they'll come take the tape down. I saw Audie come in from the field and stick his head inside the barn but Creed wasn't there so he walked right on around to the front porch and lifted the tape and went on in. He doesn't know what it means. He doesn't know anything about tape, not that kind or any other kind. I suppose maybe he's seen them use it on Rockford or somewhere but that doesn't mean he understands it. To him that tape's just a decoration. He probably thinks it's the Fourth of July.

Tom didn't have but two uncles left and in spite of that I hadn't seen him around. He was never much for coming by their place when he was growing up. I think I understood that. They were alien to him. Just one generation away and they were like a tribe of cannibals to that boy, even though his own mother had come up among them. I'd blame it on DeAlton but I don't think that's entirely fair either. DeAlton always knew his way around a farmyard, even though you might not know it to look at him. First on that onion farm of his father's and then selling for Dobson. He'd go from one place to the next like the Fuller Brush Man, but with a trunkful of milking equipment instead of brushes. He kept coveralls in the trunk and he'd pull them on right over his suit and tie, and a pair of old Redwing boots that he'd probably worn for digging onions back before he got his own ideas. A man makes use of what he owns and where he's been, and DeAlton was no different that way. He never could sell a thing to those Proctor boys, though. Not that they had two nickels to rub together. They did everything just the way Lester did before them and they never made any complaint. I don't think they even knew the world had changed.

The last few years have been different, at least in the summertime. I mean with regards to Tom coming around and all. Ever since he's been grown up and working he's been out to the farm a couple three times a week. Sometimes more. Sometimes to visit and sometimes not. It's none of my business what he's up to. I know that. It was none of my business when Creed built that whiskey still after he came home from Korea either, not until he needed help sweating a little copper pipe and I had a blowtorch I knew how to use. My father'd taught me. I'd never even touched that particular blowtorch before then. It was old stock that we'd brought home from the lumber yard when something new came in and nobody wanted the old. It was still sealed up in the box until Creed decided he'd start making whiskey or whatever you'd call it. He needed some other help too and I gave it to him. More than he asked for. The crawl space is still full of that old junk. I ought to have a yard sale one of these days.

Del

THEY WRAPPED THAT MATTRESS up in plastic and left it in the hall outside the lab, but you still couldn't stand to go anywhere near it. People complained. I'm told that the guard outside the morgue, which is down the hallway a little bit and around the corner, just plain refused to sit at his desk as long as it was out there. He propped open the door and dragged that old metal desk right into the morgue proper and shut the door behind him. He snaked the phone line in and did his business there. He said he was more comfortable associating with the newly deceased than with that mattress, and I don't blame him.

I'd guess he got an eyeful when the medical examiner worked on Vernon, but I couldn't say with any certainty. I've seen the preliminary report but I didn't notice any mention of a witness.

The technicians finally caved in and took samples and bagged them up and hauled the mattress back outside. Somebody got the duty of returning it to the farm. I can't say who. The crime scene is still sealed, so they probably just stuck it in the barn. Crime scene. I still don't know about that. I've read the report but I still don't know. I don't know that you ever do.

Audie

WHEN IT'S HOT that old red rooster starts itching. He woke me up in the night and rolled me right on over. I saw we were in the barn by the light through the walls and I didn't mind too much. It was different. Creed wouldn't let us sleep in the house on account of the tape. He said the tape was supposed to keep us out but I said it couldn't keep me out and I showed him but he pulled me back so I guess it worked. When we came down from the pasture at milking time we found the mattress leaning on a fencepost over by Preston's. There was a cat sniffing around it because she'd never seen a mattress out there against the fencepost before and neither had I. I thought maybe the other things they took might end up out there just like it. The ashtray they took and the blanket and the glass and Vernon's coat and so forth. Just lying around in the grass for us to find. I didn't tell Creed. We put the mattress in the barn and slept on it there and when the sun came up I looked over by Preston's but there wasn't anything else. That trooper came to visit later and he was loaded up with questions but I didn't have any time for him as long as he wouldn't let me sleep in my own house.

1938

Preston

THIS HAPPENED WHEN Lester was still alive. He didn't go the same way his wife Ruth did, or like Vernon did either for that matter. Cancer couldn't get him. He was too hard. Then again maybe it could've and he just didn't live long enough, but either way he worked like a mule right up to the end. It took an awful lot to kill him.

This was when he was still around, though. I was a senior in high school and those three boys looked awful young to me, but God bless them they did men's work. Vernon particularly, although I don't know why I say that. I guess because whenever Lester didn't have him running, his brothers did. He always had Creed to amuse and he always had Audie to occupy. You'd think a boy would take some pleasure in that but I'm not sure he did. I'm not sure he could.

Everybody knew you couldn't trust Audie with anything sharp, but Vernon had ideas of his own. He had a jackknife with a blade about four or five inches long. He always kept it sharp. How I heard it later was he took Audie and laid his hand flat down on the lid of a milk can and he took that jackknife and opened up the blade and held the point of it to the palm of Audie's hand and pulled. Just pulled on it in a straight line as nice as you please, pressing down gently all the while, as if he was drawing a picture or something, until the blade sank in a little and started making its cut and the blood came. Audie watched it come for a second like it was a magic trick or like the red was coming out of the point of the jackknife instead of from him—like it was a fountain pen, even though he didn't know the first thing about fountain pens and he doesn't to this day—until Vernon picked up the tip and showed him what was what. Audie felt the sting and he saw the cut and he began howling right off. It seemed like he didn't realize he was hurt until then. I must have been in school at the time or else I'd heard him holler and come running. I don't know if Lester heard him or if he was up in the fields somewhere, but the result was the same. The old man kept his distance like always. He'd have whipped Vernon if he'd found out.

The truth is that Vernon knew what he was up to. If anybody else had stuck Audie that way, it would have been what they call the end of a beautiful friendship. Then again nobody else would have thought to do it. But anyhow the truth is that no power on earth could diminish Audie's admiration for his big brother. Not even something that an ordinary person would take for cruelty. It wasn't normal, but you had to respect it. Vernon had Audie wipe off that cut on his pantleg or somewhere and he shushed him and he took him over to the woodpile. They picked out some sticks of wood and went back over to the porch and sat down. Vernon pulled out the knife again and Audie took one look at it and started to shake all over but Vernon calmed him down. He took the knife to the wood and cut. I guess he had a talent for that kind of thing although he never showed it but that once. He'd spied an old barn cat sitting on the fence and he pointed it out to Audie and then he whittled up the very likeness of that old tom faster than you could blink. I still have that carving, is how I know. It sits on my mantlepiece to this day. Now that Vernon's gone I don't guess he'll be doing any more of them. It's a collector's item.

He shut the knife and he set the little wooden cat on the porch rail, and they admired it the two of them. A minute went by and he picked up another piece of wood and gave it to Audie. He opened the knife and he tried to give that to him too but Audie turned away and started to shake so he had to quit for a little. They just sat and admired the wooden cat, with the knife lying there on the board floor between them. After a while he picked up the knife again and took the carving off the rail and made some little improvement to it. Maybe he cut in the slits for the whiskers. I don't know. Then when he was done he tried handing the knife over again and this time Audie took hold of it. He took hold of it like it was a live bird or something on that order but he took hold of it all the same. I don't think he's ever let it go since. The lathe came later and he's just as cautious with that.

Not that he's ever gotten much good at it for all the time he's put in. He never did have much of an eye, to tell you the truth, and now that he's three-quarters blind it's worse. But he keeps at it. He'll still do a cat sometimes or a sheep that you can make out but the rest could be anything. Some folks like it. There's a shop over in Clinton that keeps two or three of them right out on the counter and you can't tell what they are but they've got pretty good prices on them. Margaret dragged me over there and the gal running it had a sign up saying they were antiques, and I had to set her straight. I reminded her how honesty is the best policy. What she calls them these days is folk art.

Every now and then somebody'll come out here and watch those whirligigs spinning away in the yard like they're visiting some kind of an open air museum. Sometimes they'll give Audie a little money if he'll part with one. They don't give him much, but he doesn't need much. He won't part with that dog one I don't guess, but he'd part with most of the others if you asked nice enough. I've seen cars here with plates from New Jersey, Ohio. I don't know where people find out about it but they do. The whole yardful of those things just creaking away, and it all started with that knifecut on the palm of his hand on the milk can lid. You could say it's just one more thing he owes his brother Vernon. That's how he'd put it, I think. Just one more thing he owes his dead brother.

Ruth

PRESTON HATCH COMES HOME with a girl. She isn't a pretty girl, but Preston isn't a handsome boy either. She is from a good family in town and she radiates the certainty that she is something special and that Preston is privileged to be courting her. She carries herself in a fastidious way and she holds her head erect and her nose elevated and she keeps her face composed into a supercilious mask, even during moments of repose, as if to offset the failed dull frustration of her ordinariness. Her name is Margaret Willbanks, and she is taller than Preston by a head, and by and by she will marry him.

Her visits begin in the springtime. The days are not yet long but they are getting longer and the world is greening. She and Preston sit on the porch and he admires her and she ignores him utterly and smokes Chesterfield cigarettes, one after another, to ward off the warm pasture stink already rising on every hand. Preston has a little tenor banjo that he plays for her amusement, and the looks that pass across her face suggest that she does not know whether to be amused by it or appalled. Preston keeps his eyes on the fretboard and does not notice either way. He plays pretty well, but he will give it up and lose the knack once they get engaged. "After she'd taken the bait," he will say, "I was able to quit fishing." And Margaret will roll her eyes.

His banjo music draws the boys from the farm next door and Margaret's presence draws them too. Vernon nearing the edge of manhood and Audie right behind him as usual in both chronology and position. After they finish their chores they leave the barnyard and cross the narrow dirt lane to the Hatch property and stroll up the gravel driveway as nonchalant as a pair of boulevardiers. Six-year-old Creed overtakes them sometimes, his feet clapping up a flurry of dust. He knows where they are headed even if they like to pretend that they do not. Then the three of them slouch against the side of the elevated porch with their backs to Preston and Margaret and their hats tilted down over their eyes, sucking on stems of new grass, listening as the mysteries of music and romance unfold all at once.

"The Three Chevaliers," Preston calls them under his breath, having taken Margaret to see that debonair Frenchman in The Merry Widow and desiring to continue harvesting the benefits.

The Three Chevaliers are always caked with cow manure and they smell worse up close than the fields do at a distance, so Margaret scowls in their direction no matter what Preston calls them. Sometimes she catches Vernon shooting her sly looks from beneath his cap, which gives her the willies. He does not seem to be modestly appraising her as a boy from the town would, but evaluating her in a kind of raw and strictly material way instead. As if assessing her market value. For milk or meat or reproduction. There is an animal quality to the looks he gives her, and as she endures them she wonders if this kind of thing might underlay every single impulse in the civilized world. Even the innocent glances that she receives from boys in the town. She wonders why she keeps coming out here, and then she lights a Chesterfield and looks over at sweet homely Preston and catches the near-swoon in his eyes and wonders no more.

The truth is that the boys don't know much about women. They have their mother and their little sister Donna and the teachers at school, but beyond these their world is a kind of male fortress. To them Margaret looks like royalty, as inaccessible as she is incomprehensible. Like their mother and their father she smokes cigarettes, but she smokes pristine store-bought Chesterfields instead of rolling her own and that only adds to her mystery. Vernon slips one of them from her pack one afternoon when she has gone inside to use the facilities. He slips it from the pack where it lies open on the railing and he slides it into the breast pocket of his overalls just as nice as you please. Nobody sees, not even his brothers. Later he goes up into the woods and smokes it down to the filter but he does not think much of it. He does not think much of the kind his parents smoke either, but at least they've never made him feel that he is having to draw the smoke through a stopper. In the end he concludes that the best thing about Margaret is the power of her lungs.

The Three Chevaliers bring little Donna with them one afternoon. Whether they think she might enjoy the music or just mean her as a distraction is long past knowing. She is two years old and mobile. She is as filthy as her brothers, but for reasons of her own. As they leave the barnyard, Vernon tries wrangling her into his arms but she kicks loose and will submit only to holding Audie's hand as they cross the little dirt lane. She follows the sound of the banjo music like a scenting hound and climbs onto the porch and makes a try for Margaret's lap, but Margaret rebuffs her.

Vernon

WE ALL DONE IT TOGETHER. I took the cigarette and Audie pulled a hair from the horse's tail and I sent Creed into the house for a darning needle. I seen a cigarette explode in the funny papers once but I don't know where you'd get a thing like that. Something would blow up a cigarette. That weren't the idea anyhow. I seen Margaret didn't like our smell and she didn't like our sister either so I thought maybe she ought to smell something worse. We took that cigarette and strung the needle with horsehair and run it right down through the middle of it like running it down a pipe. We run it through and back three or four times I think. I trimmed the loose ends of it with my knife. Audie was pretty good with the knife but I didn't want to take no chances that he'd cut himself or cut that cigarette or crush it down or bleed on it or something like that. Ruin it someway. Then where would we be. We'd have to start over.

Audie

VERNON HAD BROWN FINGERS against the white. He said he had to be careful how he handled that cigarette but he had brown fingers against the white of it and some of the dirt rubbed off and I thought we were done for but it didn't turn out that way. She was watching Preston and listening to that banjo music of his and she didn't notice. She just took it and lit it right up. She didn't look.

Vernon

I SLID THE CIGARETTE back in the pack just the same way I took it out. We stood against the porch and waited. I did anyway. I waited. Me and Creed. Audie turned to see what Margaret was up to but I give him a slap and he come back around. Then he seen the way I was just standing there against the porch like always and he copied me at it. He stood there with his back against the porch waiting. He was shaking some because he couldn't tell what was going to happen next. I asked Preston would he play that song my brother likes and he said your brother Audie and I said yes that brother my brother Audie and he played the song. Turkey in the Straw I think. It set Audie's feet moving and calmed him down some. About halfway through I heard her strike a match and that was that. Audie always did love Turkey in the Straw.

Margaret

THEY WERE JUST BOYS. We were all just children, really, although Preston and I surely didn't think so at the time. Why should we? A year later we'd be an old married couple. Another year after that, he'd be in France.

I don't think the Proctor boys liked my intruding into their world. I was an outsider. A foreigner. A girl, frankly. They weren't any more comfortable around girls then than they are around women now. So they punished me by putting that horsehair in my cigarette and letting me smoke it. That's the way I always understood it. Perhaps there was less to it than that. But everything's open to interpretation, isn't it?

Good heavens, it's a wonder I kept on smoking after that day. It's definitely a wonder I ever went back to Preston's parents' house. If he hadn't taken my side and run those boys off, I don't believe I would have. And then where would I be?

My understanding is that the boys got a good scolding from their mother, but that's as far as it went. I'll bet their father had a good laugh over the whole thing. I was sick to my stomach for two days, and I'll bet he had a good laugh at my expense.

1965

Audie

WE NEVER BUILT anything much but we sure could tear down. My brother Vernon with the sledgehammer and Creed with the crowbar and me collecting the nails that fell out. They were those old square ones, black iron. You can't get those old square nails anymore but here they came falling down and bouncing in the plaster dust and there I was collecting them up. That was my job. My brother Vernon gave it to me. The nails left little trails where they bounced. Some of them were still in the uprights or the lath or both and those I had to pull out with the claw hammer. It was broken but I made it work all right. My pockets got full and the one with the hole in it leaked nails down my pantleg and right on out. You can't get hold of those old square iron nails anymore and I liked the look of them. I could put them to use.

Tom

HE WAS A FASTIDIOUS BOY, happiest in the round of his own regular habits, and nothing about the Carversville farm interested him. Not the green fields that lay around it and not the hard mechanics of working it. The animals were the worst. The scratching of a hen on the board floor of the front room would drive him into the yard. The low wet rooting of a hog made his gorge rise. From the chickens to the sheep to the weary old workhorse, every one of the animals seemed to him inscrutable, treacherous. He hated even the harmless dog, Skip, a mottled mongrel of uncertain heritage and vague origin. Boys may like dogs as a rule, but Tom had no time for Skip.

His father brought him, to demonstrate how far they'd come. To demonstrate it to himself, to the boy, and perhaps to his wife as well. Maybe even to the brothers, although they didn't seem to care much about anything other than the work that lay in front of them. DeAlton loved bringing Tom with his white tennis shoes and his neat dungarees and his spotless tee shirt out to the place where it all began. The place where his mother had come from.

"Do you know what grows best on a farm like this?" he asked Tom as the three of them turned off the main drag from Cassius and started up the dirt lane. "Opportunity!"

Tom sat and looked out the window, panicky and wide-eyed. The Hatch place next door looked ordinary enough, but he didn't trust it. It looked like a house that had been plucked from a regular street in town by a tornado or something and then dropped down way out here in the fields all queer and disorienting. It made him think of The Wizard of Oz, which in turn made him remember the flickering image of the Wicked Witch of the West cackling in the storm outside Dorothy's window. Whenever he watched that movie, he was always relieved when things finally settled down and the color came on and Dorothy wasn't in Kansas anymore. He thought Kansas looked like Carversville.

"Yes sir," said DeAlton. "A place like this grows opportunity like weeds. Opportunity to improve yourself, for one thing. Why, just look at your mother!"

She shifted the plate of cookies she had riding on her lap. "You know," she said to her husband, "I'd think a place like this might even present the opportunity to sell a milking machine, don't you? Provided a person made a little effort." She surely knew that this wasn't true, but it was a topic that never failed to deflate him a little.

DeAlton rolled up his window against the rising dust and Tom did the same. He hit the gas and the car flew over a couple of bumps and he yanked the wheel hard and spun it into the yard. "We've come a long way," he said as he hit the brakes. "And I don't mean just up from town."

*

Vernon put a thin blanket on the horse and tied a rope around her neck. They didn't own a saddle and they never had. It would have taken an unusual sort of saddle to fit this particular beast, with her abrupt swayback and her weak shoulders and her bloated stomach that seemed to be getting worse. He guessed maybe she had cancer too or was getting it. There was still plenty of use left in her all the same. Say what you want about her conformation, she had Percheron blood somewhere and she would be a long time losing her strength.

The boy inquired about her name and the uncle told him that he could give her one if he wanted. They'd never seen the need. Tom put a little thought into it but decided he'd leave well enough alone. Instead he stood perfectly still in the corner of the barn, as if by not moving he could prolong this moment of disengagement. Make it last until it was time to go home. He watched milky light pour in through the cracks between the boards. He watched dust motes and chaff rise up and take to the air like spooks. It all got in his nose and made him sneeze. Vernon laughed—a sound like a horse—and he said the mare was ready if Tom still wanted that ride. He had never wanted it but he moved toward the horse anyhow, and as he did Audie materialized from around an edge of the track door without ever opening it wide enough for a cat to pass through. Vernon indicated Tom and gave Audie the rope and told him not to hang himself with it.

Tom approached the mare as if he were approaching a bomb. As if his uncle were holding a detonator instead of a length of rope. Audie put the rope in between his teeth and bent down and made a step from his hands, and thus he helped Tom climb onto the mare. Before they left the barn he reached into his pocket and drew out the better part of one of Donna's cookies, oatmeal raisin with a dusting of lint and silage and God knew what else. Smiling through his whiskers, he offered it to his nephew. "No, thanks," said Tom, thinking that what looked like a raisin might be almost anything.

DeAlton

I SEE YOU BOYS are doing a little remodeling.

No, that's good. I like it. It kind of opens the place up, don't you think? A person needs some room. A little elbow room. A little room to stretch out, make himself comfortable.

Hey, thanks. I don't mind if I do. Your sister won't ever bake for us at home. Not for the old home team. No sir. Not anymore. She used to when we were first married but I guess she kind of ran out of gas for that sort of thing.

Isn't that right, Donna? Isn't that right?

Now don't bother with that, honey. Quit that. There's no cleaning that up. You try every time and it's no use. Besides, there's all this plaster dust everywhere. But like I said, honey, isn't that right? About when we were first married?

She used to bake just all the time, Creed. All the time, but not anymore. The only way to get a pie or a plate of cookies out of this woman is to come out to the farm. "Come on out to the farm with me, she says, and I'll bake everybody an apple pie." That's what she says. And I have to confess I'm a sucker for it. Not that I wouldn't come out anyway. You know.

Now that's a delicious cookie right there, honey. Oatmeal raisin? Are there walnuts in there too?

Nice. I thought so.

To tell you the truth, I never knew why you boys needed the two rooms here to begin with. It was just the usual, I figure. I mean it was just the way folks ordinarily set things up. A bedroom here, a living room there, what have you. The usual. But now you can lie in bed and watch TV all the way over there by the door. That's what I call luxury. That's what I call living. I guess you could move the set over here by the bed if you'd wanted to, but that would make things kind of cramped.

Oh. I see. Well. If the outlet doesn't work anymore then you don't have much choice in the matter. So yeah. This is what I'd call an innovative solution to the problem. Good thinking. A big room like this with the bed and the kitchen table and the fridge and the TV all at once? That's living. Man oh man.

1985

Tom

HE KEPT A LITTLE DOPE in the car, even though he knew it was probably a bad idea. It was in a baggie, right there in the glovebox where any cop would be sure to look right off. He had put the first of it there the summer before, kind of by accident on account of he'd been in a hurry and he wasn't thinking, and then once the glovebox was contaminated and all he figured that he might as well just keep it up. Maybe if he got stopped and they looked in the glovebox and found that much they'd quit, instead of just finding a few traces and deciding to search the whole damn car.

He stopped where his uncles' dirt lane met the pavement and rolled himself a joint and lit it. Just a skinny one. Some of the grass stuck to the red spiral of the cigarette lighter and he wondered if a cop would look there too if one stopped him. At least he wasn't drinking. He knew guys who didn't just drink and then drive but actually did both at the same time, guys from the construction site and guys from the community college, and it never failed to freak him out. Fazio, the foreman on the job, showed up every morning in his big red pickup with his big red forearm hanging over the doorsill and a can of Genesee standing right there in his big red hand, the can dressed in a little foam jacket to keep it cold. The foam jacket was day-glo orange and it had VERNON DOWNS printed on the side of it over and over. They gave them out at the track on weeknights, to drum up business. Fazio thought it made the beer can look like it might be a Coke.

He turned north onto the paved road and hit the gas but the old VW didn't do much. The road was nothing but hills all the way to Cassius and beyond. The VW had to work hard. The sun was down by the time he got to the beach. He had a little apartment that he rented on the second floor over a body and fender shop on the edge of town, just past the last of the bars. The body shop was closed at night and he was working days so it didn't matter how much racket they made, banging on fenders or whatever. The whole apartment stank, though. That penetrating plastic smell of solvent got into everything. It made it hard to breathe, and now and then he worried that just living here might be causing him some sort of long-term harm. Plus he was afraid that if he lit a joint or a cigarette the whole place might go up one of these days. On the other hand, that same fear was helping him cut down on the smoking. So you took the good with the bad.

He parked the VW in the body and fender lot and sized up a couple of new wrecks on either side of it but he didn't go straight into the apartment. Instead he walked down the main drag toward the water. The rides were going full blast, with kids screaming and carnival music blaring and lights shooting out every which way. His parents had never taken him there when he was growing up and he didn't have much interest in any of it now, but he stopped and watched the carousel go around for a few minutes. He smoked a cigarette and watched the little kids going up and down on the horses. The horses made him think of the old horse on his uncles' farm, long dead.

He crushed out his cigarette on the sidewalk and went on past the Clam Shack and Harpoon Gary's without giving either one of them much thought. Growing up around here, he never saw the names of these places as either ironic or aspirational. He never much saw them at all. The places and their battered signs were just what they were. Fixtures. Both Larry's and the Shack had big decks that looked out in the general direction of the water, and both of the decks were crowded with summer people and people who'd come over for supper from Cassius and Verona and maybe as far away as Rome, the summer people wearing beach clothes and the locals still dressed for work. The beach looked eastward across the lake, so these places on the water did a pretty good business around sunset. At least in the summer. Come winter they'd be shut.

He kept walking until he got to the Woodshed, which was on the other side of the street, just across the bridge, above where Fish Creek emptied into the lake. Beyond it were a couple of campgrounds and some empty docks but that was pretty much it. Kids hollering on a swingset somewhere in the dark, in competition with the screaming from the rides back in the direction he'd come from. Neon beer signs buzzed in the windows. A cardboard sign on the door advertised LADIES' NIGHT, but there weren't any ladies around when he walked in. Then again it was early.

Preston

MARGARET AND I'D BEEN to the movies and we came home late. The night was plenty clear I remember. There was a big wide moon and a lot of stars. You might be surprised at how few stars you can see in town, compared to what you see out here. Even though it's not a big city it's big enough that the stars have to compete with street lamps and headlights and whatnot. It's darker out here in the country and the sky seems to light things up more. Anyhow we pulled up and something caught my eye over at the Proctor place.

Creed was in the back yard taking in laundry. Sheets, it looked like. I pulled up by the barn and stopped and put it in park and got out. Margaret stayed. Those boys didn't keep a washline up, so he'd strung rope in between the barn door and the rear view mirror of the schoolbus. Not the busted one on the passenger side, but the other. The one on the passenger side tore off the day it got here and the other one broke not long after that. I think the conveyor picked up a rock and maybe flung it somehow. It was either that or I don't know what. You've got to watch out around a farm. That's the lesson. The glass is still all over. Regardless I spied him taking in sheets and that wasn't exactly the usual thing never mind in the middle of the night, so I stopped and went over to ask him what the holiday was. Those boys never were much for laundry.

He said his brother'd been having trouble holding his water. I thought he meant Audie. That's what a person would think and I told him so. He said no, it was Vernon. He'd been having the trouble for a while and they were just now getting around to washing out the sheets. They'd got to the point where they couldn't stand it anymore, and they had to wash them out because they didn't have money to buy new—not so much as once, to tell the truth, and definitely not on a regular basis if Vernon was going to keep at it. Coveralls they could get a year's use out of and buy more from Philipson's in Cassius and then burn the old pair, but not sheets. Not if Vernon was going to have that kind of trouble every night. Creed stood there by the schoolbus with a look on his face I could see in the dark. Like a man sizing up something he doesn't much like the appearance of. The start of something or maybe the end of it.

Tom

TOM WAS NEVER going to pass for tall, but the low ceiling in the Woodshed gave everybody who came in the door a kind of unconscious stoop and he wasn't any different. The front room held a long bar with nobody at it or even behind it, and a couple of bowling machines with polished wooden lanes that you lubricated by shaking out some kind of wax from a canister with holes in the lid. It looked like greasy yellow popcorn salt. Instead of balls they used round metal pucks that weighed enough to do some damage. Tom had taken one of them in the eye late one night and he still had a swelling that was beginning to look like it would never go away. The yellow wax stung your eyes, too. He remembered that. He'd had to go in the men's room and bend over the sink and rinse it out, and then get some ice for the swelling. He never did find out who threw it.

The back room was a bunch of little tables clustered around a low stage covered in astroturf. The astroturf was melted in places from dropped cigarettes and it probably amounted to a huge fire hazard, but it was sturdy and it provided good footing no matter what got spilled on it. Sometimes they had a band but not tonight. Once upon a time they'd had strippers on the weekends, but now that was just a fond memory shared by a handful of old-timers, vets of the Second World War who'd come home and gone straight to the Woodshed with visions of Betty Grable in their heads. Every now and then one of the old dancers, a heavy-set bottle blonde from somewhere up on Fish Creek, would stop in and get up on the little stage and shake what she still had just for old time's sake. There were always a few tips in it. Her knees were going fast, though, and conditions had reached the point where she was starting to need help getting up onto the astroturf. Before long there wouldn't be anybody left who wanted to give her a hand, anybody left who even remembered those glory days.

REO Speedwagon was cranking from the jukebox and a few regulars were hunched over the tables, working at getting drunk. One of the guys called out to him, calling him Tommy Boy, which he hated. It drove him back out into the front room. He settled on a stool and got out his smokes and lit one of them and pulled on it hard. He was pretty sure it made the buzz from the dope he'd smoked on the ride over rise up a little bit, and that was good, but on the other hand it might have been all in his head. He sat knocking his lighter on the bar and Sal came out from the back at the sound of it, thinking somebody out there was impatient.

"Oh. It's just you."

"Just me." Tom drew on the cigarette again. "That's right."

"You're early." He put a glass under the tap and pulled Tom's usual.

"Sometimes I like to get a head start."

"I can see that."

It was a while before the place filled up. A bunch of college kids on summer break were working the bowling machines. Most of them looked like regular kids out of Cassius High—home from wherever, doing factory work or construction for a couple of months—but two or three of them were all decked out with pressed jeans and those alligator shirts with the collars turned up and they looked like they might have come over from Syracuse or someplace just to see how the other half lived. Tom's natural inclination was to hate them for that, but he tamped it down. The bar itself was mostly regulars except for a couple of girls at the other end. One of them looked predatory and the other one looked dazed. He'd never seen either of them before, he didn't think. He drank his beer and watched everything. The jukebox ran through ZZ Top and Van Halen and Wang Chung. That awful "We Are The World" came on but somebody gave the machine a good kick and the needle skipped and the changer pulled up some Elton John instead. Tom didn't hear any complaints. A couple of men approached the girls and smiled at them and put a little money on the bar. They drank for a while but they all seemed kind of nervous with it except for the predatory girl, who was kind of dancing without getting up from her stool. Tom sat and drank and wished he'd gotten to them first. Watching them a little in the mirror. They were younger than the college kids and he was older all of a sudden. What a world. Time just went by no matter what a person did.

Around eleven Reed showed up. Reed was his last name. His first name was Karl but he never went by it. He'd been too cool to hang out with Tom in high school, but things were different now. Now he sold real estate in Cassius and Verona and sometimes over here at the beach, and even though he'd made some money he'd never figured out how to grow up. He'd peaked in high school—when he'd quarterbacked the football team and gotten the head cheerleader and all the usual what have you—but that was that and he was still stuck in it even though it was all over, even though it was half a dozen years ago and he was going to fat and losing his hair and coming to places like this to check out the women and score a little dope from Tom Poole, whom he'd never even condescended to greet in the hallowed halls of Cassius High.

Tom liked it. All those years Reed had had something he'd wanted—a lot of things he'd wanted, come to think of it—and now the shoe was on the other foot. "Hey, buddy," he said when Reed came in. The way a person says it who isn't your buddy and doesn't want to be. Just relishing the sound.

"Hey." Sal brought Reed a beer. There was an empty stool next to Tom's and he took it. Tom lit a cigarette and Reed looked at the pack and raised his eyebrows as if he'd never seen anything so terrible. "You still smoking those?" he said. "They'll kill you one of these days."

"Thanks for the input."

"I'm just saying." He leaned back in his stool and made himself comfortable, acting like he was still first-string on the varsity team or something. Like anybody still cared or even knew. Old habits.

"I hear you. And I'll tell you what. I'll quit smoking the minute you lay off the cheeseburgers."

Reed sucked it in a little and smiled. "It's the munchies, man. I got nobody to blame but my favorite dealer."

Which got the attention of the college kids over at the bowling machines.

"Sure," said Tom. "Everything's always my fault." He raised a finger and Sal brought him another beer. He waited until Sal was gone and then he lowered his voice a little. "I don't deal, anyway. There's dealing and then there's growing. Two completely different things."

Audie

THE BED SMELLED LIKE HER. It was nice and cool after a hot day and it smelled like her and it smelled like the wind and it made me think about how she used to hang the sheets out before she went on ahead. It made me remember. I told Creed and he said if I wanted to lay down someplace that smelled that way every night then it was up to me to do the wash. This time though he did it and he took all the credit for it. I thought it was just as much Vernon's doing but I didn't say. Not the washing I mean but the need for the washing. Creed wasn't happy while he was at it and Vernon said he'd do it himself when he got done feeding the pigs if he was going to be so finicky about his bedlinens but Creed didn't let him. He told him it couldn't wait. He told him it had to be done right then and he did it himself and then he stayed mad at Vernon.

Tom

SOMEHOW THE GIRLS at the end of the bar got wind of things and shook off the two men who'd been buying them beer all night. They worked their way down to the end of the bar where Tom and Reed were sitting. The one still looked kind of dazed and the other one still looked kind of like she wanted to bite somebody, but the beer was starting to push them both toward a kind of woozy middle ground. They were beginning to look like anybody else. Tom asked could they buy them a couple of drinks and Reed laughed and said maybe they ought to card them first just to be on the safe side. You had to be nineteen. Ha ha ha. The way he said it gave Tom the creeps. Like Reed was some kind of dirty old man, which would make him a dirty old man too. The college kids were still working the bowling machines and the ferocious girl kept looking over at them. It made Tom kind of angry and a little bit sad at the same time. He blamed it on the beer. Dope didn't play that kind of games with your head.

The dazed girl had taken one of his cigarettes and was lighting it off a little votive candle that she'd taken from a table in the other room. She put her face up near his and over the music from the jukebox she asked him what kind of games he was talking about in particular.

He looked at her like she'd just read his mind.

She blew smoke out the side of her mouth and asked again. This dazed-looking girl who had read his mind and couldn't have been more than seventeen if she was a day. When he didn't answer right off she pulled on the cigarette again and let the smoke leak back out while she said that even though he maybe hadn't meant to say it out loud she'd heard him anyway. She had ears like an elephant. Her father always said so.

He said he hadn't meant anything by it. Then he said her ears didn't look all that bad, they sure as hell didn't look like the ears on any elephant he'd ever seen, and he pushed her hair back behind one of them with his finger. The dazed-looking girl smiled at him and asked if he was sure he hadn't meant anything when he'd said what he'd said about dope. Seeing as how she sure could use a little.

Tom checked and saw that his buddy Reed was doing less well with the ferocious-looking girl, which he decided was just too damned bad. It was about time Karl Reed got used to living in the real world.

1945

Preston

WHEN THE U.S. ARMY called me up, Margaret and I hadn't even found a place of our own. We were still staying with my folks. We were still looking around and saving up, so for lack of anyplace better she just kept right on where we'd been, up in that attic room, with me going off on the troop train and then stationed down in Texas for a while and then sent to France after that. I've got no time for a Frenchman to this day. Here we were, the U.S. Army, liberating their country and saving them from Hitler, and we had to pretty much sleep on the ground. Not just when we were in between towns, but all over. I remember this one farmer wouldn't even let us sleep in his haybarn. Imagine that. The U.S. Army, come to save their sorry derrières.

I learned resentment in France. That's one thing the army taught me.

And I guess I grew up while I was over there, even though I was already an old married man when I left home. What you are and what you think you are can be two different things. When I came back I was a changed man and things were changed here at home. They kept right on changing. That's how it was everywhere after the war.

With Lester gone, Vernon had pretty well taken over the farm. Ruth was still with us, but other than what you'd strictly call the women's work, which was up to her, the boys ran the place and they'd let it go pretty far downhill.

Which was saying something. Not that I don't understand. Minus Lester, there was a lot more work for everybody. The acreage and the livestock and all the rest hadn't changed, just the hands available to work it. A whole lot can go wrong in two years.

Anyhow I grew up while I was in France and the older of those boys grew up while I was away. By grew up you know what I mean. Not that I got near any of those French girls myself. But a boy goes through certain things no matter what. In France or on a farm. A French girl can't teach you anything you can't learn about in a cow barn. Audie was slow in a lot of things but I don't guess he was slow in that. The way I hear it, he was the reason they put up the door. The door between their mother's room. He wouldn't stay out of there on his own and she couldn't keep him out and to tell you the truth nobody knew what he might try sometime. He's never been a very big individual but he was getting his growth. Not that I hold anything against him. It's the way he was built. But they put up that door on account of him and once it was up Ruth about froze to death all winter. It didn't even keep her middle boy out unless she put a chair against it from the inside, but it sure kept out the heat.

I came back from France in October and she was already complaining that with winter on its way she didn't know what she'd do. She thought she'd freeze to death. I told Vernon that his father'd always promised to knock a hole in the wall that'd let in the heat from the stove, and Vernon said a hole didn't seem too much for his own mother to ask for. He guessed he could handle it, but I said there was more to it than he might think. I'd help. I was already back working at the lumber yard then. I told my father what Ruth needed and he told me help myself. I got a matched pair of register grates, one for the kitchen wall and one for the bedroom. Not big. Maybe eighteen inches on a side. Those and some screws and some sandpaper and a little patching compound and a can of paint. My father owned plenty of tools so I borrowed everything else we'd need. You couldn't count on those boys to have anything. If I hadn't been there they'd probably done it with a sledgehammer.

Ruth

THE ARMY HAS MADE Preston thinner than he was before—thinner than he will ever be again—and between that and his newfound discipline and his sharply pressed khakis he brings an austere and military air to the project. Just the way he holds himself inspires confidence in the Proctor boys. They respond to him as if he were their commanding officer. Ruth takes Donna out on the porch and calls to Creed but he won't come. He is all eyes. Eleven years old and all eyes. As if in the marking of the square and the sawing of the hole and the prying loose of the lath and plaster he is present at the revelation of some mystery unseen by ordinary men. Something very nearly constituting religion.

They have moved everything from the front room onto the porch. The table, the chairs, the chest of drawers. The rag rug and the washtub and the ice box. Preston tells Audie to hang a bedsheet over the cabinets to keep sawdust and plaster dust and God knows what other kinds of filth from getting into things once they start cutting. He marks the wall with a carpenter's pencil and a square. He drills into the corner for a place to start the saw. He works carefully and surely. When the piece is out he drills through the four corners of the hole into the opposite side and goes around into the bedroom and marks those corners with the square and the pencil, and the brothers watch the procedure as if he is performing magic or summoning spirits.

He cuts the second hole and marks where the screws will go. He has brought his father's electric drill from home and he shows Vernon how to use it to make the pilot holes. When Vernon pulls the trigger it jumps in his hands like a something rabid, which draws laughter from everyone but Vernon himself. The first time he touches the bit to the wall it skitters off across the plaster but Preston tells him that's all right, he's brought some compound to fill it with and some paint that nearly matches. Later on Audie gives the drill a try and he does no better. They hand it over to Creed for the last couple of holes, and having watched the missteps of his older brothers he takes to it instantly. It must weigh half of what he does, but he shrugs and says there's nothing to it. Then he puts it down on the floor and goes off to fetch the screws from where Preston left them on the table, just as cool as you please.

1990

Audie

THE TROOPER CAME and took my brother in the car. It was pretty early in the day but we were finished milking and we had a minute just to sit. The cows were back up in the pasture and the truck from the co-op would be along soon, so I had a minute. You don't get a lot of time to yourself. I had a field to plow but I didn't want to get out there and have to come back when the truck came. I would have gone if Vernon was there to stay behind but he wasn't. So I just sat on the porch waiting for the truck. I was carving some. Then here came that trooper up the road with that big blue car of his throwing up dust. He got out and he was full of questions and he took my brother off.

Preston

VERNON WASN'T EVEN IN the ground when they started after Creed. I don't believe that's right. I don't believe that's any way to do things. A man should have an opportunity to put his own brother in the ground before the authorities start giving him the third degree about it.

How can anybody hope to get a straight answer from a man whose brother isn't even in the ground? A man who isn't even given time to grieve his own brother has been punished enough.

When I picture it I see Creed sitting at a table in a dark room with a hundred-watt bulb hung right over his head, and even though I guess that's not the way they do it outside the movies it's still what I see when I think about it. Poor Creed. I'll bet that's how it seemed in his mind, too. Like he was getting the third degree in some cop show.

Tell you the truth the first thing I thought when I saw them go was it might have been Creed's idea. The way he was just walking along there behind Graham like a puppy. Docile, I'd call it. Like the two of them were going on a fishing trip. That's how it looked. Like Andy and Opie. Every morning since I quit work I go downtown and have breakfast, a bunch of us drink coffee and shoot the breeze and what have you, and I was just coming out of the garage to go when I saw them out there like that. One behind the other, going toward the car.

I said a puppy, but a lamb to the slaughter is what I should have said.

I pulled up alongside the car and I got out. I said my good mornings to Creed and Graham both, but they were pretty quiet right back. Audie was up on the porch. His head was faced our way and his hands were shaking. He had his knife in one hand and a piece of wood in the other and I wished that he'd calm down. I was hoping the wind would come up and start those whirligigs turning. That'd been the best thing for him. I don't believe he could see Creed going from up there but he knew he was going. His eyes looked black and kind of shaded over and his lip jumped a little under his beard. It wasn't like he was going to cry but more like he was going to come apart. I guess Creed wasn't the only fuse they lit that day.

Del

WHEN I DROVE OUT to talk with the Proctor brothers I didn't have any fixed idea about bringing either one of them back to the barracks with me. It just turned out that way. We sat on the porch and I asked both of them some questions, but not many. What they'd seen, what they remembered. What time they'd gone to bed that night and what time they'd woken up. What they'd watched on television the night before. They couldn't agree if it was The Simpsons or Roseanne. I don't know which of them was right about that since I don't watch a lot of television myself, but I can check the papers. That's easy enough. Maybe they watched both. It doesn't mean anything anyhow. They were just a few questions I was asking.

After a while I asked Creed if he would mind coming back to the barracks with me, and he said that he wouldn't mind provided we didn't take too long. He had chores to do, and I could see that he was concerned about seeing to them, but he didn't hesitate to come. I think it was kind of an adventure in his mind. I let him ride up front. I didn't think there was any harm in granting him that little dignity, although you could make a case that it gave him the wrong impression as to his circumstance. I did try to be clear about all that, though. A little ways out of town I got his attention and we went through his rights. First I went over the letter of the law and then I explained everything again just as clearly as I possibly could in very simple language. Creed Proctor doesn't possess a great intellect. He's a person who's very easily confused. I did everything I could for him in that department.

He didn't want an attorney. He made that clear. I asked him if he was certain and I went so far as to determine that he knew exactly what an attorney could do on his behalf. The importance of it. He assured me that he knew all about that from watching the cop shows on television. The cop shows and the lawyer shows. He knew what a district attorney was and what a defense attorney was, and he knew how they'd take opposite sides. I was persuaded that he knew what he was giving up, or else I wouldn't have let it go.

He didn't want a defense attorney. He said it just like that. He said he had no use for a defense attorney. I made sure he knew that he wouldn't have to pay for it if he couldn't, but he was adamant.

Creed

DEL GRAHAM ASKED if I wanted us to stop at McDonald's before we went to the station but I said no. I had my breakfast already. He said how about just a little coffee and I said no I didn't care for none. I said I seen from the television how they always have a pot of coffee at the police station so I guessed we could do without McDonald's.

I told him I had to be home by lunch for chores. Audie was all by his lonesome. He said he didn't know when we'd be finished. He couldn't make any promises. He said we'd get some hamburgers at lunchtime if we wasn't finished and we needed some. He was crazy about McDonald's I guess.

Del

FIRST WE TALKED about the farm. We talked about his parents and his brothers, and how they'd had it growing up. Those men lead an isolated life. They see the regular world on television and then in the morning they get up and go back out into a different world all their own. It must seem like a dream.

The sister intrigues me, though. Donna. How did she cut herself loose?

One thing you notice is that there's been a lot of sickness out there. A lot of pain. Hardly anybody in the family has a full set of fingers. The mother died of cancer thirty years ago, and Vernon's body showed any number of tumors that the medical examiner identified as quote unquote potentially malignant. That's as far as they take it. There was a large one in his throat. What looked like skin cancer in a number of places too, which is what you'd expect from a man of his age doing outdoor work. Probably more of them elsewhere, but we don't know yet. I should think that the tumor in his throat may have obstructed his breathing a little, but that would be up to the medical examiner. We'll have to wait for his final report.

I don't know what killed the father.

Vernon seems to have developed bladder problems on top of everything. According to Creed he couldn't hold his water. The bed was always wet. Creed volunteered that information. I hadn't questioned him along those lines, because I didn't remember anything in the report that would have suggested it in particular. It would certainly explain the condition of the mattress, although I guess it really could have been any one of them doing it. Or all three. The lab work may tell us more, but to my mind Creed's statement was telling.

It got me thinking down certain lines.

People were coming and going in the outer office and I could hear them muttering to one another about the smell. They kept their voices low, but I knew what they were talking about. I didn't think Creed needed to hear that, so after a while I shut my door and switched off the air conditioning and opened up the windows. There was a little cross breeze coming through and it made his beard flutter. Sitting there, he looked like the old man of the mountain. Rip Van Winkle. Somebody from a fairy tale. He's not nearly as old as he looks, though. It's just that the years have been unkind to him. My own father, for example, is a good bit older than anybody in that family, substantially older than Vernon, although you'd never know it to look at him. He retired out of the school district with a good pension. That's one of the things he raised me to seek out in this life, a good pension. I ended up here. How's that for an indication of the world I was brought up to live in.

Audie

THE MILK TRUCK CAME and he was full of questions just like that trooper. He wanted to know when the funeral would be but I couldn't say. I said I guessed we had to dig a hole first. He could keep an eye out for that if he wanted to know about the funeral. He asked where Creed was and I said he'd gone off.

I hoped he would be home for lunch but lunch time came and he wasn't home. I was out in the field where I belonged and by the sun it was time but he wasn't home yet so I just kept going. Some days I never want to get off that tractor.

Creed

WE WAS HAVING a nice talk. I had a cup of coffee and there was a breeze through the window. It was nice just to set. I told him Audie needed me back to home but he wouldn't bring me. He had a million questions. After a while he pushed a button on the telephone and said would somebody go get us some hamburgers. They done it straight off. I seen them go, through the window. They come back with the hamburgers and some fries too and a couple little apple pies and we had more coffee from the pot. I was thinking we ought to get Vernon in the ground, and I asked him where they had him and he said in Syracuse at the morgue. The county morgue. I said how about that, Vernon got to Syracuse before me. How about that. I said I ought to be going home once we got done eating. We finished and somebody come in and took the bags. Then we talked for a while more and then he begun talking about how I killed my brother. He had me talk about it too. Before he would bring me home we had to work it out between us. We had hamburgers for supper too.

1985

Tom

THE DAZED-LOOKING GIRL was named Shelly. She still looked dazed come morning, so Tom figured it was a regular thing with her. They got up and there wasn't any coffee in the apartment so they put on some clothes and walked down the street to Dickie's. The body and fender guys were banging away downstairs and Tom was late for work in Utica, but he decided what the hell. Either he'd go in late or else maybe he'd just make it a long weekend. Fuck the overtime. You had to make allowances.

The waitress brought coffee without asking. Tom ordered scrambled eggs and Shelly asked for a slice of that coconut cream pie that Dickie's was famous for. When it came he asked her where she had to be this morning.

"Noplace special. It's summertime."

Tom sat watching her work on her coconut cream pie, trying to persuade himself that she looked like college material.

*

She grew up in Canastota and she had a brother just a little bit older than Tom. She said he always called her baby and Tom could too if he wanted but he didn't want to. That was all right, he said.

It was turning into a good day to sit on the beach but first they had to get some Slim Jims and a bag of chips and a couple of six-packs. At the register Tom splurged on two packs of cigarettes, different brands, his and hers. He had a foam cooler they used for the beer. The store was out of ice and the lake water was pretty warm already, so he filled the cooler up with water from a hose alongside a house that faced the beach. He and Shelly tried lifting it but they couldn't. So they tipped it over and emptied it on the guy's driveway and walked it down as far as the hose would reach and filled it up again but only halfway this time. Then they worked it down the rest of the way, picking it up sometimes and sometimes sliding it on the grass and then on the sand. They left the hose.

The beach was full of kids. There was a playground over by the snack bar with an iron carousel that wouldn't stop going around and around, sending up a screech that Tom thought was going to saw his head in two. Shelly watched the kids jumping onto it and flying off again. She had a dreamy look in her eyes that Tom thought made her look like a babysitter. You'd never get that innocence back. She turned from the carousel and leaned back on her elbows to look out over the lake. He did the same. The water smelled better since the sewage regulations had gone in when he was a kid, but he still didn't feel like getting his feet wet. He didn't even own a suit. He lived right here, and he didn't even own a suit.

Shelly said her brother was the one got her started smoking. Dope, she meant, not cigarettes. She could hardly remember when she hadn't smoked cigarettes. The dope came later, when Nick was out of two-year college and living back home and she was what, maybe fifteen. Nick was a bad apple. That's what her father used to say: His son kept coming back like a bad apple.

"I think he meant a bad penny," Tom said. "It's a bad penny that comes back."

Either way, he was the best brother there ever was. He always treated her like an equal and he trusted her to do anything she wanted. Anything at all. That was why she'd left her parents' place and moved in with him.

Tom finished his beer and started another one and looked over at the girl and then back down at the lake. He'd been in trouble with fathers before, but never with brothers. He wasn't sure how much he liked the idea. Then again if Nick was such a bad apple they might turn out to have a lot in common. They might share a whole world view. How about that.

Preston

TOM HAD SOME BUSINESS or other up in the hayloft. I always thought it was funny how when he was a little boy and DeAlton'd bring him out he'd sneak around like he didn't dare touch anything, and now that he was all grown up he felt different. I always got a kick out of that. The irony of it. How he'd come to see the use of certain things. I believe that's something that happens to a man when he gets his growth. He starts seeing the use of things he never cared about or understood before.

Tom was in the hayloft and the rest of us were on the porch and Vernon was saying how his throat hurt. He had a sack of horehound drops that he sucked on when he wasn't chewing tobacco. He'd take them one right after another. I don't believe they helped even the slightest little bit. I think he knew that, but I guess he always hoped for the placebo effect. He had his left hand in his lap and he was rolling up little pellets of stuffing from the chair with his right hand when he wasn't rubbing at the place on his leg where that tooth from the harrow went in. They say Audie has a nervous problem, but it runs right through that whole family. There isn't one of them could keep still if you put him on the payroll for it. It goes all the way back to Lester and maybe beyond him.

We knew when Tom came down because we heard his car doors open and shut. First one door and then a little wait and then the other. He was fooling with something in the car. Vernon said he hoped Tom would come around to the porch and pay his respects before he went home, on account of he was tired and didn't want to get up. He said he'd just as soon sit right there and if that no-good nephew of his didn't see fit to bother coming around then so be it. They all could do without. But after a few minutes Tom did come around. He had a little plastic bag and he put it on Vernon's lap, and Vernon gave him a look like it was trick or treat. He just lit right up. I had a suspicion about that bag but I didn't know for sure. Not then. When Tom told his uncle he ought to be careful since that right there was a good fifteen dollars' worth I knew.

Creed knew the same. "If that's fifteen dollars' worth," he said, "I don't know why I been fooling with feed corn." Words to that effect. You couldn't blame him.

Vernon asked him could he chew it because he didn't care much for smoking anymore and Tom said that wasn't how most people used it. He didn't know if chewing it would work or not, but he couldn't make any promises and since that little bag was worth a good fifteen dollars of anybody's money why take chances with it. Most folks either smoked it or made brownies. Vernon said he wasn't much good in the kitchen so he thought he'd just stick with the regular way. Tom had some papers in his pocket and he gave them to him and then he left.

I'd heard that before about the brownies, but I'd always thought they were just pulling my leg. It turned out it was true.

Audie

VERNON WAS FEEDING TURKEYS through the window. He had the feedsack lifted up and he was tossing in handfuls and the turkeys were jumping behind the glass. I couldn't hear them holler but I knew they were. Behind the window the air was all feathers. Vernon was smoking and there was smoke in the air outside and feathers inside. I was over by the woodpile. Tom drove up the road and he parked by the barn and came on around. He was coming about every day. He waved and I waved back. He went toward the barn but then he saw Vernon feeding the turkeys and he went there right off instead. He was in a hurry. He didn't wave at Vernon like he waved at me. He just went straight over to the bus where Vernon was feeding turkeys through the window.

Tom

YOU HAVE TO TELL some people everything. Take, for example, the old farmer alongside the schoolbus with a homemade cigarette dangling from his lip like a regular smoke. Just working on it slow, the way anybody might work on something he'd lost the savor of. The thing was stuck to his sunsplit lower lip, it had been there so long. Dangling, dripping ash and weed. Tom just about blew his top.

He stamped over to where his uncle stood not even sucking on it and he snatched it out of his mouth. He almost put it in his own but reconsidered. The turkeys were squawking in the schoolbus and he could barely make himself heard over their racket. "You don't do this in the yard," he said. "And you don't do it that way. You roll it up tight and you suck it in and you hold onto it. It ain't a regular smoke. You keep it in your lungs. You concentrate on it and you get the value from it. And above all you don't do it in the goddamned yard."

He pinched it out and twisted it up and stuck it in his uncle's breast pocket, then he thought better of his haste and gave him an apologetic pat right there where he'd put it. Just over his heart. He turned his back and went off across the dirt yard and up to the hayloft for some of what he kept there, and then back down to the car. He had dirt on his hands from the hayloft ladder and he rubbed it off against his pantlegs before he got in. Shelly was in the front seat and they were headed someplace. She put up a hand and waved to Audie over by the woodpile and he waved back, tentative, looking like he'd fallen in love.

1939

Preston

THE OLD MAN was made of nails. I never saw the haybale he couldn't lift or the mule he couldn't drive or the roofline he couldn't walk with his eyes shut. The weather he couldn't withstand. He was a figure from a world that was pretty much gone even then, and you knew right off there was something about him you had to respect even if you might never understand it.

He knew how to last, is what it was. He knew how to endure and he knew how to bend things to the way he wanted them. He used whiskey for medicine and entertainment both. And if you were smart you didn't cross him. That goes without saying.

What else? Like I said, it took an awful lot to kill him.

Audie

WE WERE COMING DOWN the road from school and we saw him up ahead and he was on the tree. Everything was white all around. He had his arms out straight and he was on the tree and he wasn't moving any. That wasn't like him.

Ruth

ON A FARM IN WINTER, the very work of survival will keep a man alive. The warmth he generates by chopping wood for the stove, by working the pump to fill the frozen trough, by shoveling a path to the barn door to admit the cows. If he is to live he must remain in motion, and so he hastens through the world with a shroud of his own weather wrapped tight about himself. The margin is thin.

The boys have gone to school in their rags, smelling richly of woodsmoke. In the classroom their pungency will be enough to distinguish them from the other boys and in fact to tell their history, here at this juncture where coal is king and oil has made inroads and only the poorest of the poor still keep wood-lots. Creed's garments are the thinnest of the three for having been handed down the most. He wears them doubled and he makes no complaint.

Lester hunches his shoulders against the cold and stands in the barn smoking. He knows he should not, he understands fully the risk of fire, but where else can he go. He has finished the milking but he lingers here still, unwilling just yet to forfeit the great hot stirring of these massed animals. Soon he will open the door and send them steaming into the pasture one by one and two by two, but just now he moves among them, alive to their rising warmth, traversing the narrow spaces between their bodies like a ship through ice. Overhead the wind sighs in the hayloft.

Preston

WE WON'T EVER KNOW why he left. I would say he was after a little whiskey, except when I went in the back bedroom later there was a good half bottle of it right there on the floor. Then again I don't know how much of it he'd go through in a day or a night or whatever. I wonder how much you can know about anything.

Anyway he was done with his chores and the roads were clear enough and I imagine he wasn't expecting any trouble. Who does? It's in some people's nature I suppose, but not most. By the time a man gets as far along in life as Lester did—he was what, pushing toward forty when he died—by the time a man gets that far he generally expects more of the same. More of what he's already seen.

Life's taught him that. So off he went. Ruth stayed to home. She never even knew he was gone till we brought him back.

He always said you could count on a mule for surefootedness. Eight or nine months out of the year he'd let the horse draw the wagon, but not in the winter. Come the first snow he'd go in the barn and fiddle with that harness until he got the mule into it. He could have used the setup he kept for the plow but he never did. I don't know why. Lester had his own way of doing things. The wagon rig was old and the older it got the harder he had to work at it. Pieces stiffened up and other pieces broke. When he was done some parts of it were slack and some parts of it weren't quite slack enough but it worked all right. The mule didn't much like it, but then a mule doesn't much like anything.

Ruth

OUT HERE THERE is no such thing as a main road. Nothing exists that cannot trace its beginnings to a farm track or a game trail. Everything winds and nothing sees traffic. Back behind the clopping mule Lester tops a rise and hunches forward against the crosswind and starts back down, threading between high snowbanks under a sky as blue as water.

The mule plods on, hoofdeep and kicking up clods. The wagon wavers side to side. Skating slanted over ice the bald wheels lose their purchase, and sliding they gain on the steady mule. The chain traces go slack, sag down toward the snow. The singletree strikes the beast across her hind legs and draws from her one complaint of a lifetime's litany. The impact urges her on. The man pulls the brake lever but the wheels only lock and skid. The rear goes out, unluckily to the left, and the wagon nearly wedges itself across the road but recovers. The delay has cut certain slack and righted some of the rigging that binds mule to wagon: harness and traces and singletree. All is right with the white world. They reach the bottom of this hill and plod through drifted snow and rise again with the next.

An upward slope is harder for the mule but easier for the man. He rests. He reaches into his coat for his flask and he finds it. He unstoppers it with his teeth and holds the cork in his rein hand and pours fire down his throat. He puts it back and goes into an inner pocket for tobacco only to have the wind take it. He curses this loss, this life. Where he is bound he can buy more makings, but he has not counted on the expense and his wallet may be low. He refuses ever to run a tab. He has raised his sons to do likewise when their time comes. Separate honor from mulishness if you can.

This upward climb is rimmed with evergreens, natural windbreaks on both sides that block the snow. The mule's hooves strike sparks from plain stone undrifted. Where that thieving gust came from he cannot tell but such is forever his lot and he shoulders it. Atop the rise the mule hits snow again and the wagon does not. Not right off. Which throws them out of rhythm once more and sets the stage for what will come on the downhill course. Pure physics. The wagon's dead weight. The steady mule. Ice and lost traction, slippage and slack chain.

The mule, struck from behind by the singletree a second time, has used up such patience as she possesses. She balks and stumbles and the wagon swings, fishtails, the outside wheel striking the snowbank and piercing its uncompacted depths, drawn low by gravity. The man barks at the mule, menacing her with threats. She strains and the wagon sinks. She staggers. One leg goes off the road as well and then another, the angle between mule and wagon gone entirely wrong. Chain snaps. Ironwork strains. Harness leather tangles and tightens. The bit jams and the mule screams, headed facedown in snow. She flails and falls and the man is flung forward from the box. He tumbles down and down, entangled, arms outstretched. The mule strains and the traces tighten and he is pinned by chain. The singletree snaps in two, flies free, and the ragged place of its raw breakage pierces his useless coat. In the shoulder only, but unstanched and thus sufficient. The mule expires. The man fights on but cannot last forever. The bright day descends.

Lester

DAMN THE MULE and damn the road and damn his going out on it. Damn the cold. Damn the busted tree. Damn everything done and undone. Damn those boys being womanraised now, and that middle one left unfixed.

Preston

I DON'T KNOW why we brought him on home. Nobody there had any use for him that way.

Ruth

HOURS PASS AND SNOW FALLS, clinging to the bloodstiff coat and covering it, making of the dead man an old sailor saltcaked and mastmounted. The wind whips and the sky goes dim and none but the mad would be out. Ghoulish gray weather into which the schoolhouse pours its homebound charges.

It is in this light that the boys find their father.

Pent up all day, they have exploded from the schoolhouse door and scattered down the farm roads like shot. The empty world offers them no resistance. Up the hill they come, slowed not even by the slope, until the first—Audie, that is, the middle—makes his discovery. White on white on white. He knows his father before the others do. He knows the hump of the mule and the half-sunken wreck of the wagon. He knows that everything he knows has changed. He begins shivering but not from the cold, and his running takes on a new urgency.

The boys clutch and grasp at their father to no avail. Nothing comes loose. Not the chain about his chest and not the broken singletree thrust into his shoulder. Not even so much as his hat. Frustrated and heartbroken, they lave him in tears that only fall and freeze.

They debate who should go for help. Creed is the fastest. Vernon is the oldest. Audie is the least trustworthy with details. Creed is all for someone's keeping their father company as long as he is not the one do to it. Vernon believes it is his own duty to deliver this news. Audie has claim on the discovery and is owed something for it. But in the end it is a flannel coat that forces their decision. Audie's is the warmest of the three, so he will stay behind. He waits by a snowdrift until his brothers are out of sight and then he climbs up the cold curve of the mule's flank and presses himself against his chained and riven father. Shivering from the cold. Shaking from his nature. Awaiting revelation.

1960

Preston

WINTER CAME and I guess they finally gave up. I heard the hammering clean through the plate glass window. Sound travels in the cold. Margaret and I were finishing up our coffee before we went to church. I drained my cup and rinsed it out in the sink and got my overcoat and put my galoshes on. People in those days wore galoshes. Overshoes. They buckled up the front and you tucked your dress pants into them. I went out and started the car and walked on down to see what those boys were up to.

They were in the barn, going through the wall where it met the house. That's where the jakes was. They had an axe and a pry bar and an old two-man saw from somewhere with one of the handles busted off. I don't know where they ever got that. It must have been in the hayloft or somewhere from back when Lester had the place or even before. When the original owner took down the trees the first time, however long ago that was. Before this land was even farmed. Anyhow between that big saw and the axe and the pry bar they were just manhandling things. Busting everything down with no rhyme or reason. Studs and all. You never saw demolition until you saw those three at it.

I sized things up quick and I hollered at them to stop and they did. I nearly asked why they didn't just go through the house if they wanted to get at the facilities but then I remembered. Ruth's old room. That place was either holy to them or haunted, I never knew which. Maybe both. So they had the idea of going this way instead.

Those boys looked like a bunch of cavemen. Even filthier than usual, what with the dryrot from the siding and the cow manure that'd built up on the walls and whatnot. They stood there in a half circle looking fit to tear down anything you might build, just for the contrariness of it. Just because they could. I went over and pointed out a couple of uprights they'd exposed and said they'd best leave them right where they were unless they wanted the house to fall down. Maybe the barn too. Vernon said how would they get into the toilet with them in the way and Audie said he thought he could make the squeeze all right. He didn't mind. Creed looked at me. He didn't say a word, he just looked at me since he knew I'd have an idea. He was the smart one because he recognized there were things he didn't know.

I marked those uprights with a mechanical pencil I keep. I just put big X's all up and down so they couldn't miss them. I said you leave these alone for now and when I get back from church we'll figure something out. I marked some other places on the barn wall too, where I didn't want them to go beyond. Then I heard Margaret slam her car door and I went out. I made a note to myself to stop at the lumber yard on the way home and pick up a sack of lime to throw into that pit. I'd lived alongside those boys since I was twelve years old, but I couldn't get my mind around how bad that jakes was going to smell when they got it opened up. It was going to set some kind of new world record.

*

I left my galoshes in the car once we got to church. I'd already ruined the floormats but I didn't see any point in bringing cow manure into God's house, not that I guess he cares much himself. He invented cow manure right about the time he invented cows. But he's got some followers around here who'll complain about the littlest thing.

*

I was raised up to expect Sunday dinner and Margaret was raised up the same way. I don't mean supper. I mean having your main meal right after church. We don't always eat at home, though. A big Sunday dinner is a lot to cook for two people and I don't care to burden Margaret unless her heart's in it. As a rule we don't go anyplace fancy. We like the Dineraunt on Madison Street in Cassius or Valentino's on the road to Utica. If the weather's poor or we're in a hurry we come straight back and just swing by the Homestead over in Madison. It's on the way and the food's good and they don't rob you. The Rotary meets there is one way you can tell. I gave up Rotary a long while back but if those cheap-skates meet in a place it's generally all right. That's one thing I learned.

We were in a hurry that day on account of the boys. We stopped at the yard and got a sack of lime—two sacks—and I hosed off my boots and the plastic floor mats before we went any farther. I sprinkled a little lime around down there too, just for Margaret's benefit. You don't stay married without paying attention to that kind of thing. There's little signs.

We swung by the Homestead and parked. The parking lot goes around both sides of the building and our side was pretty near empty, but I didn't guess it would stay that way for long. They make a chicken and biscuits platter on Sundays that I don't know what their secret is but a person just can't make any-thing close to it at home. No offense to Margaret. I think they must use that broaster they keep in the back somehow. I had my mouth all set for it.

We went in the side door by the nice dining room where the Rotary meets, not the old section up front which is the original diner they expanded from and still looks it. The tables weren't set up back there yet so we went on around. We went around past the rest rooms, and right there at the counter in front of us sat the Proctor boys, big as life. There was nobody near them for twenty feet in any direction. To tell the whole truth I saw one little old couple come in by the storm door and catch sight of them and turn right away, right back to their car. The woman had a cane and all and she was having a little trouble walking on the ice but they quit and went somewhere else instead of staying there with those three.

I don't believe the boys had been to the Homestead before, although I know I'd spoken highly of the chicken and biscuits platter they serve on Sunday. That's what Creed and Vernon were having. Audie was having a limburger cheese sandwich on rye bread with onions, which is another thing that'll drive people away. Thick slices of a Wampsville red onion on top of cheese that smells like a dead man's armpit. Margaret and I greeted them kindly and went on over to the other side of the room. The waitress came and I promised her a good tip to make up for the lost business and she laughed. That saved her an apology, I guess.

The boys finished about the time our meal came. They raised their hands to Margaret and me and filed out grinning. Audie was patting his stomach. He looked full up and happy. The waitress took their plates away and wadded up their placemats and scrubbed the counter and sprayed it with Lysol. She had a boy come out and run a wet mop over the floor while she went around and sprayed the stools. When she was done with that she held the can up high and let loose a few good long shots of it into the air just to make sure. She came over by us and asked if we'd please cover up our meals with a napkin so she could fumigate some more but I said don't bother. It was all right. That platter of chicken and biscuits smelled just like ambrosia.

Creed

IN THE BARN Preston stopped us and made us hold off but that was all right because we got to have a nice lunch. He told us before we should go there and we never went. It was a good place though. It turned out he was following us around and a little after we got back home he come on over. Audie took a nap and I waited with Vernon till he come. Audie was in the stall snoring. Preston didn't ask where he was. He had a tape measure and we got started cutting wood and then Audie sneezed and Preston found out where he was all right. He laughed like Audie done it as a trick. We all laughed. Audie roused up and come over scratching.

Preston

THE SMELL WASN'T ANYWHERe near as bad as I'd thought it'd be but I spread a little lime around anyway. Emptied one bag right down the hole just in case. Everything was all dried out good down there. It looked like a display in a museum, showing how the Egyptians did their business a million years ago. Once we were done with that we cut a header out of barnboard and doubled it and toenailed it to the uprights. We did the same on the inside. Then we went up two feet and did it again just because we could. Reinforced it left and right. Found some old lumber that was straight enough and cut four jack studs and scabbed them on. I didn't want that house falling down or the barn either. You never know how those old places were put up but you can bet they made them better than they make them now. I was counting on that.

I don't think I breathed for a whole minute when we sawed through the uprights, but everything held just fine. To this day nothing wobbles any worse than it ever did. We took the wood and nailed it on alongside the jack studs while Audie went in and out through the empty hole like he was doing magic.

I said I'd bring a door from the lumber yard but they didn't care for one. They had an old plastic shower curtain they hung up on nails. I guess it served their purposes all right. To my mind a door would have been a big improvement. It would have made all the difference in the world. The jakes being right there in the barn with no more divider than a transparent shower curtain, a man had no reason to think himself any better than a beast.

1990

Donna

A COUPLE OF TROOPERS found her at the nurses' station on the third floor, where the mood was somber. It takes something serious to lower the spirits of a group like that, but a death in the family will do it. The troopers picked up on the mood and were even less expressive in their manner than usual, nearly to the point of a kind of negative affectation. "My brother always loved Dragnet reruns," she told them as they went into an examining room together, "and I'm starting to feel like I'm on one."

"We're sorry, ma'am," said one of the troopers. He meant it but he didn't mean it the way it came out.

Mainly they wanted to know about Vernon's relationships with his brothers. She said his relationships were fine although they weren't exactly ordinary. They asked what she meant by that and she said her brothers stuck together in a way that most people don't anymore. A way that most people probably can't even imagine. Whether it was from their close relations or from the demands of farm life or from something else, something more primitive, she didn't know. Sometimes she thought they had a kind of group consciousness, if that made any sense.

"Like ants," said one of the troopers. He looked like he was about to tell her something he'd learned on the Nature Channel and then he looked like he'd thought better of it.

She went on undisturbed. "What one of them thinks of doing the other one does. Especially with Vernon and Audie. They were always that way."

They asked her about Audie's troubles, because one of them had seen him on the porch that first day. He'd arrived with the emergency technicians and he'd taken note of Audie on the porch with his head tilted back and his eyes glazed over, listening to his whirligigs turning in the wind from over the fields. Donna said he had always been that way but had never been diagnosed. What was the point. They asked about his eyesight and she said he had been going blind for some years. As for his speech, you had to know him. They asked how she guessed he would get along without Vernon since they'd always been especially close and she said she didn't know. He was strong as an ox physically, but otherwise he had always been what she called fragile.

Speaking of health, they inquired as to Vernon's. She said he'd seen Dr. Franklin a few years ago but nothing had ever come of it. They asked about access to his medical records and she said don't bother. She said they were free to look at them and if they needed her to sign anything as next of kin she would, but in her professional opinion it would be an utter waste of time. One of the troopers said that was all right, it probably wouldn't be necessary on account of the autopsy and all. Then he went a little bit pale and apologized again.

Del

I ASKED CREED how long Vernon had been having that bladder difficulty he'd mentioned. I asked if he'd had any trouble breathing. If he'd snored heavily in the night and so forth. I don't know what the medical examiner could have done to corroborate something on that order as a cause of death—sleep apnea or what have you—but at that early a stage I don't think it pays to exclude anything. You listen and you ask questions and you see where the answers take you.

Creed reported that his brother's bladder trouble had grown more frequent over the last several years, he couldn't say how many, and that it was only recently that it had gotten out of hand. His brother didn't snore, he said. Audie was the one who snored. He demonstrated a variety of the noises that Audie makes in the night. Creed is a voluble individual once you get him going. I think he has a lot stored up. He likes to talk, and contrary to what you might think he's quite able to make himself understood in great detail. He enjoys conversation.

I made notes as we went along. I asked his permission to do so and he granted it. After a while I called one of the other fellows to come in and help. Burnes. He took notes and he listened but he didn't put in much. The conversation stayed between Creed and myself. At one point Creed went back and did a little snoring for Burnes' sake, just to catch him up, and Burnes got a kick out of that.

Their mother died of cancer, and Creed was persuaded that cancer had been about to kill Vernon too. Not that he'd been diagnosed. Medical care was unheard of out there. If you want to see what happens to a human body under pretty harsh conditions and without the benefits of modern medicine, you could do worse than look at those men. They're a case study.

Burnes got everything down.

Margaret

IT WAS GETTING DARK, and there were no lights on in the house. No lights at all. I don't mean to suggest that they usually kept the place lit up like a Christmas tree, but they didn't go around in the dark either. At the very least they'd have the television going. Preston and I had been out all day. I don't even remember where we'd been, although you'd think I would, there was so much going on. But we'd been gone for the better part of the day, and we came back after supper and there were no lights on. We decided that they must all be gone. Not all, I mean. Both. It takes time to adjust your manner of speaking after a person passes away.

The tractor was in the yard, so Preston said they couldn't have gone very far. He thought maybe they'd taken a walk up to where they kept that still of theirs, perhaps to have a drink in honor of Vernon. Their father always liked his liquor. He was a wicked man. I didn't know him well. So Preston put on his work boots and took a flashlight and went up. I think he might have been looking forward to having a taste of their whiskey himself, if they'd asked. I don't know that he'd ever drunk any of it, but I believe he'd always been curious.

Creed

DEL GRAHAM BROUGHT in this other one named Burnes but he stayed quiet. They was nice boys. Nice fellers. It was awful good to set with that breeze blowing across and no work. I felt like I was on vacation and I told them so and they laughed about that. It weren't a vacation for them I guess. They always had it that way. Indoor work and a pot of coffee and all the McDonald's you want. That ain't hard to take and I said so.

We talked about how Vernon died. Del Graham thought he might of snored himself to death but I said no. I never heard of a person doing that. I didn't know you could. Audie ain't done it yet but maybe he will.

It got later and I used the bathroom and Burnes come along with me. I guess he had to go too. I don't know when I ever drunk so much coffee. I asked Burnes if we was about done and would he take me back home and he said it was up to Del Graham. Del Graham was the man in charge.

Del Graham said if Vernon didn't snore himself to death then he wondered how it happened. I told him it was the cancer but he said it weren't big enough. I said cancer don't need to be big it just needs to be cancer. I said I never heard of a big cancer or a small. I didn't know it come in sizes.

Del Graham said maybe Vernon had some help besides the cancer. He said maybe it wouldn't take much. Just a pillow or a hand while he was asleep.

Burnes wrote everything down steady. My belly started to growl and I said how about some more of them hamburgers if they were still buying.

Del

BURNES WENT AND WROTE UP the confession while we had our supper. I believe he got it right or I wouldn't have asked Creed to sign it. I wouldn't have expected him to.

1985

Tom

AFTER A COUPLE OF HOURS he tipped the cooler out into the sand and he put the lid back on the top of it and said he ought to take her home.

"We were just there," she said. "I'm happy down here by the water."

"Not my place," he said. "Yours. You know. Home." She must think he was a hermit or something. Maybe a sex maniac, wanting to go right back in the middle of the day for crying out loud. Then again once she'd seen that he was talking about her place instead, she'd probably think that he'd had enough of her. It was always a tightrope. He wouldn't have even brought it up except they'd kind of run out of conversation and the wall clock on the snack bar showed close to noon and if he left now he could drop her off and make it to Utica by the end of the lunch break. Pick up an afternoon's work and stay however late it went. They sorted out the full bottles from the empties and put the empties in a wire mesh basket in the sand by the snack bar, a couple of young mothers in bathing suits and coverups keeping an eye on their kids from a bench and looking at the two of them like they were derelicts. Like they were scavengers taking something out instead of putting it in. Then they put the full bottles back in the cooler and went and got in the car.

Her brother's place was half a house in a little neighborhood that ran up against the edge of a black muck onion farm. Driving Shelly there he wondered if maybe they were passing by the place where his own father grew up. They were always going out to his uncles' farm in Carversville, but they hadn't been to his grandfather Poole's place in years. He'd pretty much forgotten how you got there. It was as if this part of DeAlton's life had never even existed. He thought his father had the right idea about that.

He pulled up to the curb and she got out and asked was he coming. He said he didn't think so. He thought he'd go over to the job site and put in some time. He didn't know how much value she put on a guy keeping it together like that, doing the solid citizen thing, but there it was. She could take it or leave it. Beer and dope didn't grow on trees last time he looked.

She said that was all right. She wrung her hands together behind her back and he thought she looked like a little kid standing there. He could imagine how it had been, growing up on this dead end street with the air full of onion stink. Maybe riding a bike up and down if she had a bike. Then he remembered that this was just her brother's place and she'd grown up somewhere else and he should quit being such a sap.

Preston

VERNON WOULD SIT on the porch and smoke his marijuana, big as life and twice as foolish. I was over there once or twice while he was at it. He said Tom had told him not to do it in the yard but he figured the porch would be all right. A man's home is his castle, he said. What a man does in his own home is nobody's business. His brothers nodded their heads to that like a bunch of old sages. The Three Wise Men. We sat out there one afternoon I remember and one night. It was late but there was a breeze still. Vernon wound up a little cigarette of it and Creed put a chaw of Red Man in his cheek and Audie asked for a little of the Red Man too rather than be left out. They were all of them going at it. Audie was whittling too, even though it was too dark to see. His vision was going anyway. You could hear the knife.

They say a marijuana cigarette smells like rope but I think it smells more like a muskmelon, kind of sweet and mossy but with a little spike to it. It's a nice enough smell, if I'm allowed to say that. Not that I'd ever think of taking it up myself. After a little while I asked Vernon if he'd started seeing things yet and he laughed at me. He said you don't see things. He said it wasn't like that.

He kept on laughing like he had one over on old Preston Hatch and I guess he did. He was the expert. He was a regular Timothy Leary in that crowd.

It did seem to relax him some and make him talk a little more. He didn't suck on those horehound drops when he was smoking it. Maybe his throat didn't bother him so much. We sat there in the dark and he started humming something. I couldn't believe my ears. I don't think I ever heard a note of music out of those boys. Not so much as a whistle. I used to play a little tenor banjo myself, but in the Proctor house music wasn't a useful enough thing to waste your breath on. I heard Vernon kind of humming now, though, in spite of that catch he had way down in his throat. The catch in his throat made it buzz a little. What he was humming sounded like a lullaby, something I suppose he'd have learned from Ruth. I guess he had to go that far back to come up with something. You use what you have. We all sat quiet. Audie stopped scraping his knife. There were headlights out on the main road. The whirligigs turned in the little wind from across the pasture.

Tom

HE HAD HER NUMBER and he called it that night from the phone in his uncles' house. He'd been up by the still tending his plants by flashlight. He'd hated like hell to be up there advertising himself, but tomorrow was Saturday and it was supposed to be a nice hot sunny day and he hoped maybe Shelly would want to go to the beach with him again, and if she did he had to get the plants tended while he had the chance. Plus with the overtime and a few beers with Fazio and some of the other guys afterward he hadn't finished in Utica until practically nine. He'd parked and gone around the back of the barn and straight up into the woods because he thought he'd seen his uncles on the porch and he didn't want to waste time jawboning with those old men. He had work to do if they didn't mind.

*

In the morning he drove out to her place past onion farms crawling all over with tractors. He didn't think at all about his uncles, surely finished with the milking by now and on to something else, out in fields of their own with their noses aimed at the ground. It was Saturday. He parked in front of the house and got out. It was one of those double houses whose owners hated each other and didn't care who knew it. Each side was a different color. One porch was screened in and the other wasn't. There was a paved driveway on one side and a dirt track on the other. Even the roofs were different. He guessed that the side with the peeling paint and the unscreened porch and the blowing dirt was where Shelly called home, and he wasn't wrong.

The brother hollered from inside when he rang the bell. The screen door was rusted out and Tom could see him through it a little, filtered by the disintegrating squares of it, sitting in a chair watching the television. Some kind of cartoon. It had his attention and he looked like he didn't want to get up but after a second he did and he came toward the door. He was maybe three-quarters as big as Tom, and Tom wasn't big. He looked like he was put together out of spring steel and leather belting. He had on black jeans and a black motorcycle vest with a little fringe. "I don't know where she got to," he said through the screen.

"I'll wait."

"All right." He made no move to open the screen door. He just stood there behind it, a cigarette burning in one hand and ash dribbling onto the rug.

"You're Nick."

"You got that right."

Tom smiled big, his father's son. "She mentioned you."

Unmoved, the brother turned back toward the television and started to drift in that direction like a man in a trance. "You can stand there all day or you can come on in."

Tom went in. He sat down on the couch and looked at Bugs Bunny for a few minutes, until a commercial came on and the brother barked his sister's name—loud—without anything other than his jaw moving. It was like a trick. He had the dark deep-set eyes of a maniac or a hypnotist and he sat there fixed on a Cocoa-Puffs commercial with a cigarette burning in his right hand, and then suddenly his mouth dropped open wide and that was it. Tom thought he looked like the mechanical dummy in the glass box that told fortunes in the arcade. He'd never cared for that dummy. He didn't trust it. Whatever it had to say to him he'd rather find out on his own.

After a minute the show came back on and the brother pulled hard on his cigarette and said that he understood he and Tom had a mutual interest. It took Tom a second to realize that he was talking about dope.

1971

Audie

MY FATHER TAUGHT my brother Vernon how to shoot and when the time came Vernon passed it on to my brother Creed. Creed was too young before. Nobody ever taught me and that was all right. I had no interest in it and I still don't. I guess I could shoot if I had to. I've been around it enough that I'd know. Sometimes we'll get squirrels or a rabbit for supper but that's all. Nothing bigger. I remember my father getting a deer once but we don't use his old rifle these days. See that. I know there's a difference.

Donna

THAT SON OF HERS. It was getting so she hated to bring him. She hated even to raise the idea.

They owned two cars now, DeAlton's great big blood-red Ninety-Eight and her little green Chevelle coupe, so on weekends the whole family didn't need to do everything together. DeAlton could throw the clubs into the trunk and go play golf, and she could bake up a rhubarb pie and go visit her brothers. But getting Tom to come to the farm was harder every time, even though

DeAlton was less and less crazy about letting him come along to the country club and ride in the cart. She knew that his reluctance meant he was playing with a certain group of fast-living friends who spent more time in the club-house than they did hitting balls, but she tried not to let that bother her. What bothered her was Tom's stubbornness.

His uncles loved him. She took no end of pleasure in witnessing it. To visit the Carversville farm without Tom was to let that go, and nobody was better for its loss other than perhaps Tom himself and then only in his own selfish imagination. He brought to the farm a kind of light and uplift, and she hated to deprive her brothers of its benefit. In turn his uncles could teach him a world of things. Things she didn't even know and things that DeAlton had long ago rejected. Useful things.

Today, though, she had him along. DeAlton was busy all week at the State Fair, where he and Roy Dobson were in the Science and Industry Building demonstrating the very latest in milking technology. They had a thirty-foot booth decked out like an operating room, all gleaming steel and shining glass and soft red rubber tubing. Every hour on the hour they'd lift an exterior door and admit one prize-winning cow or another and show the world exactly how it was done. DeAlton hated the whole thing. He hated it like poison. He hated wearing the coveralls and he hated showing his wares to the ignorant and he hated the public degradation of these poor innocent cows. Dobson Milkers got less and less profit from the Fair with every year that went by—DeAlton would come home fuming about the little kids and maiden aunts and pencil-necked bookkeeper types who'd gawk at them as if they had no previous idea as to where milk came from—but for Roy Dobson it was an inviolate tradition. He'd sold his first machine at the State Fair, and that was that.

Tom had asked to go along but DeAlton had said no. Noplace on earth was more deathly boring than the Science and Industry Building, and noplace on earth was less suited to an unsupervised boy than the rest of the fair. Any kid worth his Wheaties would say nuts to the blue ribbon livestock and the horse jumping and the Porter Wagoner concert, and head straight down to the girly tent on the midway. God help him he might even figure a way to sneak in. DeAlton figured he still had a right to have that conversation with his own son, and he'd do it on his own damn schedule.

Out of both generosity and self-defense, Donna put together some sandwiches before they left home. Baloney and cheese on white bread. She baked a rule of peanut butter cookies and put them in tinfoil. They stopped to pick up a couple of sacks of chips and she thought about maybe getting some of that smelly cheese that Audie liked but at the last minute she couldn't bring herself to. Tom would be miserable enough without having to witness that. She had sponges and buckets and a mop in the trunk, along with a pair of rubber gloves and a million kinds of cleaning products. Tom had only himself.

Vernon

WE HAD THAT DOG forever or one just like it. They was just always around. One of them might hunt and the next one might not. They come as pups usually. Pups nobody'd have. I guess if you pay good money for a dog you expect something out of it but we never paid a nickel. So this one would hunt and the next one wouldn't and you never could tell until they got their growth. This last one won't hunt for shit. He's about wore me out on dogs.

DeAlton

NOBODY CAN MAKE YOU go for a horseback ride. I don't know what's the big deal about a horseback ride anyway but nobody can make you take one so quit it.

I know you're growing up. I know. I already said you didn't have to.

Hey. Now that's not a bad idea. Just one problem. You'd need to be Dan Blocker to be too big to ride that horse. She's what they call a Percheron. At least part of her is, somewhere. So just say you don't want to if you don't want to.

That's right. He's Hoss on television. Dan Blocker.

Anyhow you've got to go with your mother today and tomorrow she'll bring you on over to the fair. I promise. I'll be there today like I said but I won't enjoy it. We've all got to do things we don't like. Even your old man. Sometimes especially.

Donna

HER BROTHERS MOVED like the ghosts of drowned men traversing the ocean floor. Their white hair and their white beards wavered in the light wind as on deep currents. They went slowly and methodically, as if they and their aims were older than time and long past any need for urgency. The longer she lived in town, the more she took note of this antique strangeness of theirs. And seeing them now as she came up the dirt lane—Audie bent over the tractor, Vernon feeding the chickens, Creed dragging a spade toward the barn—she pictured her three brothers preserved in grainy black and white or some aged murky sepia. Perhaps not even that. Perhaps a woodcut.

Yet the two oldest had walked the earth for not even a century between them. The youngest was not yet forty and looked half again that. Work and woe had done to these men not their worst but just their usual, which was enough.

They heard her car coming and they looked up in unison like cows. Audie's hand shook and he dropped his screwdriver into high weeds and he vanished after it. In a moment he came up grinning, put the screwdriver in his breast pocket, and went toward the car. If he had known how his eyesight would dim in the years to come, he would have filed away this moment of happy recognition so as to call it up in darker days. Instead he just went. His lips and tongue were stained red and the white of his beard at the corners of his mouth was stained red too, and inside the car Tom recoiled as if his uncle were one of the living dead so recently advertised on the theater marquee in Cassius. Audie was as speechless as they were and as implacable too. He came toward his nephew with his right hand outstretched and there was red not just on his mouth and in his beard but on his grasping fingertips.

Not blood, though. Just the juice of raspberries.

"I hope you didn't eat them all," Donna called out Tom's window. The vagueness of it did little to ease her ignorant son's alarm.

Audie planted his red hand on the sill and made it clear that no, there were all kinds of berries left. He could show Tom where they were. Donna opened the trunk and took out a bucket meant for other duties. She handed it to Tom and told him to hose it out before he put berries in it, as though any kind of sanitation were possible within five miles of this place.

Preston

THEY WENT UP toward the edge of the woods. There's no end of raspberry bushes up around there. I don't know whether they're on my place or theirs but it doesn't make a difference. If a person's got a stand of wild raspberry bushes that he never even planted in the first place and he can't manage to share them with his neighbor then it's a pretty sad world. The dog went along as I recall. The dog always liked that boy but the feeling was never mutual. Not that I knew of.

I sat on the screen porch watching them go. Tom kind of picked his way around the edge of the bushes but Audie dove right into the middle like it was a swimming pool. That's what happens when you live on a farm your whole life. A few prickers don't bother you anymore. He came back and reached out and grabbed the boy by the arm and took him in. The bushes were taller than Tom in places but Audie's head stuck up. I hope he was putting as many raspberries in the bucket as he was eating because he was eating plenty. He always did. Not that he made any show of hiding it.

I watched them for a while and then I went back to my book. I was probably working on a Zane Grey. How that man could write. I read a while and I didn't think it would take them long to fill up a bucket.

After maybe a half hour I heard a truck come up the road. The tanker from the co-op had already come and gone so it wasn't that. I didn't think anything of it. I looked up and saw Tom and Audie sitting by the bushes eating raspberries. Some dust blew across the pasture. I heard the truck engine start up again and the gearshift grind and somebody hollering. There was a sound of chains and slipping metal, that hard sound you hear. A shriek, and then something lowering down. I put my book on the little side table and went out the screen door into the back yard where I could see what was what. I hate to be nosy, but a person can't concentrate with that kind of noise going on. Not even on a Zane Grey.

*

The truck was a plain stake-bed with no markings on it. It was so rusted through and beat-up that the Proctor boys could have owned it themselves if they'd ever wanted to own a truck. I couldn't decide what color it was and I was looking right at it. It had a ramp in the back, and a couple of men I'd never seen before had pulled it out and lowered it down. One young and one old. The young one had on a ball cap and the old one didn't. He was bareheaded and his head was sunburnt. They looked like father and son. The older one shook hands with Creed and they got to talking while the younger one went into the barn where Vernon was.

They looked like they were up to no good, and even though the Proctor boys aren't stupid they're as innocent as they come. Naive. Credulous might be the word Margaret would use for it. So I went down. The older man was named Tubbs and sure enough it said Tubbs around the other side of the truck where the paint wasn't all worn off. I never found out if the younger one was his son but I think so. They had a similar way. There was another word on the side of the truck along with Tubbs and I should have guessed it from the look of things. I shook the old man's hand and he said he'd come for the horse. That old part Percheron mare. A bigger animal that was any less use would be hard to find unless you went to Africa or someplace. The Proctor boys were sold a bill of goods when they bought her and I didn't think they were going to get out the other end of it any better with this Tubbs.

I asked him what he was paying and he told me it was none of my goddamned business. Creed told me instead. I thought about it a minute and then I looked him in the eye and I said by golly I didn't know the horse was dead already.

Tubbs laughed right out loud. He shook his head and said that's how much I knew about his business. Creed laughed right along with him. That old mare is just as alive as you or me, Tubbs said. He said if a man had a dead horse he'd need to pay somebody to haul it off and here he was giving good money for it.

I said I knew that. I said I just thought his price was a little bit low. The money he was putting up was just about what the bones and the hide were worth. Plus maybe the tail too if he had a customer for it.

He didn't like that much.

I asked him if he'd weighed that mare yet and how much he was getting for a pound of horsemeat on the open market. Seeing as how a live horse would yield up horsemeat and a horse part Percheron would yield up plenty.

He said a deal was a deal and I asked him to show me the papers. He said there weren't any papers and he didn't have to take that useless old nag off anybody's hands unless the terms suited him. He pulled out his keys and made like he was going to get back into the cab of the truck but he didn't. He shook his finger at Creed and said he was doing him and his brothers a favor. Asked him why he'd let me go sticking my nose into their goddamned business anyhow.

Creed put his hand on my shoulder and said something I never in all the world expected to hear. I think he must have gotten it from one of those lawyer shows. I don't know how he'd saved it up but he did. You never know what's in a person's mind. He looked Tubbs straight in the eye and said he'd better get used to paying attention to me because I was his trusted business advisor. Just like that. His trusted business advisor.

I've never been so flattered in all my life.

Tubbs said all right maybe we could renegotiate the numbers a little, and I said OK let's get down to it.

Audie

WE STARTED DOWN from the bushes. We were all over with raspberry juice and coming down with the mop bucket almost empty. I hoped my sister Donna wouldn't care. I was thinking she might want to bake a pie but she never baked a pie here. Only at home and brought them. I was thinking Tom might want a pie but he had his fill of raspberries already. So we were just coming on down. That old Tubbs was there with his truck, and he had the ramp down, and he was talking to my brother Creed and then Preston. He looked mad. His head was red and his face was getting red too. One from the sun and the other from Preston. Preston looked like he was giving old Tubbs what for.

Vernon came out of the barn with the mare. Tubbs' boy was with him. Tom took one look and said he wasn't interested in going for a horseback ride today and I told him that was all right. I said that mare wasn't taking anybody for a ride. Not anymore she wasn't.

Preston

THE BOY CAME RIGHT OVER big as life. I'd never seen him take an interest in a horse before, but he sure had an interest then. I guess he'd either put down the bucket or left it with Audie. He'd definitely set aside any ideas he had about picking any more raspberries. He came straight up to where I was hammering things out with Tubbs.

His eyes were lit up and I could see DeAlton Poole in them. His old man. He said he'd heard the mare was on her way to the glue factory. He wondered where the glue factory was and how it operated. Tubbs told him for Christ's sake there wasn't any such thing as a glue factory and the boy said he was a liar because there was glue wasn't there so there must be a glue factory someplace and Tubbs said maybe so but he didn't run any goddamned glue factory. If there was any glue factory it was somewhere else and somebody else ran it. He could only speak for his own operation. The horse wasn't going straight to any glue factory anyhow. They'd haul her back to the slaughterhouse and take her to pieces first.

Tubbs got a little cagey right about then, and I could see he was torn between peacocking around for that curious boy on the one hand and leveling with me on the other. I told him to go on ahead, I knew where the bear shit in the buckwheat, and he said all right. Then he turned to Tom and stuck up the fingers of his left hand and started counting off what would become of every part of that mare. Where it would go and how it would end up. Animal feed and shoe polish and soap. Gelatin and paint and glue. He taught that boy a lesson I don't think he'll ever forget. Opened his eyes for the first time I believe they'd ever been opened on that farm.

I figured a lesson like that was worth about twenty dollars, so I let him keep that much extra.

1936

Preston

LESTER ALWAYS HAD A DOG. I believe he loved a dog if he loved anything. He had this one mixed breed when the two older boys hadn't quite gotten their growth yet. Creed would have been in short pants if they'd owned a pair of short pants. He was in Audie's old coveralls, rolled up. Donna was just a baby and she doesn't figure into this.

Lester used to do some work for an old man out on Middle Road named Lawson. He kept horses. Some of them were his own and some of them he boarded. Lawson claimed to be a veterinarian but I don't believe he ever had a license. He kept dogs, too. Lester always said if you were short a dog you could go out there and find yourself one. You might even find the very same dog you were short. Probably would. That's the kind of individual Lawson was. Everybody around here knew him.

Anyway he taught Lester a few things about animals. Lester had his faults, but he always took good care of his livestock. A horse, a pig, a sheep, I don't care what it was. A dog or a chicken. He used to keep Rhode Island Reds. Now the time I'm talking about, Lawson gave him an old pair of rusty hand clippers he used to use on some kind of stock, I don't know what. Not sheep. A long-haired goat maybe. Those clippers were like a big set of pliers with a sliding blade where the jaw would be and a spring in back of that. An adjustable comb in front of the blade, mounted on screws. There were two or three different combs you could swap out, all of them rusted up. I think he might have given it to Lester as payment for something. That would have been just like the both of them. He gave it to Lester and it was worthless to him but he took it anyhow.

Nobody had anything then.

I don't think Lester's family ever knew about the depression or recognized they'd gone through it. It was all the same to them. My father started our new house in 1931 and we moved in the next summer and I thought we were moving in alongside what these days you'd call a bunch of Okies. They looked like they'd grown up out of the dirt and now here the dirt was strangling them back down. Choking them right off. Of course that was just my own idea, coming from town the way I did.

Ruth

THE MEN WHO ARRIVE to frame the new house work as silently as things conjured. Spirits or elves or carved statues brought to life. Only one among them ever speaks—the one who appears just once or twice a day and not for long, the one who wears not coveralls but a light woolen suit, the one who upon removing his fine jacket and hanging it on a nail shows himself the privileged inverse of his workmen. Narrow shoulders where theirs are broad, and thin arms where theirs are solid iron, and a contented little pot belly where they have none to speak of. In his difference he reigns over them and causes them to do his bidding, for his will has given them life in this dead time.

There is a boy with him now, a child older than hers but not by as much as perhaps he thinks. With a wary eye he proceeds heel and toe down a suspended plank or a narrow nailed beam. Arms out like a boy flying. She has worked at sweeping the yard with a corn broom and as she has worked she has seen him and she has seen too that this wariness of his is not confined to the placement of his own footsteps but takes in as well the rolling countryside and this poor dirt farm and herself and her own two children, Audie and Vernon, at play in the fields. They keep their distance, her boys. They send looks her way that ask if they might introduce themselves to this new child and she sends looks back that say they might if they want to and still they do not. They lack the courage for any such transgression if transgression it is. For his part the balancing boy signals no openness to them or even curiosity. He walks and he wavers. He keeps his gaze low and his arms high. In the field the younger boy begins to do the same, heel and toe, arms outstretched, until his older brother tackles him.

Audie

MY BROTHER WENT FIRST. My mother said don't do it in the house since she didn't need to be sweeping up after that mess too, so all four of us went in the barn. My father and us three. Vernon sat on a bucket and I sat on the ground and waited my turn. I had Creed on my lap watching. My father said you take your shirts off now or you'll wish you did. He said you'll itch like hell. Vernon told him the regular man had a white sheet and put a little bit of paper wrapping around your neck but our father told him the regular man cost money and we didn't need the regular man anymore. We didn't need any white sheet when we could take our shirts right off in the barn. He took out the clippers. If I'd gone first I don't think I'd let myself holler like Vernon did, but since Vernon hollered already it didn't make any difference. Those clippers pulled more than they cut. Our father greased them up and took a file to the blade and tightened the screws but that didn't help any. I bawled just like Vernon did and there was bloody hair on the dirt floor and some on my knees where it fell. Just pulled clean out. It could be that he got better at it as he went from one of us to the next but I don't think so. When it came his turn Creed didn't holler even though he was the youngest. He didn't cry either. He just took it.

Preston

MY FATHER OWNED a mower ran on gasoline and he had me push it around the yard once or twice a week. He was always a great one for getting the first of anything. He had connections from the lumber yard. I suspect it was a demonstration model he talked somebody out of. Anyhow I was pushing that gas mower around the yard and over the sound of it I heard the worst kind of hollering you could imagine. Just a terrible racket. Bleating and crying and carrying on. I thought maybe Lester had gotten some new sheep and was notching their ears, but that wasn't it. It wasn't any sheep. I cut the engine and looked down the hill and one after another those boys came tearing out of the barn like he was firing them from a gun. Vernon first. He ran out and stuck his head in the water trough and blubbered around some. Then Audie came out and he did the same. The crying and hollering stopped then but I went down out of curiosity and no sooner did I get near than here comes Creed flying out the barn door just like the first two, only when he made for the trough they grabbed his arms and legs and stuck his whole self straight in.

With those haircuts they looked like a family of porcupines. They were all bleeding a little but not too bad. You could see it trickle down their necks and around their ears and there was some in the trough. The water had a pinkish tinge to it if you looked at it right, unless that's just how I remember it. My memory may have colored things. Either way I said they ought to drain the trough and fill it up again if they didn't want their father taking it out of their hides. He'd say the animals didn't want to be drinking that and then they'd have to drain it out and pump it full again anyway and on top of that he'd give them a licking. They did like I said. Later on I guess I'd have done it myself and saved them the trouble. By later on I mean years. But I was just finding my way with those boys then.

The old man learned a little about giving a haircut, but not much. Around our own house when I was wasteful with anything my own father would say we ought to start economizing and for a first step he was going to let old man Proctor cut my hair. He never did it though.

1990

Creed

BURNES HAD THIS PAPER where he typed it all out. Del Graham told him to. First he went across to McDonald's and then when he come back he give the hamburgers to Del Graham and then he went off somewhere and typed it all out. He kept a Big Mac for himself I think. The coffee was out so Del Graham made a fresh pot. He said he didn't know if he ought to make it regular or unleaded since he didn't know how long a night it was going to be. He hoped maybe unleaded. I said I didn't care. There was nobody much around except us. One feller up front and a couple of other fellers at their desks but that was it. All the lights was on though. Somebody had a radio going and the police radio was going too. It weren't busy like during the day.

I asked Del Graham when was I going home and he said pretty soon. He said he'd take me once Burnes came back and I read his paper and signed it. Burnes was putting down everything we said about how Vernon died and Del Graham wanted me to see if he got it right. I said I didn't mind checking what he typed out but I wished he'd hurry up since I didn't have all night and Audie was home all alone. Del Graham didn't know Audie. He knew who Audie was but he didn't know him.

Burnes

FRANKLY, I was just glad to get a little fresh air.

Del

WE'D BEEN AT IT since the morning and we were all a little bit frayed around the edges. It wasn't that there'd been anything adversarial about it. Not by any means. It just makes a long day. For a person like Creed, who's not accustomed to the back and forth, it can be especially difficult. And then there's the fact that you've got him talking about things that he'd probably rather not talk about. You've got him going over them again and again just to get them straight and understand what happened. As much as that's possible.

While Burnes was typing up the confession and it was just the two of us in the office, Creed got a little agitated regarding his brother. I had an officer call out to the house but there wasn't any answer so I had him call the neighbor instead, Mr. Hatch, to see if he could go over there and knock on the door. I didn't want to send a car out. I thought the brother had seen enough police cars for one day. I thought if Mr. Hatch could just check on him, that would be enough to reassure everybody. I didn't think we'd be much longer anyhow. The officer rang back and said he'd gotten Mrs. Hatch and her husband was on his way to see about the brother. That made Creed feel a little better. He was very lucid, there's no question about that. Once he was reassured about the brother he asked if we could bring home a hamburger for him when we went, and I said I thought we could probably arrange that.

Burnes brought in four copies of the confession, one for each of us and one more. We cleared the table and sat around it. Right off Creed said he had difficulty reading without his glasses, which I took to indicate at least some measure of illiteracy, although I suspect that he must be able to read at least a little. I know he's had some schooling, but I don't know how much of it took.

Preston

CREED COULD NO MORE read that paper than he could talk Chinese.

Creed

THEY BRUNG ME some reading glasses but I can't say they helped too much. That paper had a lot of words on it I didn't know. Burnes was awful good with words. Del Graham said he'd go over it out loud if I wanted but I said he didn't need to. I said if I run into something I couldn't make out I'd ask. He read parts of it out loud anyhow and I didn't tell him not to.

This was after supper and my stomach was growling from too many hamburgers in one day. Restaurant food don't always agree with me. I said so and Burnes showed me to the bathroom again like he thought I'd forgot where it was since the afternoon. I looked out the window and seen the cars sitting out there in the dark. I was thinking about Audie.

A lot of what was on the paper was about how Vernon died and what all I had to do with it. I told Del Graham that's how we talked about it all right but it's not the way it went. I never said it was. Burnes got it all just right the way we talked about it even though he used some different words. He did a good job. Del Graham read some of it out loud and explained it here and there and I said if that's what those words mean then that's what we talked about. But that don't mean it's what happened. It's only what we talked about. Del Graham said wasn't I telling the truth before and I said I was but it sounds different now, the way Burnes put it on that paper. Real things and things you talk about and things somebody puts on a paper sound different. They sound like different things.

The phone rang and Del Graham said maybe it was Preston, but it wasn't. I said I thought it was time to go home. Time to go see about Audie. Del Graham said he'd let me know when that time come and then he'd take me himself in his own car.

Del

I WANTED TO HAVE a witness from outside. You don't necessarily have to do it that way, but it can carry more weight if there's any question. I also wanted to get Creed out of the barracks and back home. That was an enormous priority. Keeping him around wasn't doing anybody any good, and at that point there was certainly no urgency about making an arrest. The clock would start to run and the district attorney would have forty-five days and he'd probably use them all up. There was no need to stretch it out like that. Vernon wasn't going anywhere, arrested or not. I had some more questions to ask other people anyhow.

So I said why don't we get in the car and bring the papers with us and just shoot on over to McDonald's across the street. I thought we could kill two birds with one stone. We could find somebody to watch him sign, and we could pick up something for his brother while we were at it.

The night was still pretty warm when we went out. Creed kind of shook himself when we got outdoors in the fresh air. He was clearly happy that we were on our way, and I was very glad to see that. It had been a long day. We went out through the back and got in the car, but when we drove around front the restaurant was closed. The golden arches weren't even lit up. They usually stay open pretty late, but now there was just one light on in the back and one car. I admit I must have lost track of the time. Rather than stop and knock we kept going. The Mobil station has a little convenience store attached to it and I figured we'd stop there and accomplish pretty much the same thing.

Creed said he didn't think he had to sign anymore if he couldn't get McDonald's for his brother and I told him no, that wasn't the case at all. That was never the case. He only had to sign because the document was his accurate statement. He didn't have to sign in order to get something for his brother to eat. There was never any relation between the two, never any quid pro quo. Of course I didn't put it exactly that way. I can't say how he'd gotten that idea into his head, except we'd had a long day and he was pretty tired out. He certainly hadn't mentioned it earlier, if he'd been thinking it.

He said all right, he understood, but he didn't want to sign now anyway. He'd changed his mind.

I think maybe just being outside in the car had done it. Being on the way back home. I wished we'd signed in the office when we had the chance. I certainly didn't feel that we could go back. Even if that weren't coercive, it might give that appearance.

We got to the Mobil station and I got out all by myself and bought some microwave pizza for his brother. When he saw me coming back his face lit right up, and when I opened the car door he said he'd changed his mind again and he would sign the confession after all. Just like that. I have to admit that it might have been the microwave pizza that made the difference. I didn't want to take him out of the car so I gave him the pizza and went back in and got the cashier and switched on the dome light and all three of us signed right there in the lot. We signed four copies and I gave one to Creed. After that I got him home just as quickly as I could.

1985

Audie

I COULD HEAR my brother Vernon swallowing hard. In the daytime he sucked on his cough drops but at night he got dried out and I could hear him swallow. That cancer in his throat was like a stopper. He was trying to swallow around the cancer and what he was swallowing didn't want to go down. I couldn't listen. I thought maybe the next time it wouldn't go down and what then. So I got on my side and set my one ear against the mattress and put my hand over the other one. Then I pushed against my brother Vernon so he'd know I was there.

Tom

THE PARKING LOT alongside the Woodshed faced the beach but there was a fifty-yard stretch of dead trees and scrub in between. Low grass and a couple of junked cars and garbage blown over from days when the wire baskets on the beach overflowed, which was most of the time. Tom and Nick went out to the edge of the lot and over the little concrete barrier and down toward the beach, crunching over dead grass and newspapers and increasing amounts of sand. Tom always marveled a little at this part, how you went from ordinary upstate dirt to beach sand just like that. Who needed the ocean, he always said, when you could walk to the lake? Not that he ever convinced himself. The lake was dirty and hot and it had all this crap around it. Still, it was close to home.

They sat on a couple of concrete blocks and smoked, passing the joint back and forth. Tom said it was decent stuff and Nick said he knew that.

Tom asked where it came from.

Nick said he couldn't say.

Tom said couldn't or just wouldn't.

Nick laughed.

Tom said maybe that black onion muck behind Nick's half of a house was all right for growing dope.

Nick said he wouldn't know anything about that.

Tom said maybe just around the edges.

Nick said what, did he look like the agricultural type or something.

Tom said well shit you could go and turn the same question right back on him, couldn't you. And then where would you be. How far would that get you.

Nick said maybe farther than you'd think. He said Tom didn't look that long from the farm when you came down to it.

Anybody else, Tom might have gotten his back up.

*

Even though it was only Thursday night, there was a band working the back room. An old-timey outfit called Luke and the Smoky Mountain Boys. Tom went through on his way to the men's and he was pretty sure the guy introducing himself as Luke wasn't the same guy he'd seen doing it during the first set. This one was a dignified little dude who looked like a bookkeeper and the other one was a big galoot with coke-bottle horn-rims under a white cowboy hat. Maybe there were two Lukes. Maybe there was no Luke at all and they let everybody in the band have a turn like they thought it was funny. Then again it could have been just the dope. Regardless, he hated that scratchy old time music and it wasn't worth waiting through a whole other set to find out who the hell Luke was. It wasn't even worth asking Sal or somebody. He used the men's and that was that.

Back out in front he found Nick talking to somebody he didn't know. A tall guy, dark, with a little mustache that looked like a scar. He had taken Tom's stool, and he was smoking a long thin cigarette and leaning over to give Nick a

look that could have hypnotized him. Very intense. Tom thought he was probably an Italian. He saw plenty of Italians at the job site in Utica every day, and he
always figured they must be connected to the dope business somehow. Just because. He kept a low profile around the job site on that front. He had his hands
full already.

He came around the bar and slid in next to the tall guy and said something
on the order of that's my beer right there if you don't mind.

The tall guy didn't even turn to look at him. He just ducked his shoulder a
little bit to give Tom access to his beer. He certainly didn't make any effort to
give the stool back. Tom decided he looked like Xavier Cugat. He had that Cu-
ban's arrogance.

Tom drank a little and tried to listen in on their conversation, but Cugat
was talking in something below a whisper. Plus he had an accent that made his
voice kind of dip and rise and slur around the corners, like the coaster over in
the amusement park. Tom drank a little more and lit a cigarette. After a minute
or two Cugat left off and Nick stuck out an elbow and pushed him back a little.
He said while you're at it this is Tom. This guy right here. The guy I was telling
you about.

Cugat swiveled slow, like a cat stretching, and he fixed his hypnotic eyes on
Tom. He eased out a slow smile. It made that skinny little mustache of his slide
outward and up at the edges and get even thinner. Like a paper cut that hasn't
healed over.

"Hey," said Tom through his cigarette.

Cugat slid a hand toward him. "Tom," he said, "I am very pleased to meet
you." He was still using that roller-coaster voice, but he'd turned up the volume
on it a little. "I am Henri."

A Canuck, then. That explained a few things. The Canuck bowed like
some kind of old time parlor magician, his black hair parted up the middle and
slicked back. Tom half expected him to reach over and fish a quarter out of his
ear.

Nick said Henri was from Canada and Tom said he'd figured that out.

Nick said hey he could be from France couldn't he or he could live right
around here and still have an accent since there was no law against having an
accent that he knew of and Tom said he guessed that was pretty much true but
he'd been thinking Canada anyway for some reason.

Henri reached inside his jacket and took out his cigarettes—a flat box of
those Matinees—and Nick looked from the pack to Tom and back again as if

this were the secret, as if Tom possessed x-ray vision and had looked through the Canuck's jacket and identified his country of origin by his smokes. Fine.

"So—Tom," here Henri paused to light up, making everybody wait for the rest of what he had to say as he fitted the Matinee between his lips and hunted down his Zippo and spun the thumbwheel and fired up the cigarette and squinted against the rising smoke and inhaled dramatically and held it for a second and then another second and then finally blew it out again, "I have heard a great deal about you." It was turning out that Henri had an unnerving habit of talking in complete sentences, and he wasn't big on getting them out all at once.

Nick bounced his eyebrows up and down and said yes, Tom was the guy he'd been talking about all right. Henri'd come all the way down here from Montreal and he couldn't go home without seeing Tom. Yes sir, the three of them sure as shit had a little something to do if Tom was willing.

Tom was pretty sure he was. In the back room Luke and the Smoky Mountain Boys were caterwauling about some guy tracking a dead girl's footprints in the snow, but he blocked it out of his mind and took a quick look at Henri's Matinee cigarette and began to envision for himself a future in international trade. Then they had a few more beers and didn't talk about anything for a while.

Preston

YOU'D THINK AFTER all this time you might start looking at it as a turkey coop, but I don't guess anybody ever will. It'll always be just a schoolbus with turkeys in it. I guess it's the color. There's nothing else in this world the color of a schoolbus. They call it yellow but it's not quite yellow, and it's not orange either. I'd say it's something somewhere in between margarine and Velveeta. It's not a natural color. Then again I guess if we wanted kids to grow up natural we wouldn't put them on a schoolbus in the first place.

The bus where the Proctor boys keep turkeys isn't quite that original color but it's close. At least most of it is. They got it third-hand or maybe fourth from an old hippie over near Whitesboro. I understand he got it special for that big show down by Woodstock. The show wasn't really in Woodstock but everybody said it was. That's what they called it. Woodstock.

Where that old hippie got the bus to begin with I never heard. After the show was over though he came back and drove it around for three or four years—you'd see him in it here and there, just going to the grocery store or something or maybe to work, if he worked—and then I guess he got sick of putting gas in it. This was during the energy crisis. He pretty much junked it in a field out behind where he lived. You could see it from the Thruway if you knew where to look, especially during the wintertime when the leaves were all down. He'd painted it up psychedelic for that concert, so it got to where it was kind of a landmark.

Then one day it just wasn't there anymore. I was coming back from Herkimer on business and I always kept an eye out for it but it wasn't there that time. I didn't know where a person would take a junked schoolbus all dolled up like that or who'd want one, but from then on every time I'd go by I'd miss it. It was kind of like a pulled tooth. You'd notice it by its not being there. Anyhow a week or or ten days later I was taking Margaret out to supper at a place over on the road to New Hartford and I thought we'd go by where that old hippie lived and just take a look on account of we were there anyway and I was curious about it. Sure enough. Wouldn't you know that bus was in the barn and he was giving it a fresh coat of paint. It was pretty much that original schoolbus yellow or as close to it as he could get. I don't think you could match that color without the specs on it. He was using a roller on a pole, just rolling it on like he was painting a house. He was covered with it himself. I think he had as much on himself as he had on the bus. I said to Margaret I bet that's latex housepaint he's using and sure enough it turned out later that it was. It didn't stick for beans and you can still see the psychedelic paint job in places. I guess he was trying to reform that schoolbus. He figured he'd take the hippie out of it so somebody'd buy it from him. But you can't cover up a schoolbus with latex housepaint. I figured even an old hippie would know that much, but that one sure didn't.

Tom

THEY LEFT THE WOODSHED and stood around in the parking lot. The lake was making some little lapping noises out past the scrub and the junk but they could only hear it when the wind turned the right way. Otherwise all they could hear was the noise from the amusement park. Bells ringing and rollers screeching on rusty tracks and that awful circus music from the carousel.

Nick asked Tom if he had his car with him and Tom said he thought he was still man enough to walk the four blocks from the body and fender place under his own power.

Nick said the two of them would go back there with him then, but Tom said no. Business and pleasure. Whatever they were going to do they would do right here in this lot or maybe in some other lot even emptier than this one, but they wouldn't do it at home.

Nick said that was pretty much what they had in mind and he was just trying to make it easier. He thought they could do it in the body and fender lot maybe. Tom said was he nuts. The body and fender lot was lit up like they were selling used cars over there. The body and fender guys had a thing about security. They had a couple of closed-circuit television cameras set up. No way they'd do any business in the body and fender lot, not unless Henri here wanted to end up in a foreign jail. By which he meant, you know, an American jail. Which would be foreign to him.

Nick said fine you go get the car and come back and pick me up, and we'll follow Henri. Tom said where to and Henri said, in a complete sentence, that Tom would most assuredly find out soon enough.

Tom went and got the car. He didn't fetch any more dope from the closet upstairs because what he had in the glove box would do for a sample. If Henri wanted to buy more they could work it out based on that. When he got back Nick was waiting and Henri was behind the wheel of a big Caddy whose idle was even lower than the inaudible lapping of the water in the lake. Henri put the lights on and Nick jumped into the VW and they took off. Tom asked how long Nick had known this guy Henri and Nick said forever. Nick said he appreciated Tom's help and Tom didn't know what he was talking about but he didn't pursue it. He kind of appreciated Nick's help in connecting him up with this guy, but he let it go. After a few minutes and a half-dozen false starts where Henri would touch his brakes to size up some parking lot and change his mind at the last second and hit the gas again, they came to a campground that seemed to suit him. It was dark. There were a few trailers there but not many, most of them permanently dug in. None of them had any lights on. They belonged to summer people, gone home to Syracuse or Rochester, though Henri didn't know that. Henri cut back to his parking lights and Tom did the same and they drove among the trailers until they were out of sight of the road.

DeAlton

TELL YOU THE TRUTH I liked it better before you threw all that yellow on it. You had something before. You had something that belonged in a museum.

I'm not kidding. You've got to be future-minded. You've got to take the long view.

I know. You've got a point. Maybe someday but not now. You park that thing outside the Everson Museum in Syracuse they'd just haul it away even if it still had all that psychedelic shit on it. They don't know the value of anything.

But I still don't think you've done it any favors with that yellow paint. Or yourself either, as far as that goes.

So what do you want for it?

Fuck. You must be crazier than you look, and that's saying something.

Hey. You know I don't mean anything by it. Not after all we've been through.

Good. That makes me feel better.

I know you know.

So what'd you pay for it new or whatever?

Christ Almighty. You must have been plenty high.

Yes sir, I knew you then and I know you now.

You missed a spot above that taillight. Right there.

And these days it doesn't even hardly run. I'm surprised you got it into the barn. Tell you the truth I don't see how you're going to get out from underneath it.

That tire's almost bald right there. And the other one too now I look at it. Plus you could get high just sniffing the seat cushions. You probably don't notice it anymore but I don't know how you'll ever get that smell out. You're going to need yourself one understanding customer. You're going to need one majorly simpatico dude.

Oops. There's another spot you missed right there.

All right. I'll tell you what. Why don't we add up what I owe you, take away a hundred for my trouble, and see if we can't work out something that doesn't hurt either one of us too much.

I know. I know.

Hey, it's your choice. You wait though, you'll end up paying somebody else to haul it away. Plus if this thing gets in the wrong hands you're in deep shit.

Jesus. Have you ever even thought about running a shop-vac through it? A broom? You ever emptied the ashtray? That's what they call evidence, pure and simple. Don't you doubt it for a minute.

All right. Good. This is your lucky day, old buddy. Be glad I came along when I did.

Preston

YOU NEED A SPECIAL LICENSE to drive a schoolbus. It's not a Class A I don't think, but it's something like it. Not the same level as what you need for driving a semi truck but it's on that order, on account of the technology's different from a family car. The gearbox mainly. So you could have just about knocked me over when I came around front on the riding mower and saw that yellow schoolbus stuck in the turn and DeAlton at the wheel. At least he wasn't hauling kids. He nearly tipped it over in the ditch.

We had a circus getting it out. I mean three rings. It took all five of us and the tractor and the Buick I was driving then. We could have used the horse if she'd still been with us but she wasn't. Audie drove the tractor. He always had a touch for it and even now when he can't see so good he still gets the fussy work. One of these days he's going to run that thing into the woods and kill himself, but he hasn't done it yet.

A state trooper came along at one point and asked if we could use any help but DeAlton waved him on. The trooper volunteered to get up in the bus and steer if we wanted but he said no thanks, we could handle it ourselves. DeAlton looked a whole lot cooler to that state trooper than he did to the rest of us. He made it seem like we had the whole operation under control, which if you know the Proctor boys was questionable to say the least. I think the way he spoke so cool to that trooper gave Creed and Vernon a little faith that we might actually get the job done, so that was all right.

It took the better part of the afternoon and we lost the passenger side mirror on a fencepost, but we got that bus up the dirt lane and put it behind the barn. We hoisted up one end and then the other with a block and tackle so we could take the tires off and set it down square on the dirt. Dug it out a little on the front end where it was high. DeAlton said you could live in it if you wanted to or you could keep chickens in it or maybe turkeys. He said if his uncles wanted to look at it the right way he'd just expanded their living quarters by a hundred percent. They could sleep on the benches. Pipe heat out from the stove. He thought I could probably help with that and I guess I could have if it hadn't been the dumbest idea I'd ever heard.

Vernon asked him what a valuable addition like this was worth and DeAlton said he thought he'd never ask. I'd have gotten in between them over that deal, but they're family.

Tom

HENRI POPPED THE TRUNK and then ran around to unscrew the light bulb from the trunk lid.

"That's one careful dude," said Nick.

"He'd been all that careful," Tom said, "he'd have ditched that bulb already." Not that he would have thought of it himself, but saying it made him feel superior.

"Still," said Nick. "You've got to respect the dude. He's cautious."

They both opened their doors and Tom reached up to switch off the dome light, wishing he'd thought of it about a half a second before. While his eyes readjusted to the darkness he turned to Nick and asked him why Henri had the trunk open anyhow, but Nick didn't answer. He was gone and the door was closing behind him. Tom put one leg out onto the gravel and then remembered to get the baggie from the glovebox, which wasn't easy in the pitch dark and with as much beer as he had in him. He hoped there were some papers in there but he couldn't remember.

When he got out Nick already had the VW's hatch open. He looked at Nick in the light that bounced off the lake from the stars and asked him what he was doing and Nick said wasn't it obvious. He couldn't take that shit home on his motorcycle now could he. There was a little bit more than would fill up the saddlebags in case he hadn't noticed. And sure enough there was. Over behind the Caddy, Henri had switched on a little penlight and was passing it over a trunkful of grass. Bricks of it in plastic wrap and bales of it in burlap sacks. There must have been two hundred pounds, maybe more. Nick got an eyeful and nodded his head once, and Henri cut the light. He clearly wasn't interested in whatever little bit of dope Tom might have wanted to talk about.

1960

Audie

I HATED MY MOTHER'S NAME on that stone all those years just waiting. Now she was under and waiting with her name. Creed called the headstone man but he didn't come right off. He was the son of the man put it in. That's how long it'd been since my father went on ahead. The father carved for my father and the son carved for her. All she needed was the numbers because the rest was already there.

Ruth

THE SUMMER PASSES and her sons cut the hay and bring it in and the late rains wash the low hummock of her grave. Rivulets run from it. Grass sprouts up and weeds. In the woods the leaves turn and fall. Preston Hatch comes up with a garden rake over his shoulder and a pocketful of seed, and he roughs up the earth of the grave and he plants grass. He gleans hay from the cut field and covers the seed over. He bows his head and says a prayer but not for rain. That much he counts on without reservation, and snow too with the changing of the seasons.

When the monument man comes up the dirt lane he stops at the house next door as the more promising of the two. It has been raining lightly all afternoon and he is in a foul mood for having to work in it. He has a ball cap and a three-day growth of beard and a cigar screwed in between his teeth like a carriage bolt. Margaret comes to the door when he knocks, and without even withdrawing the cigar or saying that he is sorry for her loss he asks which way to the stone. She points up the hill. Then she points over his shoulder to the Proctor house and advises him to go there first, since it isn't her grave and it wasn't her mother who passed away to fill it. It was theirs. Their mother and their grave. And he'd better learn to feign a respectful measure of sympathy if he plans to be spending his time among the bereaved.

"Yes ma'am," he says, and he touches his cigar to the brim of his ball cap and leaves.

The brothers are in the barn. He goes to them without moving the truck, his feet sticking in the barnyard mud, and they come out to meet him halfway. Which of them has made out the words on his truck will stay a mystery.

"Whyn't we go on in," he says when they have made their introductions. Tilting his head toward the barn.

"Not with that seegar lit up," says Creed. Just like that. Seegar.

"Sorry," says the monument man, extracting the cigar and hiding it behind his back and blowing smoke leeward from the corner of his mouth. "I should know some folks don't care for the stink." It is the first sympathy he has shown. "My own wife, for example."

"It ain't that."

"I don't hardly notice it myself."

"It ain't the smell," Creed says. "You don't want no fire in a haybarn." He laughs either at the idea of it or at the monument man's ignorance. Maybe both.

The monument man looks over at the barn as if a sprinkling of hot ashes might do it a world of good.

"You're welcome to chew if you want," Vernon says. Showing his own wrecked teeth.

"That's all right," says the monument man. "I got work to do anyhow." He sticks the cigar back between his teeth and he yanks down his ball cap to shield it against the rain, and then he walks back to the truck.

*

He drives up through the pasture to the edge of the little graveyard. He pulls around to the wooded side of it where there is more protection from the weather and less chance the tires might get stuck if the rain gets any worse. It sure does seem to be settling in. A wind has risen from the east. He gets out of the cab and compares the stencil he cut in accordance to his father's old records against the lettering already on the stone and decides it's all right, and satisfied he takes a towel and rubs the stone dry and marks it and mounts the stencil to the face of it with rubber cement. He masks off the stone around the stencil and puts down tarps to catch the sandblasting compound. The air compressor he leaves in the truck bed since he has plenty of hose.

It won't be a long job. Just the two digits. He can't afford to waste effort on it because his father sold these packages complete and now that the old man is in the ground himself the time and materials are coming straight out of his own pocket. The old man probably made five or six of his long solitary fishing trips to Saranac Lake on the work his son has yet to finish. It's all there in the contracts, so there isn't a thing he can do about it. If there's anything these old timers know how to hang onto it's the paperwork for a headstone. He's learned that lesson once or twice.

He preps the sandblaster and puts his goggles and his gloves on, and he knocks the dirt out of his respirator and puts that on too. He takes off one glove to check that the stencil is glued down tight and won't go anywhere or leak compound around the edges and ruin the stone. He puts the glove back on, then he goes back to the truck and pulls the rope on the compressor. Beneath the sound of it he picks up the shuddering gun and kneels on the tarp he's spread over the grave and squeezes back the trigger.

For a moment it's raining everything. Water and sandblasting compound and pulverized granite. Against the onslaught the monument man settles his mind and counts steadily, metronomic by long practice, and moves the gun evenly across the face of the rock. One pass and he releases the trigger and then another pass from the other direction. After this second pass he stops and puts the gun down and sprays water from an Indian pump over the stencil and assesses the cut. His father would have disconnected the gun and blown the cut clean with compressed air but he is not his father and he hates to waste motion and it's raining anyhow. Once he is satisfied as to his progress he begins again, confident that he knows within a pass or two how many it will take to finish. Thinking as he goes that he knows of no work more permanent than this.

Wondering will his own children take it up when he is through, but thinking it unlikely.

He releases the trigger and rubs a fist over his goggles and turns to look left, down the hill toward the house and the barn, where amid the fierce cloud of grit and granite borne downwind like the locusts of old he spies a single figure upright. The voiceless brother. Silhouetted there against the red sun, his hands covering his face and his elbows lifted up like wings. Enduring the torrent of rain and rock. The monument man nods to him in acknowledgement of whatever might have brought him here, mistrust or curiosity or even love, and then he turns once more to finish his work.

Preston

I BLAME my own impatience. If I'd waited to plant the grass until after they'd come to put the year on the stone I don't guess I'd have had to do it twice. But to tell the truth it seemed like they weren't ever going to come. And then it'd been winter and what then. So I planted it once and it began to come up pretty well and then they came to work on the stone and it got all trampled down again and I had to do it over. I didn't mind. You owe some things to the dead even if they're not your own dead. I guess in some way they're all your own.

1954

Creed

I LEARNED TO LIKE a drink over to Camp Drum after I come back from Korea. Not before. Before I went liquor just put me in mind of the old man. He was a drinker and he had a brother drank too. Uncle Walt. We called him our drinking uncle. He was an awful drunk. He's dead now. My mother didn't have no time for him but she was stuck with my old man. Stuck till he died too like his brother. I think that's why I never got married yet. I seen her and how it was and I never wanted nothing to do with it.

There was quite a few drinkers in my squad up to Camp Drum. One boy from Tennessee said he liked to make his own back home. His own whiskey. He said he made it out of corn and I said we had enough corn back to the farm for that. We had plenty. The cows wouldn't miss a little of it. I decided I'd make my own like he did even though I weren't much use in the kitchen. He said it weren't a kitchen you needed and he showed me. He drew it all out the best he remembered it. He said you didn't want it anywhere near the kitchen. You wanted it a good distance away. He said the main thing you needed other than the parts and the corn was good luck to stay away from the law. I thought he was joking. He was a great one for jokes. I still got that paper he drew me. That boy from Tennessee.

So that was what we done at Camp Drum. There weren't much else to do since we was all through with the war. Our part of it. Old Camp Drum sets up there near Canada. I guess the army wants to watch out in case Canada comes down like North Korea did but it never happened that I know of. It was cold up there and there wasn't nothing to do and you could get a drink pretty easy. Some boys like that one from Tennessee were in the habit already when we got there. I don't guess Camp Drum'd seemed so bad if I'd gone there from home but I come straight from Korea. So I got to like whiskey all right. Not too much. I could afford it on my army pay but I knew when that give out I wouldn't be able to. I begun saving up the last I got of it for parts like that Tennessee boy put down on paper for me.

Preston

IT TAKES A CERTAIN KIND of individual to put on pounds in the U.S. Army. Most men lose some, or at least they look it. The ones who've been overseas anyhow, which Creed sure had. People don't think much about Korea anymore but he went through something over there, I guarantee it. I don't know what it was but he did. There's no getting out of a situation like that otherwise.

Men in the service overseas get broader in the shoulders maybe but aside from that they slim down. I know I did. Some fellows will say their years in the army were their best years, but mine weren't. Not by any means. Still I was probably at my best when I came out. Physically, I mean. Margaret would tell you. Creed came back all filled out and grown up. I swear he looked like a different species from his brothers, but it didn't last. Farm work will do that to you. It'll build you up for a while and then it'll wear you back down. Back down even farther than you started if you let it. The Lord giveth and the Lord taketh away, and working a farm will do the same thing.

He seemed to keep his distance a little when he got back. He hiked home from the train station just the same way I did. Nobody'd said he was coming. This was on a Sunday morning and Margaret and I were on our way home from church in that blue Nash. We drove right on past him. I eased over toward the other lane to give that soldier walking some room and we went right on. I didn't recognize him from the back and I sure didn't recognize him in the mirror. I didn't even think. It was Margaret who said Creed. My goodness, she said, there goes Creed Proctor walking and we went right on past him. Home from Korea and we went right on past. We had to turn around and go back.

*

Compared to him, his brother Vernon looked old. He came limping across the barnyard when we pulled up and you'd have thought he was Creed's own father, dragging his leg behind him from that accident with the spike tooth harrow and dragging Audie behind him too like he was on a short rope. He never lost that limp until the day he died. But here he came plugging across the yard like Creed was the prodigal son and he was the father. I don't know what kind of animal they'd have killed for his welcome home dinner if they'd seen him coming. They didn't have the turkeys then. Probably a chicken. Those Rhode Island Reds they kept used to be a good eating chicken. Anyway Creed got out of the car and his brothers clapped their arms around him. I'd never seen them do that before and I never saw it again. When I was in Washington with Margaret on that bus tour we took they showed us the Iwo Jima monument and it never had the same effect on me as the sight of those three in the barnyard. I know Iwo Jima was my war, but that statue didn't do a thing for me. Picture those three Proctor boys, two sets of coveralls caked with cow manure and one set of U.S. Army khakis pressed sharp. There's your war memorial.

Ruth

WITH DONNA FINISHING high school and her brother home from the war, it is a time of awakening and transformation. She will be the first of them to graduate and the first to go on. She has set her sights on the two-year college in Morrisville and she gets in without half trying. She could have gone anywhere. She could have become anything. Between the height of her ability and the depth of her need she is without practical limitation, but Morrisville is the school closest to home. She rents a plain room in the attic of a house in the town, moves her things out, and never entirely returns.

Creed behaves as if farming were light work after the rigors of army life. The truth is that while he was gone his brothers have learned to make do without him, so upon his return he is a spare hand. He moves from task to task as if he has been granted vast supervisory powers, suggesting needless improvements to practices unchanged since his father's time. He studies Vernon as he tosses haybales down from the loft and critiques his form, saying that he had better start lifting with his legs if he doesn't want back trouble one of these days. He improves the ramp to the chicken coop with new cleats that it does not need. He shows Audie how to hotwire the tractor with a jackknife, and then he laughs to see him dance away with one scorched hand jammed between his knees. He says he learned all about that from working in the motor pool. All but the dancing part anyway. Ha ha ha.

Evenings he sits by blue television light and studies the plans he got from the Tennessean. When he knows them by heart and can envision in his mind every element of their fitting together he takes his money and asks Preston for a ride to town. He says he needs some things at the hardware store.

What kinds of things, Preston wants to know. He says that the overlap of inventory between the hardware store and the lumber yard generally surprises most people, including himself. Creed ticks off the list on his fingers. A tub with a lid. Copper tubing and pipe. Fittings and elbows and reducing couplers. He gets no further than that before Preston interrupts, saying that if he wants a drink of whiskey it would be easier to purchase it by the bottle.

Creed says he doesn't know what he's talking about.

"Don't insult my intelligence," Preston says. "Not if you want my help with your science project."

Creed clears his throat and reaches into the pocket of his khaki trousers. The crease in them is long gone and they're stiff with the same excrement that stains every inch of his brothers' coveralls. They don't look any great distance from the burn barrel themselves, even though Ruth is still doing her best to keep up with the laundry. So much for the transformations of Korea. He unfolds the paper like a treasure map and hands it over.

Preston pulls off the road and studies it. He takes a pencil from the glove box and makes some notes. His mind begins working with questions that he knows Creed could never answer, but he figures that they can at least make a start and work out the details later on. Get a little help from men who know the specifics.

When they reach the lumber yard he insists on using a proper boiler instead of the jerry-rigged cut-and-welded monstrosity that the Tennessean's diagram calls for, and he advances it to Creed out of inventory. The truth is that he writes it up on the bill of sale as miscellaneous hardware, n/c, figuring he'll take it out in bad whiskey or at least entertainment.

Preston

IF HE'D PUT that thing together the way his army buddy told him, Creed would've beat Vernon to the graveyard by forty years at least. I don't know which one of them was crazier, him or his army buddy, but I never met the army buddy so I'm at a disadvantage. They say whiskey makes a man do funny things but I guess the want of it can make him do funny things too.

I knew some people in the plumbing and heating business, and my father had a pretty good relationship with old Roy Dobson who invented that milking machine. Between us we doped out what that Tennessee boy either didn't know or didn't see fit to write down. Some of these men I knew from church. They were all churchgoers, good God-fearing Christians every single one, but the idea of a whiskey still had a taste of sin about it that was one hundred percent irresistible. I guess naughty is the word you'd use. We were all over that job like a troop of Boy Scouts on a girly magazine. Creed never knew what hit him.

Years from now, when these buildings have all fallen down and the school-bus has rusted away, one thing will be standing on this property and it's that whiskey still. Solid copper and high grade stainless steel. Some of it built on site and some of it assembled down at Dobson's welding shop by the old master himself. NASA couldn't have done it any better. People to come will find it up on that hillside like a moon lander or something and they'll scratch their heads trying to figure out what it is. I don't guess they'll ever figure it out. It'll be our little mystery. A message from the past. *This is how we did things.*

1990

Audie

I DIDN'T KNOW what we had to eat in the house but I never stopped working so I never found out. Butter on bread I guess but I don't know. I meant to stop but I got busy and then it was milking time again so the day was already gone. I was hungry but the cows wouldn't wait. One thing Vernon taught me is the cows come first. They know what time it is when you don't, but they're not too good at waiting. When they're ready you'd better be ready too. It took me a long time all by myself. The man came from the co-op and he had to wait or come back so he came back and I still wasn't done so he had to wait since he had no-place else to go. It was the end of the day and Creed still wasn't back.

Margaret

PRESTON HAD IT in his head that Creed and Audie might be up by their whiskey still having a drink. I suppose it made sense, with Vernon just dead. You could see how they might want one. I didn't know that they kept their whiskey up there where they made it, but I suppose they might have, hidden in the woods. Or maybe they just made it fresh and drank it right away. I wouldn't know. They weren't hillbillies staggering around with clay jugs, I can tell you that. That would have been their father.

So Preston went up with his flashlight. I had just settled down to watch television when the phone rang. The phone hangs on the wall in the kitchen, so I stood there listening and looking out the window at the same time. It was a state trooper calling. I didn't get his name, it went by so fast. He said Creed was still at the barracks in Cassius—he didn't say they were questioning him, but I knew that's what he meant—and they were wondering if we'd seen Audie. He must have been young, because he pronounced it like the car instead of like Audie Murphy.

Who remembers Audie Murphy these days? Old folks, that's who.

I said no, we'd been out all day—I still can't remember where, isn't that just the strangest thing?—and when we'd come back we hadn't seen any lights on but Preston was heading over right now to check. The trooper asked if I would be so kind as to call back when we knew something and I said yes I would, but that's not the way it turned out.

No sooner had I hung up than I saw Preston's flashlight coming back down the hill. The beam of it was bouncing up and down with that abrupt walk he has. Nobody else could have been carrying it, not to my mind. We've been married for fifty-one years. There's nothing he could do that I wouldn't recognize, and vice versa. He didn't come straight down the hill toward home but across toward the farmhouse. Across the ridgeline and down through the pasture. Every now and then he'd walk through a little patch of moonlight and I could see that he was all by himself, even though I'd guessed that already. If he'd been with Audie he'd have been going more slowly, both because he wouldn't be hurrying to track him down anymore and because Audie doesn't go anywhere very fast. You know these things after fifty-one years, even without the moonlight to help.

Ruth

HE COMES PAST the graveyard where she lies alongside Lester and he walks across the ridge to follow the slope of the pasture down. Aware of the dew settling in the grass and the dampness on his pantlegs. Threading among the cows, entirely careless of where he steps but glad that he changed into his workboots out of the dress shoes he's had on all day. Thinking how quickly things can go to ruin from one innocent mistake.

He smells the night everywhere and the cows on either side of him and the silage from down in the barn as its scent rises on a light southerly breeze. He hears the creaking of iron spindles and wooden dowels aturn against iron fittings and wooden frames in the yard around front. He pictures Audie on the porch listening or down among them listening. The work Audie loves best, come to life. The clouds clear and he switches off the flashlight and keeps going. The creaking grows louder the nearer he gets. A half a hundred voices raised in the night and crying out. The earth turns and the sun shines somewhere and the temperatures shift and the wind comes up and these things—these creatures, for what else are they but created—these creatures cry out in their half a hundred voices. He pounds his damp boots on the dirt of the yard and scrapes a clod from one heel and enters the barn and finds the light switch. Just a couple of chickens and a duck and some cats. The cats look startled by the sudden illumination but the others are as insensible as bugs. He switches off the light and goes around front.

He sees the crown of Audie's white head as he rounds the corner. He is on the porch, upright in the overstuffed chair that Vernon always claimed for his own. He sits like a man entranced, not plucking tatters from the chair and rolling them into pellets the way his brother did but absolutely still and moveless in the dark. Faint blooms of light creep over his face as cars pass on the main road below, but he is blind to them. Preston jingles the change in his pocket by way of announcing himself and Audie twitches. Preston speaks his name out loud and Audie recoils. Preston steps onto the porch and Audie drops from whatever trance he had lulled himself into and turns his head in his direction and begins to shake with such unearthly intensity that the little wooden feet of the overstuffed chair chatter on the board floor as if the chair means to bear itself and its poor palsied burden off to some more hospitable place.

"Where'd your brother get to."

Audie makes no answer.

"That's all right," he says. "You take it easy and I'll go find him myself." Beginning to reach for the screen door, unsure of what to expect, thinking that Creed could not still be with the trooper after all this time. Wondering where is he.

Audie struggles to indicate that his brother is not in the house.

"I didn't think so," Preston says. "I guess that trooper didn't bring him back yet did he."

Audie says no. The word as it emerges draws itself out into a howl less suited to a man than to a wolf. Forlorn and yearning and isolate. It quavers at the end when his breath fails and it rattles like some last exhalation and then he gasps himself back to life. Reduced to tears, collapsing on the big overstuffed chair into a position perhaps even less than foetal. In the yard the whirligigs scrape against themselves.

Preston comes to his side and kneels down. His knees hurt. He wants to go see about Creed but he can't. He places a hand on Audie's shivering side and at the touch of it Audie withdraws as if he's been branded.

That rooster. Vernon give it to me. We was boys.

Creed

FOR ALL I WORRIED about him my brother'd already ate his supper. Margaret fed him a pork chop I think and some sauerkraut and some mashed potatoes. I brung the microwave pizza Del Graham bought at the gas station but he didn't want any part of it. He said he was too full already thanks to Margaret. He set there at her kitchen table patting his belly and saying it. He said why didn't Margaret keep the microwave pizza. She had it coming.

Preston said he wanted to see Del Graham so he went out but I don't think he got to him in time. Del Graham was pretty satisfied with his paperwork I guess and he pulled out quick. He had a lot on his mind. Not just Vernon I don't think. When I was getting out of the car with the microwave pizza he asked me about a marijuana cigarette they found and I didn't let on Tom had any connection to it. I told him Vernon used that stuff for the cancer and it just grew. It just grew around. Things grow on a farm whether a city boy knows it or not and that marijuana just grew like the rest. Del Graham laughed and he said he thought I was right about that. He was a city boy so what did he know. I didn't say a word about Tom so he never found out.

1947

Preston

EVERYBODY IN THE FAMILY just doted on that little girl right from the start. She was the last to come and she was the first one that wasn't a boy. Her mother was always a mystery to me, but judging by the way she favored Donna I always thought maybe when she married Lester she married down. I don't know why I say that because I don't know a single fact about her life before. It was just a feeling I had. Like she hoped her daughter could be what she was supposed to be herself. You expect that with boys usually but not with girls. I don't know why that would be. Maybe things are changing. Anyhow there's no question those boys rose up above their no-account father and Donna surpassed her mother with nursing school and all that, so I guess everybody got their wish.

Donna and Audie had similarities even though you might not think it. Each one of them was the younger of a pair: Vernon and Audie, Creed and Donna. They were what, ten years apart? That's a big gap. Until Creed came along Audie'd been the youngest for a good long while and I think he got used to it. It suited him. Folks either expect the world from the youngest child or else they baby him along. Sometimes a little of both. So they had that in common. Anyhow Donna was just a little thing in elementary school around the time I'm talking about. Her mother dressed her like a doll, at least as far as she was able.

Being the one girl she didn't get hand-me-downs, or at least not directly. The ones she got probably came from the Salvation Army or the church. She certainly didn't get them the way Creed did, him being third in line. I guess if she'd been a tomboy she'd have fit right in and been able to carry on the family tradition, but she wasn't a tomboy so she didn't have to. I don't guess her mother would have let her be one. So she wore a dress to school every day. Not that I guess she smelled any better than the rest of them.

*

One day Vernon came along and asked me if I'd run him down to see that fellow Driscoll over by the creek. That's Cassius Creek, not Fish Creek. Fish Creek runs into the lake. Cassius Creek runs I don't know where, it just runs. Driscoll has a sawmill down by the creek. Back when he was younger he did a little bit of every kind of woodworking there might be any call for. Not just sawmill work. He'd take down a tree if you needed one taken down or he'd haul it away if it came down all by itself. Then he'd cut it up and dry it out in a couple of barns he kept and sell it back to you or somebody else. He had a couple of big planers and some joinery equipment and he did some carpentry and even a little bit of cabinetmaking. In those days Driscoll used to be a kind of a one man band when it came to wood.

He'd come the summer before and taken down a cherry tree from up along the top of the pasture that'd been hit by lightning, and now he'd called back and said he had some wood from it for Audie. For his whirligigs. I don't know how they had the details of that transaction worked out. The cherry tree was worth something to him and hauling it away was worth something to the boys and the lumber he got out of it was definitely worth something to pretty much anybody. Those little bitty pieces Audie put into his whirligigs weren't worth anything. They were just scrap.

When Vernon came near he had Audie with him but he didn't mention anything about Audie going. Just him. I said why didn't Driscoll just drop off that little bit of wood when he was out driving around, but he gave me a look and leaned in toward me so Audie couldn't hear and said there was more to it than that. I asked him what and he laughed and said it was a secret, and I said not from me it isn't. Not if I was doing the driving. He said a secret was a secret and then he just shut up, grinning. I said all right I'd take him if he was going to be that way.

I tell you what, it turned out to be a fool's errand.

The first thing was, Driscoll didn't have enough scrap lumber to fill up a milk crate. It wasn't worth the gas to drive over, and this was when gas was twenty-five cents. The second thing was, it turned out we didn't go for the lumber anyhow. That was a ruse on Vernon's part. The real reason was Driscoll had an old wood lathe he was getting rid of, and Vernon wanted it for Audie.

I said to Vernon now how in the world am I supposed to get that home in my car. He said he thought we'd have better luck with the car than with the tractor, and I had to admit he had a point. Driscoll threw a switch and shut down the saw he was running and came hustling over under a full head of steam and said what was wrong with him. Couldn't he wait a week for Christ's sake. He said he'd told him on the telephone that he'd bring that lathe out to the farm next week. No charge. Just to get rid of it. Provided he could wait that long.

Well, didn't Vernon look sheepish. Disappointed and sheepish both. I told him it was all right. His brother had waited this long and he could wait another week. I said remember he didn't even know he was waiting for anything in the first place. Vernon asked was I sure we couldn't take it to pieces and get it in the car some way and I said I wasn't about to take it to pieces and Driscoll said he didn't have any time to fool with it now. He'd bring it out in a week.

Donna

WHEN IT ARRIVED on Driscoll's truck, it looked bigger. Driscoll had a crane mounted on the back for wrangling tree trunks and sawn wood and with the help of it he'd gotten the lathe on board all by himself. He backed the truck all the way up from the main road and got out and stood all alone in the dirt swatting at flies with a straw hat, looking like he'd made a terrible mistake. Like unless someone appeared directly to give him a hand he might just tip the whole thing into the barnyard like the trash it was and leave it there to rust. The Proctor boys were slow in materializing, but one by one they detected his presence and emerged from their various secret occupations. Young Creed lowering himself from the hayloft. Vernon stepping from behind the house, buttoning up the fly of his coveralls and squirting a jet of tobacco juice at the dog.

Audie piloting the tractor down from a high cornfield, mounted on it like some pale rider. They converged, already a gathering of spirits, wordless.

"I ain't got all day," said Driscoll.

Ruth and Donna poked their heads around the corner of the porch and came down into the dooryard as yet only lightly populated by Audie's makings. A live rooster pecking, and another rooster of wind-driven wood making as if to peck. A man sawing timber. Something with wings.

Vernon got Audie's attention and climbed up on the truckbed and put his arm around the lathe as proudly as if he had fathered it himself. He said it would belong to Audie from now on but Audie had trouble getting the drift. Vernon looked disappointed but he kept on. He paced off the dimensions of the lathe and went into the barn and paced them off again and came back out and said he'd miscalculated. It wouldn't fit where he'd thought. Driscoll's shoulders fell and he uttered a curse, not the day's last. He said he reckoned he could take it to the dump then just as easily as not. Vernon's shoulders fell but he uttered no curse to match Driscoll's, his mother and his innocent little sister being present after all.

Creed suggested the hayloft. Driscoll tilted his head back to study the old barn and concluded that he didn't believe it would support a good snowfall much less woodworking equipment. Creed said he might be surprised. Driscoll shook his head and swatted flies and whistled through his teeth. Creed said if Driscoll hadn't lifted a haybale lately he would be surprised for certain, for they were far heavier than a man might think and the loft held mountains of them just fine. Driscoll put on his hat and said all right maybe it wasn't such a stupid idea after all, and he went in to size up the timbers and came out not entirely satisfied but not about to hold back progress either. It was their barn.

Vernon

DRISCOLL THOUGHT IT WOULDN'T WORK but he was wrong. We used the block and tackle. We hoisted it right up and in through the door just as easy as pie. I sent Audie up to clear a place for it first while Driscoll backed the truck around and we untied the straps he had on it to hold it down. He had it tied down good so it didn't fall off. I went up and showed Audie how big a space to clear and he cleared it. We hung the block and tackle from the beam and lifted it up. When we got it in I said Driscoll ought to show us how to work it and he said plug it in first he didn't have all day. We didn't have juice up there it turned out but that was all right because it didn't take a regular plug anyhow. Driscoll said we had to have a two-twenty line if we wanted to run it or else we could just keep it for a decoration. He laughed about that. How we'd have it for a decoration in the hayloft. He climbed down laughing and he was laughing when he drove off. Preston put in the juice for it later. He was always handy. He was always a good friend. Then he showed me how to run it and I showed Audie.

1986

Tom

SHELLY MADE IT out of high school and her parents threw her a graduation party, but since they didn't know about Tom he never got invited. Not that they would have had him anyhow. He wouldn't exactly have fit in with the family and friends that were spread out under the big elm trees in the backyard, although it turned out there was an unsanctioned secondary party under way in the paneled basement rec room that would have been just his kind of thing. Nick was in charge of it. It had been his idea, and he'd brought along the refreshments in the saddlebag of his Indian: Two pints of Southern Comfort and a baggie of Panama Red and a sack of Fritos. He'd gotten the dope from an old hippie over in Whitesboro and it had cost him a fortune. But this was a special day, after all. No use settling for his usual, scraps and scrapings of the stuff he distributed for Henri. So while the burgers sizzled on the grill outdoors, Nick and Shelly and a couple of cousins from down near Ithaca took turns standing by the open basement window, inhaling fiercely and blowing jets of smoke out into the side yard. Between that and shots of Southern Comfort, the graduation party was going along just fine.

Tom was home, dreading Monday and thinking about his future. The winter past had been a period of drudgery and dread and unreasonable dreams—doing some interior maintenance work for Fazio in a couple of apartment buildings he managed for some other Italian guy, watching the calendar creep toward springtime and a resumption of the construction work in Utica, contemplating a future when he could throw it all over for steadier and more profitable work in the recreational pharmaceuticals line—but now that the seasons had turned and he'd settled back into his summer routine he was wondering if anything would ever change. The weather had been damp so far but sunny enough and the grass he'd planted over at his uncles' place was coming up strong but not strong enough to stake a person's future on. He'd planted a little more this year but it didn't seem like he'd ever grow enough to make a difference unless he went full-time into farming like the prior generation had. And he sure as shit had no interest in that.

Audie

UP I CLIMBED and the higher I went the darker it got. I came to the trapdoor and pushed it open and it hit something. The light turned gray and swimming. With the trapdoor up I saw better. I saw the light and the dust swimming in the light. I stuck my head out and sneezed from the dust and I banged my head on the trapdoor. It wouldn't lie down flat because something was in the way of it. I wanted it to lie down flat. How I go to the hayloft is I climb up and open the trapdoor and I keep going the rest of the way on the ladder that goes on up against the wall and I come out to the side and close the trapdoor all the way shut again so I don't fall down it and break my neck like Vernon says. Then I get what I came up for. I always do it the same because I'll need to if my eyes keep up the way they're going. I wouldn't fall in if I didn't shut it because I know right where it is and I can see the dark of it and the shape of it but I like knowing. I'm used to it. I might not even notice when my eyes get worse if I keep doing everything the same way. The lathe is up here still but I don't use it too much. I was up to fetch wood. The trapdoor was bumping on something that belonged to Tom. He keeps things up there and sometimes he makes a mess. This was a couple of plastic buckets and a bag of fertilizer tipped over. I didn't clean it up but I moved it.

Donna

SHE MADE AN APPOINTMENT for Vernon with a doctor she knew. He said that he would see her brother as a professional courtesy, but she would be on her own for whatever tests he might need. Medicaid would cover some of it and she knew a social worker who could arrange for whatever help might be available from the county. There was always a way. If her mother taught her anything growing up, it was that there is always a way. How else could she have raised four children on nothing?

The doctor's name was Franklin. He was a general practitioner of the old school, drawing near to retirement. A widower. He could recall the days when doctors spent half of their hours traveling from sickbed to sickbed with nothing to rely on but the contents of their black bags. He believed still that a man with a sharp eye and a good ear could accomplish certain commonplace miracles with a stethoscope and a tongue depressor, a scalpel and set of good forceps, a curved needle and sufficient thread. He kept up with the latest information but he was cautious about putting too much stock in it. His bag still sat on the top shelf in the front hall closet, pebbled and snapdragon-mouthed, full of old se-crets.

His office was in a square, hip-roofed, three-story house opposite the for-mer Cassius hospital, which was now a nursing home populated mainly by the indigent. Both properties were once the best in town, but with the passage of the years they had slipped downhill together. Thus had Franklin's patients aged with him and returned in this new guise. He joked that one day he would walk across the street to make his rounds and they would keep him. He believed that it would not be such a terrible fate, for at least he would be among friends.

The day was young and the office was empty. Donna delivered her brother to the nurse guarding Franklin's door from behind a massive desk of black wal-nut. Mrs. Waverly was her name and she had been with Franklin since the days when her position required that she wear a curved white cap starched as stiff as whalebone. She ushered Vernon into an examining room and weighed him on a scale minus his shoes. She took his temperature and his blood pressure. Vernon remarked that so far he hadn't received any treatment that his sister could not have given him at home if they'd had a scale and whatnot, and she laughed po-litely and told him to be patient. She made some final notes and pulled a paper gown from a cabinet and asked him to wait until she shut the door and then remove his coveralls and put on the gown. She said it tied in the back.

The stink of Vernon Proctor in the closed room, undamped by the thin barrier of his clothing, was the smell of some ailing beast gone to ground in a long-used den. Franklin knew to expect such a smell from the residue of it that lingered in the hallway and from a quick pantomime on Mrs. Waverly's part, but he was struck by the sour animal pungency of it all the same. Some things are worse than we can imagine in advance. A lump or a cough can only hint at the multifarious complexity of the cancer etched upon an X-ray, and that image in turn can only suggest the ramifying reality of the disease at work in a living matrix of ruined tissue. Some things are worse than we can imagine and fifty-odd years in practice had taught him this again and again. So although nothing had quite prepared him for the precise stink of Vernon Proctor naked in a closed room, he persevered.

He sat on a stool with Vernon before him on the examining table. He asked how long it had been since Vernon last saw a doctor and Vernon recalled the incident with the spike-tooth harrow which had not required a doctor visit and the subsequent blood poisoning which had.

"So you're an old-timer like me," said Franklin, clapping a hand on the examining table alongside Vernon's draped leg. "Nobody calls it blood poisoning anymore."

"Is that so."

"These days they call it fifty different things, depending. All fifty of which they treat like blood poisoning."

Vernon laughed and Franklin observed his teeth, warily, his mind clicking.

Franklin smiled and nodded and moved smoothly to the business at hand. "Your sister tells me you haven't been feeling your best."

"That's right."

"She's a fine person, your sister."

"I guess it runs in the family," said Vernon. He was having a pleasant enough time of it now, in spite of sitting naked on a table with nothing between him and the world but a sheet of pale blue paper. To tell the truth he had feared doctors all along or at least mistrusted them, given his mother's fate. But this wasn't so bad.

"Runs in the family," said Franklin. "I guess maybe it does." Then he cocked his head and something shifted behind his eyes that changed everything. "Donna tells me you have some specific complaints, but I'd really like to hear about them from you."

Vernon swallowed. "I guess the main one's cancer," he said.

"Cancer," said Franklin. He paused, waited, thought. "I knew your mother," he said.

"She died from it."

"I know."

"I got it like she did."

"Whereabouts? Whereabouts on your body?"

"My throat that I know of." Touching it with a knobby finger. "My pecker."

Franklin did not doubt that either of these could be true, but he mistrusted Vernon's diagnostic skills. "How does it feel, exactly?"

"I can't swallow too good. Sometimes I can't hold my water."

"That probably wouldn't be your pecker, but it might be something connected to it." Franklin sat nodding, assessing such of his patient as he could see without lifting the blue paper. Vernon's skin a wrecked Rorschach of sun damage. The calf of his right leg puckered on both sides around the old wound. One finger sheared away at the second knuckle. "You saw a doctor for that too, I suppose." Pointing to that last. "One of your many engagements with the medical community."

"No," said Vernon. "My dad done that on the stove. I cut it off and he cauterized it."

Franklin drew breath.

"I don't know what become of the rest." Sitting under the blue paper, holding the hand up and studying it as if it possesses vatic properties, his mind going back to the missing flesh and bone as to some lost opportunity for divining. "I was a boy. I never did ask what he done with it."

1955

Creed

MY BROTHER BLAMED IT on smoking but I don't know. Smoking ain't what killed my father before her and he smoked his whole life. What killed him was a goddamned mule.

Ruth

HER COUGH SHAKES THE HOUSE. In cold weather it emerges on smoke and steam. She usually has a cigarette burning but even when she does not her breath in the frigid house is white like all the rest. At least in her cold back bedroom, never mind the grate. Not that she does not appreciate the work that went into it or the compassion. She remembers the day they put it in, Vernon and Audie and Creed and Preston. She remembers how they cut the hole in the wall and filled it back up, all for her comfort. She does not have the heart to say how far the actual fell short of the intended, but they all know. They all know by the blankets they bring her when the weather gets cold and her cough shakes the house.

She relies on her sons and she relies on her daughter gone off to nursing school in Syracuse and she relies on the cancer that will kill her if she lives long enough. Her breath comes hard. She lies awake in the black of night listening to the gunshot bursts of sap exploding in distant trees. She coughs blood and she balls tissues and drops them to the floor alongside her cold bed and she waits. Morning does not come and death does not come either and so she lights a cigarette in the dark and listens to the bursting of trees and the snoring of her grown sons in the next room. The three in one bed. Then and now and forever and ever.

Preston

AUDIE HAS A LONG MEMORY. You have to grant him that.

Audie

I WANTED HER to stop was all.

Ruth

HER MIDDLE SON goes from the house to the barn, from cold to colder still. Opening the door just a crack and sliding through it and closing it again. There are chickens in the barn, chickens and an old horse and a wind that howls between the barnboards where the drifts have not yet blocked its entry, bearing snow that spills over itself and tumbles down its own alluvial flanks like sand.

He has something hidden in the breast pocket of his coveralls. He stops and unbuttons his coat and presses his fingers against the fabric, fearing that his passage through the narrow doorcrack has squashed his treasure flat. Cursing his careful thoughtlessness. But the denim is shitstiff and his fingers are frozen and he cannot determine much. He creeps along the wall, stepping in snow, toward a bright window where he can draw the thing out and look. Chickens scatter. Cellophane gleams. A half pack of cigarettes shakes in the snowlight. Crushed yes but not beyond salvaging. He takes one out and holds it like some venomous thing alive and bent on treachery. Runs his fingers along it to nurse it back to shape. Blows into the pack to expand it and shakes out the rest and does the same, restoring them one by one. All is not lost.

He climbs to the hayloft where the wind howls wilder yet. The lathe has a worktable built into one end of it and he clears it off. A single electric bulb crusted with sawdust hangs low above it and he switches it on. He puts the cigarettes down on the worktable where they skitter, windshifted. He reaches into the pocket of his coat and draws out a darning needle he has kept there, stolen likewise from his mother. Through the eye of it a hair from the horse's tail, just as he remembers. He sets it down on the worktable and it slides a little and he recovers it and stabs it through his cuff for safekeeping and then he takes out the first cigarette and applies himself to it. Squinting. Summoned here as to the nightdark shop of some poor shoemaker, working wordless magic.

Preston

HE SURE DIDN'T MEAN IT as any joke. Not like they all did with Margaret that first time. What he wanted was to kill his mother's taste for cigarettes, which by then was going to take a whole lot more than a little bit of horsehair. I don't know that it would have done her any good if it'd worked. If she'd taken the hint and just up and quit. Probably not. It was probably too late. Maybe she would have breathed better toward the end but it still would have been the end.

To hear Vernon tell it, she smoked the first one that evening without even taking note of the difference. The house was shut up tight and it raised a stink like you wouldn't believe and she didn't even take note of it. Most people it'll make sick to their stomach quick enough. That's how far gone she was even then, and she still had a few years left. Creed got his coat and went out into the barn for a little fresh air but Audie just sat there and took it. He was waiting to see what would happen and he wanted to be there when it did. Vernon stayed with him. He knew what was up. He wasn't anybody's fool. And he figured he ought to be there right along with his brother.

After she smoked the first one Audie went in to check on her and the smell was worse in there but she didn't seem to mind it. He sat down at her bedside for a while and she lit up another. That one must have been the last straw. I guess it got to her stomach directly without going through her nose because the next thing you know, up comes dinner. She wasn't eating much by then, but it came up.

Audie

I THOUGHT SHE WAS DYING. I thought I'd done it. I thought I'd brought it on.

Ruth

VERNON DOESN'T KNOW which of them to care for first. The woman or the man. His mother choking on sour vomit in her bedclothes or his brother gasping and aquiver on the floor. He calls out for Creed but Creed does not answer. Perhaps he does not hear. He cannot know the extent of this, and so Vernon does not blame him either way. The cigarette still burns on the bedlinen and he squashes it out in a pool that looks like eggwhite. The fallen match has gone dead on the floorboards but he grinds it out with his toe for good measure and glares down at it and then grinds it out all over again. It is something he can be sure of. His mother doubles over and vomits once more, emptily this time but with no less force than prior, and then she brings herself erect. With an arm to each side she steadies herself against the effort and pulls in a crippled half lungful of air. He pats her on the back and utters some apology or promise and goes to his brother, calling for Creed again as he steps around the foot of the bed. He kneels and wraps himself around his quivering brother Audie and enfolds him there upon the cold board floor and they lie together a moment like Union soldiers spooning. Audie calms a little. His breathing steadies. One leg thumps the bedstead in a doglike rhythm and Vernon reaches to suppress its beating. His mother either speaks or merely gasps but either way it is sound of some vengeful haunt making its ragged accusation. So Vernon rises to his knees and goes to her again, telling Audie to get up if he possibly can and go fetch Creed.

1990

Preston

I WANTED TO GIVE that trooper a piece of my mind but I didn't get there quick enough, so I just watched him drive off and balled up my fist and shook it in the air and came on back into the house all steamed up. Madder than a wet hen. I'd have set Creed down right there and talked to him like a Dutch uncle if they hadn't already put him through the wringer all day and half the night. So all I did was ask who they'd gotten him for a lawyer. He looked at me like I'd turned into a talking sheep or something. Like he knew more about these things than I did. He said he didn't need any lawyer, and I knew then. I said everybody needs a lawyer and if you can't afford one they'll appoint you one. They've got to. He knew that from his cop shows. I knew he knew it. He gave me a look that said it was just now dawning on him for the first time, and Margaret put out her hand and made me stop. There'd be time in the morning she said.

I wasn't just mad on account of Creed but on account of Audie, too. We'd given him some supper and he was all right, but those troopers should have been ashamed of themselves. You don't call a neighbor to check on somebody like Audie. Maybe you do if you're a relative from out of town or something, but not if you're the damn state police and you've got men in patrol cars on every road between here and Albany. You send somebody out is what you do.

You send somebody out. After I brought him back home Margaret told me to call the barracks, but I didn't call because I didn't want to give them the satisfaction. I'm not working for the State Police. I wasn't then and I'm not now and I don't plan to start up anytime soon. Their whole problem was they were too busy coming after Creed.

*

The first thing I did come morning was give Mary Spinelli a call over in Utica. Her father used to do my father's work and she has the practice now. I knew she wasn't the lawyer for the job on account of she mainly does wills and trusts and real estate and like that, but I thought she ought to know who was. She flat-out couldn't believe they'd kept Creed all day and never given him access to counsel. I could practically hear her shake her head over the telephone. She said she'd read about Vernon in the paper and she knew a little something about farm boys like the Proctors and if a fellow like that was ignorant enough to refuse a lawyer that meant he was ignorant enough to require one. Too ignorant not to have one. Which was my thought exactly. She didn't go so far as to say the troopers had taken advantage of him but I knew what she meant. She gave me some names anyhow, and I wrote them down.

I let them finish the milking before I went over. I still had a full head of steam up. Margaret tied me to the table and made me drink another cup of coffee. She makes it weak so it didn't do me any harm. I looked up the numbers of those other lawyers in the phone book and drank my coffee and kept an eye out the window, and once the co-op truck had come and gone I went over.

I asked Creed if he'd signed anything and he said yes. I asked what. He told me he'd signed what they'd talked about all day, he and Del Graham and some other fellow Burnes. A trooper I figured. All day and half the night. All day and half the night without a lawyer. Never mind. Whatever it was he signed I didn't think it sounded too good. I asked him what it said and he told me he had a copy right there I could look at if I wanted and read it for myself. He had it folded up into the breast pocket of his coveralls. It looked about a million years old already when he took it out. I don't know how long he meant to keep it in there but I was glad I got my hands on it. I told him I'd give it back to him after I made a photocopy down to the library. For posterity.

Del

I SENT THE PAPERWORK to Ben Wilson's office early the next the morning. It was my interview and it was my confession and I sent it over myself. It was going to be a busy day around the district attorney's office, and I thought even as I was sending it over that it would end up on the bottom of somebody's in-basket just by default. If only for a little while. They were expecting the final report from the medical examiner too. I thought that that would be of some interest. I didn't expect there would be anything there to contradict the confession and it turned out that there wasn't. There were some developments I hadn't thought about or even imagined—the semen, mainly, which suggested I'm not sure what to this day, maybe nothing—but there wasn't anything to contradict the story as Creed had laid it out. I didn't think there would be. I was confident that we'd done a thorough job. I thought he had explained it all pretty well.

You try to understand how another person's mind works. I think that's the hardest thing. It surprises you sometimes. But unless you understand how another person's mind works you can't necessarily make sense of the evidence in front of you. Take that bed. Take those men. Two of them left alive and one of them dead. Whatever evidence is left on the bed is so ephemeral as to be useless. It tells one story as well as it tells another. If you weren't there you couldn't be sure. Reading it is like trying to hear a tune somebody whistled last week. You can't do it.

There's evidence on the body, but it might mean anything. What I first took for a sunburn turned out to be something different, burst blood vessels, maybe a sign of strangulation. What looked like a cancerous growth in the neck wasn't, not according to the pathology report. So the thing you thought might have killed a man becomes a thing that couldn't possibly have killed him, considering that it wasn't cancerous. On the other hand if a person believes he's got cancer and he's dying from it and everybody around him thinks the same thing, then just the idea might kill him one way or another. It might help. It might contribute to the circumstances and aid the process.

So you try to understand how people think, and sometimes it surprises you. People don't always see things the same way you see them. But if you listen carefully enough—respectfully enough—and if you pay attention to the things that matter to people, sometimes you'll hear a story that not only explains things you already know, like the burst blood vessels and the urine in the bed, but things you haven't even heard about yet, like Vernon Proctor's not having had cancer in the first place. And how he might die from it anyhow.

When those things start coming together, you start thinking maybe you know. At least to the extent that you can ever know anything. Which I suppose is why they invented the courts.

Preston

I GOT SO WORKED UP I came off without my change, so Margaret had to fish around in her purse for money to put in the photocopy machine. She drove us for that same reason. I forgot my keys and my wallet. Plus I just kept on reading and rereading that paper the whole way. I couldn't believe my eyes. It was just one fabrication after another, with some mark at the bottom that was supposed to say Creed Proctor. You could tell just from that. Just from that mark. There were two signatures down there that mattered and the only one of them that suited the words typed out underneath it was Del Graham's. He had handwriting like a schoolboy, every letter of it just so. Creed's was only a scribble. He might have made that scribble but I don't guess he ever said those words.

In a nutshell the paper said he killed his own brother. It said Vernon was out stone cold and he'd wet the bed as usual and that woke Creed up. It said Vernon was snoring up a storm from the lump in his throat. The lump that had him sucking on horehound drops all day and started him smoking marijuana even though there wasn't anything on the paper about that little transgression, thank God for small favors. According to the paper he was making a racket and Creed had finally had enough of it and he couldn't go back to sleep and he couldn't abide the sound of his own beloved brother suffering anymore and wetting the bed every goddamn night in the bargain and so he pinched Vernon's nose and mouth shut and put him out of his misery. Just like that. Put him out of his misery. And Audie never even knew a thing about it until the morning. That's what it said on the paper, over a scrawl that meant my name is Creed Proctor and I said this.

I know Creed Proctor. He never said that. He never even read it.

1986

Donna

WHILE VERNON PUT his clothes back on, Dr. Franklin asked him if he'd ever had supper over at that new Chinese restaurant, and Vernon said no. He and his brothers didn't eat out much. They never had. The Homestead was good enough for them. Franklin thought that by the homestead he meant the farm, until Vernon waxed rhapsodic over the chicken and biscuits platter they put out on Sundays and he realized that he was talking about the place in Madison where the Rotary met. He said he'd been thinking about the new Chinese restaurant because they sold dinners where you chose a certain number of dishes from one column and a certain number of dishes from another column, and that was pretty much the situation in which he found himself now that he was looking at Vernon. Between the misshapen moles on his skin and the alarming state of his blood pressure and the nameless abnormalities visible in his ears and throat, between his stated complaints about the lump in his neck and the malfunctioning of his pecker, never mind the fact that he'd never had a prostate exam until five minutes ago or a colonoscopy in all his sixty-one years or even the barest minimum of blood work, it was hard to know where to start.

Vernon asked him what they did for cancer these days, as if the direct approach would be the best.

"It would depend on the cancer," said Franklin. "If there were one."

"They never done much for my mother."

"I know," said Franklin.

"They just took blood till she about run out of it."

Franklin made some notes in a folder. "We've learned an awful lot since those days." He put his pen down and looked up and smiled. "As much as I hate to mention it, we'll need to take a little bit of your blood too."

Vernon nodded.

Franklin asked if he wanted to know what they'd be looking for.

Vernon said he knew. The same thing they looked for with his mother.

"Not exactly," said Franklin. "We're a long way from that."

Vernon brightened. "You don't take blood for cancer no more then."

"I mean we're a long way from a diagnosis," said Franklin. "This is just the first step. A little preliminary investigation. Cholesterol. Blood sugar. That sort of thing. Just to see what you're made of."

He said he'd write everything out for the lab at the hospital and he asked if Donna would be coming soon to pick him up, and Vernon said that she would.

Tom

HE CAME DOWN the outside stairs with his teeth brushed and his hair combed back wet and a cold beer concealed in a foam jacket advertising Byrne Dairy. When he was growing up Byrne Dairy had delivered milk from door to door, but they didn't do that these days. Now they ran convenience stores like everybody else. Come to think of it he didn't know if they were even in the dairy business anymore, with cows and everything, although his father would certainly have known. Not that Tom cared. Fuck Byrne Dairy. Like everybody else they'd given up on production and gone straight into merchandising. Like everybody else but him, anyway. He was still stuck hammering nails and hoeing weeds. His life was an argument against evolution if there ever was one. Fuck Byrne Dairy and all they stood for.

With the beer in his hand he walked toward town and the beach. Past Harpoon Gary's and the Clam Shack and Dickie's, where the line for tables was already out the door. Summer people in sandals and beach coverups alternating with old folks dressed up for church. His head hurt, and if it weren't high noon and no shade in sight he would have stuck to the shady side of the street. Not even the Fourth of July yet, and all these people. All this heat. He skirted the beach and went into the amusement park and watched the rides for a while. Old man Coletti grinned at him from behind the grating of the ticket booth and hoisted a foam-jacketed can in a kind of conspiratorial toast. A few girls about Shelly's age came sailing through and bought tickets and got on the carousel, all candy apple mouths and pale winter skin. They looked like children. He followed old man Coletti's eyes as he watched them get on the carousel, and it made him kind of want to punch somebody. He wasn't sure who.

The Woodshed wasn't open yet and he walked on past, over the bridge and toward the beat-up playground equipment and along the old docks. Only a handful of boats were in, a couple of them looking like they had been there all winter. Sitting low, probably full of water. He didn't know anything about boats, but that couldn't be good. He finished his beer and stripped the foam jacket from it and jammed it in his back pocket and threw the empty can into one of the boats from where he stood. Two points. Past the boats was the campground, and it got him thinking.

*

He was sitting on the front porch when Nick came home, just one more telltale difference between Nick's half of that little split house and the nicer half. Drinking a beer and smoking a cigarette on the old naugahyde couch that took up most of the disreputable side. Shelly rode in on the back of Nick's motorcycle. She looked happy to see him but by the way she came up the steps she was either a little drunk or a little high or maybe both. She went on in the house and didn't come back out. Nick took a seat on the couch next to Tom and Tom blew smoke and looked at him from behind the screen of it as if Nick had done something terrible to his own sister, which was kind of turning the tables. Maybe now they were even.

Nick pulled out a cigarette and took Tom's to light it. He still had on his mirrored sunglasses. The ash broke off Tom's cigarette before the other one caught and it fell down between Nick's knees and melted through the naugahyde in a heartbeat. Just like that. Right through and down into the stuffing. Tom had the presence of mind to slosh a little beer down the hole after it, and Nick laughed and pulled out his own lighter. He seemed a little drunk or high too.

Tom asked if maybe he'd been using some good stuff for a change instead of that crap from Henri and he said yes as a matter of fact he had. He and his sister and a couple of their cousins had recently partaken of a baggie of Panama Red that he'd obtained from an old hippie dude in Whitesboro. The one who used to have that psychedelic bus out back of his barn but didn't have it anymore. You couldn't get weed anywhere near that good from Henri. The old hippie was Tiffany's and Henri was K-Mart. Tom had seen the stuff they'd loaded into his car that night, hadn't he? Strictly mass market. You could tell just by looking.

Tom was a little hurt and he asked why Nick hadn't come to him if he'd wanted something better than his usual. Nick said he probably would have, but since it was for Shelly's graduation and Tom wasn't even invited it didn't seem right. Tom didn't get any less hurt and he started to ask how come he wasn't invited until he realized it was probably a stupid question. Then he raised the idea he'd come over to talk about, which tied right in to everything now that he thought about it. How would Nick like to start selling a better class of merchandise?

Nick said his regular customers couldn't afford a much better class of merchandise, and what was he talking about anyhow?

Tom said he was talking about diversifying. He said he was talking about putting together a partnership that would, as he put it, enable them to capitalize on one another's strengths. His own in supply, and Nick's in distribution.

Nick looked down at the smoldering hole between his knees. Inside the house, the toilet flushed and water ran.

Tom said what he meant was that they ought to go into business together. He had a strong crop of the good stuff coming on and Nick had a list of regular customers who might be interested in it. He had the hayloft of his uncle's barn, while Nick had been crazy enough to keep the stuff in his own bedroom. He had that nice roomy VW fastback with folding rear seats while Nick was still jamming dope into the saddlebags of that useless Indian motorcycle.

Nick said hey don't make fun of his ride, and Tom said he wasn't making fun of it. He said he was thinking about the night Nick himself had just mentioned, when they'd had to use the VW to haul a ton of weed back from the beach. So much for the mighty Indian.

Nick said okay he had to grant him that but what about Henri. He and Henri went way back. They had an arrangement.

Tom said he wasn't talking about replacing Henri's stuff but adding his own on top of it as a little something special. For customers who appreciated a Michelob instead of a Genny every now and then. Nick knew customers like that, didn't he? Guys who'd recognize the difference between that Canadian crap and something made in America?

Nick said Henri's stuff wasn't from Canada, it just came through there.

Tom said he knew that but he was just saying Canada to differentiate.

Nick said he didn't know if they even grew dope in Canada, on account of it was pretty cold up there.

Tom said it didn't matter.

Nick said he supposed it didn't. What mattered, now that he thought of it, was how much cash Tom planned on putting up. Tom said no cash, and Nick glared at him. Tom said hey wait a minute. Hadn't it occurred to Nick that this high quality locally grown weed would sell for twice as much as Henri's did and was therefore tons better than cash? Plus he was throwing in the aforementioned transportation and warehousing. They'd keep careful records and split everything fair and square. He'd taken a bookkeeping course in college.

Nick nodded and looked either bewildered or thoughtful. After a while he said maybe Tom was right but he'd have to advise Henri when he came down with a carload next month, let him know who was who and what was what and who was doing what to whom, and Tom said maybe it would be better if they just kept it between themselves for right now.

Donna

HE DID NOT HAVE even that little bit of blood work done. Nothing his sister could say would change his mind. He came home and told his brothers that after a complete going over from top to bottom Dr. Franklin had decided that he had cancer and that he would need the same blood treatment their mother had endured through all those terrible years. "It didn't do her no good and I ain't going to let him try it on me," he said. "I ain't going to let him get started." He sat in the overstuffed chair on the front porch and he sucked on a horehound drop and he plucked cotton batting and he said that he believed he would do better against the cancer by holding on to his blood than by dribbling it out a little bit at a time, and his brothers thought that he just might be on to something.

There was a commercial on television for some kind of health-food diet, and each time it aired he dropped whatever he was doing. He had it memorized from front to back, all sixty seconds of it right down to the music (which he whistled through his teeth while he was at the milking) and the rapid-fire legal disclaimers (which echoed in his mind as he lay awake in bed trying to swallow around that lump). He dreamed without ceasing of how his life would improve if only he could afford to buy the products advertised during that hectic tele-vised minute—some kind of natural supplements and supercharged vitamin pills—and one day he spied Preston sitting on his screen porch and he went to him.

Preston had retired from his father's business but he still went in most days. The fellow he sold it to didn't mind, although sometimes he wished that he and the old-timers who came in to chew the fat with him would adjourn to some place other than his service desk. The seasonal area, maybe, where he'd put in a line of picnic tables and lawn furniture that they could test out. Or McDon-ald's, where the rest of the geriatric crowd went. But then they'd have had to pay for their coffee instead of drinking his for free all morning long. Nonethe-less he knew there was a world of experience floating around in those old gray heads, a regular encyclopedia of homegrown construction, and if a person was working through a knotty bit of plumbing repair or framing work or whatever, he could do worse than to show up here and seek their wisdom. If he were in really deep trouble, he should make sure to bring doughnuts.

Preston was home from the lumber yard now, and napping on the couch when Vernon came over. Vernon stood on the ground alongside the screen porch and said his neighbor's name, not going up the two steps or even knock-ing from down where he was. Preston opened his eyes just a slit and saw him there outside the screen, deferential as ever, one of those famous Three Cheva-liers of old. Vernon coughed and cleared his throat and coughed again, and Pre-ston came fully awake. Sitting up and telling him to come on in.

The farmer sat on a hard chair just inside the door. Margaret kept a pair of them there and although the reason was never made plain—she hated to think of the Proctor boys' shit-stained coveralls coming in contact with her uphol-stered furniture, even though the stuff out here had passed through the house and would be on its way to the Salvation Army soon enough—he seemed to prefer the hard chair anyway. He settled into it with his boots squared before him on the board floor. He may as well have been at the milking. "I been to the doctor," he began.

"I heard." Preston rubbed the back of his neck.

"I guess I can't keep nothing a secret."

"Your sister told Margaret," said Preston.

Vernon nodded and pinched his lips between what teeth remained in his head.

"She also told her you won't have your tests done."

"I guess that'd be my business," said Vernon.

"Tell you the truth, what she actually said is you're a stubborn old mule. That's your whole family's business."

Vernon explained his belief that the medical community would fail him as surely it had failed his mother. He said further that he couldn't exactly afford the latest in medical care anyhow and Preston said he understood from Donna that there might be fewer problems in that department than he'd think, with Medicaid and all. Vernon grunted. He sat for a minute. Margaret was running the vacuum cleaner in the house and both men listened to her work.

After a while Vernon brought it up: "I been considering them supplements."

Preston had heard everything, but not this. "Supplements."

"All-natural vitamin supplements."

"All-natural."

Vernon nodded. "All natural. They come in a powder. You mix a little in with your water or your coffee. Your Tang."

"For Christ's sake," said Preston. "If you want to go all natural, you'd better quit drinking Tang. A glass of orange juice'll do you more good than a glass of that Tang with a spoonful of some all-natural whatever mixed up in it."

Vernon chewed his lip, abashed.

"There's nothing all-natural about Tang. You think they drink that shit in outer space because it's natural? They drink it because it lasts forever without benefit of refrigeration." Margaret was drawing nearer with the vacuum cleaner, and he raised his voice over the whine of it. "Have you been watching the television?"

"I seen this show all about vitamins."

"You turn it right off. You forget about it. They just want your money."

"It's what they call an all-natural supplement," said Vernon.

"It's pure snake oil," said Preston. "There's nothing in the world more natural than leaf tobacco, and look where that gets a person. If you don't mind my saying, look where it got your mother. If I were you I'd drink a little more orange juice and watch a little less television. And I'd keep my money in my pocket where it belongs."

Which left Vernon without a dream in the world to trust.

1967

DeAlton

IF YOU THINK it's bad on a farm in the summertime, you should spend a little time there in the winter. Not the farm where I grew up but your uncles' farm. That's what I'm talking about. Where I grew up was the height of civilization compared to that. It was like the goddamn Waldorf. Don't tell your mother I said that. She'd have a fit.

I know. The whole winter's like one long vacation on account of she doesn't take you out there much and I don't blame her. I don't blame you either. I had enough of that a long time ago.

No we're not going to stay very long. We're just dropping off. Your grandma expects us for Thanksgiving over at the Waldorf.

I'm just kidding. Get in. Watch out. Mind that platter. That right there is the best meal your uncles are going to have all month. Maybe all year. I wouldn't mind a bite of it myself right about now. How about you?

Never mind that.

Ow. She put any napkins in there? Check around for me, huh? There might be something in the glovebox.

Tom

THE SKIES OF NOVEMBER had been low and gray but until now the snow had mostly held off, leaving the landscape a barren and windblown waste. Such patches of white as there were, hidden in the deep woods and pushed up alongside the roadways, were withered and pockmarked and cancerous-looking. Gunshots of wind howled in hard gusts over the high fields, and the leafless trees offered no resistance. Now and then a black bird would shoot past the window of Tom's father's station wagon, crying, propelled by wind and by its own impulse to vacate this place of comfort withheld.

The drive from town was one hill after another and the view from the top was always the same. Muted shades of brown and gray. Shorn fields encroaching on wind-ravaged farmhouses, not so much as a chained dog visible. A countryside full of that same old homegrown desolation. They saw no other cars. The wind tore woodsmoke from farmhouse chimneys and sometimes Tom could smell it for a second as they went past. It smelled like his uncles' house. His father asked if he'd remembered his mittens and he reached into his pockets to produce them. It was warm in the car and it smelled like Thanksgiving and he didn't think he'd be needing mittens. He knew there was a shortcut from out here in Carversville to his grandmother's onion farm in Wampsville, but he wasn't sure where it was. His father knew all these back roads.

They climbed the last hill to the farm and saw smoke coming not just from the chimney but from a big fire in the yard. Wind yanked at the smoke, and they turned up the dirt lane and went toward the fire. His uncles' silhouettes were visible against the moving smoke and visible within it. Tom thought they were crazy to be outdoors, but then again he didn't blame them. Their house offered so little comfort. They were doing some kind of work in the barnyard, Audie throwing scrap wood onto the bonfire and Vernon emptying a bucket of water into a vat already steaming over the coals and Creed yanking angrily at the block and tackle that hung from the beam over the hayloft door. Smoke and pale steam and the cry of metal gone to rust. They looked like devils, fiercely industrious.

Tom's father said he hadn't seen this coming but he guessed they'd arrived just about in time. "You take this platter into the house and come right back," he said. "This is going to be educational. You'll be able to write a school report on this. What I Did On My Thanksgiving Vacation."

Tom ran off and slipped into the house with the red rooster gleaming darkly on the stove and slid the platter onto the kitchen table and came running back. His father was leaning against the car and he leaned beside him, hugging himself against the cold. Thinking he was missing the Macy's Thanksgiving parade for this. They were supposed to have a giant Snoopy balloon this year and everything. The World War One Flying Ace, aloft on his doghouse.

Audie had given off stoking the fire and was just now disappearing behind the shed, dragging a rope. Vernon was spreading canvas tarpaulins on the cold ground. Creed had gotten the block and tackle unstuck and was arranging a big wooden worktable they'd moved out into the yard from the barn. There were knives laid out on it and shears and big bent scrapers that looked like tools meant for performing dentistry on a race of giants.

Audie emerged from behind the shed backwards, pulling a spotted hog. The hog didn't want to come and it weighed a good bit more than he did but he was determined. Slowly he mastered it. The ground was frozen solid and slick in places and he used it to his advantage, placing his feet with care and yanking on the rope when the hog's hooves were gathered over particularly perilous and glassy spots. Eventually the resistance drained out of the beast and it came along doglike. As if this were its own idea after all.

The hog was curious about the bonfire and curious about the table and curious about everything. It cocked a gleaming demonic eye toward the snapping flames and thrust its snout under the first tarp it came to. Whuffling, raising up the canvas with its hot breath. Audie yanked hard to keep it moving toward where Vernon and Creed stood holding two ends of the rope that hung down from the block and tackle. Creed had tied a loop of chain to his end and Vernon was poised as if to climb his, reaching up. They stood waiting, wordlessly urging their brother on.

"You much for bacon?" DeAlton asked his son.

No answer.

"I just love it myself. I can't ever seem to get enough."

Tom breathed through an open mouth, pushing out pale smoke into the smoky air. He took his arms from around himself and reached down toward his pockets for his mittens but missed and kept on going instead, entranced and mindless, as Audie drew near to his brothers. The boy tensed and held his arms flat to his sides and pushed back against the car door with his shoulders and his hands. His fingers and his palms were damp with dread, and in the cold they stuck to the frozen door a little. Flesh against ungiving metal.

Audie brought the hog near to his brothers and Creed slipped the chain over one hind leg and drew it tight. Audie dropped the useless rope and hastened without a word to Vernon's side. Creed stepped away backwards, toward the table, around buckets of lye and ash and a barrel half full of salt. His movements had about them a strange disembodied grace. Vernon stood on tiptoe and hove on the dangling rope and as he reached the bottom of his stroke Audie stretched up and grabbed on above him and he hove in turn and thus they went on straining, hand over hand, a pair of old salts raising sail. Up went the hog, thrashing. Deceived, furious, disoriented, it screamed but not for long. Creed rolled back his sleeve and took up a straight knife and stepped toward the beast's swaying bulk like a duelist or a dancer, and with one thrust he drove the blade beneath the breastbone to sever the unseen artery. He drew back his hand and his arm red. Vernon tied off the rope. Audie watched, vibrating. The hog lived briefly while its hot blood drained away, spattering and streaming, pooling onto the frozen dirt and warming it and merging with it. Creed dipped boiling water from the vat and sat the dipper on the table and let it cool a little and then poured it out over his red arm and rolled his sleeve back down satisfied. There would be some waiting now.

DeAlton tipped his hat to his brothers-in-law and said he'd love to stay all day, but they had to get going. They were expected over at the Wampsville Waldorf. He said he would pass their greetings on to their sister.

1990

Preston

IF YOU LIVE LONG ENOUGH, you'll owe a debt to everybody you know and some you don't. If you live right, they'll owe you back. That's why it didn't cost anything to get Vernon's hole dug. I know a fellow named Johnson over in Valley Mills who rents out a backhoe. He works by the job or by the hour. He's not particular and he does a good job and he stays busy all the time. I guess I threw a lot of work his way when I had the lumber yard, although you couldn't have proven it by me. He says I did so I guess I did. You talk up people who do a good job and he does a good job. Anyhow between the state troopers chasing Creed around and Audie gone half crazy with grief and lonesomeness nobody was paying much attention to the necessities of getting Vernon under the sod. How I saw it, the medical examiner or the coroner or whoever would keep him so long and no longer and then what. I called the undertaker. Not the one who buried Ruth but his boy. That's a business that runs in families. I told him I was acting on the authority of the deceased's brothers, which I would have been if I'd had the chance to ask them for it. I told him to get in touch with the troopers and figure out his end, I'd figure out mine. Then I called Johnson over in Valley Mills and asked him what a hole that size was worth. He told me my money wasn't any good.

I remembered how that bureaucrat came out from the state when Ruth died and told me we couldn't bury her in her own plot, so I didn't bother getting permission. I asked the undertaker to keep quiet and he said he would. I walked up that afternoon with a square and a steel tape and a snapline. I don't go up there as much as I used to. I go slower when I go. The hill's gotten steeper. I'd see Vernon go up there with a scythe sometimes when the grass got long, but I don't know who'll take care of it now. Audie, I guess. He'd want to.

I paced off the hole and measured it with the tape to make sure I'd gotten it close enough and I marked it. I made sure it was right in line with Ruth and Lester's. My stride was always just a hair short of three feet but I guess it might be a little less now, and that's why I brought the tape. After I finished I stood alongside the one headstone up there and took in the view. It was a cool dry afternoon and the air was as clear as it could be and you could see almost to Hamilton. Green everywhere you looked. I'd forgotten that view. It did my heart good to spend a little time up there, and to imagine those three having the benefit of it. I'm not a religious fanatic and I don't think I'm overly sentimental and I sure don't believe in ghosts, but when you get to be my age you think about things. The things you'd miss, if you'd miss things.

Johnson came early the next day, when the boys were just about through with the milking. He was on his way to some paying job and he didn't even bother to load the backhoe onto a flatbed, just drove it right on over. I heard him coming and I saw him turn off the main road and start up. He had a line of cars backed up behind him for a mile. None of the drivers looked like they were exactly enjoying the wait. I thought if they knew he was here to dig a hole for a person to lie in forever they might count their blessings, but you never know with people.

Audie and Creed came out when they heard the backhoe. They came out slapping the last couple of cows on the flanks and looking for the co-op truck but the co-op truck wasn't there and it was the backhoe instead. I don't know how many forward gears a backhoe has but it's not enough. It made an awful racket. The cows ignored it completely. You'd be amazed what a cow can ignore. Johnson pulled up short and asked me where to, and I climbed up alongside the cab and pointed. He asked me was this the farm where that ignorant sonofabitch murdered his own brother and I said I didn't know what he was talking about. I said I hadn't heard about any such thing and he said he didn't know how I could have missed it. It was all over the place.

He put it back in gear and we headed up. Through the gate into the pasture. The gate was open to let the cows back through after the milking and I thought somebody ought to shut it. Creed or Audie. While I was thinking that I looked back over my shoulder and what did I see but those two boys standing on the rear bumper of the backhoe and hanging on for dear life just the same way I was. Creed jumped off and closed the gate. Audie just rode on along, bumping up and down and side to side as if that backhoe man Johnson wanted to shake parts of him loose. Creed got the gate shut and ran after us and jumped back on again. Up we went and across the ridge, with those boys holding on like they always did on the tractor when Vernon used to drive and they'd climb on. On a farm you take your excitement where you can find it. Those boys always knew that.

I directed Johnson to the spot. Creed and Audie knew where we were going. Nobody told them. It wasn't any secret. We all got off and helped Johnson lower the stabilizers and chock the wheels. We just did as Johnson told us. He took off his hat and scratched his head and cussed a little bit, saying whoever picked the spot for Vernon's hole wasn't much experienced with running a backhoe since it was flatter over on the other side and this side was going to be tricky. Looking right square at me the whole time. Just pulling my leg a little, but meaning it too. The way a fellow will.

Before he climbed back on he asked Audie if those were his parents under that stone and if this hole was for his brother. Audie nodded yes and he said he was sorry for his loss. Sorry but glad they could be in the ground right here at home and glad that he could help with it. He never said word one to Creed. Not that day.

Ben

WE HAD A LONG WAY to go, but I thought it was all going to be straightforward enough. The confession was huge, although I suppose it could have been better witnessed. The thing about it that gave me a little agita was the timing of it, by which I mean how late in the day it was. When a person signs a confession after normal business hours, people will start thinking about coercion. You take a shopkeeper who works until ten o'clock every night, or a secretary who has to pull a few evening hours now and then, and you show them a confession signed at nine-thirty PM and they'll start to wonder why. They'll picture a couple of cops in a room with a lightbulb hanging down over a man's head and the man tied to a chair. Cops with saps in their hands like in the movies. I don't know why. That's the image they get in their heads and you can't entirely get it out no matter what the truth is. The truth is of course that the state police would never have taken that confession if they didn't believe it to be accurate. I don't know Del Graham very well on a personal basis, but I've worked with him a number of times and I've taken testimony from him often enough. He's as square as they come.

From an evidentiary point of view, this was going to be a complex case. The body. The bedlinens and the various bits of clothing. The contents of the room. The histories and the personalities of the parties involved. To say nothing of the confession, which as I saw it was bound to be disputed. There were going to be a lot of details and it was going to be complex. A complex case is sometimes hard to make fly, because you can very easily wear a jury out with too many facts. Even if the whole thing fits together like a jigsaw puzzle, you need to remember that some jurors don't have the patience to work a jigsaw puzzle. Most of them don't. These days people have short attention spans, and no list of instructions from a judge is going to change that. So the upshot is that as litigator you have to consider the whole narrative, by which I mean not just the story of what happened or the internal logic of the evidence itself but the way that the story and the evidence fit together to make a kind of perfect sense that you can't get out of the world any other way. People like to believe that the truth is simple, so as a prosecutor you have to talk about these complex things in a simple way. I'm not saying people are stupid or simpleminded. But since they like the world to make sense, you have to keep everything direct and straightforward. Above all—and I know this sounds cynical—you have to keep it interesting. I know. You'd think a murder trial would be interesting enough. But you have to remember how much television people watch these days. On television, everybody's problems are over inside of sixty minutes. Minus commercials.

Some of the most interesting things in the confession didn't have anything to do with the brother's death, at least not directly. Like how the three of those grown men slept in the same bed. I could see how three little boys might do that but not three grown men. That information alone establishes certain questions in your mind. The semen on the deceased's clothing establishes some of those same questions, or amplifies them. I didn't know what if anything that might have to do with the events surrounding Vernon Proctor's death, and if anything I was afraid it might distract the jury. If we ever got to a jury.

The same went for the marijuana found on the scene. I don't think people mind much if a couple of old men out in the country want to use a little marijuana or even grow it for their own consumption. What people don't like is if they start killing each other. People will want to put a stop to that.

1988

DeAlton

IF YOU'D SAVE YOUR MONEY and get a decent car, you wouldn't have to borrow your mother's when it won't start. I've got to move around a golf date so I can bring her home on account of you.

It's a guy I've been working on from down by Binghamton. He's got a big operation I'd love to get into and I'll do it one of these days. You watch. I'll do it, because I don't give up easy. You know that. He's a piss-poor golfer, though. I don't think he devotes enough time to it.

Now don't smoke in there or I'll hear about it from your mother.

And I'm not just talking cigarettes either, ha ha ha.

Hey, don't look at me like that. I've been around the barn. I knew Woodstock before it was Woodstock. And don't kid yourself, sonny. People have been smoking that stuff a lot longer than you might think.

Yes really. Your old man. I know.

You and your little friends didn't invent it, that's all I'm saying.

All right. Drive safe. Don't park where anything'll get dropped on it or your mother'll have your head.

And gas it up before you bring it back.

Preston

I'D GO OVER THERE in the evenings sometimes and sit on the porch alongside Vernon, and when I'd come back home Margaret would say I smelled like an opium den. Like some kind of Turkish harem. I guess that was one way to smell after you sat with the Proctor boys for a little while, and it was better than most.

You smell like a seraglio, she said one time. I didn't even know what that was. You live with Margaret, you learn as you go along.

Anyhow Vernon was smoking marijuana a good deal that second summer. In the evenings he'd stay at it pretty steadily. I think for a while he'd been keeping a plug of it under his lip while he was doing his chores but that didn't seem to work out. I don't imagine it tasted all that good, but then again I don't imagine Red Man tastes all that good either. So what do I know. I used to smoke a little now and then but I never had any interest in chewing tobacco.

He said Tom was a good bit more generous now than he'd been before. He said Tom would pretty much give him all the grass he wanted. That's what he called it, grass. Just like that. It sounded funny coming from Vernon, an old dirt farmer who knew what regular grass was all right. How he'd just pick up that other meaning and go with it, like it was the most natural thing in the whole world.

He said Tom was a good boy and he knew how to take care of his dear old uncle even if Dr. Franklin didn't. If you think I'd argue with that you're crazy. We'd sit and talk and Creed would sit with us and Audie would be over there on the steps working on a piece of wood with his jackknife. He liked the smell of that marijuana all right. That wet muskmelon smell of it. You could tell. He sat on the steps with his eyes kind of lit up and a happy little grin on his face listening to us talk and just carving away. Some of the things he carved you'd thought he was high on marijuana himself if you didn't know better. Jaggedy things and big swoopy curved things and little strange knobby things that looked like bugs or some kind of bacteria you'd see under a microscope, all blown up bigger than they had any right to be. I don't know what he thought he was up to. Right to this day city folks and by that I mean folks from the actual city, not Cassius and not even Utica, city folks will come out here and ooh and ahh at the most outlandish of them. The weirder the better. Smooth looking little fellows in black outfits and big horn-rim glasses like they used to wear in the fifties, sometimes two by two if you know what I mean, they'll size them up and take out their wallets and open wide. Audie only takes cash.

Anyhow I was glad to hear that Tom was being more generous than he used to be. It gave me a little bit of faith in him for a change. I knew why it was, or I thought I did. Ever since the springtime I'd seen him show up at the barn a couple of nights a month, maybe two or three in the morning, with this other fellow. I'd call the other fellow a greaser, if they still have greasers these days. He was little but he looked hard. Not the kind who goes out of his way to look hard, but the kind who's just exactly the way he is and that's the extent of it and he doesn't give a damn if you notice or not. You'll notice just fine when you run up against him. That's what I thought and I've lived a long time and seen a lot of different people. He and Tom would come at night in that VW of Tom's and haul a load of something up into the hayloft. I'd take note because my bedroom window looks right down the hill toward the barn door. That and about the time I turned sixty I gave up sleeping the night.

I knew what they were putting up in the hayloft, and I wondered what my obligation was relative to it. I thought it'd been one thing when he was growing his own and storing it up there. That was a hobby, kind of like his own way of following in his uncles' footsteps whether he wanted to or not. But one thing leads to another, and now here they were bringing drugs in from somewhere else. Drugs and probably trouble. Just the greaser fellow alone meant trouble as far as I could see. I sure didn't want to mess with him. On the other hand at least Tom was sharing the wealth with his poor old sick uncle Vernon, so I guessed his heart was still in the right place. His father would have gotten Vernon hooked and then started charging him for it. That's the kind of salesman DeAlton is. So maybe there was decent Proctor blood in Tom after all.

Tom

HIS UNCLE TRIED to give him a little money once but he turned it down. Not because he couldn't use it, although he was definitely doing better now that he and Nick had the business rolling, but because he didn't like the way it came out of Vernon's wallet all stiff and crusty. A twenty dollar bill, twenty perfectly good American dollars, and it looked like it had been buried in a manure pile for a hundred years. It smelled that way too. He'd said no thanks, really, he couldn't take money from a sick relative.

Thus had he discovered at least one of his limits.

*

Nick had a bad habit of keeping Henri's phone number a secret. He wouldn't give it to Tom even when it made sense to, like when after one misunderstanding or another the phone company had cut off his service for a month.

"I can't remember whether Henri said he was coming down on the fifteenth or the sixteenth," he said to Tom as they motored down Route 5.

Tom was doing exactly one mile under the limit, having adopted out of self-preservation the driving habits of an old maid schoolteacher or a drunk. He hated it, but it was a cost of doing business. You made accommodations. "Call him up and find out," he said.

"I guess it don't make no difference. We'll just be at the Woodshed either way."

"Call him and find out. What's the big deal?"

"No big deal. What's the big deal if I don't call him?"

Tom took his eyes off the road for two seconds. "What's got into you?"

Nick shifted in his seat and looked out the window. "Look. If you don't want to inconvenience yourself two nights in a row you just stay home. Watch some television. I'll go on the fifteenth and if he shows up I'll call you on the pay phone and you'll come on over. If he don't come we'll know that the fifteenth was the wrong night and you'll come with me the next night because we'll know. The sixteenth."

"That's not the point."

"Then what is?"

"How come you won't call him is the point."

"Because I don't need to. Henri's a busy man. I don't want to look like the kind of an asshole who can't mark my own calendar and remember when I'm supposed to be somewhere."

"What about if that's the kind of an asshole you are."

"Shut up."

"Give me the number and I'll call him."

"I thought we were in this together. You and me."

"We are. That's why I'll call him if you won't."

"No."

"Then you'll call him."

"Why."

"Because depending on when he's coming, I might need to rearrange some things. I might have a customer who needs something he can't have until he gets here, and if I don't know when he getting here I don't know what to tell the customer."

Nick screwed up his mouth. "You ain't the milkman."

"I know that."

"Tell him he'll get it when he gets it."

"Look. There isn't any such customer. It was hypothetical."

"So what's your problem?"

They drove past a Byrne Dairy and Nick said he could use a cup of coffee so they turned around and went back. There was a police car in the lot and Tom pulled up right next to it. He hadn't meant to. He was distracted. But once he was there he figured why the hell not. He had the same rights as anybody. The cop had his windows rolled up and the air conditioning on and he was working on a Little Debbie fruit pie behind the tinted glass. Before Tom shut down the VW he turned to Nick and said, very slowly and patiently, "I didn't have a problem until you wouldn't make the call or give me the goddamn number."

"So?"

"So is this some kind of power thing? I've got as much right to talk to him as anybody."

Nick got out of the car saying he and Henri went way back and that was all he was going to say on the subject.

In the end, Tom had to get Shelly to go through the stuff in her brother's room looking for some piece of paper that might have a Canadian phone number written on it. There was only one. The number belonged to Henri. He was coming on the sixteenth, but Tom went along on the fifteenth anyway so as not to rock the boat.

1932

Ruth

SOME THINGS THERE ARE that will not freeze, whiskey in a flask among them. He slides the slim leather-wrapped thing into the breast pocket of his coveralls like a charm against bad luck. The flask is battered enough to have warded off an army of devils, for in years past he has variously dropped it and fallen hard upon it and used it for a hammer. But it still holds whiskey and that is as much as he requires of it.

He gathers up what else he will need. Fishline and hooks. A square of hard cheese for bait. Matches just in case. Vernon and Audie watch him until he says that if they mean to come along they'll put on their coats right now and fetch in some firewood for their mother. She has said she doesn't have enough to last and the baby will be keeping her indoors. Then he works newspaper into his tall rubber pack boots and puts on his second pair of socks over those he is already wearing and shucks on his coat to leave. In the barn he pulls a saw from under a pile of rusted tools and puts it under his arm and finds a coal shovel against the wall and hoists that over his shoulder. In haste the boys stamp their feet and drop the wood and say goodbye to their mother and the new baby. They promise to bring him back one of the million things he has not yet seen in the world, a flapping fish, and with wet eyes he glares back at them. They kiss their mother and slip out the door into the barn, and then out the barn door to find their father's footsteps already filling up with snow.

The creek runs above the property and along the farthest edge of it, and in summer it tumbles milky over rocks and plummets into deep round pools that it has hollowed out for itself. The next farmer owns the land and the creek and the falls too if such things can be owned. A half mile below and far from sight of any road or habitation the creek empties into the weedy stillness of Marshall's Pond and where it goes from there Lester has never wondered. There is fishing in Marshall's Pond summer and winter both, but the snow is coming down hard and he thinks he might better keep to the creek.

He knows a natural pool where in summer a sunken log provides cover for trout, and although he has never dropped a line there in winter he reasons why not. Surely fish are creatures of habit. Surely they lack such powers of cognition as might compel them to vary their behavior by the season. Besides, there is a high flat rock above the water where he can arrange his things and sit comfortably with his legs dangling just as he does in summer. Watching the line and drinking a little. In the summer to cool down and in the winter to warm up. A fine miracle of transformation.

The boys catch up to him and in a line they crunch over the snow toward the fence. Audie wonders aloud if his father has brought a fishline for each of them and Lester says no particular setup will belong to any particular fisherman if they plan to eat. This is not a competition or a pleasure trip in case he hasn't noticed. Audie wonders if this means he cannot have his own fishline and Lester says yes that is exactly what it means. Audie sniffs and looks at the snow and walks. Vernon pulls his hand to stop him short and lifts his earflap and whispers that he will let him have his if he keeps quiet about it. It will be their secret.

A wind barrels out of the west and the trees bend and a frozen rag caught on barbed wire makes a hard horselike whickering. The snow is deep here at the margin of the property, three-quarters of the way up the fenceposts and nearly overtopping the last strand of wire. They sink into it but not far. Lester stands for a second with his bootsole on the top strand and the boys flail over it in a panic and he lifts his boot and moves on toward the line of bent trees that marks the creek. They draw near. Small branches and twigs clothed in old ice and clacking.

The falls is frozen buttermilk, long ropy strands of it descending. By some mysterious power, water moves beneath it. Lester stamps up to the rock ledge above the pool and kicks away the snow that covers it and drops his tackle and stamps back down. He sends the boys up. "Don't touch them lines," he says. He uncorks his flask and swallows some and corks it again. He edges toward the water, not trusting the ground underfoot, holding to a sapling that bends and showers down snow and ice in clumps. He slips and recovers but drops the shovel. It falls and tips in slow motion and lands handle-first on the ice and he follows it warily, testing as he goes. The snow is thin on the ice and the ice curves like windcut stone and he hears the water running beneath it. He takes up the shovel and clears a space. There is a crack here, round-edged, and dark water gleams below it. Between his native impatience and this lucky opening he decides that he will not need to use the saw after all. He strikes the curved ice with the sharp fore-edge of the shovel and after repeated blows it cracks. Chunks fall in and bump downstream and collect. He strikes some more and thin cracks spread both where there is no snow and where there is and more chunks fall in and he judges that he has opened a target large enough to hit from the high rock even in this wind. He regains the bank and leans the coal shovel against a tree and stoops to collect two thin branches snapped off and fallen. Then he stamps up to where the boys wait.

He squats in the center of the rock and arranges his tackle. The boys gather around, aping his pose, their little hands hanging down between their knees. Vernon takes up the thin branches and gives one of them to his brother while their father finds the hooks and untangles the lines and makes them up. He hands the lead sinkers to Vernon and Vernon tries fixing them to the lines but the lead is too cold and his hands are too cold and he ends up using his teeth instead. Lester tells the boys that he would notch the poles if he hadn't forgotten his jackknife and they know this already for they have helped before and have done it themselves fifty times the same way. Audie has an idea. He gnaws at the growth end of one branch until he has notched it. He yields it up proudly, his mouth all ice and bark, and his father laughs. "You're all right," the old man says, handing him the other to chew on.

They bait the hooks with cheese. Lester sits on the edge of the rock and the boys sit to one side of him, Vernon first and then Audie. Through their thin trousers the cold knits them to the spot. They lower the lines into the hole and wait, listening to the wind and the water. Lester has one pole and the boys have the other and they do not argue over it. Instead Vernon has given it outright to Audie and now sits warily watching him, on the lookout for some slip.

Lester clamps his pole between his knees and finds the flask. He unstoppers it with his teeth and takes the cork in one hand and drinks, the flask tipped straight up and gurgling. The boys watch, shifting their gaze from their father to the lines in the dark water below and back again. "You watch them lines," he says. The lines waver in the water and the wind and they are difficult to track from here. He presses the cork back in and slides the flask into his pocket and sits restored against the cold.

Vernon says maybe the fish are all sleeping or frozen and Audie says maybe the fish are all dead. Their father says they had better not be or there'll be short rations tonight. Vernon says what if they have all gone downstream to Marshall's Pond and his father says all right if he wants to walk all the way down there in the snow to find out it's no skin off his nose. Vernon sighs. Lester takes another drink of whiskey. Audie squirms where he sits and the line jumps and he yanks on it hard. The line and the baited hook and the lead sinker all fly out of the hole in the ice and everything lands in a snowbank and Audie laughs. His father does not. "Get that back in the water if you mean to eat," he says.

"He thought he had a bite."

"I know that. He didn't have no bite. Not yet."

"But he thought."

"I know what he thought and he didn't have no bite. That'd be no way to set it if he did."

Vernon takes the pole to get the line back in the water and gives it back to Audie and they sit for a while. Audie is nervous and he watches the line as if it has threatened to bite him. Lester uncorks the flask and drinks and corks the flask again and what movement there is in the water is current only.

"He needs a bobber," says Vernon.

"He'll learn to get along without."

1990

Audie

THEY NEVER CAME to take down the tape so the time came we just took it down ourselves. Took it down and went on back in. Nobody ever gave us any trouble about it.

Preston

THE THING WAS, he wasn't even charged. He wasn't held over and he wasn't charged. I guess the troopers figured they were doing him a kindness by letting him go home. All I know is it didn't cost them anything, because there sure as hell wasn't any gamble to it. It's not like Creed Proctor was what you call a flight risk. They knew where they'd find him all right. Where in hell would he go? He'd never been anywhere.

And if they'd charged him and set bail, how could he have come up with the money? He didn't have two nickels to rub together. Everybody knew that. So that's what I mean by the troopers figured they were doing him a kindness.

Either that or they just didn't want to get saddled with him for as long as it was going to take.

I had those lawyers' names that Mary Spinelli gave me and I started calling them. I didn't have any way to judge one from another, so I just got prices. You wouldn't believe what the going rate is for that kind of work. I'm surprised anybody in this country can afford to stay out of jail. I'll bet the jailhouse has more poor men in it than rich ones, and I'll bet I can tell you why.

Mary's name helped and a few of those lawyers gave me a little free advice. Things to keep an eye out for. I appreciated that and once I'd talked to all of them I sat Creed down. I said with that confession he'd signed it wasn't going to be long before somebody came out here to arrest him and charge him with Vernon's murder. He said Vernon never was murdered and I said not according to that confession. According to that confession Vernon was murdered in cold blood and he'd done it by his own hand. He said well that was just what it said on a piece of paper and they couldn't prove nothing by that. It was just a paper. I got so fed up I could have done him in myself, regardless of what the law had in mind.

Margaret

PRESTON WASN'T SLEEPING MUCH in those days. People talk about female troubles, but he was having male troubles. He'd get up in the middle of the night to use the bathroom and he just couldn't get back to sleep no matter what. Then the business next door got started, on top of everything.

I knew what he was worrying about, even though all he'd say that he was worried about was Creed.

We had a little money. We have a little, I should say. There's my retirement from the school district. We do our best to live on that, as far as it goes, that and our Social Security. The fellow who bought the lumber yard doesn't always pay his note on time. He'll call and he'll say he can't make the payment because he's had a bad month or because he has some big contractor stringing him along or whatever. Preston says he understands and lets him go just this once, although by now I don't know how many just this onces there've been. More than I'd like to hear about, probably. I'll hear him on the telephone saying, "I remember February was always hard," or "Old man Kinney never could pay a bill on time and I guess his son's no better," and then I'll know I ought to think about making the pot roast stretch through another meal. My husband has a good heart and sometimes it gets him into trouble, so we keep within our means on my school retirement and the Social Security if we can't count on the lumber yard anymore. That's what he was up worrying about half the night. He didn't have to tell me.

Ben

THE MAIN THING I didn't like was the older brother. Audie. It wasn't that I believed he would contradict anything we already knew if we got him on the stand. I just always kind of wished we didn't have him. That we didn't have to deal with him.

From what everyone said—and by everyone I don't mean the gossips around the courthouse or the big talkers at the Kiwanis Club or even the stories in the newspaper; I mean the troopers who'd seen him and the investigators from my office who went out there in a professional capacity and actually tried to take his statement—the older brother was something of an enigma. Nobody ever suggested that he might be involved. On the other hand nobody was one hundred percent sure about what he really knew—including, I began to think, the man himself. When you started with that much uncertainty and added in the descriptions in the paper and the talk on the street and the stuff that got written in letters to the editor and what have you, it was a classic case of the blind men and the elephant. I'm not saying that people saw what they wanted to see in Audie Proctor, and I'm not saying they saw themselves by any means. He was too particular for that. Altogether too colorful.

But for an individual without a lot of endearing personal traits, he was oddly sympathetic. Weirdly sympathetic. People in this area have gotten pretty well removed from the agrarian way of life even though it's still right at their doorstep, and here came this curious little man—I've heard him described as looking like a hermit or Rip Van Winkle or a prophet from the Old Testament—here he was in the flesh, reminding them of something they had come from but had let themselves forget about. Something they'd put behind themselves without even knowing it. Everybody in this county probably has a little bit of milk from that farm every day, in their cereal or whatever, and here he was to remind them of it.

There was power in that, I think. People were curious about him at first and definitely a little repelled, but it all had a way of turning into something that I can only describe as compassion. I'm not saying people saw what they wanted to see in Audie Proctor, but I'm not sure they were seeing Audie Proctor either. Not entirely.

1988

Tom

THE LANDLUBBER LOUNGE at Harpoon Gary's was cave-dim at noon, lit mainly by some strings of Christmas lights worked into dusty fishing nets that drooped down from the ceiling over the bar. The lights blinked every now and then, making the broken fiberglass lobsters and the big satanic plastic crabs suspended up there loom like props from an old science fiction movie. Revenge of the Appetizers. DeAlton sat studying them and nursing his summer drink, a rum and Coke. He hated this place, he hated all of these places at the beach, but it was far enough from home that nobody he knew ever saw him come in and nobody he knew ever saw him leave. Donna didn't like him having a drink. Not ever. He figured that it must have something to do with her old man, even though she'd been only what, three or four when he'd finally bought it.

It was cold in the lounge and it was no warmer in the sunlit dining room when he finished his drink and went out there to sit down and order a sandwich. They'd serve at the bar but those plastic lobsters and crabs gave him the creeps, so he sat all by himself at a square formica table with an advertising placemat on it, looking through the picture windows over the beach. He had a little buzz from the rum and Coke and that was enough to last him. He refused a menu and asked the waitress for an iced tea and a club sandwich on white toast, light on the mayonnaise. He studied the placemat. It was sponsored by the Chamber of Commerce but dominated by various arms of the Coletti family, who had run the beach as long as he could remember. Dickie's Family Restaurant. The Clam Shack. Harpoon Gary's right here. Plus the Sea Breeze Cabins and the Beachcomber Motel and the Little Starfish Day Care Center. Not to mention the beachfront amusement park, where old man Coletti still ran the ticket booth and kept his hand in the till. The iced tea came and he poured two sugars into it from packets that advertised their manufacturer on one side and Coletti's Cone Zone on the other. In case you couldn't get enough sugar for free.

The lunchtime crowd began to trickle in. People with flip-flops and damp cover-ups and the shapes of their wet bathing suits soaking through their shorts and tee-shirts. Not one of them working. Not today. Not like DeAlton Poole, who had places to go as soon as that club sandwich came and he got it eaten and cleared himself out of there. He tried to remember the last time he'd taken a day off and he couldn't. Other than Saturdays and Sundays, which he had to admit even to himself was a better deal than he would have gotten if he'd stayed around the onion farm. But still. The life of a milking machine salesman wasn't exactly paradise.

The sandwich came and he opened it up to check the mayonnaise and put it back together. He picked up the iced tea and held it up to the picture windows to see if the sugar had settled out, and he put it down and stirred it again. That was when he noticed his own son, sitting out on the beach in an aluminum lawn chair. He had his back to him and his shirt off but it was Tom all right. Sitting there taking the sun and smoking a cigarette and fishing around in a foam cooler for a beer. On a Tuesday. How dare he. Wasn't he supposed to be working construction somewhere?

DeAlton took his time eating his club sandwich. He watched his son put out his cigarette in the sand and unwrap a Slim Jim and substitute it for the cigarette in between his teeth, sitting there like Roosevelt with the stupid thing just waving around. Sitting there watching the world go by. Looking at the girls in their bathing suits and not being subtle about it. DeAlton envied the beer and the beach chair and the boldness with which he looked at the girls. He even envied the cigarette, having quit a long time ago under Donna's orders. About the only thing he didn't envy about the whole scene was the Slim Jim, and as long as his son didn't see fit to show up at his construction job on a routine basis he could keep eating those things for lunch instead of enjoying a nice club sandwich in a nice air-conditioned place like Harpoon Gary's. He certainly wasn't going to go out there and invite him in.

*

He finished his sandwich and got a free refill on the iced tea and mixed in some sugar and sat nursing it. Cleaning up the last of his potato chips and keeping an eye on his son through the window and checking out a twenty-something girl who'd come into the dining room with her bikini soaking through a USA for Africa tee-shirt like an X-ray. He couldn't help himself. She caught on after a while and shot him a look and although he would have sat for longer if he could, he figured right then it was time to ask for his check. He was due at a farm over toward Peterboro in an hour or so and he didn't need long to get there. He paid his check and went out into the parking lot and followed a little sandy trail full of footprints over to the beach. It was hot in the sun so he took off his sportcoat and the sun on his bare forearms was even hotter. He thought about the Bedouins or whatever they were, those wandering tribes in the desert, and how every time you saw pictures of them they were all covered up like that Lawrence of Arabia. It made sense when you thought about it. He put on his sportcoat again and walked over to where Tom sat, sinking into the sand as he went and getting his shoes all filled up with it.

"Hey, Sonny boy. Catching some rays?" His voice came out louder than he meant it to.

"Hey." Tom turned around in the folding chair, all nonchalant. But with the look of a high school kid caught with a cigarette in the boys' room.

DeAlton hardly knew where to start. The lassitude, the beer, the fifteen or twenty cigarette butts arrayed in the sand alongside the folding chair like ruins in the desert. He made his decision and nodded down toward the crumpled butts, acknowledging them as evidence of Tom's having been sitting out here for a while. "That Fazio's giving you an extra long lunch hour, is that it?"

What was Tom supposed to say. "I'm not working for Fazio anymore."

"How long's this been going on?"

"A while now."

"You didn't tell me."

"I didn't think I had to."

"You didn't tell your mother."

"I didn't think I had to tell her either."

DeAlton pushed the toe of his loafer against the folding chair. "Move," he said.

Tom did. He vacated the chair and sat down gingerly on the lid of the foam cooler, not quite putting his whole weight on it.

DeAlton sat in the chair. He settled into it and folded his hands behind his neck and leaned his head back. "Now this," he said, "is living."

Tom indicated the cooler. "You want a beer?"

"You kidding?" said DeAlton with his eyes shut against the sun. "I've got to work. And don't distract me from my point. Like I said, this is living."

"I know."

"You've got it all worked out, if you can do this on a Tuesday afternoon."

"I guess."

"What are you, working nights?"

"Kind of."

"Kind of."

"I'm kind of working all the time, Pop."

DeAlton squirmed his butt around in the seat and said, "Kind of working sounds pretty nice to me. I could go for a career in kind of working."

"Now come on. That's not what."

"You think they could use me?"

"Come on."

"Are they hiring? Are they kind of hiring?"

"Come on, Pop."

DeAlton slitted his eyes open just the least little bit and cocked his head toward Tom. "Because I could kind of use a job that let me kind of sit on my ass all day and look at girls in bathing suits."

"It's not what you think."

DeAlton kicked the cooler. "You're right. There's refreshments too."

Tom leaned forward. "Look. I'm making money. I'm paying my bills. You want more than that?"

DeAlton picked a little bacon from between his teeth. "I could use a straight answer."

"I'm working."

"You're not working for the Italians, are you?"

"Not hardly."

"The Italians with the suits, I mean. Not that big fat dope Fazio."

"No. I'm not working for any Italians."

"Good. I don't want you running numbers or something like that. You want to do that, you can get a job over at Vernon Downs. A square job."

"I'm not running numbers. I don't even know what running numbers is."

"Good." He checked his watch. "Keep it that way." He considered the time and decided what the hell, that farmer over near Peterboro could wait. He toed the foam cooler again. "On second thought," he said, "how about giving your old man one of those nice cold beers you got."

Vernon

I GIVE UP SMOKING a long time back but it didn't do me no good. I didn't give it up on my own account. I always liked it and I'd kept up with it if it was up to me. I done it for Audie. He wanted me to give it up ever since our mother passed. She had cancer and Audie got the idea I was in line for it too and I guess it turned out he was right. It was either quit or wait for a horsehair of my own inside a cigarette and I wasn't in no hurry for that so I just up and quit. I told him I quit and I quit right then. That same day. I started up with Red Man about the same time. Audie didn't have no complaint about that and I didn't either. Sometimes he asked for a chew and I give it to him all right. He wasn't much for it but he'd give it a try every now and then and I didn't see no harm in it.

Anyhow I quit but I still got the same cancer killed my mother. I got my own though. I didn't get it from her. Cancer ain't like a cold. You don't catch it but it catches you. Since I got the cancer I'm back to smoking but it's different since you don't smoke grass the same way you smoke a cigarette. Tom showed me. He gives me all I can use but I don't use too much because it's still smoking no matter what you put in the paper and maybe it might make the cancer worse. I don't know. It don't take much anyhow. I smoke a little of it and I feel better. I don't swallow no different than I used to around the cancer but it don't bother me so much either.

Preston told me to drink more orange juice one time and I tried it but it didn't do me no good. Not that I could tell.

DeAlton

I THOUGHT IT WAS just a hobby. I thought you were just growing a little for yourself and giving some to Vernon.

By God I've got to say I never saw you as the agricultural type. My own son. I spend my life running from a goddamn onion farm and you go running right back to it. Like you're some kind of a throwback.

No, I'm just kidding. Of course I'm just kidding.

I know it's dope and not onions. I know that and I don't care. It takes more than that to impress me. I've been around onions and I've been around dope. You've got to be a little more cautious with the one is all.

I know you are. I know. But the more you grow the bigger the risk.

Yes that's my way of asking how much you're growing.

Well shit. That's not very much. That's not very much all. How can you live on that?

I don't care how good it is. That little bit isn't enough to maintain any kind of standard of living. It's not enough to let a person sit on the beach all day looking at girls and drinking beer. It never was that I knew of and I don't bet it is these days either.

Because a nickel bag is still a nickel bag and five dollars isn't worth two dollars these days. You've got to allow for inflation.

Do I look ignorant to you? I know about running a business. You've got fixed costs. You've got storage and packaging and transportation. You've got supplies and hardware. You've got your drip lines and your timers and your pressure reducing valves and your.

Why you goddamned amateur. You don't just throw it in the ground and hope for the best. Dope ain't onions, and you don't even do that with onions.

1932

Ruth

A THIN DRIZZLE of freezing rain comes up but they pay it no mind. Soon something bites, and before Audie can notice or react the fish has nibbled free the cheese and made off with it. The hook comes up bare. Audie squalls and his father squalls too, each in his own way.

"How'd you like it if that was your dinner just swum off?"

Audie makes no particular answer and his cry of disappointment goes on as if the thought of hunger troubles him no more and no less than the mere loss of that lively fish, and from the well of his son's stubbornness Lester draws more anger. He reaches around Vernon and knocks the back of Audie's head with his knuckles and only the boy's hat responds, not the boy himself, tilting forward and cocking crazily over his eyes. Lester snorts and reaches into his coat for his whiskey and while his gaze is downcast Vernon fixes his brother's hat.

Lester has the cork between his teeth. Vernon spies it and has an idea and asks if his father has a knife, and Lester says if I had a knife I'd notched them poles myself. Can't you remember that. Vernon says how about we just break that cork in half then and use it for two bobbers or not break it and use it for just the one. That way Audie can catch something.

His father breaks it with his teeth and makes two rather than have none for himself and he strings them up and rebaits the hook. He sets down the open flask on the rock by his haunch and he eyes it from time to time. He feels in his hip pocket for a rag that he might improvise a stopper but he finds none. Vernon shivers at his side and it startles him and his leg nudges the flask. It tilts away by a few degrees and wobbles and rights itself. He worries that he might get no fish out of this enterprise and lose his whiskey in the bargain.

Audie's bobber sinks a little and comes up again. The boy tenses and Vernon puts a hand on his knee. Wait. The bobber bounces again and goes fully under and Vernon lets up. Now. Audie pulls on the line and sets the hook and brings up a perch, a big one, writhing, frigid as the ice it came from. The boy shivers with cold and delight. Vernon pulls out the hook and Lester takes the fish by the tail and strikes it hard against the stone to stun it or kill it and either way it lies still. Green and yellow and glistening on the gray rock.

"Bait up some more of that cheese," their father says. "While your luck holds out."

Audie fumbles with it but Vernon helps and back into the water goes the hook. Lester's cork floats steady on the little current but Audie's dips again, and soon he has pulled up another fish. Lester curses and kills it and hands his own pole to Vernon and tells him why doesn't he try his luck instead, his brother's so goddamn handy with a fishpole. They do, and while they sit shouldering one another with their eyes on those two corks shouldering one another the same way, he resorts to his flask. Soon enough Vernon's cork dips and he pulls up a fish and Lester kills it with a slap more aggressive than required.

The cheese commences to dwindle and so does the whiskey. Lester closes his eyes and listens to the sighing of the wind and the hard thin pattering of the rain and the whistling of his own breath. Three fish icing on the rock and then a long wait when nothing happens but the slow nibbling away of bait and the slow diminishment of the whiskey in the flask and the slow faint whitening of the frozen world. The boys pull up their hooks empty and rebait them. Audie wonders if the fish have gotten too smart for them but no sooner has he suggested it than two more tug at the bait and the corks bob, one to each boy. Lester opens his eyes and shakes his head to clear it for he could swear he has seen four fish come up. Either the whiskey or the frozen rain stuck to his eyelashes. He swabs at his face with the back of his hand and he helps unhook the fish and he kills them one by one.

Five nice perch. With Creed still suckling, five nice perch will be more than enough for the four of them. But Lester is warm from the whiskey and the fish will easily keep in this weather—they will all but keep in the bedroom, the house is so frigid—so why not continue as long as their luck runs and the cheese holds out. "Let your old man show you how it's done," he says to Audie, holding out his hand for the pole. "You caught your limit."

Audie cries and shrinks away and Lester wrenches the pole from his hands all the same. His hip strikes the flask and it tilts and he recovers it, but rather than take any further risk he raises it to his lips and drains the rest. His lips adhere to the frosty neck and he pulls it free uncaring. A little blood. Into the pocket with the flask.

Vernon has already baited both hooks and they lower them into the water. Nothing. Nothing for the longest time. Just the pattering of the frozen rain and the sighing of the wind in the treetops. And then, just when a person of ordinary patience or stubbornness would have abandoned hope, Vernon's cork jumps a little and he brings up another fish, this one the largest yet, and his little brother Audie laughs both to see it break the iron surface of the water and to see his father's own cork still floating hopelessly alongside it. Lester reaches around and raps the laughing boy's head again and this time his hat flies off, spiraling downward into the frozen creekbed. Pellets of rain strike his close-cropped hair and melt down into it. Lester reaches over for the fish but Vernon gives him the pole instead. He takes off his own hat and screws it tight onto his brother's head and slides down the icy face of the rock into the narrow passage that the creek has cut.

"Let Audie get that," says his father. "He's the one dropped it."

Rather than explain and suffer the consequences, Vernon does not answer. He scrambles over icy rocks to where the hat has come to rest and he kneels on the ice to retrieve it, tugging it free from a clump of brush where it has landed and standing up again to beat it dry against his knee. He puts it on and pulls the earflaps down and ties them underneath his chin, not against the cold but against his father's ongoing injunction that he let that damned hat be it's Audie's to look after. He sees his father's jaw working and he points to his stoppered ears and he shrugs, scuffing down the edge of the creekbed through the snow toward the place where they climbed up to begin with. Watching his feet. Beneath the high rock, and under the catenary of the one fishline still dangling there. His father's. He looks up, thinking to get himself a fish's eye view of a fish's fate, and he sees two pairs of bootsoles and one branch pole and two curious faces looking down. Freezing rain strikes his face and he blinks and sticks his tongue out to catch some. He spins a little to see it come spiraling hypnotically down from above the trees. Then he loses his balance and slides backward on the frozen rain and on the layer of snow beneath it and on the layer of ice beneath that and first one foot goes into the water and then the ice breaks clear beneath the other foot and then in he goes completely.

The creek is shallow but not here. Here in this pool it is well over a man's head and deeply treacherous, even in the summertime, with its sunken log and its walls of tumbled stone jointed by cunning time in ways fit to catch an unwary limb. Vernon goes under and bobs up again, not in the clear space but beneath the ice, and with one foot against the submerged log and the top of his head against the ice and his eyes closed against the dark water he cannot judge up from down.

His brother screams and begins to shake, his whole world cast into the void.

His father curses and drops the pole and it skitters down the rock face into the creekbed. He calls the boy's name. No answer from the wavering black pool. Whiskey-addled and panicking, he cannot decide which route to take to the cursed creekbed, straight down the rock face or along the icy path behind him.

On the rock Audie shakes like a boy puppet, wooden with cold.

Lester stands and takes off his glove and reaches into his pocket for whiskey by way of fortification but he comes up short and curses himself for the instant thus lost. He hollers at Audie to sit up straight and he turns and races down the path, half sliding.

Underwater Vernon exhales.

Audie does not sit up straight.

Lester loses his footing and goes down on his ass. His hand ungloved scrapes against a rock and his knee through thin coveralls scrapes against another and he leaves two patches of blood, red on gray. Freezing rain merges with them and the red bleeds pale into the new white and Lester regains his feet and goes on. Soon enough there will be no sign of his passage. He lurches toward a sapling and takes it in his bleeding hand and hangs from it to make the last turn onto the margin of the creekbed.

Vernon opens his eyes and sees light and pushes himself toward it.

From the sapling Lester moves to the edge of the hole in the ice. The branch pole slants across the opening and he takes it. He sees the mirage of his own fish son moving beneath the surface. Kneeling he pokes the end of the branch into the water.

Audie's cries go on.

"Hush, you," and "Come on, boy," says Lester, alternately to each child.

Vernon breaks the surface. His father tells him to grab on but for all the response he gets he may as well be speaking to an otter or a dead man. His son's eyes are closed and iced over, and apart from certain small movements as may be attributed to the water itself he might be recently dead or near enough that it might not matter. Tears of frustration from Lester. Frustration or frustration combined with something else. He has half a mind to strike the bobbing boy with the branch to rouse him or at least vent his own fury and no sooner has he drawn back than Vernon opens his mouth gasping. His eyes too.

Lester looks from him to his other son, one leg just visible over the edge of the high rock where he lies in his misery, shaking leaflike and beating against stone.

The boy Vernon looks like some ghastly spirit of the waters, emerging from the black pool blue and white. He lacks the strength to grip the pole so his father edges toward him on his belly and takes his two hands in one of his own, soaking himself in the bargain.

1990

Preston

MARGARET WANTED ME OUT of the house one morning since I wouldn't quit storming around and making her miserable on account of Creed, so she sent me down to the lumber yard and when I got down there what's everybody talking about but Creed anyhow. It was in the paper but I didn't take the paper anymore. It'd been in the paper two or three times. The Cassius Courier was a daily then even though it's a weekly now. It was a daily then and it was mostly advertising. Advertising and the funnies and the police blotter was about all there was to it. That's why I stopped taking it.

Anyhow it'd been in the paper and it'd been on the news out of Syracuse and Utica when I was too busy looking after Creed and Audie to waste my time watching the television. Everybody knew the whole story and nobody believed it. Nobody. By God, who would. You'd have to be crazy.

That fellow Ben Wilson hadn't been talking to the reporters yet, but there were other people in his office who were. An unnamed source in the district attorney's office speaking on condition of anonymity is what it said in the Courier. I don't know but what it was Wilson himself, now that I think about it. If one person in the office will do that I guess another one will, and it usually goes all the way to the top. The top man sets the tone.

It'd be just like Wilson. I wouldn't put it past him.

For Christ's sake that's not speaking anonymously. It's just spreading rumors around.

Plus some reporter'd come out to the farm and talked to Audie. This was a fellow from the Syracuse paper. I don't know when he got out there that I didn't see him but he did. Maybe it was that same day the troopers talked Creed into making up that confession. That same day Margaret and I were gone wherever. Anyhow he had a camera with him and he took some pictures, and the old farm didn't look too good when they printed them up in the paper. It looked like a bad place where anything could happen. A place you'd want to get away from. I wouldn't be surprised if folks in the city just browsing through took it for a western movie set or a dust bowl farm from back when nobody had anything and you couldn't wait for time to pass and things to get better just so you could maybe quit starving to death. That's how it looked.

The reporter didn't get much out of Audie. I guess when he came out from Syracuse he didn't have any idea what he might find. I thank heavens he ran into him though and not Creed. That'd been trouble right there. That was another reason I knew we had to get those boys a good lawyer just as quick as we could do it. I figured we needed a spokesman of our own. I say we. You know what I mean.

But anyhow until right then I hadn't thought about the papers. I'd only thought about the law. And now there I sat behind the service desk reading the stories and my blood pressure was going through the roof, thinking how we had ourselves one agreeable idiot and one half-mute on our side and they had people in the district attorney's office whispering to reporters no questions asked.

I don't call that speaking anonymously. I'd go so far as to say it's the first step toward tampering with a jury. I've seen a few lawyer shows myself. I ask you how on earth a person was supposed to get a fair trial if everybody inside of a hundred miles had heard those fellows in Wilson's office whispering about him like that? Off the record is worse than on, as far as that goes. They knew what they were up to.

And don't tell me about a change of venue. You take the Proctor boys off that farm for two weeks either one of them and they'll die dead just from being homesick. You don't have to be a genius to see that. You want to kill either one of them that's the way to go.

Audie

VERNON WAS THE OLDEST and now he was gone on ahead and I was the next in line. I asked Creed about that and he said I didn't have the cancer Vernon had. He said it was cancer that killed him and not being the oldest. I said I thought maybe it was not holding his water too and Creed said not holding your water won't kill you. That didn't have anything to do with it. I said I didn't care I meant to keep holding mine right up to the end and Creed said that was a good idea. We buried him on the hottest day that summer.

Donna

THIRTY YEARS HAD PASSED since Tuttle had come out from the church in Carversville to put her mother in the ground, and as the time had passed he'd been replaced by one young preacher after another. A series of innocents thrust from the seminary into the field, alike in their enthusiasm for the Lord and alike in their goodhearted ignorance of His creatures.

This new one was different. A woman of late middle age, perhaps five or six years older than Donna herself. Her name was Monroe. She'd retired early from teaching school and put herself through the seminary in Rochester. She had a husband who'd worked all his life in a shoe store in Rome, and she had three grown children and seven grandchildren counting one who'd died in his first week on this earth. All in all, she liked to say, she had seen a good bit of life and she desired to do the Lord's work nonetheless. She dressed in black from head to toe and people took her for a nun and as a rule she did not see fit to disabuse them. The black, her public secret, was for the grandchild.

She and Donna sat on the screen porch of the house in Cassius like sisters. Whenever DeAlton came home he liked to turn on the air conditioning but Donna had never cared for it, so when the hot weather came she naturally retreated out onto the porch. Just because something cost money didn't mean it was good. He never saw it that way.

Donna and the preacher sat in a pair of new white wicker chairs that creaked. "I believe these two could carry on the conversation without us," the preacher had said as they settled in, and Donna had half hoped she was right. That by some miracle the conversation could go on without her. It would have made things easier, seeing that the last time she'd had anything to do with a church she'd been in the company of that other fellow, Tuttle, up in the same little family graveyard where they would all be heading tomorrow afternoon. But the preacher skipped right over any kind of holy business and got straight down to it.

"Tell me about your brother," she said. "Vernon."

Considering how interested everyone else had been in Creed, this simple question was gift enough. "There's not much to tell," she said.

"Oh, there's always something."

"He was a simple man."

"There you go." The preacher smiled. "That's something."

"To tell you the truth, he grew up in a simpler time."

"We all did."

"Only he never left it."

The preacher adjusted her hand on a small and battered black volume in her lap, which Donna had taken for a notebook. She saw now that the edges of the pages were gilded. A New Testament with the Psalms. Just the essentials. The preacher caught Donna's eyes on it and neither concealed it nor disclosed it further. "He was a good bit older than you." It was not a question.

"Eleven years. Vernon was the oldest, and I was the youngest. Am. I am the youngest."

Light dawned. "Your parents kept trying until they got a daughter."

Donna cocked her head. "I'd never thought of it that way."

"I'll bet they did." The preacher gave a broad smile. "Why else would they keep going through three boys in a row?"

"Boys are useful around a farm."

"I'll bet your parents kept them busy."

"They sure did."

"And then when your time came, they let you go your own way." The preacher let her gaze wander around the sunporch, the more or less manicured yard, the late-model Toyota in the driveway.

"I guess they did. Pretty much."

"That's what happens when you wait for a child. My husband and I did the reverse. We had our two girls first and then our boy. Of course they're all grown up now."

"Mine too. My one."

"They go their own ways."

"They do."

"Time goes by."

"It does."

The preacher's fingers rubbed at the gilt edges of the book in her lap. Donna got the impression that she might be about to turn the conversation toward other ends, so she half rose from the creaking chair and made an offer of some nice cold iced tea and the preacher said yes that would be a pleasure and a relief on this hot afternoon. She said she'd help Donna get it and Donna didn't say no, so they went together into the cool kitchen.

Del

PEOPLE TALK. Things get out. In a perfect world it wouldn't happen, but this isn't a perfect world and it does. Then again, in a perfect world people wouldn't die under mysterious circumstances.

It could be that's just it. If the world were perfect, Vernon Proctor would pass on in his sleep exactly the way he did and nobody would give it a second thought. But we know things. We suspect things. Our brains start working on them and we can't help it. We want it all to be perfect and it's not perfect, it isn't going to be, but we keep trying to make some sense of it.

A hundred years back, I don't know. Things were different. Fifty years even. You go to the doctor and he asks what did your grandparents die from and you realize you can't say. People died, that's all. When there was any record they had different words for things or they used the same words we use now but they meant something else. The words meant something they might have been sort of unsure about, but it didn't make any difference. It didn't change things.

I guess we've come a long way. We're all experts in everything now. We might just be the poorer for it.

Anyhow people say things who shouldn't say things. An old fellow like Vernon dies and it wouldn't make a ripple under normal circumstances. It's nothing out of the ordinary. My men went out there because Creed Proctor called us. The emergency technicians went out there because of the same call. No big deal. Simple as that. An unattended death we'd have had to look into it anyhow. We went out the next day because the medical examiner found some things and we had to see about them. A reporter can look at that from any angle he wants—it's all there on the public record, or he could come straight to me for a statement—but until somebody in the district attorney's office begins shooting his mouth off there's no reason to start talking about murder. And there's definitely no reason for everybody and his mother to know about how that poor old man signed a confession.

But you have to think it through all the same. So when I first heard about it I wondered if maybe the story had come from the night clerk at the Mobil station. The one who witnessed. The one who sold us that pizza for Audie. I thought maybe he'd gotten an idea about talking to the newspaper, but if he had they wouldn't have said what they did about an unnamed source in the district attorney's office. That would have been a lie. An unnecessary lie. And as little as I trust the Courier, I think I was starting to trust Ben Wilson's office a little less.

1989

DeAlton

HOW YOU DIDN'T KNOW this road was back here I'll never know.

You bet I'd call it a road. You can drive on it it's a road.

If I'm putting up money then you're going to have to take the bad with the good. Get used to it. We've got plans to retire on that money, your mother and me, not just this little bit but the rest of it I'm going to have to pump into this operation, and we're going to want it back with interest. That's why they call it interest. I'm here looking out for my interest.

That's right.

I say we're going to want it back but I mean me. If she knew about this she'd kill the both of us.

Ow. Watch your head. This'll get better in the summertime once the mud dries up.

I'm all right. You all right? This damn VW's got no padding anywhere. It's like riding around in a damn freezer chest.

So. How many ways you got to get up here?

Just the one? Just the one straight up through the pasture?

Unbelievable. How in hell have you stayed out of the penitentiary all this time?

Well now you got two ways up. We'll find a couple more, quick as we can. Maybe park down by Marshall's Pond and come up cross-lots. Blaze a trail. We'll get around to it. The main thing right now is to get this shit moved up and finish digging out the trenches and run the drip lines without that busybody next door deciding he ought to start taking pictures for his scrapbook.

It's a figure of speech. Preston's an old woman is all and he doesn't miss a thing. He thinks he runs the world. That's why we had to go to Canastota for the parts. You think I'm buying this kind of merchandise from anyplace Preston Hatch hangs around you're crazy. He'd ask what I needed it for and I'd tell him I was thinking about maybe starting up a little garden and he'd say he didn't know I had the room out back for it and I'd say well maybe I was going in with a neighbor or something and he'd say that was a pretty good idea and why didn't I bring him some nice tomatoes when they came on. And he'd be waiting for them. He wouldn't forget.

That's why we had to go to Canastota. You can't be too careful.

Audie

THEY COME AT NIGHT SOMETIMES. Tom and that friend of his. People say if you sleep the night you're sleeping like a baby but a baby will be up crying all hours. I know that from when Creed and Donna were little. They'd be up hollering and my mother would be up with them. I guess I must sleep like a baby then. Up half the night.

The first time they came I thought it was burglars. Vernon was making that hard swallowing noise he makes and I couldn't sleep and I heard them come. I got out of bed and I got a stick of firewood and I didn't turn the light on since it wouldn't do me too much good. I didn't open the door but a crack and I slid out into the barn and they were loading. The two men. One of them had a little penlight he shined at me and somebody said hello Uncle Audie how you doing it's just me Tom. I asked if they needed my help and they said they didn't. I went on back to bed. It was the three of us in it. This was a while back and Vernon hadn't gone on ahead. Not yet.

Tom

HIS FATHER SAID it was all about leverage. Not the mechanical kind but the financial kind, although in the end it came to the same thing. He'd put money into Tom's crop and they'd multiply his yield by five or six times and then they they'd have some leverage over that Nick. Make him into a junior partner if that. Leverage was the only thing little creeps like him understood. Once they had Nick where they wanted him they'd take that leverage and a little more of DeAlton's retirement money—as much as it took to get noticed—and go talk turkey with Henri up in Canada. Take it right to him on his own turf. Put their offer on the table and tell him take it or leave it if he wants to play with the big boys. They had other places they could get the low-end crap he was selling if it came to that. There was Mexico, wasn't there. Mexico made more sense than Canada. You didn't have to be a genius to see that. Canada for Christ's sake. Henri could go sell that garbage to the Eskimos if he didn't see things their way.

In the end they'd have the Canuck selling to them at their price and Nick doing the grunt work and a happy future lined up for everybody. Everybody meaning the Poole family.

In the meantime, it was dirty work. Dirty but familiar. Back when DeAlton was barely out of short pants, he'd helped his father build an irrigation system for a newly broken field. He'd maintained that one and others pretty much like it until he'd finally grown up all the way and broken loose of his old man and gotten the hell out of the onion business, but he couldn't deny that the experience had served him well. He prided himself on being able to help out if some old farmer he called on was having trouble with a water system. When it came to ingratiating yourself with these old-timers, by which he meant selling them a truckload of milking equipment, nothing beat a readiness to get your hands dirty. That was one lesson it wouldn't hurt Tom to learn.

For a water source they thought about the creek back in the hills, but the slope was steep and the pressure might be too great. They didn't want that. So they settled on hooking into an old waterline that Tom's uncles had put in sometime back in the fifties or sixties. Who even knew what it was meant for? Maybe to pasture cows up there someplace or maybe to water the grass in the graveyard even though it was a good distance from there. It was uphill of the graveyard though so maybe they'd had a trench. The tap was rusted open when they found it and the line was dry so it was either broken somewhere or shut off. Tom said ice had probably busted it during the winter sometime but his father said if it was busted there'd be water running wouldn't there and there wasn't any. Sure enough the line was just shut off at the wellhead. They wrenched it back on and all of a sudden there was plenty of water up there, as if the line had been put in just for that purpose, and since it came straight from the well there'd be no telltale bump in the water bill. You had to think these things through, DeAlton said. This was the stuff they didn't teach you at the community college.

The spring passed and summer came on again. Tom found himself busting his ass up in the field more than he'd have liked, all alone at that, but his father had to work and to tell the truth he enjoyed the chance to be all by himself without the old man plaguing him. There was no income from the dope yet and there wouldn't be for a while, so right now he was more or less an indentured servant to a bunch of green sprouts. A bunch of green sprouts and DeAlton Poole. His father had him wearing different shoes every day of the week and taking a different route up every time he went and looking for his own tracks as he did and it was starting to make him a little crazy. One minute he was a dirt farmer and the next he was some kind of secret agent and either way there wasn't much glamor to it. Sometimes late in the day when he'd come walking down through the pasture and see his uncles waiting for the co-op truck he'd have an impulse to embrace the three of them like brothers in arms, like they were all members of that Solidarity from over in Poland, but he never did. He'd have needed two showers, one for the dirt and one for the cow shit, and he had places to go.

Preston

I KNEW DEALTON'D STUCK his nose into it. I could tell you when it happened, right down to the day.

DeAlton's been a disappointment to me. I never knew his father all that well but I knew him enough to speak to. They were from over by Wampsville someplace, so he didn't come in much unless he needed something that Willis didn't have over in Canastota. He was a gentleman, I'll tell you that. Neat in his habits and prompt in his payments and never an unkind word, not from Leon

Poole. I never knew his wife. Maybe she's to blame for how DeAlton turned out.

The old man did stink like onions though. I'll tell you that.

Anyway Donna deserved better. She worked to get away from her beginnings and DeAlton worked to get away from his, but it wasn't the same thing. There's ways to get away and there's ways to get away. And by get away I guess I mean grow up. Donna got away from a little place with a pretty narrow horizon. DeAlton got away from the onion stink but that's as far as he got, and I'm not even sure that entirely took. Like I said there's ways and there's ways. There's ways to and there's ways from. Donna went to and DeAlton went from. But regardless of what he had in mind he never went very far.

That's not always a bad thing. I never left my father's lumber yard except to go to France, and even that wasn't my idea. I stayed in that lumber yard all my life, but when I was done it was a different place than it'd been under my dad. We'd expanded into the lot next door and we'd leased the railroad yard across the tracks and we'd bought the old depot building and made it over into a little boutique for home goods. Margaret picked out every single thing in there by hand and she did a good job. My father never would've thought of that. Then again the depot was a going concern in his time. Six passenger trains a day when I was a boy and then down to four and then down to one in each direction and then that was the end of it. The train that brought me back from the war dropped me off at that depot and it was the same for Creed. Generations came back that way from everywhere. Generations left too.

I tried to keep an open mind when I saw DeAlton and Tom going up there with their carload of pipe and whatnot. DeAlton's father taught him a few things and from the look of it I guess DeAlton passed a couple of them on to Tom. That irrigation system I mean. Not that I would have put it together the way they did. They took a few shortcuts, made some compromises I wouldn't have. Then again I wouldn't have done it at all. So that's how much my opinion on the subject is worth.

I was in the graveyard when I first saw them go by on the old tractor path. The one along the treeline up toward the creek. Nobody uses that path too much anymore. Not even Audie, and he does most of the tractor work. He just goes cross-lots. I was up paying my respects to Lester and Ruth and I saw them go by in Tom's car with the back open, loaded up. I didn't go over on account of I knew they were up to something, but I did have a look after they went home.

They didn't get much done that first day but they came back every day until they were done, just like it was a regular job.

That first week I got more exercise than I get in a year, going up and down to check how they were doing. Margaret thought I'd gone crazy. Once or twice I thought about fixing a couple of their mistakes but I never did. It just about killed me to leave them alone, but DeAlton would have been suspicious. Tom, he probably wouldn't have noticed a thing. Or else maybe he'd have thought they had elves.

1932

Ruth

CERTAIN THINGS ARE SAID to sober a man in a hurry. Peril, shock, ice water. The combination works on Lester and if it does not entirely overwhelm the whiskey then it does at least subdue it. His woes are everywhere at once and his mind goes everywhere with them. He drags Vernon from the water and clasps him tight, wringing out water in sheets. The boy shivers like his brother Audie and his teeth chatter like the bones they are and he gasps but seems unable to speak. As if some mechanism within him has frozen solid.

Lester debates giving him his coat. To wrap the boy in it now will only soak it through and cost him the use of it and then where will they be. He hesitates and shakes his head to clear it. The boy is freezing. Anyone can see that. His skin is blue beneath the white of the ice. He lets him go and nearly permits kindness to overwhelm what passes in this instance for sense, stepping away and half removing the coat and then deciding otherwise. If he freezes to death there will be no one to aid the boys.

Vernon's hair is frozen. His hat, Audie's hat, still hangs beneath the ice, a dim and shifting shadow. The ties of it, come loose in the fall, reach around the edge of the hole and flutter in the black water like slow pennants. There is no use for it now save as a reminder of the younger boy. Lester tells Vernon to wait here and then he tells him to come on and then when neither admonition makes the slightest difference or even seems to register he picks him up, staggering. As he lifts the boy, one foot slips back and finds thin ice that cracks beneath their combined weight and he lurches forward. Careening toward the rocky bank, utterly lacking purchase. They spin and swoop and recover and the wet boy has already soaked his coat through and he wonders why he did not just give it over to begin with. What kind of monster he might be.

They reach the pathway to the high rock and he sets Vernon down. He asks how he is doing and the boy does not answer, which could mean anything. He considers the wisdom of perhaps giving him his coat now, but the useless old thing is half soaked through so why bother. Instead he pulls it about himself and heads up the path. Calling for Audie. "You come, boy. We ain't got all day. Your brother's fell in the water in case you ain't noticed."

But Audie does not come. When Lester reaches the top he is still lying on the stone, whimpering and shaking and banging first one leg and then the other against the hard world. He has let go of the pole and it has slid off the far side of the rock, hook and sinker and line and all, each of them worth good money, and Lester curses him for his carelessness. The very tip of it is still within reach and he bends over his son to grab it but a tremor passes through Audie and his fingertips just brush it and down it goes. He strains after it and falls short. Perhaps it will be recoverable in the spring, but not now. With the back of his frozen hand he cuffs the boy and that seems to wake him up.

He takes him by the collar and hoists him bodily. The boy's feet skitter on the slick rock as he brings him up and the father lets go of his coat and the boy crumples down again. The father gives him the toe of his boot. "Get up, you." The boy rises to his knees like a beggarman and his blue eyes turn upward to his father but his father sees them not, for he has already turned away. "Get up if you're coming, and bring them fish. I can't do everything."

*

In his arms the boy is but a groaning log. A stiff rotten thing pulled up from the deep and conjured into some kind of life that is not life exactly. Lester trudges through deep snow, following the footprints he made earlier, sinking into his own covered-over tracks and remaking them. They reach the barbed wire fence and rather than stretch it down for Audie he stumbles straight across and Audie stumbles after him. The boy catches his pantleg and tears it and catches his sock and tears that too. He cries and keeps going. What will his mother say. He keeps crying and he works to catch up.

Lester shifts his hold on Vernon to apply a little warmth to new places. Against his icy coat the boy's face is blue and he unbuttons and wraps the hard fabric partway around him, at least so far as he can and still keep moving. Perhaps that will help. Within his breast pocket the flask presses against the boy's head and he can feel the hardness of it with his arm but he leaves it where it is and looks back instead to see about Audie. "You'll cry plenty if you left them fish behind." Audie wails but Vernon in his arms makes no sound at all.

Soon they will see the barn and the house. Just over a rise and down. The wind picks up but they do not notice it. They squint and keep on. The clouds scud low and the rain comes in pellets. They top the rise and slide down through the pasture, too fast for their own good. They teeter and they tumble and they send up snow. There are trees in low wet places down here and the cows are sheltered among them and Lester knows that he should see to them but not now.

He calls out his wife's name although she would have to be looking out the bedroom window in order to see them and that window is covered over with feedsacks to keep out the cold. He calls nonetheless and the sound causes Vernon to stir just the slightest. He calls again and Audie joins in, perhaps only for the companionship of it.

He turns. "You left them fish you'll holler all right."

The pasture flattens out as they near the barn and the snow is less deep for having been blown elsewhere, off into low spots and up against the buildings in drifts. They push on through it and Lester hauls the barn door open a crack and they slip inside. Out of the wind it is warmer already. He bellows his wife's name again and this time she comes. "Whyn't you boil some water," he says as he staggers in through the door. Only that.

She has the good sense not to ask how this has come about. She merely takes Vernon and tells his father that she will see to him. He can pump the water and set it to boil. This chore being hers by custom, he balks. She says he will get it done faster than she can, and still he refuses. She says that doing it will warm him up, and he gives in at last. She takes Vernon to the bed over on the cold side of the house then she thinks better of it and strips away his clothes and wraps him in a blanket and brings him back to the cherry red stove. Sitting there in the straight kitchen chair, rubbing color back into him. Lester strips off his own wet coat and throws it steaming on the floor in front of the stove and starts working the pump. Audie stands hugging himself against the wall, shivering as he does, and a single green fish slides from his coat to lie dead on the plank floor. His father laughs for the first time in eternity. The boy laughs too. Then he spreads wide his arms and the icy fish come showering down.

1990

Margaret

MONEY CAME IN from all over, and for some reason I got the job of handling it. Better that it fell to me than to some others I could name. I'm a trustee at the church and I've been bonded for counting what comes into the collection plate, although nobody thought to ask that. They just started handing it to me. I suppose I have an honest face. At least we know where every nickel went.

Preston got it started. He was storming around here one morning, going on about how the Proctor boys were never going to be able to pay for a proper lawyer if they lived to be a thousand, and I suggested that he ought to go storm around the lumber yard for a while instead of bothering me. I won't deny that it was purely self-defense on my part. We've been married a long time and you get to know your limits. So he went to the lumber yard and sat down with his old cronies, and to hear him tell it the money just started to appear. It wasn't just a trickle, either. People opened their wallets who didn't know Creed Proctor from Adam. People opened their wallets who'd never spoken a word to him their whole lives and surely wouldn't have sat on a stool alongside him at the Homestead, not and been able to keep their suppers down. People opened their wallets who couldn't afford to.

Preston said Creed could have his choice of the best lawyers in the county with that kind of money, but Creed let Preston pick for him.

Del

I WENT UP to the farm for the burial. I can see how a person might interpret my being there as intrusive, but Creed and I had squared things between us and I thought he'd understand that I was there for honorable reasons. By which I don't mean law enforcement. I was there for him. You don't go to a funeral for the sake of the dead. You go for the living, and that one I went to for Creed. No matter what might come next.

It was one of the nicest services I can remember, and I've been called upon to attend some. I didn't know the pastor and I doubt very much that she knew the deceased, but you'd never have guessed that from the sound of it. She spoke plainly about life and death and she didn't soften anything too much. I never knew Vernon, but from what I know of his brother I think he would have appreciated that. On a farm you live around death your whole life.

Not a lot of people came out and those who came out didn't shed many tears. Creed sniffled some but he might have had a cold. He stepped away in the middle of the sermon and blew his nose with one finger the way a farmer will. He just let fly into the tall grass and came back mopping himself with the back of his hand. I don't think anybody thought the less of him for that, although it did complicate the receiving line a little if you let yourself think about it, which I tried not to.

Donna welled up some, you could tell. She had a lace handkerchief in her sleeve and she pulled it out early on. That husband of hers was no help to her whatsoever. DeAlton, his name is. He and his son—I ought to say their son I guess, but he seems to take after the father—he and his son didn't seem overly distressed. They both had what I would describe as a little bit of an attitude. Even at a funeral. It was as if they would rather have been somewhere else and didn't mind your knowing it.

Audie was the one who got overcome, and he got overcome enough for the whole family. I don't know exactly what his problem is. He doesn't have epilepsy, and I don't think he has what they call a seizure disorder, but there's definitely some kind of a fit that comes over him. That's about the only word for it, although the older generation might call it a spell. An episode. The cliché is to say that a person shakes like a leaf but in his case it's the truth. It's a terrifying thing to watch. You think you should do something for him. I've wondered if it might have anything to do with the trouble he has communicating. Maybe if he could just say what's on his mind everything wouldn't get all bottled up and have to shake itself loose the way it does. That's how it seems to me, although I guess it's not a very scientific way of looking at it.

Lester

THE FIRST INDIVIDUAL to work this earth was the first to lie beneath it and it came to pass in the same way for his sons after him, the first to work it the first to end his work. Vernon Proctor was brought home and lowered down already half decomposed, preserved and dipped and shot through with chemicals sufficient to last forever, but already cut to pieces and thus well on his way. The casket was closed and the truth went unspoken. The mere facts of life and death. If everyone knows a thing then why say it.

1989

Tom

NOT LONG PAST SUPPERTIME on a sunny day in the middle of September, Tom was in the hayloft and the hayloft was heaven. A light and steady breeze drifted in through one open door and out through the other, keeping the hanging stems in constant motion. Like palm fronds being waved over a pharaoh's bald head by half-naked slave girls. That was how it seemed to him. The temperature was perfect for both man and marijuana, and the air smelled good up here too, like lush green plants and fresh cool breezes from somewhere else and money. Mixed with the smells of cows and cow manure from downstairs, but you couldn't have everything.

He'd put in a long couple of days getting the buds trimmed and the stems hung out on clothesline and the rest of it, the tender little stuff, set out to dry on screens that he and his father had dragged back from the municipal dump in Cassius. DeAlton had worried that it was going to be too hot up in the loft but they didn't have much in the way of alternatives and the results for the last few years had been plenty fine hadn't they so that was that. Even DeAlton Poole couldn't very well argue with success. Besides, if today was any indication of how the next few weeks would go, the weather was going to be perfect. Absolutely primo.

He squatted in the doorway and looked down, watching his uncles going about their work like ants. Mindless and automatic and driven by something even they couldn't fully understand. Audie and Vernon had been out in the high field since sunup, harvesting corn for silage. Creed had been mending the fence up by the graveyard. Somewhere in the pit of his heart Tom allowed himself a little throb of gratitude for everything they did, by which he meant how they went about the hard work of practically starving to death around this desolate place. Without them, where would he be? Nowhere, that's where. Or at the very least out in the open, which was as good as being in the state penitentiary.

He held onto the doorframe and leaned out into the open air and craned his neck either way. The sun was getting low over the Marshall property down the hill to the west, and Nick was still nowhere in sight. Late as usual. That was all right. The work he'd done in the hayloft might look even better once the shadows came up with the dusk. It'd be like a jungle in there, all spooky and mysterious. It would seem to go up and up forever, and all those hanging stems whispering. That would be good. He stood up to stretch his legs and thought about climbing down the ladder to put a nice tidy little joint on Uncle Vernon's chair for later. The poor old bastard was getting so he shook so much that if you gave him a baggie he just spilled it all over his lap, so Tom had started rolling them for him. There was less waste that way. Plus it was kind of the least he could do, if you thought about it.

*

Nick got there just after sundown and once he'd climbed the ladder he went weaving around the hayloft like a kid on his first trip to Disney World, maybe taking in that Haunted Mansion they have. Looking straight up into the shadows with his mouth sprung wide open, positively thrilled to death. Tom said buddy what you're looking at up there is fifty dollar bills and Nick said I know it and I'm smelling them too and Tom said that's right. That's right you are. You're smelling a barnful of fifty dollar bills. Hundred dollar bills too. Just give it time.

Nick said wait till Henri hears about all this and Tom said since when does Henri need to know anything about it. I don't work for Henri. Nick said we got an arrangement with Henri and Tom said we got an arrangement between the two of us last time I checked. Henri doesn't need to know every goddamned thing I do. Nick dropped it and went on mooning around the hayloft, his head thrown all the way back, sniffing the air like a cat after its supper. The floor was covered with a layer of dirt and woodchips and sawdust and the leavings of a million bales of hay, and his engineer boots made tracks in it. From the loopy way he was following his nose around, Tom thought his trail looked like the one that that little cartoon kid in the newspaper makes, on Sundays when the guy who draws him can't seem to come up with an actual joke.

Tom pulled a baggie out of his pocket. There was some loose dope in there along with a couple of joints. He offered it to Nick, telling him that this was about the last of his own personal stash left over from last year's crop. He was welcome to it in case he needed a reminder. Nick said no he didn't need a reminder but yes he would take that baggie off his hands if he didn't mind. It'd be his pleasure.

They sat in the high doorway with their legs dangling and they smoked the first joint and they watched the night come on.

"Of course we're going to have to adjust our arrangement a little," Tom said after a while. His father had given him that word adjust. Adjust was easier for a person to swallow than change or fix or renegotiate or whatever else he might have come up with. Adjusting was what a person did to the vertical hold on a television set when the picture started flipping for no reason. Adjusting was no big deal.

Nick asked anyhow. "What do you mean."

"I mean with me supplying all this product, our old split just doesn't cut it anymore."

"Hey," said Nick. "It wasn't my idea. I didn't ask you to go to all this trouble."

"So you don't want any part of it? I can find somebody else to help me sell it if that's what you want."

Nick drew hard on the joint and his words squeaked out high on the slightest drift of pale smoke. "I didn't say that." He handed it back to Tom. "We still got Henri. We still got Henri's stuff is all."

"I know. We'll split that the same as always." Tom took a long pull and held it in his lungs and sniffed a little air in on top of it. He studied the joint to see if what was left was worth the trouble and then he handed it back to Nick. "You just got to start treating me the same way you treat that Canuck is all. As far as this goes. This stuff right here." Raising his shoulders and cocking his head to indicate the roomful of dope behind them in the dark.

"I guess you got a point."

"It's an adjustment. Like I said."

"Right," said Nick.

"I don't hear you arguing with Henri. I don't hear you telling him you want to go fifty-fifty."

"All right," said Nick. He rubbed out the joint in the hard palm of his hand and crumpled the paper and threw it into the yard and licked the rest off with his tongue. "Hey," he said. "Look over there. Is that the Big Dipper or what?"

Preston

THE FIRST THING IS, you don't smoke in a barn. Least of all in a hayloft. You don't have to be very smart to figure that out even if nobody ever told you. Margaret gave me a telescope for my birthday that year, with a tripod and everything, and I had it set up on the screen porch. It's so dark out back you could just about run an observatory. Cassius isn't a big town and Carversville isn't even a town at all, but if you go there at night and look up at the sky you won't see very much. That's not the way it is out here in the country. Out here there's no light except the lamppost I keep on a timer and I had that turned off. Margaret was in the front room at the other end of the house with the television on but you couldn't see that from the screen porch. So there I was in the dark looking at Venus I think it was and just kind of finding my way around the heavens on account of I was pretty new at it when what do I see but this little orange dot going back and forth, way up in the hayloft door.

I knew who it'd be. I'd heard Tom's friend come up the dirt lane on his motorcycle while Margaret and I were having supper, and Tom'd been here himself all day and all day the day before that too. I'd about come to the conclusion that he wasn't working anymore unless you called what he was doing up by that old still working. Which I guess it is if you look at it that way, but that's not how you think of it as a rule. You don't think of it as a job, I mean. A regular job you'd go to.

So I knew the two of them were up there, and I just hated like hell to see it. To see a perfectly good dirt farm being turned into some kind of opium den. A seraglio, like Margaret says. I thought about how that land had produced so much over the years. The way it smelled in the spring and summer, good smells and bad smells both. How it had supported Lester and Ruth all those years and then their children one by one. And now to see it come to this. I wondered where was the justice in it. If this was the way everything would go sooner or later.

I turned the telescope on the hayloft and Tom and his friend looked like a couple of big old giants sitting up there. They looked like something you'd find at the top of a beanstalk. That marijuana cigarette they were smoking could have passed for a comet the way it moved back and forth, getting brighter when they pulled on it and dimmer when it just sat. Which wasn't for very long, let me tell you. It didn't look like they wanted to waste any of it.

I kept an eye on those two until the cigarette went out and then I quit holding my breath and looked at the stars for a while. It's amazing what you'll see. Then they went and lit up another one and I had to keep an eye on them until that one was gone too.

1954

Audie

IF I WAS DONE with the tractor he would take that or if I weren't done he would just walk. When he was done with his own chores he was done and he didn't care if I was done or not. Vernon either. He'd just wash up and go. Even if we hadn't done the milking yet. I think it was the army taught him that. Just get your own chores done and don't worry about the other man. Plus he was kind of giving orders to Vernon and me all the time even though I guess in the army he probably just took them. I'd come back through the pasture and I'd see him going down the dirt lane or maybe already down there turning toward Cassius and I didn't know where he was going but I knew he was through working for one day.

Preston

LIKE THAT OLD SONG used to say: "How you gonna keep them down on the farm, after they've seen Paree?"

Ruth

HER NAME IS VELMA, a name which in these days is just coming into fashion and will not stay in fashion for long. Her eyes are deepset and her nose is sharp and she favors lipstick the color of fresh blood. She keeps her thick dark hair pompadoured in the front and brushed close on the sides and pinned back into a pony tail that hangs down inside a sling of black netting. The first time Creed Proctor sets eyes on her he decides that this is the woman he would like to have serving him his supper every night of the week, and for a while he will nearly manage it.

He still has some army pay. When he came home he used a little of it to buy his mother a brooch at the Woolworth's in Cassius and he used some more of it to buy hardware for the whiskey still, but the rest he has kept in a carton under the bed with his clothes and it has been burning a hole there for weeks now. He and his brothers have taken the tractor to the feedstore in Cassius and they are coming back with the stake-bed wagon loaded down behind it when they pass the Dineraunt on Madison Street and Creed happens to look in through the window. There she stands behind the counter, working the register and looking up at some customer in the most earnest manner. The light is just perfect and the plate glass window between Creed and the woman inside seems to fall away. Even the lettering on it. There is no reflection to separate the two of them and no glare of sunlight from anywhere and no arch of handpainted letters spelling out MADISON STREET DINERAUNT — GOOD FOOD. Just Creed and the dark-haired woman and nothing in between. He realizes all of a sudden that he is hungry but he does not say anything. He isn't going to stop now. Not with Vernon and Audie to drag along. They'd probably think they could beat his time with any girl but they'd be wrong about that. They're just a couple of hayseeds who've never seen anything worth looking at in this old world. He'll come back sometime soon. He'll make a point of it.

*

His most immediate problem is those army khakis. He's been wearing them every day since returning from Korea, and as hard as he has tried to go easy on them they just won't stay clean. His mother washes them every Saturday morning with the rest of the laundry and she presses the creases back into them with an iron heated up on the stove, but her disease is already beginning to weaken her and the filth never comes out entirely and the heat of that big rusty iron just seems to set it in. She apologizes every time she hands them over. He sizes them up and tells her that it doesn't make any difference, but it does and she can see that, but there is no help for it.

He takes them now from the carton under the bed and unfolds them and lays them out, picturing the girl behind the cash register and despairing in his heart. He simply cannot go down there dressed this way. And he certainly can't go in his coveralls. He considers washing these poor things himself and he considers asking his mother to try again but neither course seems promising. So he folds them and puts them back in the carton and slides it back under the bed where it belongs, and when the day is done he takes them out again and brings them across the yard to Margaret Hatch. She has a brand new Bendix Duomatic in the basement, and it washes and dries both. Margaret tells him that she will do her best to get the stains out, but that if he really wants to preserve his uniform the way Preston preserved his from the second war then he might want to stick to wearing his coveralls around the farm from here on out. He says he knows that. He says he isn't interested in keeping them but in wearing them. She sighs and says they won't last then and he says he'll be careful. He promises to bring them out only for special occasions.

Margaret

PRESTON GAVE ME that Bendix because he always had to have the very latest of everything. I never got a word in on the subject. He just brought it home one day. He meant well, but the truth is it was a step backwards from what I'd had before. Not that I'd ever tell him that. Not in a million years. Not even now.

Creed's uniform was hopeless, with that awful Bendix or without it. I took it straight to the dry cleaner's, and even they had a terrible time with it. I don't believe they so much as charged me, they felt so bad about how little they'd been able to do. They'd even replaced a couple of buttons that were missing, no charge.

Creed, though, he was thrilled to death. It just goes to show.

Ruth

WITH THE EXCEPTION of his mother and his little sister, Creed has always found women completely inscrutable, captivating in a nearly mystical way, and troublous as snakes. They've borne watching, but beyond that he has never known what to do with them. Even at Camp Drum, among soldiers possessed with the romantic impulses of French legionnaires and the self-restraint of Siberian tigers, he was at a loss for role models. He would go with men from his barracks to seedy little taverns around the base and get a glass of whiskey and sit at the bar with his mouth shut and his eyes open, wondering how it was that these fellows could talk so easily to any girl about anything at all. Wondering how they'd gotten so smooth with the offer of a drink or a cigarette and where they found the courage to invite these strange creatures to dance with them, cheek to cheek.

By the time he'd worked up the courage to try his own luck, he'd been mustered out and sent home to Cassius on the railroad. And now here he is on his way into that same town all over again but on foot this time, wearing his pressed khakis and keeping up a brisk military pace in spite of the heat. His shadow stretches across the fields and his boots raise dust. He covers the six miles to the city limits in a little more than an hour and a half and it is another fifteen or twenty minutes to the far end of Madison Street, and when he pushes open the door he realizes that he is ravenous. The place is air conditioned and the difference in temperature hits him hard. He shivers and he feels the long wet stripe down his back go icy. The spots under his arms too. There are booths and stools and all of the booths are taken but that's all right. That's fine. He doesn't want a booth. He sits on a stool by the cash register where he saw the girl before, as if she were some vision that might appear only in that one particular spot. He keeps his arms pressed tight to his sides and he waits for her to come around from the back and take his order.

When she comes out her face is flushed pink and she is adjusting the shoulders of the sweater she has to wear because of how cold they keep the restaurant. She apologizes for making him wait, saying that she likes it better back in the kitchen where at least there is a little bit of warmth but that's no excuse. She knows it. She reaches into her apron pocket for a pad and a pencil and asks him what he'll have. He looks from her to the menu and he chews his lip. She says she is sorry but there aren't any specials tonight. They sold out an hour ago.

He'll have to come in earlier next time. But the meatloaf is good and so are the pork chops and can she get him some coffee while he makes up his mind.

Creed says coffee will be all right. What he really wants is some ice water but he doesn't know if it's all right to ask for two different drinks. Even one hot and one cold. She disappears to fetch the coffee and take care of some other customers and when she comes back she has both the coffee cup and a glass of ice water and he tells himself that he has made a very fine decision in coming here. He takes a sip of the water and studies her nametag with a kind of alarming intensity and then he tells her thinks he'll have the meatloaf if it's anywhere near as good as she says it is. He says it in tones so serious as to border on accusatory, as if she has tried to work some fraud upon him and he means to call her bluff.

She says it is every bit that good and it comes with green beans or carrots on the side and does he want his potato baked or mashed. He asks do the potatoes come with the meatloaf or are they extra. She says they come with it and he says in that case mashed. He squints down at the menu and up at her again. As for the carrots or green beans why doesn't she pick. She touches the nametag on her sweater as if to dust from it whatever is drawing his attention. The green beans, she says, on account of she hates cooked carrots like anything, and he says all right.

She says it'll be out in two shakes, hon, and he very nearly faints.

Hon.

Later he will blame it on the heat.

*

He eats with a mechanical intensity, sawing the meatloaf into regular cubes and spearing each cube with his fork and loading up mashed potatoes on the back of the fork and shoveling it all in upside-down. He cuts the green beans into pieces and he spears great quantities of them with the fork as if he is loading hay and he shovels them in too. When he is finished he takes rolls from the basket and tears them in half one by one and mops up the last of the gravy, and then he sits back on his stool and smacks his lips and inhales as with the satisfaction of a job well done. As an afterthought he reaches for the water glass and drains that too. The waitress comes by and he points to his gleaming plate and says he guesses they might not even have to wash that for the next customer.

She says she doesn't know about that but she marvels at it anyhow. He checks her nametag again and says I guess that'll be all for me tonight, Wilma, and she does not correct him. When the check comes he pays it exactly, down to the cent, counting it out twice over in dimes and nickels and pennies. Then he goes out into the dying heat and walks on home, light as air.

1990

Audie

EVERY TIME that fellow Del Graham came before, he came for Creed.

Donna

SHE BEGAN GOING OUT to the farm more often, as if wanting to substitute herself for her dead brother, as if hoping somehow to fill the gap he'd left behind. As if such a thing were necessary or even close to possible. Driving out there one noontime she saw Tom's car parked half in and half out of the barn and she turned right around in the middle of the dirt lane and went straight back to the hospital, thinking there was no need for the two of them to be there at once. She didn't know what use Tom might be around the farm or how he'd gotten off work to help his uncles with whatever they were up to, but that didn't matter. He was thirty years old and maybe he was finally growing up a little. She'd have to remember to mention it to him. Or maybe not.

Creed and Audie were out there all by themselves when Del Graham came the next time. He drove out on his way to work, plenty early but still late enough to be certain that milking time was over. The co-op truck was barreling around the corner onto the main road without even slowing down and the driver hit the brakes hard when he caught sight of the police car. Del just smiled and waved him on. If there's one thing that won't wait it's milk. Milk and the cows it comes from.

When he got to the barn it was empty and the house was empty too. He rapped on the screen door and called out their names, Creed and then Audie and then Creed again, but no answer came. The door bounced open of its own accord but he didn't go in, he just stuck his head through and called again and sniffed a couple of times and squinted into the dim room and that was that. Without the veil of the rusty screen, the place looked exactly as it had looked when he'd been out here before. Everything had run so far downhill so long ago that there wasn't much left to be altered by either use or time. Even the flypaper, stiff gluey twists of it hanging down from the ceiling over the table, over the bed, over the sink, had caught its limit.

He closed the door and pushed on it and pushed harder waiting for it to click shut but the spring latch was rusted out. He went on down from the porch and around into the barnyard. Dust collected on his shoes and he stamped them and thought this is how it begins. A little bit at a time. He cocked his head, hearing the sound of a tractor from somewhere up in the high fields, and hearing it he followed along the way he'd gone on the day of Vernon's burial, letting himself through the gate and taking the path up into the pasture. It was pleasant up there, green and breezy. Trees stood in places, making little pools of shade that drew some of the cows but not others. Another small mystery.

He found them near the graveyard, Audie driving the Farmall tractor and Creed watching him from beneath a tree at the edge of the field. Creed had a can of Dr. Pepper and he lifted it to Del on sight, grinning like mad. Del thought if you scrubbed away the grime and gave him a shave and maybe fixed his teeth a little, you couldn't have told him apart from some well-heeled playboy type greeting you at the country club. He had that same manner.

Del came over to the shade of the tree but he had to shout above the noise of the tractor going past. "I came to see your brother."

Creed pointed to Audie with the hand holding the Dr. Pepper can, one crooked finger straight out. It was short by one knuckle but it pointed well enough.

"I see him. I need to ask him a couple of questions."

"He'll be done in a while," Creed said. "I come up to keep an eye on him. He don't see too good no more."

"I know," Del said. Then: "How about you take over, so I can borrow him for just a bit?"

"All right," said Creed. He put the can down in the grass and stood up, clapping dust out of his pantlegs, and then he went out into the field hollering at Audie to stop right where he was.

Preston

I SAW HIM GO and I thought I knew what he was up to. I didn't know how he'd found out about that marijuana field but I didn't care. He'd need a search warrant and I guessed he had one, either that or he was just going to talk to the boys for a while and have a little look around and pretend to just kind of stumble onto it. That was all right with me either way. I figured it was about time. So when he and Audie came back down together you could have knocked me over with a feather just about. I could still hear the tractor going. I figured Creed was driving it since Graham and Audie were coming down through the pasture together. Graham had a hold of Audie's elbow the way you'd do it if you were showing a blind man where to go. Like he thought Audie couldn't find his own way.

They were coming down the hill but they were coming slowly. They were talking back and forth. Graham would say something and then he'd turn his head toward Audie and Audie would say something back but you could see that Graham didn't understand it. He'd get kind of squinty-eyed and curl up one corner of his mouth and cock his head at an angle. Then he'd say something more and you could tell he was probably asking the same question all over again. I didn't feel sorry for him. I felt sorry for Audie. Audie'd shake his head and kind of draw it back like a lizard or a bird or something the way he does. A turtle. Kind of making his neck short and wagging his head back and forth quick. He looked worried. Graham would nod and pat him on the arm or take his own hand off his elbow and rest it on his shoulder like they were the best old friends in the world, but Audie didn't ease up any you could tell. I could see him winding up. I could see him just winding himself up real tight.

I went into the back hall and got my hat and then I went into the kitchen and asked Margaret if she'd call that lawyer on the telephone. Chapman. His business card was on the corkboard. When I'd sat down with him the first time I didn't think we'd need him for Audie, but things change. I wasn't going to let the same damned thing happen to Audie that happened to Creed. Next thing you know he'd be signing some piece of paper and they'd have the both of them in the pokey together. I was thinking maybe the troopers couldn't make up their minds between them so they'd let a jury choose or else just go for the Daily Double. Convict them both. I wasn't going to stand for that. I meant to nip that in the bud. Margaret got up to call that lawyer and I went out.

The door slammed behind me and I let it. Graham heard it go and believe me he pulled up short. For a lawman he looked an awful lot like a kid who'd been caught with his hand in the cookie jar. I don't mind telling you that.

Del

PRESTON HATCH WANTED to drive Audie to the barracks in his own car, which seemed like a good idea. I went on ahead and they came along when they got themselves situated. It didn't take long. To tell the truth they almost got there before I did. Preston has something of a lead foot. But you could say he was on official business, so I didn't make any remark on the subject. I just let him go.

The five of us would have been a tight fit in my office, so we talked in the small conference room. Al Chapman and Preston Hatch and Audie Proctor took one side of the table and Burnes and I took the other. Burnes was recording. I'd never met Chapman before that day and I wasn't impressed with him. His first misstep, as far as I was concerned, was making Preston and Audie cool their heels in the lobby waiting for him to show up. That was disrespectful. Mrs. Hatch had phoned his office while I was out at the farm and she'd gotten him on the line and I'd gone into the kitchen to speak with him, and he'd said that he'd meet us down at the barracks right away. It took him well over an hour and a half to get there and that was only from downtown. He must have had something more important to do. I didn't ask. It wasn't any of my business. I had paperwork to keep me occupied in the meantime, but Preston and Audie just had to sit and wait. Burnes took them out some coffee but neither one of them drank any of it. From where I sat in my office I could see them on the couch with the coffee cups on the table in front of them. They had their heads together but they weren't drinking the coffee, so I sent Burnes out to see if perhaps they wanted a Coke or something instead. Something cold. Hatch said no but Audie said yes although I don't believe he drank that either, once he got it.

Once Chapman got here he took Audie and Preston into the conference room to go over what they had to go over. When he closed the door he didn't look as if he was happy to see Preston and he didn't look any happier about it when he opened the door again and came out. He looked like he'd figured out that he was stuck with him for better or worse. He fully expected me to object, no question. Before we'd even sat down he jumped on me with both feet. He insisted on his client's behalf that Mr. Hatch be permitted to stay and participate in the questioning, since otherwise Mr. Proctor's statements might be misunderstood both by law enforcement officers and by his own representation. He said having Mr. Hatch in the room was equivalent to bringing in a translator for a foreign speaker and I said fine. He said if I didn't see it his way he could do a little research into the subject and quote me chapter and verse and file some papers but it would cause a delay and I said fine, really, I had no problem with Mr. Hatch. I had no problem with Mr. Hatch at all. I was the one who'd let Mr. Hatch come in the first place, for exactly that purpose. Chapman hadn't expected that. I think he might have preferred the delay, but he didn't get it.

Audie had a powerful smell about him in that small conference room. There's only the one window and Burnes opened it up all the way, but it didn't help much because there wasn't any cross-ventilation. You couldn't open the door and get some, either. Not with the questioning under way.

I began by asking Audie what had happened the night before his brother died. Asking if he remembered anything in particular. He said something to Preston and Preston cleared it with Chapman before he said it to me. Audie and his brothers had watched some comedy program on the television. He couldn't remember what. Then they'd watched the news a little and switched off the television and gone to bed as usual. I got the impression from how he said it, from the cadences and the details, that Preston was giving me his words accurately. And it matched well enough with what I already knew.

I asked him how Vernon had seemed that night while they were watching the television and later on when they were going to sleep, and he said he'd seemed the same as usual. No different. He'd made no complaints.

I asked had they all slept side by side in the one bed the way they usually did, and he said yes. I asked in what order and he shook his head as if he didn't understand the question. He kept shaking his head and he wouldn't look at me. So I asked in a different way. I asked who slept on the side of the bed against the wall and who slept in the middle. He started picking at the edge of the table with his fingers as if he wanted to strip the veneer away from it. Preston took his one hand by the wrist and looked at me, wondering if that was all right to do, and I told him it was all right without saying it out loud. Just by the way I looked back at him. He got Audie's hands down in his lap and Audie calmed down at least to some measure. Preston asked him the question again for me, which I thought was good judgment on his part. It was better than my asking it myself, and this time Audie answered. Creed against the wall, Vernon in the middle. That fit with the way his brother had described it. As for Vernon's being in the middle, it also fit with the presence of the urine stains. Although they'd been all over the place, really.

By then I'd decided I ought to back up a little and take it slower if we were going to get anywhere at all, so that's what I did.

1989

DeAlton

I NEVER LIKED DRIVING this far north after Thanksgiving time. Once the hard weather settles in. It's too risky. Old man Roy Dobson's been after me to expand the territory up here about as long as I can remember—up toward the border, I mean, not over it, I don't think he ever had anything in the way of an export license—but I've never seen the sense in it. If a man can't make a living selling milking machines in central New York, he probably can't make a living at all.

I said an export license. Don't you know anything? I never went to college and I've heard about an export license.

Anyway I guess we won't need one. That's the beauty of this line of work. Import, export, who gives a shit. And no taxes either.

I wish they'd get the plows out earlier. I thought they called this a main highway.

If you were going to keep this up on a regular basis I'd say get a different car. Nothing fancy. I don't mean that. Maybe four-wheel drive. Just something less conspicuous than that VW.

I don't care if you scraped the stickers off. You can still make out some of them if you look.

Anyway the trick is to get that Henri to do the hauling. If he's coming down with a carload anyway there's no sense going back empty. Anybody can see that. We want to stay out of the transportation business and let him stay in it. That's job one on this trip.

What's he drive anyway?

See, that's way too much car. A car like that just draws attention. That's why we brought your mother's. You want to maintain the right profile. Low but not too low.

Damn it the customs agents could be his own mother and father and it wouldn't make any difference. You don't smuggle dope in a Cadillac Eldorado.

That's a good point. He'll have our stuff in there going north. That's right. But you can't control every damn thing. I'd rather lose a shipment in his fancy car than get caught with one in my own.

It's under the spare tire. I put some dirty old shop towels and newspapers under the spare tire and it's under that.

Now shit. Shit. I tell your mother to keep an eye on the washer fluid but she never does. It's good for her to take a little responsibility for herself in that line, but now look where it got me. Shit shit shit. I can't see a goddamn thing. I'll pull over and you squirt on some of that deicer and we'll see how that helps.

I think there's a gas station this side of Cicero might be open.

Donna

HE SAID DOBSON wanted him to make a run to Quebec, and her car had the newer tires on it plus it got better gas mileage. Dobson paid the legal twenty-five and a half cents a mile regardless, and there was no way DeAlton Poole was going to bother impressing that old fool's customers on his own dime. Not all the way to Quebec.

Tom

THERE SURE WAS A LOT of French stuff up there. Tom couldn't believe it. The road signs would have been enough, never mind the billboards and the food and the newspapers and everything else. He and DeAlton got in early, so they parked the car and had something at a little coffee shop on a side street. Tom couldn't get over the menu. He kept saying it was like they were in a foreign country and his father shook his head and said they were and Tom said well yes he knew that but still. Then they got back into the car and parked where they'd been told to park and walked around the corner the way they'd been told to walk and knocked at the locked door of a restaurant the way they'd been told to knock. Then they waited. There was a little gray snow on the sidewalk and they stamped their feet in it to stay warm.

They heard some sounds from inside, the slamming of a door and maybe some footsteps, unless it was from the building next door or upstairs. The noises faded to nothing again. DeAlton looked at his watch and asked Tom if he was sure they were here on the right day and Tom said yes. DeAlton said he didn't like to be kept waiting, giving Tom a look that made him feel as if the whole thing was his fault. As if Tom had willfully gone into business with somebody whose idea of a good time was making DeAlton Poole freeze his ass on a street-corner in a foreign country with a baggie of marijuana in his coat pocket. Like this particular indignity had been planned from the start.

Tom stuffed his hands into his pockets and lifted his shoulders up around his ears. "I can hold onto that bag if you want me to," he said.

"I'm not handing it over in the middle of the sidewalk. Not even to my own flesh and blood." He shivered. "Although by rights you're the one should be in charge of it. I've got to quit putting everybody else first. It's like I said about your mother. Until you're in charge of your own washer fluid, you don't think about it. You never have to grow up."

"Live and learn," said Tom. And with the creaking of a latch and the turning of a key, the door slid open. It wasn't Henri behind it. It was an antique individual in rumpled chef's whites, not much more than four feet tall, with a towering and very grimy toque pushed down to his eyebrows. He had bright little eyes like marbles in gray dough and pretty much the same little scar of a mustache that Henri wore. He needed a shave. "You have come to meet with Henri," he said, stating the obvious. Speaking in complete sentences, just like his boss.

"Right you are, Chef Boyardee," said DeAlton. "Now lead on. I don't know what you're used to, but we're not the kind of men that like to wait."

The place smelled like paradise and purgatory. Paradise from the swinging doors to the kitchen, and purgatory from the cigarette smoke that lingered everywhere. The little man shut the door and locked it and led them back through a series of barely lit dining rooms, where bits of glass and polished hardwood gleamed like secrets. "Boiardi was an Italian," he said, throwing the words over his shoulder with a palpable contempt. "He sacrificed everything for commerce." Evwysing. "I, on the other hand, am French."

"Right," said DeAlton. "I know some guys who fought in the big war, and they told me how you French boys feel about compromise."

The old man stopped short and DeAlton very nearly stumbled into him. For an instant he was pretty sure that the little Frenchman was going to spin around on his heel and nail him in the gut with a sucker punch. It would have been just the sort of duplicitousness that he should have been expecting. But instead the little man swept open the hidden door to a private dining room and pointed within, his little gray faced twisted into a scowl. This was it, the end of the line.

"Thanks, pal," said DeAlton. "Let me know when you've cooked up something I can buy in the Acme."

"Don't hold your breath." The little man sneered beneath his mustache, and marched off toward the kitchen.

*

Henri let the smoke trickle slowly through his lips and he didn't speak until it was all gone. Then the words rode out on a long string of delicate little coughs. "So what are you saying to me? Is this my competition?"

"You wish."

Henri looked puzzled.

"You wish it was your competition. You wish you had something to compete with it." DeAlton's tone had an oiliness that only slightly masked something volcanic underneath. "Now look here. I just promised to buy twice our usual from you in the future, so trust me when I say I know the difference between the stuff you're selling and this stuff."

"I see." Henri turned the joint in his fingers, studying it from all angles. He lifted up his shoulders and drew down the corners of his mouth. "So. If this is not my competition, then why do you bring it to me?"

"Because you're in the distribution business, same as we are. Only we've started doing a little production of our own." DeAlton nodded to indicate the joint in Henri's hand and the baggie on the polished walnut tabletop.

"Ahh. Long ago Nick told me that he grew a little. I had no idea."

"This doesn't have to do with Nick. Nick doesn't know the first thing about growing marijuana. I'm the one who knows about growing marijuana."

Henri pursed his lips.

"And thanks to me, we've got a ton more of this than we can get rid of all by our lonesome."

"A ton?"

"Figure of speech."

"I see. You have a ton that is not a ton, and you want me to dispose of it on your behalf."

DeAlton showed as many of his teeth as he could. "I wouldn't put it that way. How I'd put it is I'm giving you the opportunity of a lifetime."

"Ahh," said Henri. He looked wearily from DeAlton to the joint and then back again, as if no power on earth could impel him to accept this burden. The joint had gone out, so he lit it again and drew on it. "Life," he said as the smoke trickled out, "is full of opportunities. A businessman must be careful as to which he accepts."

"Accepts?" As if he didn't understand the word.

"Accepts."

"Look." Reaching out for the baggie. "We didn't come up here to talk you into anything."

Tom coughed.

DeAlton got his fingertips on the baggie and began drawing it toward him.

Henri just watched it go.

"We didn't come up here on a goddamn sales call," said DeAlton. He got the baggie to the edge of the table and left it there.

Henri nodded.

Tom coughed again.

DeAlton reached for the smoldering joint and extracted it from Henri's hand and pinched it out. "This shit sells itself," he said. He rubbed it between his thumb and forefinger, letting bits of ash and paper and grass filter down to the tabletop.

"Perhaps it does," said Henri, "but not always. It does not sell itself to me, for example."

"Come on. An ounce of this is worth two pounds of that crap you're pushing."

"That may well be the case." Henri sighed, "but I have only a professional interest in such things. I am not a connoisseur like yourself."

DeAlton narrowed his eyes into something you could slide a coin into. "I don't like your attitude."

Tom coughed.

Henri fired up a Matinee. "I did not say that you were incorrect." Then, looking to Tom: "Did I say that your father was incorrect?"

Tom shook his head.

Henri creased back his smile so far that his mustache just about disappeared. "Ahh. I did not believe that I had. But as I say, I am open to the idea that you may be right about the quality of this merchandise."

"I'm right about it all right."

"If you are—"

"I am."

"If you are, then I shall consider putting myself into a position from which I may help you get rid of it, as you say."

"You know that's not what I meant."

"Forgive me. I am but a poor Frenchman, and I am handicapped in the refinements of your language. I can make use only of such words as you have given to me."

DeAlton

THAT WENT PRETTY WELL, considering.

Nah. Not on your life. Until you've been an a few sales calls, you don't know how bad it can go. But as long as you maintain control of the situation you'll come out all right in the end. Take it from me.

Some guys, your real hardasses, they'll want free samples. They'll want a unit they can hook up to every goddamned cow in sight and use for a month or two and then give back if they don't like it. If it doesn't meet their expectations. If it doesn't perform as promised.

Can you believe that? What performs as promised? Nothing.

You've got a point. I admit it. That high class dope lives up to expectations, absolutely. In spades. That bullshit about it selling itself? I meant every word of it.

I know you know.

Anyway at least he didn't want free samples. That's the worst. Once a guy gets his heart set on free samples it's tough to get him turned around. He doesn't see the value in what you're putting in front of him.

Some guys don't know the value of anything.

Anyway the main thing is we've got him taking care of the transportation. And we've got him opening up new sales territory. North of the border, without benefit of an export license. What do you think of that? And so what if we had to give him a little bit of an introductory discount? I've given away a whole lot more than that in my time.

Like they say, we'll make it up in volume.

Tom

THEY WERE IN WATERTOWN by suppertime, off the highway and motoring down a commercial strip jammed with opportunities to partake of good old American chow. None of that French stuff. DeAlton said he was buying to celebrate their success and they ended up at either a Bennigan's or a Friday's, Tom could never tell those two apart. Out the window was the ruin of one of his old favorites, a place that served hot dogs steamed in beer, one of the last in a chain long gone belly-up for reasons that he would never understand. Bennigan's or Friday's or whatever it was served beer too, though, so that was some consolation. They each had a couple over dinner and then they picked up a six-pack for the road.

It was plenty cold when they got back in the car but it warmed up in a hurry and they took off their coats and tossed them over into the back. Tom remarked as to how the bottles clanking around his feet weren't getting any colder with that fan blowing hot air on them. DeAlton said he wasn't ready to start on those yet but Tom could go on and help himself if he wanted, which he did. That made five left and the car getting warmer still. Tom said he didn't think he could drink the rest fast enough and DeAlton said he'd better not even think about it if he knew what was good for him. He said to pass him one and Tom did, and then he grunted and handed it right back and Tom twisted the top off and handed it back again. DeAlton nearly spat his first mouthful back into the bottle, it was already so warm.

He pulled off the road under a bridge where there wasn't much snow. Tom asked what was up, and DeAlton said he was going to give him one last lesson for the day, free of charge. "Find that paper bag the beer came in," he said, and Tom reached over and fished around in the back seat until he came up with it. "Now put the beer back in it." Tom did, and the bottles clanked hard against each other, and DeAlton said, "Not just loose. Put that carton back together where you tore it and put the bottles in it staggered where they won't bang too much and then put that back in the bag." Tom did. "Now roll the top of the bag down tight and put your window down a little bit and see if you don't get any ideas."

Tom did as he was told, and he sat with the window down and the beer in his lap for a few seconds. DeAlton sat too, just waiting for the light to dawn if it was going to or for it not to dawn and for him to have to explain everything, sitting behind the wheel in his shirtsleeves as the temperature dropped and a few flakes of snow flew in from out of the dark. Sipping at his beer. A couple of pairs of headlights loomed and flashed past and Tom finally got the idea. He stuck the bag out the window and put the window back up most of the way and then he clamped it tight with the rolled-up top of the bag on the inside and the beer hanging out there in the cold.

"That's my boy," said DeAlton, and he grinned and hit the gas hard. The heat came back up quick and they still had a couple of hours to go.

1954

Vernon

HE WAS A GREAT ONE for giving orders when he come back from Korea. None of us went for that too much. None of us but him, and he liked it just fine. It put me in mind of my father.

Later on he got that whiskey still running and he took up a little drinking and that put me in mind of my father too. We always got along pretty good without that kind of thing. Ever since the old man died. Drinking and giving orders. Bossing folks around.

Audie took to it better than me. He didn't mind following. He always was a great one for following. A person or orders either one.

Problem was it got so Creed weren't pulling his weight. He done chores but he done them his own way and some of them wasn't even chores needed doing. He done his wash two three times a week when my mother wouldn't do it for him. Extra wash I mean. Just his army uniform. I thought if he'd do some of the wash he ought to do the rest of it but he didn't think like that so every Saturday morning my mother still did it and he weren't no help to her. Donna come over from school sometimes to help but not always. Then when he was doing his wash he was too busy to do nothing else. And even when he kept up with his chores he did them kind of light. Like he give up sweating. It got almost like he was right back in Korea except he needed feeding and he weren't sending home no pay.

Preston

THERE WASN'T ANY QUESTION what Creed was up to. He was going courting. He'd set his cap for somebody, is how they used to say it. Two or maybe three days, along about suppertime, I'd seen him start down the road with that old three-legged mutt they had back then trailing behind him until its legs gave out. I mentioned it to Margaret and her eyes lit up and she clapped her hand over her mouth and fessed up about the uniform. Like it had been a secret between her and Creed and now it was out. I asked her if he'd said anything about a girl when he'd come about his khakis and she said no, but the both of us put two and two together.

A young fellow that age it was to be expected.

Then again this wasn't just any young fellow. It was Creed Proctor. I don't remember he'd been lucky with a girl ever. Of course I can't speak for what might have happened over in Korea or even up to Camp Drum. A lot of things can happen to a young fellow in the service. Things he might not be in a hurry to bring home. Not all of them will have to do with what you're required to do regarding the enemy, either. Some of them you come up with yourself, or among the other fellows. Out there in the big world.

Anyhow the Proctor boys had always been shy around girls as far as I knew. Not that they were the kind of men that girls would have gone seeking out. Far from it. But then again there's all kinds of girls. A fellow I know in the car business will tell you there's an ass for every seat.

Look how Ruth married Lester. You never know who'll come along or what'll happen or why.

So even though I thought it was comical that he'd get his sights set on some little gal, Margaret thought it was sweet.

Ruth

THE AFTERNOON IS FIERCELY HOT and wickedly close and a couple of mile-high thunderheads hang in the sky like anvils. Vernon is bent over inside the henhouse wielding a short-handled shovel, scraping the worst of the chicken manure into piles by the door and pushing lumpy hailstorms of it out onto the yard, much to the irritation of the chickens. They squawk and storm around as if the flying manure is a surprise every single time, as if they have no idea where it came from in the first place. Audie is up at the edge of the high pasture underneath the Farmall tractor, unscrewing the plug to let the old oil drain out into a swale that runs along the fenceline. He has half a case of fresh oil on the wagon behind it because he can never remember how much it takes and he wants to make sure he has enough. Creed has lifted the hatch to the pumphouse and let himself down into its coolness to tap at joints and knock on valves and pretend to himself that he is forestalling future problems. Preventative maintenance, they called it in the motor pool. Pipes clang and rust rains down. He may as well be banging on the works of a nuclear generator or a rocket ship for all he grasps of it and all the good it does, but the temperature is comfortable down there below the ground and the day is hastening on and he doesn't want to begin anything too demanding. He is thinking of the girl at the Dineraunt.

He climbs out and lowers the hatch behind him and brushes cobwebs and red rust from the front of his overalls, then he bends and claps the same mess out of his pantlegs as best he can. More or less satisfied, he stretches up straight and gets a look at the sky and judges that by the appearance of things there are worse places to be right now than underground. With those stormclouds. He goes and stands in the shadow of the barn and hollers Vernon's name toward the henhouse and Vernon sticks his head out the door.

"You go on up there get Audie and bring him back," Creed says.

"If you want him brung back you go."

"Storm's coming," says Creed

"I know that," says Vernon.

"Go bring him back."

"You want him brung back you do it. I'm busy." Pulling his head back inside the henhouse. Mr. Punch on a traveling stage.

Creed raises his voice further. "He'll get hit while you fool around with them chickens and then what."

"He'll come if he wants to."

"He won't come. He'll hide under them trees and them trees'll get hit and then what."

Chicken manure flies from the door of the henhouse. "Far as I remember the old man never run home on account of a little rain."

"The old man never learned what I learned in the army. He never had my army training."

"I guess he didn't, but he done all right." Then, sticking his head back out and playing his trump, "You didn't know him like I did. You was always too little."

*

The storm does not come but Audie does, rattling down from the high pasture aboard the Farmall, grinning as if he's just taken the whole thing to pieces and put it back together again, blindfolded. Creed watches him come, imagining a spiny finger of lightning leaping from one of those great distant piles of cloud to the very crown of his brother's head, seeing the impact and the power of it illuminating him all blue and yellow before burning him to a cinder, thinking that the whole tragedy will be Vernon's fault if it happens. But it doesn't happen, and Audie draws the tractor up alongside the barn and switches off the engine and climbs down from the iron seat. He disconnects the wagon and puts the leftover oil cans in the barn and throws the empties into the trash. Then he says something that Creed does not quite catch and goes around to the front of the house to sit on the porch and carve on a piece of wood for a while. It is half an hour at least until milking time and if Creed is going to take a rest then maybe he will take a rest too. Their mother comes out and sits beside him, watching something emerge from the wood and watching the storm come on. Marveling at both of them.

1990

Del

I BACKED OFF and came around slowly to the important questions. It wasn't because I wanted to sneak up on Audie or trick him into saying something he hadn't fully thought out, but because the process was clearly so painful for him. There was no stealth on my part. My aim was strictly to acclimate him to the process of being interviewed. At a handful of points I thought again that it might be just as well to jump into the deep end in order to get it over with and minimize his distress, but then he'd settle back down and I'd decide that going slow and steady was best after all. I may have been wrong, but you play these things as wisely as you can at the time and then you try not to look back and second-guess yourself. Although I still do. I always do. Second-guess myself, I mean.

Preston

HAVING THE LAWYER THERE was my idea so I was the one who had to suffer for it. First he made us wait on him the better part of the morning, and then when he finally made his appearance he blustered around like a little banty rooster. As if it was all his show to begin with. When he finally settled down and we got going he didn't do anything I wouldn't have done on my own, except for just being a lawyer, which I guess counts for something. I don't know why.

We had to do a lot of whispering back and forth. Audie got nervous right off and I didn't think he'd stay with it for long, but Graham backed off a little on the deathbed stuff and I said how what we were doing was just like on one of those crime shows they always watched on television. He brightened up like we were putting on a show. Or like the people on those programs weren't play-acting but doing it for real and now here we were doing it just the same way they did. He'd whisper something to me and then he'd bend forward and watch me whisper it on to Chapman, all smiles. Then the lawyer would nod and tell me to go ahead and I'd say out loud what Audie had told me and he'd sit there listening to it and nodding up and down just as satisfied as a person could possibly be. He even began to drink a little of his coffee, but it had to be cold by then, so Graham buzzed somebody on the intercom and they brought in a fresh pot of it on a hot plate. Audie's eyes lit right up to see it come. He doesn't see too well but he could see well enough to make that out. You would have thought he was getting room service at the Ritz.

The problem was that it all went on for too long. Graham has a round-about way of getting at things. He's a very methodical person, and that's all right. He has to be. He has a job to do like the rest of us. I believe he wanted to take it kind of easy on Audie, but as a result he ended up going all the way back to the Civil War. He got Audie talking about how it'd been growing up right behind Vernon, and then how Creed came along next and then Donna. The things they did as children and young people and so forth. I remembered an awful lot of those things myself, since very little of what went on in that family went on inside the house. They weren't much of an indoor bunch then and they still aren't.

One of the things Graham asked about was killing. I mean as a general thing. Mercy killing and slaughtering livestock and what have you. It's part of living on a farm and he had to know that. Audie answered his questions all right though, passing on what he remembered and staying pretty calm, and I spoke his answers out again just the way he said them. Stories of his various experiences. The lawyer Chapman got impatient after a while. He asked were they here for a questioning or for an installment of This is Your Life, which was a program I remembered but I didn't think he was old enough to. He threw down some papers on the table and pushed his chair back like he meant to leave even though there was no way he would've dared do that. It was all just for show. But when Chapman got agitated Audie got agitated right along with him. Jumpy. I blame it on Chapman more than I do Graham. Audie was doing well enough right up until then and he might very well have kept it up if that damned lawyer hadn't flown off the handle and got him started.

Graham did as the lawyer wanted, and got right down to brass tacks. He asked Audie if he knew what it meant to die from suffocation. Audie cocked his head like he didn't understand the question and Graham said like strangling. Like strangling a man. Audie said he knew about that and Chapman let him say it. That is he let me say it for him. Audie went on to say he'd seen that kind of thing on crime shows on television and Chapman let me say that for him too. Audie was shaking pretty badly. He was starting to draw his neck in the way he does and he kept looking down at the table. Graham went on because he had to. He asked Audie if he'd heard about how that was the way his brother died. Being strangled. The lawyer hit the table with his fist and objected to that and Audie jumped like he'd been hit by lightning and Graham tried a different way. He asked Audie if he'd heard that his brother'd passed on from suffocation and Audie said yes he'd heard about it and the lawyer let him say that too. Graham nodded. Then he said he wanted to clarify if Audie had only heard about it, or if maybe he knew something about the subject first-hand. You can bet the lawyer raised an almighty objection to that, but Audie didn't know he was objecting because he'd kind off shut him off by then and he wasn't paying much attention to him. Only to Graham and me. Like we were two fellows with a couple of life preservers and he was drowning. He answered the question and I guess it was a good thing I was there to do his talking for him because I bent over to repeat what he'd said more or less to Chapman and Chapman said don't you dare say it. Just flat out like that. Don't you dare say it. Even to him. He said it didn't matter what the answer was since it wasn't a fair question. He cited some fancy legal reason, I don't know what. I can't say if it was a good reason or a made-up one, but either way Graham accepted it and shrugged his shoulders and moved on. That other trooper, Burnes, was writing away like mad, doing his best to get it all down. I don't know how he could have kept it straight.

About then Audie gave up and just put his head on the table. Leaned over with his hands in his lap and laid his head on the table with his eyes shut. Graham asked could he please sit up and he didn't answer. His head was kind of drumming on the table and the coffee in his cup shook in circles. I picked it up and moved it away to keep it from spilling over. Chapman said all right, that's enough, and it was. It was enough.

Donna

WHEN THEY BROUGHT her brother in, she was waiting under the portico where the ambulances pull up. Emergency had called the third floor nurses' station and she'd dropped everything and come right down, skipping the balky elevator at that end of the building and taking the stairs two at a time and tearing down the hall and reaching the portico before he did. The troopers hadn't called an ambulance. Del Graham just drove him straight over from the barracks in his patrol car, like a member of the family using his own vehicle. It was only a mile or two. Audie sat in the back with Preston. Actually he lay on his side with his head on Preston's lap. His teeth were chattering as if he were freezing to death in that bright hot patrol car and he was saying something over and over again that nobody could make out. Not even Preston. Chapman had returned to his office to see about other things.

They didn't admit him overnight, but they may as well have for as long as it took. Preston went with Graham to get his car and came back. He sat in the waiting room reading a Syracuse paper that was more than a week old and a Hollywood gossip magazine that was a lot older than that, wondering with every page he turned how many kinds of contagion he might be picking up on his hands. He didn't recognize a single soul in the gossip magazine and it made him feel old and out of touch. All those celebrities were just regular people to him. After he was finished he stood up and went over to check out the vending machines. It was going on one o'clock and he hadn't had any lunch yet and he didn't feel like finding the cafeteria because who knew when they'd be done with Audie. A package of cheese doodles caught his eye but before he put in any money he remembered the time he'd spent with newspaper and the magazine and he went to the men's room to wash his hands. He came back and got the cheese doodles and ate them, then folded up the package and tucked it into his shirt pocket rather than get up. He paged through a cooking magazine and used it to brush orange cheese dust from his trousers and he saw there on his lap the greasy imprint of Audie's old head from the ride over. He sighed.

When Donna came out from the back and found him in the waiting room, half asleep with the cooking magazine in his fist and little trace of orange powder staining his lower lip, she ran over with a panicky look that said not twice in one day.

"Hey," he said, rousing himself. "How's Audie?"

She said never mind Audie, Audie was going to be all right, how was he?

"I'm fine, fine. I rode your brother down to the barracks, and I thought I'd ride him home when he's ready."

"I didn't know. I though you'd—"

"I didn't think he ought to go in that patrol car."

"Right. That was kind of you."

"I guess. It didn't do him much good."

"We do what we can," she said. "Those brothers of mine."

Preston blinked and put down the magazine and rubbed at a little orange stain he'd found on his shirtfront, making it worse.

"They're putting him on a sedative," she said. "He's going to be fine, but it'll be a while."

"Because—"

"Because it always is. Everything takes forever. You know hospitals."

"I know this one pretty good. I've read everything there is to look at around here except the VD flyers. I had enough of them in the army."

Donna smiled and stood there for a minute, and then she sat down in the chair next to Preston's. She leaned in close and lowered her voice. "Tell me," she said, "what did they ask him?"

"Nothing special. Background stuff. The usual, I guess."

She slumped forward a little with her hands folded on her lap, shaking her head. "It doesn't take much, does it?"

"No," said Preston. "It doesn't take much at all."

Audie

I WOKE UP in the bed and all the lights were on and Donna was in the chair. I don't think those lights ever do go off. Donna wasn't there to be a nurse, so a different nurse came in and sat me up by pushing on a button and the bed moved. Donna smiled to see me come up. She said they were going to let me go home and I asked how long they'd had me to start with and she said not too long. The doctor came in to sign papers. He asked me how I felt and I said I'd feel better once I got out of the hospital and Donna said something to him and he laughed like he didn't really mean it. They had me in a dress made out of blue paper and it made a noise when he touched it. He asked me if I'd mind him taking a look at my backside before he let me go. I said I didn't have any trouble with my backside that I knew of but go on ahead and Donna said go on ahead and he sat me up straight and pulled at the paper dress. He said oh my he'd never seen anything like that in all his years. That rooster tattoo I got way back. He said had I ever got any medical care for that and I said I never got any medical care for anything until this very day. This was the first time and everybody must have done a pretty good job because I felt all right. He stood there clucking at it until he let me go and I got my clothes on and Donna brought me home. I was glad to be out of that dress. It was late and Creed had the milking done and I felt bad about that but he said it was all right. I didn't need to worry. That was what he said.

1989

Tom

"HENRI GIVE ME A CALL yesterday," Nick said.

Tom put down his beer and reached over for some Chex mix. He got a handful and picked through it to filter out the tasteless bagel bits and those hard little dried peas with the horseradish powder that they put in there to make you thirsty. He didn't say anything.

Nick went on. "He told me all about the new setup. He had an idea I might not know about it and he was right."

"What new setup?" Crunching the Chex mix.

"You know."

"Maybe I don't know."

"The deal he cut with you and your old man. Him selling our stuff up there. Us buying more of his stuff for down here."

"Oh," said Tom, going for some more Chex mix. "That setup."

"How come I had to hear about it from Henri?"

"I was getting around to telling you."

"When?"

"When I figured out how to do it so you wouldn't feel stupid for not thinking of it yourself."

"I don't feel stupid. I feel got around."

"I'm sorry."

Nick waved for the bartender's attention and tapped on the side of his glass for a refill. "I told you we go way back. Me and Henri."

"I know that. I remember."

"You can't keep secrets from old Nick."

"I know. That's why I was going to tell you any minute now."

"Especially if the secret means more work for me."

"More work, more money. I don't see the problem." Picking through the Chex mix.

"It ain't balanced. It ain't fair like it used to be. You got a cigarette?"

Tom gave him one and lit him a match. "Sure it's balanced. Everybody gets paid for what he does."

"I already don't get paid as much as you. And now I bet I'm gonna get less."

"You don't grow the stuff, and you don't process it, and you don't cut the big deals with the Canuck."

"I used to. With Henri, I mean."

"Things change."

"Now look," said Nick. He pointed at the bowl, which by now held pretty much nothing but wasabi peas and bagel bits and dust. "That right there is exactly what I'm talking about."

"What."

"That's the kind of person you are."

"I don't—"

"The kind of person only thinks of himself. No concern for the next guy."

"Oh come off it."

"Shit." Nick stubbed out his cigarette. "Here I am getting the short end of the stick, and it used to be my stick."

"Now come on."

"Remember that? It used to be my fucking stick."

"It's still your stick."

"Sure it is."

"It's both of our stick. Except it's bigger now. There's more stick to go around."

"You can't prove that by me." He looked down at the bar and then looked up again, square at Tom. "Ever heard of dancing with what brung you?"

"I'm not much for dancing."

"Like hell you're not. Henri said you danced just fine up there in Montreal. He said your daddy danced even better than you."

DeAlton

SO DROP HIM. Cut him off.

Guys like that are a dime a dozen. The sooner you learn that, the better you'll do in this life.

I know, I know, but I don't care. He can't possibly have a line on every damned pot smoker in the county. Nobody ever gave him sole rights to that information. Nobody ever gave him this territory on an exclusive basis. You didn't. I sure as hell didn't.

There's ways to find out. Use your head. It won't be a big deal.

You cut him off and get him out of the picture and the sooner you do it the better.

So what if he does? I assure you that Henri isn't going to start selling through the both of us. Who's got the money? You tell me that. Who's got the money?

That's right, we've got the money. Henri's a businessman and he's going to go with the people who've got the money. He can't afford to be sentimental. And he's sure as hell no idiot.

If you won't cut him off I will.

That's right. He's just a little fish and I'll throw him back myself if you won't.

On second thought, no. You do it. Consider it part of growing up.

1990

Donna

ON HIS WAY HOME for lunch, Graham saw Donna's car turn up the dirt lane. He thought that with her as a buffer it might not be out of line to swing by, see how Audie was doing. So he touched the brakes and made the turn, switching on the air conditioning and rolling up his windows rather than let the patrol car fill up with the dust that her car had raised.

He found them in the house. The temperature had gone up to well over ninety-five and the humidity was higher than that and there wasn't much air moving. The windows were open and the gray lace curtain poked through one of them like a tongue and hung listless against the gray sill and the gray clapboards. He didn't knock because they saw him on the porch and Donna opened the door. She was in her hospital greens and she hadn't sat down yet and she never sat down the whole time he was there. He figured he knew why.

Creed was the first to speak. "You want one of them hamburgers, you go on help yourself." Looking at Graham but pointing at an open sack that Donna had brought up from McDonald's in town. "We already had our lunch and they won't keep too good." Donna looked frustrated. Graham said thank you but he was due to make up a Rotary meeting out at the Homestead, so he couldn't stay long. Creed advised him to have the chicken and biscuits and he said he just might if they had it.

Audie had his mouth full of burger regardless of what he'd had to eat already, and he grinned at him around it.

"I just came out to see how you were doing," Graham said.

Audie made some response through the burger and Creed said his brother was doing just fine now that he had two lunches in him. The one they already had and the second one their sister brought.

Donna asked if he was here with more questions for Audie and he told her no. He didn't have any questions for Audie other than how he'd been doing since they'd let him out of the hospital. "That's all through," he said. He put out his hand to Audie and Audie took it. "I'm glad to see you're doing all right." He gave Audie's hand a good hard squeeze and Audie squeezed back as if it were a competition and he extracted himself. Then he stepped toward the door.

Donna followed him and opened it and said as they stepped out, "He's still on medication right now. A sedative."

"I wondered. It wasn't my business to ask." He drew breath and looked back through the rusty screen at the two brothers making ready to come back out. "It seems to be doing him good."

"I think he has another day or two to go. We'll see."

Graham lifted his damp shirt away from his skin. He looked around the porch and took note of the ashtray on the arm of the overstuffed chair that Vernon had always favored. There were some twists of something probably not quite tobacco in it still and he asked about them, pointing. "You wouldn't know anything about that, would you?"

"I thought you didn't come here to ask questions."

"I didn't. I just—"

"My brother had cancer. Marijuana gave him some comfort."

"You know where he got it?"

"I'd tell you he grew it himself if you'd let it drop."

"Is that so?"

"As far as anybody ever told me. They grow a lot of things around here."

"Then I'll let it drop," said Graham.

"Creed used to run a still up there in the woods," she said. "A little bit of marijuana isn't that big a reach."

"No," said Graham. "I guess it isn't. Like I said, I'll let it drop. No harm done." Then he tipped his flat-brimmed hat and left.

Del

I WOULD HAVE LET IT GO. I meant to. Not just because of what the sister said, but because those two old men had endured enough. They'd endured enough and they were going to have to endure more before it was over, so there was no sense adding to it now. Another individual might have pursued it regardless and I might have been that other individual under different circumstances, but not under these.

Imagine me showing up at their doorstep with a search warrant.

You could say I'd let myself feel overly sympathetic toward those two. That's been suggested before, and it'll be suggested again, but I don't believe it's entirely true. I was perfectly prepared to come out and make the arrest when the time came. When Ben Wilson made his decision or the Grand Jury sent down a charge or however it shaped up. I'm not rationalizing. Another man might lie to himself and say he didn't want a bunch of drug charges confusing the larger issue, when all he really wanted was to give those two a break. But that's not what I'm saying. I'm saying plainly that I didn't want those two old men to suffer over this on top of everything else. When it wasn't the least bit necessary and no one on earth would be served by it.

I'd said my goodbyes to the sister and I was getting into my car when Creed and Audie came out of the barn. Audie was saying something to his brother, and whatever it was it made them both laugh. They were very happy right then. They caught sight of me and Audie said something else to Creed and Creed passed it on. He said they were about to take the tractor and go up to the creek that lay just beyond the property line and get their feet wet for a while. They'd cooled off that way on hot afternoons ever since they were boys. He asked if I might like to come along. The sun was straight overhead and I was wringing wet so I said yes, yes I would.

Creed drove, and you would have thought Audie was on carnival ride down at the beach. To take that much pleasure from such a simple thing is most definitely a gift, although I suppose it's the kind of gift that's more or less forced on some people for lack of an alternative.

We rode up through the pasture and came to a wire gate, and Audie jumped off and opened it. We went through and he closed it again and we rode along an overgrown tractor path that must have been left over from their father's day, right along the edge of a little copse of trees that started near the family graveyard and went on for a good while. The shade felt nice and the moving air felt even better. It was along that tractor path, well past the grave-yard, that I realized I had a problem. Out there among the trees were thirty, maybe forty mature marijuana plants that I could see from the tractor. That amounts to a major crop, more than those old men could use if they lived a mil-lion years. And from the way they tooled past on the tractor, they had no idea of its value.

It put me in mind of that nephew of theirs, the one with the attitude. I wondered what his mother knew, if she knew anything. I figured I had some work to do.

We kept going and we got to the creek and Creed parked the tractor with the front wheels right in the water. We put our feet in for twenty minutes or so, and even though my heart wasn't entirely in it at that point and my mind was going a million miles an hour I must say that it was lovely. Very cool and re-freshing. Sometimes when I'm having a rough patch at work, I catch myself being envious of anyone who can finish off his lunch hour that way. But not too envious. Not entirely.

1954

Ruth

SHE SITS ON THE PORCH alongside Audie and she watches her other son go. Dressed in his khakis. Marching off into the oncoming storm with the dog limping along behind him. Stopping down where the dirt lane gives onto the main road and hollering something at the dog and going on. He's never even said goodbye. She pictures him lightning struck and dying by the roadside in a puddle of mud with raindrops pattering and no goodbyes said whatsoever and she calls out even though she knows he will never hear her and he does not.

Audie looks up from his work and mutters something and she says probably some girl. Some girl from town, the way he's been spending his money. Creed Proctor the third of her sons and the first to take this route.

Audie grins down at his knife work as if he might like to take that route himself if ever granted the opportunity.

She asks what he is carving, is it a cow or a pig she can't tell yet.

He points toward a place in the yard where he has planted one of his whirligigs just a week or two earlier, this one in the shape of a pig, painted up in the conventional pink.

Oh she says the mate of that one, and he nods.

He sits and carves on, chips flying. She asks if he will need to do some turning on this one and he points with his beak nose toward the one in the yard with its turned screw of a tail and she says just so. I see. Silly of me to ask.

Even the pigs have mates, she thinks, even the wooden ones, and she remembers her long-gone Lester and she stifles a coughing fit and she wonders how her son Creed is getting on with whatever lady friend he is most surely courting. Hoping that he does not get wet before he crosses her threshold.

Creed

THE STORM HELD OFF and I got in before the rain come down. Where I usually sit was empty and two or three places on either side of it were empty too. There were enough people in there though. It was a Friday. I remember it like I put it on a calendar. Friday means payday so there were enough people there and folks looked at me like they never seen a soldier in the Dineraunt before. That's the way they always did even though I come there regular enough and there was plenty of soldiers everyplace in them days. Soldiers was always coming and going.

I had the meatloaf. She brung it and she brung the ketchup I always liked with it since she knew me and she knew how I like to eat my supper. I didn't have to ask. The ketchup weren't extra they just give it to you if you asked for it to go with your meatloaf. I set quiet and ate my supper and people come in and people went out. In from the rain and out into it. She didn't have too much time for me since it was so busy but she checked up on me now and then the way she would.

I never usually had the dessert but that time I did. It got dark outside and you could see yourself in the glass window. People give up coming in so much. I was getting nervous. Not nervous like Audie but almost. I wanted more people to finish up their suppers and go out so I could ask her and not worry. So I had the dessert. It was a white cake and I had coffee with it and I took my time working on it. More people finished and paid up and left and I was still working. The white cake had frosting and little red flower decorations like for a birthday. I took some on my fork and I told her I guess somebody's always got a birthday at the Dineraunt and she laughed. She was laughing and mopping at the counter with a rag right there next to me and I leaned over where she was working and told her how I killed a few men right up close when I was in Korea. She left off mopping. I said I thought you ought to know about that Wilma and she said Velma. She said Velma and she told me I ought to finish up now and go on home. I said I thought you ought to know what I done before I seen if you want to go to the movies with me sometime and she said she didn't care what I done and she didn't care for the movies either. Not with me. Then she went in the kitchen and this feller in a white apron come out and give me my check himself. I think he was the boss. All of us over there in Korea done it like I said but it weren't the kind of thing you talked about.

Audie

THE DOG DIDN'T COME BACK so I whistled for him but he didn't come back then either. I went to the road to see about him. It looked like rain. The wind whipped up and there was thunder but it wasn't too close. My mother said not to go but I went anyhow. She said he'd come back or else maybe he'd stuck with Creed but I didn't know about that. I didn't think so. He wasn't dead when I found him but he was hurt bad. Some car. He didn't have but three legs when he went down there and when I found him he didn't have that many. I've seen animals cut up but this was different. What kept him alive I don't know. I picked him up and the rain started and I brought him back to the barn. My mother saw me coming and she called Vernon and he came too. The dog was awful slippery. I won't ever forget the sound he was making but I can't make it myself. My mother took one look and went in the house. Vernon got a feedsack and he doubled it over and he wrapped it around the dog's nose and held on. The dog didn't fight. He didn't have any fight left. When a dog passes on I don't know if he goes on ahead like a man does or if he just passes on and that's the end of it. If it goes that way it doesn't seem fair to dogs. Vernon put the dog in a wheelbarrow for later and I put the feedsack over top and then we had to do the milking. Creed wasn't around to help with any part of it.

1990

Tom

THE FIRST TIME that Henri came to the barn was early in January, and DeAlton had a devil of a time convincing his son that they had the date right.

"We said the tenth," Tom said, "but if it's not till two in the morning, then that makes it the eleventh. Right?"

"You want to go on the tenth at two in the morning, you'll be in for a long wait. Like twenty-four hours."

"Still. If we say always be here on the tenth of the month and he always shows up on the eleventh, why don't we just call it the eleventh?"

"That'd make it the twelfth, if we said the eleventh." DeAlton leaned on the windowsill of his son's VW and spat onto the ground. "It'd be the twelfth, and you'd be a day late."

"All right," said Tom.

"Just be out there tomorrow night, you'll be fine."

Tom lit a cigarette and blew smoke out the window into the frigid morning, past his father. "It was different when we had Nick."

"If you can't carry a few bricks of dope up and down a ladder, you're getting too soft to be of any use to yourself."

"It's not that."

"Use the block and tackle."

"I never used a block and tackle."

"Get the Canuck to do it for you"

"I doubt he knows."

"I mean get him to carry it. Up the ladder. He's got to be good for something."

"I don't know." Tom started the car and a little plume of gray smoke blew out the tailpipe. "We'll see."

DeAlton took his hands off the sill and whacked the roof of the car with the flat of his gloved hand. It rang like a kettle drum. "Manage it, boy," he said. "Take charge. Show us what you're made of." Then he stepped away from the car and went back inside the house. He was going to be spending the whole day in his little office down at Dobson's, filling out order sheets and figuring out the December expense report which Dobson was about to kill him for not having done already, and he had just enough time for one last cup of coffee before he went.

Preston

IT GOT SO THAT it was a circus over there nights. That mean-looking greaser friend of Tom's quit coming toward the tail end of eighty-nine but that wasn't the last of it, not by any means. I'd still see him ride past on the main road now and then, slow down and give the place the fuzzy eyeball. Like he was keeping tabs on things. I guess they'd had a falling out.

And then once a month this big black Eldorado with Canadian plates on it would come by like clockwork, I mean like the milkman or the mail train or something, and Tom would be waiting to meet it. It was always in the middle of the night. Two, maybe three o'clock in the morning. Right in between there. Only an old man with urinary troubles would have been out of bed to know about it, but I knew about it all right. The way things turned out, I wasn't the only one having that kind of trouble during those days. That was probably why Vernon would stick his head out the barn door sometimes and give them a hand hauling bundles from the trunk of the Caddy and vice versa. I figure he'd probably gotten up to take a leak. You could see who it was in the light from the house door, if he thought to put it on. Tom and the Canadian never once put on a light. This was back in the springtime. Vernon was still alive but he wouldn't be for long.

Nick

HE'D PRETTY MUCH DECIDED that there wasn't any goddamn decency left in the world. A working man builds a little something up for himself, and the next thing he knows some asshole comes along and takes it away. The same asshole who screws his little sister while he's at it and then gives up on her too, even though to hear her tell the story it might have gone in the other direction on account of she decided he was a Grade A loser and gave him the old heave-ho but who cares. It wasn't right either way. Loser or not he had the best dope in the county and a private line to the Canuck and where did that leave old Nick. The Canuck wouldn't even take his calls anymore. Wouldn't even let that French chef of his pick up the phone. They must have gotten Caller ID just for him. It just rang and rang.

1990

Del

MY MOTHER'S HOUSE is the very same way. Not very much has changed in it since Kennedy was in office or before.

Margaret Hatch kept a display of those little old-fashioned mustard pots on her kitchen shelves. All sorts of them. Crystal and china and pewter. What the old folks used to call milk glass. I don't know why you'd decide to collect mustard pots or why you'd give any shelf space to milk glass, but people are all different.

Preston was upstairs, so his wife and I chatted in the kitchen for a while waiting. But rather than go into the living room when he came down I said why don't we just talk out on the screen porch. I showed my pantlegs, which were still a little damp even though I'd managed to keep my shoes and socks dry, and they agreed that it would be a good idea. So we went out onto the porch where they had some castoff furniture that I wouldn't ruin.

Neither one of them looked surprised when I mentioned the marijuana field. I made it clear from the start that I didn't believe the two brothers had anything to do with it, and I think I'd developed sufficient credibility with Preston that he saw I wasn't trying to mislead him in any way. He said if those two were raising that big a cash crop they'd probably eat better. Dress better too. Maybe drive something other than a tractor when they had an errand to run, something with doors and a roof. He went on about the implications for a while as if I still might need convincing. I said I guessed he was right about all that, and he let it go.

Since it wasn't Creed and Audie growing dope up there in the woods, I asked if they had any ideas as to who might be doing it. I didn't say that I thought it might be the nephew. I left it open. Preston asked Margaret if she'd go in the house for a while. She said she didn't need to. She said she knew what he was going to say because he'd been talking about nothing else for the better part of the year. He scowled at her and said no that wasn't it. He had things to talk about with me was all. Different things. Things she didn't need to put her nose into. He wasn't polite about it in the least, which surprised me. But she stood up and smoothed her dress down and went on into the house. Just like that. They come from a different time, those two. Their ways will die with that generation.

Once she was gone Preston's demeanor changed. He actually went quiet for a minute, as if he were having second thoughts as to what he was about to tell me. Then he looked out the screen and remarked on the heat and the lack of rain and the condition of the grass in the pasture next door.

I said how about you tell me about who's growing that marijuana.

He said there was more to it than that.

I asked what he meant.

He said the marijuana crop up in those woods was worth an awful lot. The crop and the people involved with it.

I said there was no denying that.

Margaret was opening and closing cabinets in the kitchen, so he cleared his throat and got up and shut the door. Then he sat down and looked at me. He cleared his throat again and he asked how certain I was about Creed. About the confession he'd signed.

I said a confession was a confession and my opinion of it was immaterial. I said how about we talk about that marijuana field instead. But he didn't give up.

He asked if my interview with Audie had changed anything as to my feelings about Creed, and I said what interview. I said it like it was a joke and I shook my head and smiled a little so as to encourage him to laugh, to help him be more forthcoming. I guess it helped, because he quit beating around the bush. He asked if there was any chance that I could influence what the district attorney might do about Creed, particularly given that there was more to the marijuana business than anybody guessed as of yet, and his testimony might well unveil what he called a drug cartel of international proportions.

I told him I was as sympathetic to his neighbors as anybody, perhaps more, but the law was the law and this marijuana business was an entirely different case. We'd eventually find out who was raising that crop and who was buying it. We'd find it out one way or another. I told him he could choose to help or not, however he saw fit, but I'd sure appreciate it if he would give us a hand. I think he was a little embarrassed, and he certainly didn't have the will power to push it any farther. I don't know that anybody would, except in the movies or on the television. He'd made a pretty good try, though.

Once we had all that settled he called Margaret back out, and she brought some lemonade, and he told me about the international drug cartel that had been operating right in his own front yard all this time. It seems they kept to a regular schedule. He asked if I thought he'd have to testify to anything in court, and I said not if we played our cards right.

1954

Audie

IT WAS GOING TO BE a pig but I turned it into a dog instead on account of that three-legged one that died. I still had it when people came around and started pulling out their wallets but I hung onto it no matter what. Sometimes I'd give it a little new paint but not anymore. I never did part with that dog. You couldn't get me to. Nobody could. I still have it to this day.

1990

Margaret

WE'VE ALWAYS HAD a double garage, because winters are hard around here and Preston is fastidious about his cars. Not that he keeps them for that long. People at the church used to joke that he'd rather sell a car than empty the ashtray. Cars have always been his great weakness.

In the afternoon he washed mine, but instead of putting it back in the garage he left it in the driveway. Late in the evening the troopers came, Del Graham and a gentleman named Myers who was much younger but very serious and terribly deferential to an old lady like me. They backed their patrol car up into the garage and put it in the empty bay and let the door down.

I made them some coffee and we all watched the late news. Then I went to bed, and I told Preston to come with me. He said no, he thought he'd sit out on the screen porch with the troopers for a while, and even though they tried very politely to discourage him he went anyway. I may as well have stayed down there and kept them company, for all I slept.

Nick

He'd had a little bit to drink at the Woodshed, that lowlife joint where Tom most pointedly did not hang out anymore, so rather than drive around he left the Indian in the parking lot and walked to Dickie's for a few cups of coffee and a big slice of that coconut cream pie. Between the sugar and the caffeine he'd be all right. Plus he had a couple of hours to kill. Was Dickie's open that late? He'd find out.

Del

THE VOLKSWAGEN ARRIVED FIRST, then the Cadillac right behind it. They killed their lights as they turned onto the dirt lane. They weren't in any hurry, and they did their best to pretty much coast the rest of the way, that big Caddy probably never getting above an idle by the sound of it. The VW was coughing badly and it would have been quieter if the nephew had just given it a little gas now and then. He parked and the Caddy pulled up next to him. Just one or two taps on their brakes and a little red glow in the yard and everything went dark again. The dome lights didn't even come on when they opened their doors and got out.

Preston elbowed me in the ribs to remind me that he'd kept his promise. I nodded my head whether he saw me or not, and I slid an inch or two away on the couch so that he wouldn't be tempted to do it again.

The nephew opened the barn door and the Canadian popped his trunk. The sounds of the door latches and the trunk latch carried across the empty space between us. The Canadian had apparently unscrewed the bulb from his trunk lid, too. He lit a cigarette and stood in the dark for a minute while the nephew took care of something in the barn. I thought that lighting the cigarette was pretty bold of him, but that was fine with me. It suggested that he'd gotten used to not having company. At first he had his back to us, judging by the way the cigarette came and went, and then he turned around and leaned against the rear quarter panel of the car and the movement of the ember was in the clear. If it had been daylight we would have been looking right at each other across the barnyard and the dirt lane and Preston's little patch of grass. Preston held his breath. We just had to wait.

Tom

THERE WAS NEVER ANY TELLING how much junk he'd have to move around once he got the trapdoor open. Lumber and haybales and feedsacks and hand tools and God knew what else. Audie and Creed had no respect for his space, that was the trouble. And Audie was the worst, with his stupid whirligigs and his lathe and his lumber set out everywhere to dry. Tonight wasn't actually so bad. Just a shovel and a couple of planks of some sort of wood and a short-handled silage fork, the tines of which he stepped on so that it sprang up like a rake in a cartoon but not far enough or hard enough to do him any damage. He opened one door to let in whatever light there was and he cleared room for Henri's stuff, and then he picked up an armload of his own and went back down the ladder. He kicked a clear space in the hay and horseshit and set the package down for when Henri's trunk was empty and they could start filling it up again. Henri heard him and walked in with his arms full and a cigarette between his teeth. Tom told him to put that out, didn't he know anything, but he just went on up the ladder. Tom got an armload himself and followed.

They took a few more loads up and they were standing in the hayloft door, breathing hard, when a motorcycle turned up from the main road.

Audie

THAT WAS A SOUND I hadn't heard for a while. Sometimes I'd go out and help those boys unload but that new man wasn't friendly so I didn't like to bother him. The other one, the old one who used to come around before, he called me Uncle Audie just like Tom did. He was all right. I liked him pretty well and Creed did too.

Preston

I LEANED OVER to say this was Tom's greaser friend, but Graham wouldn't let me. Tom and the Canadian were in the barn somewhere, so I didn't see any harm in whispering a little. Graham was coiled up just like a wire sitting there.

Tom

THE TWO MEN BACKED AWAY from the hayloft door to watch the motorcycle come up the lane. They stood shoulder to shoulder, just out of the dim starlight, in the door shadow where Nick wouldn't see them.

Nick pulled up out of sight in front of the barn and revved the engine a little. Under the noise of it Henri turned his head and spoke to Tom. Very rapidly, but softly and without much inflection. He said how disappointed he was to be seeing this former associate of theirs appearing from out of nowhere and sticking his nose into their business, particularly when he'd done his best to sever the relationship. Just like that. Sever. He suggested that Tom, on the other hand, had perhaps not been holding up his end of the bargain. He indicated that Tom might want to make that right just as soon as possible, using whatever means might be required.

He sounded just like DeAlton, only with a French accent.

Tom decided that he'd had just about enough.

Del

AS LONG AS the motorcycle was running I thought we ought to take advantage of the noise. Myers and I got up and stood in the shadows against the house, right near the screen door. Not Preston. Preston knew to lay low. I had put some duct tape over the latch so that when the time came we could open the door and slip out without making even that little bit of noise. We waited to see if the nephew and the Canadian would come out to see about the other fellow, but they didn't. He leaned his bike against the wall and poked around in the trunk of the Caddy for a minute. I thought I saw him put something in his pocket but I couldn't be sure. Then he bent over the trunk again and lifted something else out and walked it over to his bike. It looked to be about the size of a shoebox. Dope. Probably two or three bricks of it. He put it in the saddlebag, and that was fine with me. That was just about perfect. I couldn't have asked for any more than that.

Tom

HENRI STEPPED FARTHER BACK into the shadows and lit himself a cigarette, listening for Nick's footsteps in the barn. Nick was slow in coming but the Frenchman had all the time in the world. Tom took up a post at the top of the ladder, the shovel raised over his head like a club, and when the crown of his uncle's vague head appeared through the trapdoor he did not hesitate.

1932

Ruth

UP FROM THE EARTH the water rises, bidden by the iron pump and her husband's furious working of it, bearing into the world the earth's own changeless temperature. Spill it on the barnyard and it will freeze into a sheet. Pour it into the pot and it will steam soon enough. Thus without complaint or will or agency of any sort it bears witness to its beginnings and makes accommodation to its ends.

Lester empties the pitcher into the pot atop the stove and stokes the fire and pumps more water which he slops into the pot as well, spilling a little in his haste and standing undaunted in the consequent cloud of vapor that blooms up white from the iron stove.

Audie

I SAW MY FATHER and that old red rooster in a cloud of smoke or steam or both. My father worked the pump and I was on the floor with the fish and my mother was rubbing at my brother Vernon. Rubbing at his arms and legs so he wouldn't go on ahead. Anything but that. Anything but Vernon going on ahead of her. She cried some and she didn't hide it and my father told her to stop so she hid it but she didn't stop. She just put her head down so he couldn't see, but I could see because I was down on the floor where the fish spilled. I was slid down among them just as cold and wet, and I was wiggling my legs and the fish were thawing out and I was getting colder. Vernon was sucking in the air like a fish himself but out of water and my mother was bent over him where my father couldn't see but I could.

Ruth

SHE WOULD RATHER DIE herself and she says so. To her husband this sounds like a poor bargain and perhaps even a wicked one capable of calling down some limitless and untrustworthy power, and so he forbids her making it. For his part he behaves as if work will save the boy. Work alone, regardless of intent or method or object. The mere movement of the elements pursuing themselves through the world, their friction generating heat and light and life. He catches the blue boy's shuddering breath from the corner of his eye and redoubles his efforts, working the pump like a bellows, hollering over his shoulder at Audie: "On your feet, boy. Take care of them fish."

The boy asks how.

"Don't make me tell you everything." He gives off on the handle and raises the pitcher and spills water into the pot which steams on the stove but not for long. He tests it with a finger and pours some into a basin and sets the basin on the table with the dishrag. "Try that," he says to his wife.

"I'll need more rags," she says. "Bigger. A towel."

Audie has bent to gather up the thawing fish but his father stops him. "Never mind them. Fetch your mother some rags. From the barn."

The boy runs off in a clap of cold air from the door flung wide and returns straight off with all that he can carry, a double armload of wretched dusty feedsacks lately home to mice. She accepts them and without so much as shaking loose their burden of seed and chaff and shit she plunges them into the basin and is grateful. Rag by rag she wrings them out and applies their heat to her son's pale body, and slowly he comes around.

Audie

ONE OF THEM came back to life. There was fish slime on the floor and water and ice melt and I bent to pick up a little one and it came right back to life just like that. Just like Vernon. The gills of it spread open and the mouth of it moved quick and I dropped it on account of how it surprised me. I never knew such a thing could happen. It slid down with the rest and when I tried to find it again I couldn't because after that it stayed dead.

1990

Del

ONCE THAT OTHER FELLOW who'd come on the motorcycle stepped into the barn, all hell broke loose. It was apparent that the nephew and the Canadian hadn't expected him any more than we had, so while they were tangling we drew our weapons and opened the screen door and ran down through the yard in the dark. The grass was wet. Myers and I went across the dirt lane and up to the barn door, and no sooner had we gotten there than the three of them came tumbling out as if they were being chased by something. They didn't have much to say when they realized who we were. They were a lot less trouble than I'd expected them to be, and I didn't know why until later on. We cuffed them to the Cadillac one by one, three men and four door handles on that big old boat, and Myers pulled the barn door shut while I brought the patrol car down. There wasn't any need to disturb the Proctor brothers. Not that I could think of. Myers asked if he should tape the door, but I said no. I said those old men would want to get their milking done before long, and they didn't need our tape getting in their way. What was in the hayloft would stay there until morning without our help. I radioed for a team to come and secure the vehicles, and when they turned up the lane we headed out.

Preston

I THOUGHT I'D BETTER TAKE that duct tape down off the latch before it got stuck there forever. We'd had the house shut up all night on account of the heat, so it wasn't until I opened the door onto the screen porch that I heard the cows down in the yard by the barn. Milking time had come and gone and nobody'd seen to them. The barn door was shut. They knew something was wrong even if nobody else did.

I put on my boots and went right straight down there in my bathrobe. You don't want to go walking around a barnyard in your bare feet. You could pick up one of those parasites they get in Africa, and then you'd be in trouble. I had to shoulder my way through the cows to get to the barn. I don't know how those old boys ever got that great big door open and shut every single day of their lives, except they were in the habit. Maybe there was a secret to it but I don't think so. I guess I've just gone soft. Anyhow I put my weight into it and pushed it open and went on in. A barn is a pretty dark place by and large, and I walked right on past them. The two of them on the floor over by the far wall. I went straight through into the house and the bed was empty and then I went out again and I guess my eyes must have gotten a little used to the dark because there they were, asleep on the hay. Audie was asleep anyhow. Creed wasn't going to be waking up. Not after that fall and whatever else. I checked to make sure there wasn't any question about that and there wasn't. He was cold. The shovel lay right there alongside his head and there was white hair on it and there was a little blood too.

Audie was behind his brother, up close like they were a couple of spoons. He had his arms around him. Maybe that's how they always slept. Maybe it was a regular thing. I'd never thought about it and I wouldn't know. I bent over and touched his shoulder and I said his name out loud and he opened up his eyes, the one of them clouded over and the other one not much better. I thought it was the strangest thing, how a person can go through this life and not see what you see. How he can stand right next to you and it's all different.

I helped him up and told him to go get dressed, and I covered Creed over with a horseblanket, and then I went back home to get dressed myself. I had Margaret call the troopers, then I went back down to help Audie with the milking. Graham came straight over from his place on the West Road and there was a whole line of police cars not more than a half-mile behind him, sirens and lights going, and I told him what I'd found and how I'd found it. He said he guessed he should have gone in last night. I said I didn't blame him for not going in. It was probably too late already. Who knows.

He said well then he should have arrested Creed back when he had the chance, and everything would have turned out different. He'd still be among the living. I said I didn't know about that either. I said he might have saved Creed's life just so he could die from shame in the jailhouse. It was hard to say.

Del

I DON'T KNOW how much a person is built to endure, but I believe that living under those conditions would be a test of it. Those brothers got whittled away a little at a time. Worn out and used up just going from one day to the next. It's like how a science program on television will say a rock formation has weathered and you don't even think twice about the meaning of it, until later on you realize that they were talking about actual weather. Rain, wind, some freezing and thawing. One day after another. The ordinary things that wear the world down. We have old mountains around here that are just hills now, and they're nice to look at but they weren't always this way.

A person couldn't be struck on the head and fall down from that hayloft and survive, I wouldn't think. Not for very long. That would be one sort of limit on endurance. That would be a definite one that you could know the extent of. Something the medical examiner could tell you, if you had any questions about it.

The ambulance came and they loaded the body onto a stretcher and rolled it out of the barn. I said they ought to clean off those rubber wheels before they got into the hospital and they said they would. They carry plenty of rags and various kinds of cleaning supplies in an ambulance. They have to, with the things they run across. I went over and said a few words to Preston. He was sitting on a milk can alongside the barn door, looking pretty tired out. He said he was waiting for the tanker from the co-op, and I said I hoped we'd be finished and on our way back to town before they came. That would save everybody some trouble.

Audie didn't see his brother go. He was around back by the schoolbus. He had the rear door open to feed the turkeys, and three or four of them had gotten loose just as I came around the corner looking for him. He threw one last

306 | Jon Clinch

handful of feed inside the bus and wrestled the door shut and went after the ones that were still out. They squawked and gobbled around the yard pecking at the ground and looking half crazy the way birds do, especially the big ones, and he chased after them. It was hopeless. He was bent over low to the ground with his arms out wide, walking in a squat, and he wasn't making a sound, just twitching all over and lunging around on the hard dirt and the dead grass like he was wearing a blindfold. Lurching toward the turkeys and then the turkeys jumping away when he got too close. Feathers everywhere. It occurred to me that he couldn't see them at all. He was following the noises they made. I watched him for a couple of minutes and I thought about how it was that he'd found his brother Creed's body in the dark of that barn. How he'd been able to do it. What might have made it possible.

I called to him and he turned his head my way and I wondered how he would endure the heavy weather that lay ahead. I thought it might be for the best if those turkeys just went on back to the wild or whatever they'd do. Escaped their confinement. Got run over in the road or shot for somebody's supper. It would be that much less for him to take care of. That much less for Preston to take care of. I heard the ambulance pull away and I didn't watch it go. I looked at the dirt yard full of birds and the old man squatting down among them and flapping his arms as if he wanted to fly himself, and the turkeys flapping like they wanted to fly too but they couldn't do it any more than he could, and I called his name one more time to let him know I was coming. And then I went into the yard and I helped him gather up those birds.

* * *

Acknowledgments

In literature as in life, we have a duty to see that nothing important should ever be lost. Notes of appreciation, then, to those who made this book possible.

To my parents, Joyce and Warren Clinch—who let me hear these voices and gave me many of these stories and instilled in me the urge to tie them all together. Thanks for everything.

To Wendy—who has more good ideas than she knows what to do with. Keep it up, sweetie.

To Emily—who, if her mother and I had stopped right there, would have been achievement enough for both of our lifetimes. May she and JTB always be as happy as we've been.

To David Lindgren—long-lost compadre, former partner in crime, and singer/songwriter extraordinaire. A finely-tuned reader who knows not just the place and the time but the music, too. He's still got the ear.

To Ben Hill—who did his best to help keep me legal. Any variances from credibility belong not to Ben, but to me.

To my Proctor forbears—for all they endured, including my theft of their surname.

To the Ward brothers, to all of those who cared about and documented their tragedy (including Joe Berlinger and Bruce Sinofsky, whose film *Brother's Keeper* is a marvel; along with Hart Seely, whose newspaper coverage of the brothers and their trials was both sensitive and unflinching), and to all of those who remember the Wards' story both first- and second-hand (which means more or less everybody I know in central New York).

And to Michael Ticcino—long-time creative partner at more ad agencies than I care to mention—who discovered his own true work just about as late as I discovered mine. Michael provided the evocative image for the cover of this book. You'll find more of his work at MJTiccinoImages.com.